A TEXT BOOK OF

COMPUTER ORGANIZATION

WITH MULTIPLE CHOICE QUESTIONS (MCQ'S)

FOR
Semester – II
SECOND YEAR (S. E.) DEGREE COURSE IN ELECTRONICS/
ELECTRONICS AND TELECOMUNICATION ENGINEERING

As per New Revised Syllabus of University of Pune

(Pattern 2012)

Mrs. MALAN SALE

Assistant Professor, Comp Deptt.

Sinhgad College of Engineering

Vadagaon (Bk) Pune.

Mrs. VEENA KADAM

Assistant Professor, IT Deptt.

JSPM's Jayantrao Sawant

College of Engineering.

Hadapsar, Pune.

Mrs. JYOTI SURVE

Assistant Professor, IT Deptt.

JSPM's Jayawantrao Sawant

College of Engineering

Hadapsar, Pune.

NIRALI PRAKASHAN

N 2865

COMPUTER ORGANIZATION (SE - E&TC/ELEC.)   ISBN : 978-93-83971-07-7

First Edition : January 2014

Published By :
NIRALI PRAKASHAN
Abhyudaya Pragati, 1312, Shivaji Nagar,
Off J.M. Road, PUNE – 411005
Tel - (020) 25512336/37/39, Fax - (020) 25511379
Email : niralipune@pragationline.com

DISTRIBUTION CENTRES
PUNE

Nirali Prakashan
119, Budhwar Peth, Jogeshwari Mandir Lane
Pune 411002, Maharashtra
Tel : (020) 2445 2044, 66022708, Fax : (020) 2445 1538
Email : bookorder@pragationline.com

Nirali Prakashan
S. No. 28/25, Dhyari,
Near Pari Company, Pune 411041
Tel : (022) 24690204 Fax : (020) 24690316
Email : dhyari@pragationline.com
bookorder@pragationline.com

MUMBAI
Nirali Prakashan
385, S.V.P. Road, Rasdhara Co-op. Hsg. Society Ltd.,
Girgaum, Mumbai 400004, Maharashtra
Tel : (022) 2385 6339 / 2386 9976, Fax : (022) 2386 9976
Email : niralimumbai@pragationline.com

DISTRIBUTION BRANCHES

NAGPUR
Pratibha Book Distributors
Above Maratha Mandir, Shop No. 3, First Floor,
Rani Jhanshi Square, Sitabuldi, Nagpur 440012,
Maharashtra, Tel : (0712) 254 7129

JALGAON
Nirali Prakashan
34, V. V. Golani Market, Navi Peth, Jalgaon 425001,
Maharashtra, Tel : (0257) 222 0395
Mob : 94234 91860

BENGALURU
Pragati Book House
House No. 1, Sanjeevappa Lane, Avenue Road Cross,
Opp. Rice Church, Bengaluru – 560002.
Tel : (080) 64513344, 64513355,
Mob : 9880582331, 9845021552
Email:bharatsavla@yahoo.com

KOLHAPUR
Nirali Prakashan
New Mahadvar Road,
Kedar Plaza, 1st Floor Opp. IDBI Bank
Kolhapur 416 012, Maharashtra. Mob : 9855046155

CHENNAI
Pragati Books
9/1, Montieth Road, Behind Taas Mahal, Egmore,
Chennai 600008 Tamil Nadu, Tel : (044) 6518 3535,
Mob : 94440 01782 / 98450 21552 / 98805 82331, Email : bharatsavla@yahoo.com

RETAIL OUTLETS
PUNE

Pragati Book Centre
157, Budhwar Peth, Opp. Ratan Talkies,
Pune 411002, Maharashtra
Tel : (020) 2445 8887 / 6602 2707, Fax : (020) 2445 8887

Pragati Book Centre
676/B, Budhwar Peth, Opp. Jogeshwari Mandir,
Pune 411002, Maharashtra
Tel : (020) 6601 7784 / 6602 0855

Pragati Book Centre
Amber Chamber, 28/A, Budhwar Peth,
Appa Balwant Chowk, Pune : 411002, Maharashtra,
Tel : (020) 20240335 / 66281669
Email : pbcpune@pragationline.com

PBC Book Sellers & Stationers
152, Budhwar Peth, Pune 411002, Maharashtra
Tel : (020) 2445 2254 / 6609 2463

MUMBAI
Pragati Book Corner
Indira Niwas, 111 - A, Bhavani Shankar Road, Dadar (W), Mumbai 400028, Maharashtra
Tel : (022) 2422 3526 / 6662 5254, Email : pbcmumbai@pragationline.com

www.pragationline.com   info@pragationline.com

ACKNOWLEDGEMENT

It gives us immense pleasure in presenting this book "**Computer Organization**" of second year IT students.

We are sincerely thankful to Prof. P. R. Futane, H.O.D. Comp. (SCOE) Prof. P. D. Lambhate, H. O. D. I. T. Department (JSCOE),   and all our collegues who have contributed directly or indirectly to the development of this book.

We are also thankful to our husbands for their patience and encouragement. Mr. Dipak Sale, Mr. Mohan Kadam and Vishwas Surve whose moral support and wishes have gone a long way in making of this book.

We take this opportunity to express our sincere thanks to Shri. Dineshbhai Furia, of Nirali Prakashan, pioneer in all fields of education. We also thanks to Shri. Jignesh Furia, whose dynamic leadership is helpful to all the authors of Nirali Prakashan.

We specially appreciate the efforts of Shri. M. P. Munde and entire staff of Nirali Prakashan for making the publication of this book possible, well in time.

We also thankful to Mrs. Deepali Lachake and Mrs. Shilpa Kale for DTP and Miss. Pallavi Kumari and Roshan Shaikh for Proof Reading.

1st January 2014
Pune.

Authors

PREFACE

It gives us immense pleasure to present this book on **"Computer Organization".** The book is written for Second Year Degree Course in E Engineering as per the revised syllabus.

As per the policy of University of Pune, Engineering Syllabus is revised every five years. Last revision was in the year 2009. New revision is coming little earlier, as university has introduced **Online System of Examination** from year 2012.

As per the new system, the **Online Examination** (separate Phase-I and Phase-II) will be conduced based on first, second and third and fourth units respectively. The **Online examinations** will have objective types of questions with multiple choices. End semester examination will be based on all the six units and that will be conducted in traditional way.

This book provides an introduction to the theory on computer organization. The concepts of computer organization are presented with ample numbers of examples and programs. Multiple Choice Questions are also given to test the understanding of the students.

Unit 1 Provides the Concepts of Basic Structure of Computer.

Unit 2 Provides the Concepts of Arithmetic Unit.

Unit 3 Provides the Concepts of Control Unit.

Unit 4 Provides the Concepts of Input-Output Organization.

Unit 5 Provides the Concepts of Memory Organization.

Unit 6 Provides the Concepts of Microprocessor.

My sincere hope is that the material presented in the book will be useful to readers.

Valuable suggestions from our esteemed readers to improve the text will be most welcome and highly appreciated.

January 2014   **Authors**
Pune.

SYLLABUS

Unit I: Basic Structure of Computer (6 Hrs.)

Computer types, Functional units - input unit; output unit; ALU; control unit; memory unit, Basic operational concepts, Bus structure, Software, Performance – processor clock; basic performance equation; pipelining and superscalar; operation; clock rate; instruction set: CISC & RISC; Multiprocessors & Multi computers, Historical perspective (generations of a computer).

Unit II: Arithmetic Unit (6 Hrs.)

Addition and subtraction of signed binary numbers, Design of fast adders, Multiplication of positive numbers, Signed Operand Multiplication, Booths Algorithm, Fast multiplication, Integer Division, Floating point Numbers and Operations, IEEE standards, Floating point arithmetic.

Unit III: Control Unit (8 Hrs.)

Single Bus Organization - register Transfer; performing an arithmetic or logic operation; fetching and storing word from/to memory; execution of complete instruction; branch instruction, Multi-bus organization, Hardwired Control- Design methods – state table and classical method, A complete processor, Micro-programmed Control- microinstructions, micro- program sequencing, wide branch addressing, microinstructions with next address field, perfecting microinstructions, emulation.

Unit IV: Input-Output Organization (6 Hrs.)

I/O Organization- accessing I/O devices, Interrupts- interrupt hardware, enabling and disabling interrupts, handling multiple requests, controlling devices, exceptions, interface circuits, Direct memory access – bus arbitration, Buses- Synchronous; asynchronous, Interface circuits- parallel; serial, Standard I/O- PCI, SCSI, USB.

Unit I: Memory Organization (6 Hrs.)

Memory Hierarchy, Semiconductor RAM memories- internal organization of memory chips; static memories; asynchronous and synchronous DRAM; Structure of larger memories, Cache memory, Virtual Memories.

Unit VI: Microprocessor (8 Hrs.)

The 8086 microprocessor, architecture of 8086, Pin diagram, Programming model of 8086, Logical to physical addressing, Addressing modes, Interrupt structure.

CONTENTS

BASIC STRUCTURE OF COMPUTER

1.1 COMPUTER TYPES

A computer can be defined as a fast electronic calculating machine that accepts the (data) digitized input information process, it as per the list of internally stored instructions and produces the resulting information.

List of instructions are called programs and internal storage is called computer memory.

The different types of computers are :

1. **Personal computers :** A personal computer (PC) is a general-purpose computer, whose size, capabilities and original sale price makes it useful for individuals, and which is intended to be operated directly by an end-user. Software applications for most personal computers include, but are not limited to, word processing, spreadsheets, databases, web browsers and e-mail clients, digital media playback, games. Modern personal computers often have connections to the Internet, allowing access to the World Wide Web and a wide range of other resources. Personal computers may be connected to a local area network (LAN), either by a cable or a wireless connection. A personal computer may be a desktop computer or a laptop, tablet or a handheld PC. This is the most common type found in homes, schools, business offices etc.

2. **Notebook computers :** These are compact and portable versions of PC. Notebook computers are a rapidly evolving category of small, light and inexpensive laptop computers suited for general computing and accessing web-based applications.

3. **Work station :** A workstation is a high-end personal computer designed for technical, mathematical, or scientific applications. Intended primarily to be used by one person at a time, they are commonly connected to a local area network and run multi-user operating systems. Workstations are used for tasks such as computer-aided design, drafting and modeling, computation-intensive scientific and engineering calculations, image processing, architectural modeling, and computer graphics for animation and motion picture visual effects

4. **Enterprise system :** From a hardware perspective, enterprise systems are the servers, storage and associated software that large businesses use as the foundation for their IT

infrastructure. These systems are designed to manage large volumes of critical data. These systems are typically designed to provide high levels of transaction performance and data security.

5. **Super computers:** A super computer is a computer at the frontline of contemporary processing capacity – particularly speed of calculation.

Super computers play an important role in the field of computational science, and are used for a wide range of computationally intensive tasks in various fields, including quantum mechanics, weather forecasting, climate research, oil and gas exploration, molecular modeling and physical simulations (such as simulations of the early moments of the universe, aeroplane and spacecraft aerodynamics, the detonation of nuclear weapons, and nuclear fusion).

1.2 FUNCTIONAL UNIT

A computer consists of five functionally independent main parts input, memory, arithmetic logic unit (ALU), output and control unit.

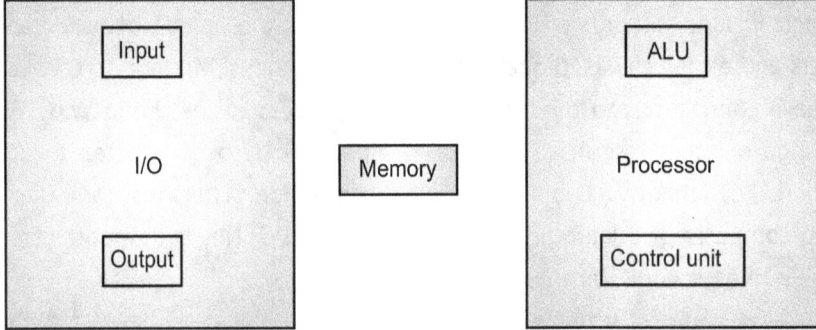

Fig 1.1 : Functional units of computer

1.2.1 Input Unit

The source program/high level language program/coded information/simply data is fed to a computer through input devices.

Keyboard is a most common type. Whenever a key is pressed, one corresponding word or number is translated into its equivalent binary code over a cable and fed either to memory or processor.

Joysticks, trackballs, mouse, scanners, digital cameras etc are other input devices.

1.2.2 Memory Unit

In computing, memory refers to the physical devices used to store programs or data. Its function is to store programs and data. It is basically of two types :

1.   Primary memory

2.   Secondary memory

1. Primary memory : The term primary memory is used for the information in physical systems which function at high-speed (i.e. RAM), as a distinction from secondary memory, which are physical devices for program and data storage which are slow to access but offer higher memory capacity. Primary memory stored on secondary memory is called "virtual memory".

The memory contains a large number of semiconductors storage cells. Each capable of storing one bit of information. These are processed in a group of fixed size called word.

To provide easy access to a word in memory, a distinct address is associated with each word location.

Programs must reside in the memory during execution. Instructions and data can be written into the memory or read out under the control of processor.

There are two main types of primary memory: volatile and non-volatile.

   (a)   Non-volatile Memory : Which is only readable by the user and contents of which can't be altered is called read only memory (ROM).It contains operating system.

Examples of non-volatile memory are flash memory and ROM/PROM/EPROM/EEPROM memory .

   (b)   Volatile Memory : Memory in which any location can be reached in a short and fixed amount of time after specifying its address is called random-access memory (RAM).

Examples of volatile memory are primary memory (typically dynamic RAM, DRAM), and fast CPU cache memory (typically static RAM, SRAM).

Caches are the small fast RAM units, which are coupled with the processor and are often contained on the same IC chip to achieve high performance. Although primary storage is essential it tends to be expensive.

2. Secondary memory : It is used where large amounts of data and programs have to be stored, particularly information that is accessed infrequently.

Examples: Magnetic disks and tapes, optical disks (ie CD-ROM's), DVD-ROM, floppies etc.

1.2.3 Arithmetic Logic Unit (ALU)

In computing, an arithmetic Logic Unit (ALU) is a digital circuit that performs integer arithmetic and logical operations. The ALU is a fundamental building block of the central processing unit of a computer.

Most of the computer operators are executed in ALU of the processor like addition, subtraction, division, multiplication etc. the operands are brought into the ALU from memory and stored in high speed storage elements called register. Then according to the instructions the operation is performed in the required sequence.

The control and the ALU are may times faster than other devices connected to a computer system. This enables a single processor to control a number of external devices such as key boards, displays, magnetic and optical disks, sensors and other mechanical controllers.

1.2.4 Output Unit

An output device is any piece of computer hardware equipment used to communicate the results of data processing carried out by a computer which converts the electronically generated information into human-readable form. Output units are the counterparts of input unit. Its basic function is to send the processed results to the outside world.

Examples of output devices Printers ,visual displays, Speakers, Headphones, Screen (Monitor), Projector, Plotter, Television, Radio, Punched card input/output.

1.2.5 Control Unit   [Dec. 12]

The control unit is a component of a computer's central processing unit (CPU) which directs operation of the processor. It controls communication and co-ordination between input/output devices. It reads and interprets instructions and determines the sequence for processing the data.

It directs the operation of the other units by providing timing and control signals. All computer resources are managed by the CU (Control Unit). It directs the flow of data between the Central Processing Unit (CPU) and the other devices. In modern computer designs, the control unit is typically an internal part of the CPU with its overall role and operation unchanged.

1.3   BASIC OPERATIONAL CONCEPTS

Instructions take a vital role for the proper working of the computer.

- An appropriate program consisting of a list of instructions is stored in the memory so that the tasks can be started.

- The memory brings the Individual instructions into the processor, which executes the specified operations. Data which is to be used as operands are moreover also stored in the memory. Most computer operations are executed in the ALU (arithmetic logic unit) of a processor.

- **Example :** to add two numbers that are both located in memory.

- Each number is brought into the processor, and the actual addition is carried out by the ALU. The sum then may be stored in memory or retained in the processor for immediate use.

Registers :

- When operands are brought into the processor, they are stored in high-speed storage elements (registers). A register can store one piece of data (8-bit registers, 16-bit registers, 32-bit registers, 64-bit registers, etc)

- Access times to registers are faster than access times to the fastest cache unit in the memory hierarchy.

Instructions:

- Instructions for a processor are defined in the ISA (Instruction Set Architecture).

- Typical instructions include:

  Mov AX, LocA

  - Fetch the instruction
  - Fetch the contents of memory location LocA
  - Store the contents in general purpose register AX

  Add BX, AX

  - Fetch the instruction
  - Add the contents of registers AX and BX
  - Place the sum in register BX

- The program counter (PC) or instruction pointer (IP) contains the memory address of the next instruction to be fetched and executed.

- Send the address of the memory location to be accessed to the memory unit and issue the appropriate control signals (memory read).

- The instruction register (IR) holds the instruction that is currently being executed.

- Timing is crucial and is handled by the control unit within the processor.

Examples : Add R_1, R_0

This instruction adds the operand in register R0, to operand in register R_0 and places the sum into register R_0.

This instruction requires the performance of several steps:

1.   First the instruction is fetched from the memory into the processor.

2.   The operand in R_1 is fetched and added to the contents of R_0

3.   Finally, the resulting sum is stored in the register R_0.

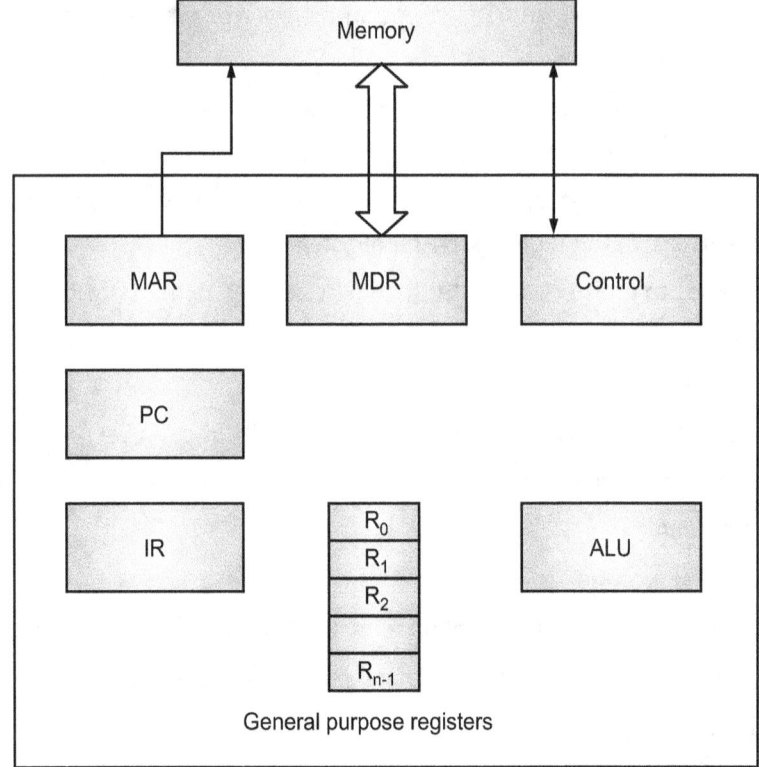

Fig 1.2 : Connections between the processor and the memory

The Fig 1.2 shows how memory and the processor can be connected. In addition to the ALU and the control circuitry, the processor contains a number of registers used for several different purposes.

The instruction register (IR): Holds the instructions that is currently being executed.

The program counter (PC) :-This is another specialized register that keeps track of execution of a program. It contains the memory address of the next instruction to be fetched and executed. Besides IR and PC, there are n-general purpose registers R_0 through Rn-1.

The other two registers which facilitate communication with memory are:

1. MAR – (Memory Address Register) : It holds the address of the location to be accessed.

2. MDR – (Memory Data Register) : It facilities communication with memory. It contains the data to be written into or read out of the addressed location.

Operating steps are

1. Programs reside in the memory and usually get these through the I/P unit.

2. Execution of the program starts when the PC is set to point at the first instruction of the program.

3. Contents of PC are transferred to MAR and a Read Control Signal is sent to the memory.

4. After the time required to access the memory elapses, the address word is read out of the memory and loaded into the MDR.

5. Now contents of MDR are transferred to the IR and now the instruction is ready to be decoded and executed.

6. If the instruction involves an operation by the ALU, it is necessary to obtain the required operands.

7. An operand in the memory is fetched by sending its address to MAR and Initiating a read cycle.

8. When the operand has been read from the memory to the MDR, it is transferred from MDR to the ALU.

9. After one or two such repeated cycles, the ALU can perform the desired operation.

10. If the result of this operation is to be stored in the memory, the result is sent to MDR.

11. Address of location where the result is stored is sent to MAR and a write cycle is initiated.

12. The contents of PC are incremented so that PC points to the next instruction that is to be executed.

1.4 Bus Structure

In computer architecture, a bus is a communication system that transfers data between components inside a computer, or between computers.

A group of lines that serve as a connecting port for several devices is called a bus.

In addition to the lines that carry the data, the bus must have lines for address and control purpose.

Simplest way to interconnect is to use the single bus as shown in Fig. 1.3.

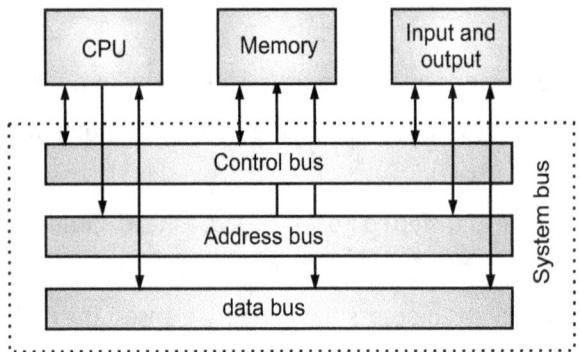

Fig. 1.3 : Single bus structure

Since the bus can be used for only one transfer at a time, only two units can actively use the bus at any given time. Bus control lines are used to arbitrate multiple requests for use of one bus.

Single bus structure is

- Low cost
- Very flexible for attaching peripheral devices

Multiple bus structure certainly increases, the performance but also increases the cost significantly.

All the interconnected devices are not of same speed and time, leads to a bit of a problem. This is solved by using cache registers (i.e. buffer registers). These buffers are electronic registers of small capacity when compared to the main memory but of comparable speed.

1.5 SOFTWARE   [May 11]

A software system is a system of intercommunicating components based on software forming part of a computer system (a combination of hardware and software). It consists of a number of separate programs, configuration files, which are used to set up these programs, system documentation, which describes the structure of the system, and user documentation, which explains how to use the system.

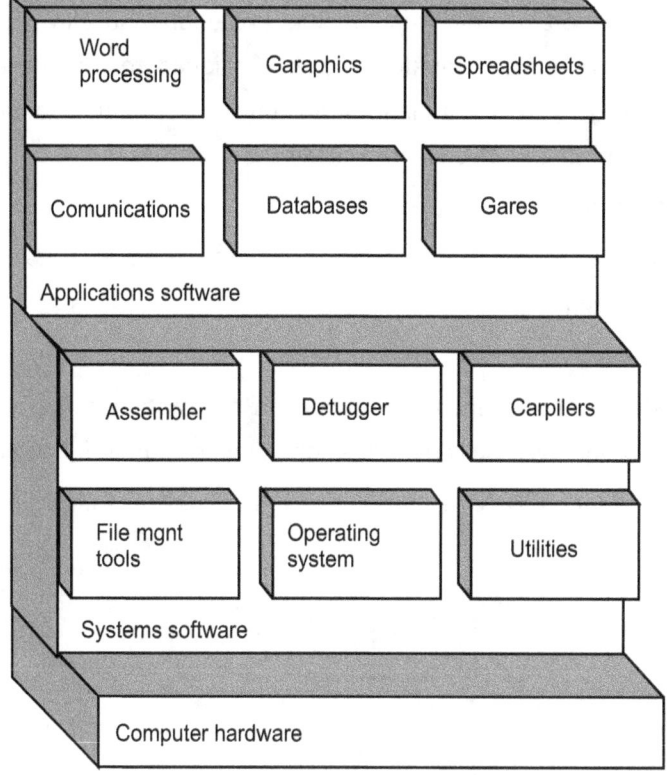

Fig 1.4 : Software

Two types of software are :

Application software : Application software is all the computer software that causes a computer to perform useful tasks beyond the running of the computer itself. A specific instance of such software is called a software application, application program or application. Common application softwares are :

- Word processors
- Desktop publishing programs
- Spreadsheets
- Presentation managers
- Drawing programs
- Accounting software
- Enterprise software
- Graphics software
- Media players
- Office suites

System software : Programs that support the execution and development of other programs. System software is computer software designed to operate and control the computer hardware and to provide a platform for running application software. The system software serves the application, which in turn serves the user.

Two major types of system software :

1. Operating systems

2. Translation systems

1. Operating systems :

The operating system is an essential component of the system software in a computer system. Application programs usually require an operating system to function.

Different types of operating systems are Real-time, Multi-user, Multi-tasking versus single tasking, Distributed, Embedded.

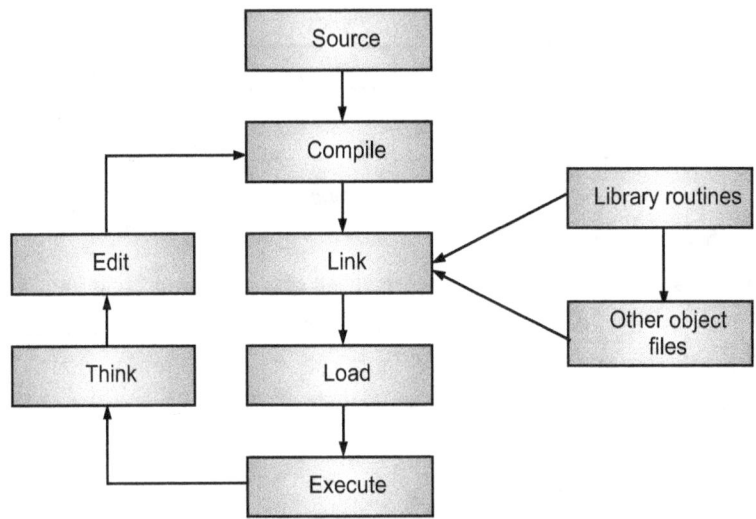

Fig 1.5 :Software development cycle

2. Translation System :

Translation system is a Set of programs used to develop software.A key component of a translation system is a translator. Some types of translators are

*   Compiler : Converts from one language to another

*   Linker : Combines resources.

This system performs compilation, linking, and other activities.

Software Development Activities :

- Editing
- Compiling
- Linking with precompiled files
- Object files
- Library modules
- Loading and executing
- Viewing the behaviour of the program

1.6 PERFORMANCE

Computer performance is characterized by the amount of useful work accomplished by a computer system compared to the time and resources used.

The speed with which a computer executes program is affected by the design of its hardware. For best performance, it is necessary to design the compiler, the machine instruction set, and the hardware in a co-ordinated way.

The total time required to execute the program is elapsed time is a measure of the performance of the entire computer system. It is affected by the speed of the processor, the disk and the printer. The time needed to execute a instruction is called the processor time.

Just as the elapsed time for the execution of a program depends on all units in a computer system, the processor time depends on the hardware involved in the execution of individual machine instructions. This hardware comprises the processor and the memory which are usually connected by the bus

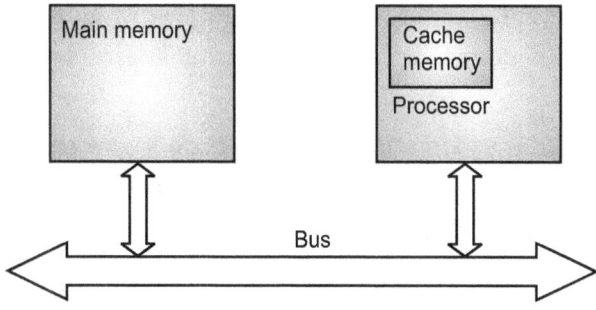

Fig 1.6 : The processor cache

Let us examine the flow of program instructions and data between the memory and the processor. At the start of execution, all program instructions and the required data are stored in the main memory. As the execution proceeds, instructions are fetched one by one over the bus into the processor, and a copy is placed in the cache later if the same instruction or data item is needed a second time, it is read directly from the cache.

The internal speed of performing the basic steps of instruction processing on chip is very high and is considerably faster than the speed at which the instruction and Main Memory data can be fetched from the main memory. A program will be executed faster if the movement of instructions and data between the main memory and the processor is minimized, which is achieved by using the cache.

For example : Suppose a number of instructions are executed repeatedly over a short period of time as happens in a program loop. If these instructions are available in the cache, they can be fetched quickly during the period of repeated use. The same applies to the data that are used repeatedly.

1.6.1 Processor Clock

Processor circuits are controlled by a clock. Clock speed is the rate at which a processor can complete a processing cycle. It is typically measured in megahertz or gigahertz. For execution of a machine instruction the processor divides the action into a sequence of basic steps that each step can be completed in one clock cycle.

1.6.2 Basic Performance Equation

- Performance means how quickly it can execute programs.
- For best performance, it is necessary to design the compiler, the machine instruction set, and the hardware in a co-ordinated way.
- Processor circuits are controlled by a timing signal called clock. The processor divides the action to be performed in basic steps, such that each step can be completed in one clock cycle.
- Basic Performance Equation is given by : $T = ((N \times S)/R)$, Where N = actual number of instruction executions , S = average number of basic step needed to execute one machine instruction , R- clock rate (cycles/sec)
- In order to achieve high performance, the T value should reduced which can be done by reducing N and S, or by increasing R.
- A substantial improvement can also be done by overlapping the execution of successive instructions. This concept is known as pipelining.

1.6.3 Pipelining and Superscalar Operation   [May. 12,13]

In sequential execution the instructions are executed one after the other. So the total time for execution depends on sum of time for execution of each instruction. Individual instructions still require several clock cycles to complete.

A substantial improvement in performance can be achieved by overlapping the execution of successive instructions using a technique called pipelining. Pipelining does not reduce the time to complete an instruction, but increases instruction throughput by performing multiple operations in parallel.

Example : Add R_4 R_5 R_6

This adds the contents of R_4 and R_5 and places the sum into R_6. The contents of R_4 and R_5 are first transferred to the inputs of ALU and then addition operation is performed, the sum is transferred to R_6. The processor can read the next instruction from the memory, while the addition operation is being performed. Then, if that instruction also uses, the ALU, its operand can be transferred to the ALU inputs at the same time that the add instructions is being transferred to R_6.

Multiple functional units are used creating parallel paths through which different instructions can be executed in parallel, so it becomes possible to start the execution of several instructions in every clock cycle. This mode of operation is called superscalar execution.

1.6.4 Clock Rate

The fundamental rate in cycles per second at which a computer performs its most basic operations such as adding two numbers or transferring a value from one register to another. These are two possibilities for increasing the clock rate.

1. Improving the IC technology makes logical circuit faster, which reduces the time of execution of basic steps. This allows the clock period, to be reduced and the clock rate to be increased.

2. Reducing the amount of processing done in one basic step also makes it possible to reduce the clock period.

1.6.5 Instruction Set CISC and RISC   [May. 12]

Simple instructions require a small number of basic steps to execute. Complex instructions involve a large number of steps. For a processor that has only simple instruction a large number of instructions may be needed to perform a given programming task. On the other hand if individual instructions perform more complex operations, a fewer instructions will be needed. It is not obvious if one choice is better than the other.

But complex instructions combined with pipelining (effective value of S $\cdot$ $\cdot$ 1) would achieve one best performance. However, it is much easier to implement efficient pipelining in processors with simple instruction sets.

RISC systems shorten execution time by reducing the clock cycles per instruction (i.e. simple instructions take less time to interpret).

CISC systems shorten execution time by reducing the number of instructions per program.

Example : RISC vs. CISC

Consider the the program fragments :

	mov ax, 10
CISC	mov bx, 5
	mul bx,ax

	mov ax, 0
	mov bx, 10
RISC	mov cx, 5
	Begin add ax, bx
	loop Begin

1.7 MULTIPROCESSOR AND MULTICOMPUTERS

Multiprocessor :

- A multiprocessor is a tightly coupled computer system having two or more processing units (Multiple Processors) each sharing main memory and peripherals, in order to simultaneously process programs.
- These systems either execute a number of different application tasks in parallel or execute subtasks of a single large task in parallel.
- The high performance of these systems comes with much increased complexity and cost.

Multicomputers

- A computer made up of several computers. The term generally refers to an architecture in which each processor has its own memory rather than multiple processors with a shared memory.

- A multicomputer may be considered to be either a loosely coupled NUMA computer or a tightly coupled cluster. Multicomputers are commonly used when strong computer power is required in an environment with restricted physical space or electrical power.

- When the tasks they are executing need to communicate data they do so by exchanging messages over a communication network. This properly distinguishes them from shared memory multiprocessors, leading to name message-passing multicomputer.

1.8 HISTORICAL PERSPECTIVE (GENERATIONS OF A COMPUTER)

The history of computer development is often referred to in reference to the different generations of computing devices. Each of the five generations of computers is characterized by a major technological development that fundamentally changed the way computers operate, resulting in increasingly smaller, cheaper, more powerful and more efficient and reliable computing devices.

1.8.1 First Generation (1940-1956) Vacuum Tubes

The first computers used vacuum tubes for circuitry, and magnetic drums for memory, and were often enormous, taking up entire rooms. They were very expensive to operate and in addition to using a great deal of electricity, generated a lot of heat, which was often the cause of malfunctions.

First generation computers relied on machine language, the lowest-level programming language understood by computers, to perform operations, and they could only solve one problem at a time. Input was based on punched cards and paper tape, and output was displayed on printouts.

The UNIVAC and ENIAC computers are examples of first-generation computing devices.

1.8.2 Second Generation (1956-1963) Transistors

Transistors replaced vacuum tubes in the second generation of computers. The transistor was invented in 1947 but did not see widespread use in computers until the late 1950s. The transistor was far superior to the vacuum tube, allowing computers to become smaller, faster, cheaper, more energy-efficient and more reliable than their first-generation predecessors. Though the transistor still generated a great deal of heat that subjected the computer to damage, it was a vast improvement over the vacuum tube. Second-generation computers still relied on punched cards for input and printouts for output.

Second-generation computers moved from cryptic binary machine language to symbolic, or assembly, languages, which allowed programmers to specify instructions in words. High-level programming languages were also being developed at this time, such as early versions of COBOL and FORTRAN. These were also the first computers that stored their instructions in their memory, which moved from a magnetic drum to magnetic core technology.

1.8.3 Third Generation (1964-1971) Integrated Circuits

The development of the integrated circuit was the hallmark of the third generation of computers. Transistors were miniaturized and placed on silicon chips, called semiconductors, which drastically increased the speed and efficiency of computers.

Instead of punched cards and printouts, users interacted with third generation computers through keyboards and monitors and interfaced with an operating system, which allowed the device to run many different applications at one time with a central program that monitored the memory. Computers for the first time became accessible to a mass audience because they were smaller and cheaper than their predecessors.

1.8.4 Fourth Generation (1971-Present) Microprocessors

The microprocessor brought the fourth generation of computers, as thousands of integrated circuits were built onto a single silicon chip. The Intel 4004 chip, developed in 1971, located all the components of the computer from the central processing unit and memory to input/output controls on a single chip.

In 1981 IBM introduced its first computer for the home user, and in 1984 Apple introduced the Macintosh. Microprocessors also moved out of the realm of desktop computers and into many areas of life as more and more everyday products began to use microprocessors.

As these small computers became more powerful, they could be linked together to form networks, which eventually led to the development of the Internet. Fourth generation computers also saw the development of GUIs, the mouse and handheld devices.

1.8.5 Fifth Generation (Present and Beyond) Artificial Intelligence

Fifth generation computing devices, based on artificial intelligence, are still in development, though there are some applications, such as voice recognition, that are being used today. The use of parallel processing and superconductors is helping to make artificial intelligence a reality. Quantum computation and molecular and nanotechnology will radically change the face of computers in years to come. The goal of fifth-generation computing is to develop devices that respond to natural language input and are capable of learning and self-organization.

MULTIPLE CHOICE QUESTIONS (MSQS)

1. Which part of the computer is used for calculating and comparing ?
   (a) Disk unit   (b) Control unit
   (c) ALU   (d) Modem

2. What are the three decisions making operations performed by the ALU of a computer?
   (a) Grater than   (b) Less than
   (c) Equal to   (d) All of above

3. The word length of a computer is measured in......
   (a) Bytes   (b) Millimetres
   (c) Metres   (d) Bits

4. Keyboard is ...... type of device.
   (a) Memory   (b) Output
   (c) Input   (d) Storage

5. Which is the type of memory for information that does not change on your computer?
   (a) RAM   (b) ROM
   (c) ERAM   (d) RW/RAM

6. Which of the following items are examples of storage devices?
   (a) Floppy / hard disks   (b) CD-ROMs
   (c) Tape devices   (d) All of these

7. Through which deice main components of computer communicate with each other.
   (a) System bus   (b) Keyboard
   (c) Monitor   (d) Memory

8. ....are used for the large scale numerical calculations required in applications like weather forecasting.

    (a) Personal computers   (b) Supercomputers

    (c) Notebook computers   (d) Workstation

9. ....unit is useful for logical operations.

    (a) Input   (b) Output

    (c) ALU   (d) Control

10. Computer accept coded information through. ....units.

    (a) Input   (b) Output

    (c) ALU   (d) ontrol

11. The function of . ...unit is to store programs and data.

    (a) Input   (b) Output

    (c) ALU   (d) memory

12. The small, fast RAM units are called. ....

    (a) SRAM   (b) DRAM

    (c) Cache   (d) None of these

13. ....is a example of non-volatile memory.

    (a) ROM   (b) PROM

    (c) EPROM   (d) all of these

14. .... converts the electronically generated information into human-readable form.

    (a) Input   (b) Output

    (c) ALU   (d) Control

15. ....controls communication and co-ordination between input/output devices.

    (a) Input   (b) Output

    (c) ALU   (d) Control

16. The program counter contains the memory address of the .... instruction to be fetched and executed.

    (a) First   (b) Next

    (c) Last   (d) previous

17.   ...... holds the instruction that is currently being executed.

(a)   instruction register   (b)   Program counter

(c)   Instruction pointer   (d)   None of these

18.   ...... holds the address of the location to be accessed.

(a)   MDR   (b)   MAR

(c)   IR   (d)   PC

19.   ...... contains the data to be written into or read out of the address location.

(a)   MDR   (b)   MAR

(c)   IR   (d)   PC

20.   ...... software is all the computer software that causes a computer to perform useful tasks beyond the running of the computer itself.

(a)   Application   (b)   System

(c)   Debugger   (d)   Compiler

21.   Word processors is a example of ...... software.

(a)   Application   (b)   System

(c)   Both (a) and (b)   (d)   None of these

22.   ...... Programs that support the execution and development of other programs

(a)   Application software   (b)   System software

(c)   None of these

23.   ...... is computer software designed to operate and control the computer hardware and to provide a platform for running application software.

(a)   Application software   (b)   System software

(c)   Operating system   (d)   All of these

24.   Operating system is a ...... software.

(a)   System software   (b)   Application software

(c)   None of these

25.   Which of the following are the two main components of the CPU?

(a)   Control unit and registers   (b)   Registers and main memory

(c)   ALU and bus   (d)   Control unit and ALU

26. Different components in the motherboard of a PC unit are linked together by sets of parallel electrical conducting lines. These lines are called......

    (a) Buses   (b) Conductors

    (c) Connectors   (d) Consecutives

27. The language that the computer can understand and execute is called

    (a) Application software   (b) Machine language

    (c) System program   (d) All of these

28. Which of the following is used as a primary storage device?

    (a) Magnetic drum   (b) PROM

    (c) Floppy disk   (d) Hard disk

29. Which of the following devices can be used to directly input printed text?

    (a) OCR   (b) OMR

    (c) MICR   (d) All of these

30. The output quality of a printer is measured by......

    (a) Dot per cm   (b) Dots per inch

    (c) Dots printed per unit time   (d) All of these

31. Who designed the first electronics computer – ENIAC?

    (a) Von Neumann   (b) J. P. Eckert and J. W. Mauchly

    (c) Joseph M Jacquard   (d) None of these

32. Personal computers used a number of chips mounted on a main circuit board. What is the common name for such boards?

    (a) Daughterboard   (b) Motherboard

    (c) Fatherboard   (d) Childboard

33. A computer program that converts an entire program into machine language at one time is called a/an......

    (a) Interpreter   (b) CPU

    (c) Compiler   (d) Simulator

34. A computer program that translates one program instruction at a time into machine language is called a/an......

(a) Interpreter   (b) CPU

(c) Compiler   (d) Simulator

35. Which disk is one of the important I/O devices and its most commonly used as permanent storage devices in any processor?

(a) Hard disk   (b) Optical disk

(c) Magneto disk   (d) Magneto Optical disk

36. I/O devices are categorized in two parts are:

(a) Character devices   (b) Block devices

(c) Numeral devices   (d) Both (a) and (b)

37. Which are following pointing devices?

(a) Light pen   (b) Joystick

(c) Mouse   (d) All of these

38. ......is device that is designed for gaming purposes and based on principle of electricity.

(a) Joy   (b) Stick

(c) Joystick   (d) None of these

39. A commonly used voice input systems are ......

(a) Micro   (b) Microphone

(c) Voice recognition software   (d) Both (b) and (c)

40. Output devices commonly referred as ......

(a) Terminals   (b) Host

(c) Receivers   (d) Senders

41. Dot matrix printer is two types is ......

(a) Daisy wheels   (b) Matrix printer

(c) High quality matrix printer   (d) Both (a) and (c)

42. ......interface is an entity that controls data transfer from external device, main memory and or CPU registers.

(a) I/O interface   (b) CPU interface

(c) input interface   (d) output interface

43. To resolve problems of I/O devices there is a special hardware component between CPU and...... to supervise and synchronize all input output transfers:

    (a) Software   (b) Hardware

    (c) Peripheral   (d) None of these

44. By which signal flow of traffic between internal and external devices is done......

    (a) Only control signal   (b) Only timing signal

    (c) Control and timing signal   (d) None of these

45. I/O module must recognize a...... address for each peripheral it controls.

    (a) Long   (b) Same

    (c) Unique   (d) Bigger

46. Two control lines in I/O interface is ......

    (a) RD, WR   (b) RD, DATA

    (c) WR, DATA   (d) RD, MEMORY

47. If CPU and I/O interface share a common bus than transfer of data between 2 units is said to be......

    (a) Synchronous   (b) Asynchronous

    (c) Clock dependent   (d) Decoder independent

48. The keyboard has a...... asynchronous transfer mode:

    (a) Parallel   (b) Serial

    (c) Optimum   (d) None

49. In ......transfer each bit is sent one after the another in a sequence of event and requires just one line.

    (a) Serial   (b) Parallel

    (c) Both (a) and (b)   (d) None of these

50. User programs interact with I/O devices through......

    (a) Operating system   (b) Hardware

    (c) CPU   (d) Microprocessor

51. Multiprocessor use......than two CPUs assembled in single system unit.

    (a) One or More   (b) Two or More

    (c) One or One   (d) Two or Two

52. Which refers the execution of various software process concurrently

    (a) Multiprocessor   (b) Serial communication

    (c) DCP   (d) IOP

53. Which is used for this and known as high speed buffer exist with almost each process?

    (a) Primary   (b) Cache

    (c) RAM   (d) None of these

54. Which consist if a numbers of processor can be accessed among various shared memory modules?

    (a) Coupled memory multiprocessor

    (b) Shared memory multiprocessor

    (c) Distributed memory multiprocessor

    (d) None of these

55. Which keeps a number of processors in which virtual storage space is assigned for redundant execution?

    (a) Coupled memory multiprocessor

    (b) Shared memory multiprocessor

    (c) Distributed memory multiprocessor

    (d) None of these

56. Intercrosses arbitration system for multiprocessor shares a ......

    (a) Primary bus   (b) Domain bus

    (c) Common bus   (d) All of these

57. Processor circuits are controlled by a ......

    (a) chip   (b) clock

    (c) none of above

58. The total time required to execute the program is ......which is a measure of the performance of the entire computer system.

    (a) processor time   (b) waiting time

    (c) elapsed time   (d) total time

59. Which is a type of microprocessor that is designed with limited number of instructions?
    (a)   CPU   (b) RISC
    (c)   ALU   (d) MUX

60. A bus organization for seven......register.
    (a)   ALU   (b) RISC
    (c)   CPU   (d) MUX

61. Instruction formats contains the memory address of the......
    (a)   Memory data   (b) Main memory
    (c)   CPU   (d) ALU

62. Which are arithmetic operations?
    (a)   Addition   (b) Subtraction
    (c)   Multiplication   (d) Division
    (e)   All of these   (f) None of these

63. SMP Stands for ......
    (a)   System multiprocessor   (b) Symmetric multiprocessor
    (c)   Both   (d) None

64. Which is a method of decomposing a sequential process into sub-operations
    (a)   Pipeline   (b) CISC
    (c)   RISC   (d) Database

65. Where does a computer add and compare data?
    (a) Hard disk   (b) Floppy disk
    (c) CPU chip   (d) Memory chip

66. Which of the following registers is used to keep track of address of the memory location where the next instruction is located?
    (a) Memory Address Register   (b) Memory Data Register
    (c) Instruction Register   (d) Program Register

67. A complete microcomputer system consists of ......
    (a) microprocessor   (b) memory
    (c) peripheral equipment   (d) all of these

68. Pipelining strategy is called implement ......
    (a) instruction execution   (b) instruction prefetch
    (c) instruction decoding   (d) instruction manipulation

69. A superscalar processor has......

    (a) multiple functional units   (b) a high clock speed

    (c) a large amount of RAM   (d) many I/O ports

70. Pipelining improves CPU performance due to ......

    (a) reduced memory access time

    (b) increased clock speed

    (c) the introduction of parallellism

    (d) additional functional units

71. In length instruction some programs wants a complex instruction set containing more instruction, more addressing modes and greater address rang, as in case of......

    (a) RISC   (b) CISC

    (c) Both (a) and (b)   (d) None of these

72. In length instruction other programs on the other hand, want a small and fixed-size instruction set that contains only a limited number of opcodes, as in case of......

    (a) RISC   (b) CISC

    (c) Both   (d) None

73. CISC machines......

    (a) have fewer instructions than RISC machines

    (b) use more RAM than RISC machines

    (c) have medium clock speeds

    (d) use variable size instructions

74. CISC stands for ......

    (a) Complex Instruction System Computer

    (b) Complex Instruction Set Car

    (c) Complex Instruction Set Computer

    (d) None of these

75. RISC stands for......

    (a) Reduced Instruction Set Computer

    (b) Reduced Intergraded Set Computer

    (c) Resource Instruction Set Computer

    (d) Resource Instruction System Computer

76. RISC systems shorten execution time by reducing ......
    (a) the clock cycles per instruction
    (b) the clock cycles per instruction
    (c) all of above
    (d) none of above

77. CISC systems shorten execution time by reducing......
    (a) the number of instructions per program
    (b) the clock cycles per instruction
    (c) all of above
    (d) none of above

78. Which is the components of computer?
    (a) System Bus   (b) CPU
    (c) Memory Unit   (d) All of these

79. System Bus Contains......
    (a) Address Bus   (b) Data Bus
    (c) Control Bus   (d) All of these

80. Which is an integral part of any microcomputer system and its primary purpose is to hold program and data?
    (a) Memory unit   (b) Register unit
    (c) (a) and (b)   (d) None of these

81. How many generation are present in computer?
    (a) Four   (b) Five
    (c) Six   (d) Three

82 .... made up of several computers.
    (a) Multicomputers   (b) Multiprocessor
    (c) Microprocessor   (d) None of these

83. Transistors replaced vacuum tubes in the ...... generation of computers.
    (a) First   (b) Second
    (c) Third   (d) Fourth

84. The development of the integrated circuit was the hallmark of the ...... generation of computers.
    (a) First   (b) Second
    (c) Third   (d) Fourth

85. The microprocessor brought the ...... generation of computers.
    (a) First   (b) Second
    (c) Third   (d) Fourth
86. The second generation of computer was based on ......
    (a) Vaccum Tube   (b) Silicon Chips
    (c) Transistor   (d) Biochips
87. The third generation of computer was made with ....
    (a) Vaccum Tube   (b) IC
    (c) Biochips   (d) Discrete Components

ANSWERS

1.	c	2.	d	3.	d	4.	c	5.	b
6.	d	7.	a	8.	b	9.	c	10.	a
11.	d	12.	c	13.	d	14.	b	15.	d
16.	b	17.	a	18.	b	19.	a	20.	a
21.	a	22.	b	23.	b	24.	a	25.	d
26.	a	27.	b	28.	b	29.	a	30.	b
31.	b	32.	b	33.	c	34.	a	35.	a
36.	d	37.	d	38.	c	39.	d	40.	a
41.	d	42.	a	43.	c	44.	c	45.	c
46.	a	47.	a	48.	b	49.	a	50.	a
51.	b	52.	a	53.	b	54.	b	55.	c
56.	c	57.	b	58.	c	59.	b	60.	c
61.	b	62.	e	63.	b	64.	a	65.	c
66.	d	67.	d	68.	b	69.	a	70.	c
71.	b	72.	a	73.	a	74.	c	75.	a
76.	b	77.	a	78.	d	79.	d	80.	a
81.	b	82.	a	83.	b	84.	c	85.	d
86.	c	87.	b						

QUESTIONS

1. Explain different types of computers.

2. What is supercomputer?

3. What are different functional units of computer?

4. Explain difference between primary and secondary memory.

5. Explain the working of ALU.

6. How the basic operations are performed in computer?

7. List out different registers used in processor of computer.

8. Describe single bus structure in detail.

9. What is difference between system software and application software.

10. How the performance of system is measured?

11. Explain working of pipelining with example.

12. What are RISC and CISC?

13. Give the difference between multiprocessor and multicomputer.

14. Describe different generations of computers.

ARITHMETIC UNIT

2.1 FIXED AND FLOATING POINT NUMBERS

Floating point describes a method of representing real numbers in a way that can support a wide range of values. Both the values are in binary. Depending upon design the hardware can interpret number as an integer or fraction. Radix point is never explicitly specified. It is implicated in design and hardware interprets it. In integer numbers radix point is fixed and assumed to be to the right of the right most digit. As radix point is fixed the number system is known as fixed point number system. With fixed point number system we can represent positive or negative integer numbers. Floating point number system allows the representation of numbers having both integer and fractional part.

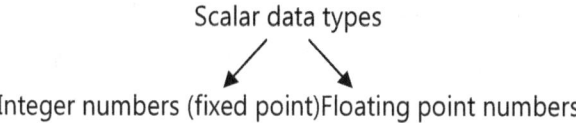

2.1.1 Fixed Point Numbers

These are represented in two forms. (1). Signed integer (–ve) and (2).Unsigned integer (+ve). Computer doesn't have provision to represent negative sign. So we can represent negative number using the following methods.

(Represents using)

1. Signed magnitude
2. 1's complement
3. 2's complement

2.1.2 Signed Magnitude Representation

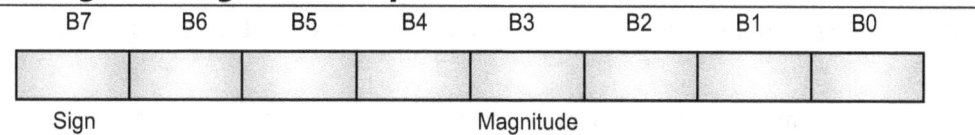

Fig. 2.1 : 8–bit signed number representations

Signed number represents negative as well as positive numbers.

The most significant bit (leftmost bit–B7) is used to represent the sign of number. If it is 0 the number is positive and if it is 1 the number is negative. For example, +7 represented by 0000 0111 and –14 represented by 1000 1110. Unsigned 8bit binary numbers has range 0 to 255. This is divided into 0 to + 127 for +ve numbers and 0 to –127 for negative numbers.

Some drawbacks are

- For addition and subtraction it is necessary to consider sign of both the numbers and their relative magnitudes
- The 0 can be represented by two ways :

  + 0 = 0000 0000

  – 0 = 1000 0000

Due to two representations of zero it is difficult to test for zero operation of computer arithmetic.

2.1.3 One's Complement Representation

In this method, negative number are obtained by complementing each bit of corresponding positive number. For –3 representation complement each bit of positive 3(0011) so you will get 1100. This operation is equivalent to subtracting that number from $2^n - 1$ that is from 1111, in case of 4 bit numbers.

Example 1 : 1's complement of $(1001)_2$.

$$1 \quad 0 \quad 0 \quad 1 \quad \text{number}$$
$$0 \quad 1 \quad 1 \quad 0 \quad \text{1's complement}$$

Example 2 : 1's complement of $(1010\ 0011)_2$.

$$1 \quad 0 \quad 1 \quad 0 \quad 0 \quad 0 \quad 1 \quad 1 \quad \text{number}$$
$$0 \quad 1 \quad 0 \quad 1 \quad 1 \quad 1 \quad 0 \quad 0 \quad \text{1's complement}$$

2.1.4 Two's Complement Representation

The two's complement number is obtained by subtracting corresponding positive number from 2^n. The 2's complement number is obtained by adding 1 to the 1's complement number.

Using 2's complement we can distinctly represent +0 and –0. As 2's complement have only +0 representation. In 4–bit numbers –8 is represented by only 2's complement system i.e. 1000. This method is popularly used in computers for addition and subtractions.

Example 1 : 2's complement of $(1001)_2$.

Find 1's complement first

```
        1  0  0  1    number
        0  1  1  0    1's complement
    +            1    add 1 to 1's complement
    ----------------------------------------
        0  1  1  1    2's complement
```

Example 2 : 2's complement of $(1010\ 0011)_2$.

```
      1  0  1  0  0  0  1  1    number
      0  1  0  1  1  1  0  0    1's complement
  +                      1      add 1 to 1's complement
  ----------------------------------------------
      0  1  0  1  1  1  0  1    2's complement
```

2.2 INTEGER ARITHMETIC

Computer process only binary number and not decimals or hexadecimals. So in integer arithmetic we process only binary addition, subtraction and division.

2.2.1 Integer Addition

Rules :

A + B	SUM	CARRY
0 + 0	0	0
0 + 1	1	0
1 + 0	1	0
1 + 1	0	1

Example 1 : Add 28 and 15 in binary.

First find the binary equivalent of 28 and 15

2	28	0
2	14	0
2	7	1
2	3	1
2	1	1
2	0	0

2	15	1
2	7	1
2	3	1
2	1	1
	0	

Binary equivalent of 28 = 11100

Binary equivalent of 15 = 01111.

Addition is

```
      1 1 1 0 0  ...28
  +   0 1 1 1 1  ...15
      1 1          ...carry
  ----------------------------
      1 1 0 1 1  ...43
```

2.2.2 Integer Subtraction

Rules for subtraction

A - B	Difference	Borrow
0 - 0	0	0
0 - 1	1	1
1 - 0	1	0
1 - 1	0	0

Example : Subtract 15 from 28 in binary

Convert 15 and 28 in binary

Binary equivalent of 28 = 11100

Binary equivalent of 15 = 01111.

Subtraction is:

```
      1 1 1 0 0  ...28
  -   0 1 1 1 1  ...15
      1 1 1   1  ...carry
  ----------------------------
      0 1 1 0 1  ...13
```

2.2.3 One's Complement Subtraction

Subtraction performed by using only addition by two numbers.

Subtract smaller number from larger number

1. Determine the 1's complement of smaller number.
2. Add the 1's complement to the larger number.
3. Remove the carry and add it to the result. This is called end–around carry.

Example 1 : Subtract 0 1111 (15) from 11100 (28) using 1's complement.

```
      1  1  1  0  0        ...28
  +   1  0  0  0  0        ...1's complement of 15
  ---------------------------------------------------
  -   1  0  1  1  0  0   carry as 1
  +                  1   add end around carry
  ---------------------------------------------------
         0  1  1  0  1   ...13
```

1. Determine the 1's complement of the larger number.
2. Add 1's complement to the smaller number.
3. Answer is in 1's complement form. To get the answer in true form take the 1's complement and assign negative sign to the answer.

Example 2 : Subtract 1 1 1 0 0 from 0 1 1 1 1 using 1's complement.

```
      0  0  0  1  1    ...1's complement of larger number 28
  +   0  1  1  1  1    ...add 1's complement to smaller no.
  ---------------------------------------------------
      1  0  0  1  0    ...answer is in 1's complement form
      0  1  1  0  1    ...final answer 13 (take 1's complement)
```

2.2.4 2's Complement Subtraction

Like 1's complement subtraction is achieved by addition.

(1) Subtract smaller number from larger number

1. Determine the 2's complement of smaller number.
2. Add 2's complement to the larger number.
3. Discard carry.

Example 1 : Subtract 01111 (15) from 11100 (28) using 2's complement.

Calculate 2's complement of smaller number

```
      0  1  1  1  1
      1  0  0  0  1       ...2's complement of 15
      Then
      1  1  1  0  0
  +   1  0  0  0  1       ...add 2's complement of 15
  ---------------------------------------------------
      1  0  1  1  0  1   ...discard carry
      0  1  1  0  1       ...13 final answer
```

(2) Subtract larger number from smaller number

1. Determine the 2's complement of the larger number.

2. Add the 2's complement to the smaller number.

3. Answer is in two's complement form. To get the answer in true form take the 2's complement and assign negative sign to the answer.

Example2 : Subtract 11100 from 01111 using 2's complement.

Calculate two's complement of 11100.

```
        0  0  0  1  1   ...1's complement of larger number 28

    +                1
    --------------------------------------------------------
        0  0  1  0  0   ...2's complement of 28

    +   0  1  1  1  1   ...smaller number
    --------------------------------------------------------
        1  0  0  1  1   ...answer in 2' complement form

        0  1  1  0  1   ...final answer 13
```

Example 3 : Subtract smaller number from larger number.

(1) 25-10

Subtract 1010 from 11001

```
    11001    ...25
    01010    ...10
    2's complement of 01010
    10101
+      11
    ------
    00110
```

```
    11001        ...25
+   00110        2's complement of 10
    ------
   [1]1111       discard carry

    1111         ...15 final answer
```

Example 4 : Subtract larger number from smaller number.

10-25

Subtract 11001 from 1010

01010   ...10

11001   ...25

2's complement of 25.

   11001

   00110

  +   1

     ——————

  00111 ...2's complement of 25

               01010   ...10

            + 00111   ...2's complement to 25

              ——————

               10001   ...answer is in 2's complement form

               01110

             +   1

              ——————

               01111   ...15 final answer

2.2.5 Hardware Implementation of Addition and Subtraction

The figures suggest data paths and hardware elements needed to accomplished addition and subtraction. The central element is binary adder which is presented two numbers for addition and produces a sum and an overflow indication.

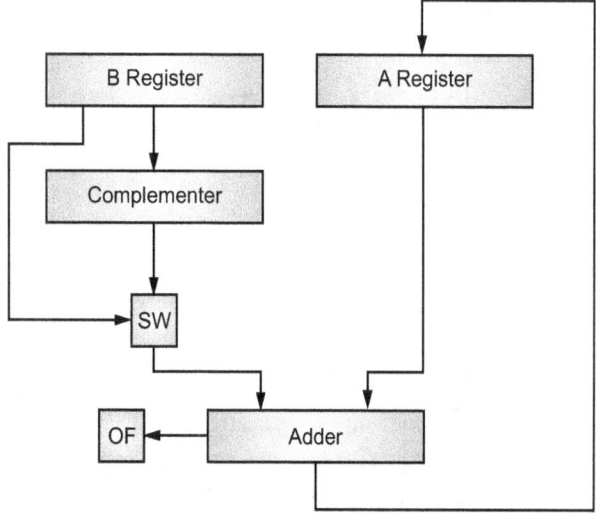

OF = Overflow bit

SW = Switch (Select addition or Subtraction)

Fig. 2.2 : Addition and subtraction

The binary adder treats the two numbers as unsigned integers. For addition, the two numbers are presented to the adder from two registers, designated in this case as A and B registers.

The result may be stored in one of these registers or in a third. The overflow indication is stored in a 1–bit overflow flag (0 – no overflow 1 – overflow). For subtraction, the subtrahend (B register) is passed through a two's complementer so that its two's complement is presented to the adder.

The logic circuit performs addition of two binary digits and produces a sum and a carry output in half adder. The circuit which performs addition of three bits (two significant bits and a previous carry) is called full adder. Three inputs and 1 output. A and B input variables and third input is C i.e. carry from the previous lower significant bit and output as sum as shown in Fig. 2.3

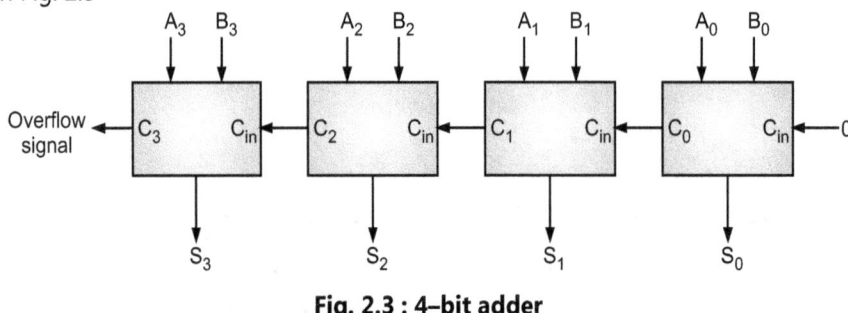

Fig. 2.3 : 4–bit adder

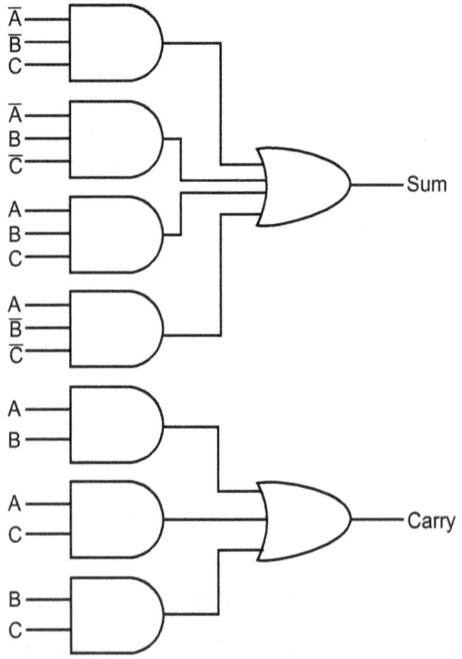

Fig. 2.4 : Implementation of adder

For multiple bit adder to work each of the single bit address must have three inputs. These implantation is shown in Fig. 2.4 which uses the AND, OR and NOT gates. Output from each adder depends upon carry from previous adder. There is an increasing delay from LSB to MSB. Each adder experiences certain amount of gate delay for lager adders the accumulated delay can become unacceptably high.

If the carry values could be determined without having to ripple through all the previous stages, then each single bit adder could function independently, and delay would not accumulate. This can be achieved with an approach known as **carry look ahead**.

2.3 2's Complement Multiplication

2.3.1 Basic of Multiplication

- The multiplication is complex operation. It can be performed by hardware and software. Multiplication process involves generation of partial products one for each digit in the multiplier. These partial products are then summed to produce the final products.

- In the binary system, the partial products are easily defined. When multiplier bit is 0 the partial product is 0 and when the multiplier is 1 the partial product is multiplicand.

- The final product is produced by addition of partial products. Each successive bit is shifted one position to the left relative to proceeding partial product.

- The product of two n digit numbers can be accommodated in 2n digits. So product of 4 bit number is 8–bit number.

Example :

		0	1	0	1				multiplicand (5)
	×	0	1	0	0				multiplier (4)
0	0	0	0	0	0	0	0		as 8-bit product take 8 bit
0	0	0	0	0	0	0	+		left shift by 1 bit
0	0	0	1	0	1	+	+		multiplcand× 1
0	0	0	0	0	+	+	+		left shift by one
0	0	0	1	0	1	0	0		final product (20)

2.3.2 2's Complement Multiplication

We will discuss multiplication of 2's complement signed operand, also we apply partial product strategy by adding multiplicand (+ve and –ve) as selected by multiplier bit.

Note that when we add negative multiplicand we must extend the sign bit value of the multiplicand to the left as far as product will extend. The technique for 2's complement method known as Booth's algorithm.

2.4   BOOTH'S ALGORITHM   [May 09, 10]

Booth's multiplication algorithm is an multiplication algorithm that multiplies two signed binary numbers in a two's complement notations. For signed number multiplication booths algorithm is used. It treats both positive and negative numbers. Three method for booths algorithm.

1.   Using recoded multiplier.

2.   Hardware implementation.

3.   Modified booth algorithm.

1. Using recoded multiplier :

The product can be computed by adding 24 times the multiplicand to the 2's complement of 1 times of the multiplicand sequence of operations by recoding the proceeding multiplier as

0 +1 0 0 –1 0

–1 times the shifted multiplicand is selected when moving from 0 to 1.

+1 times the shifted multiplicand is selected when moving from 1 to 0.

0 times the shifted multiplicand is selected for none of above cases as multiplier is scanned from right to left.

Example 1 : Recode the multiplier 0100 (4) for booths algorithm.

    0 1 0 0 ⓪   implied zero at end
     ◄────────   scan from right to left
    ⌐⌐⌐⌐⌐──┘   make pairs
    +1 –1 0   0   recoded multiplier.

Example 2 : Recode the multiplier 1100 (–4) for booths algorithm.

    1 1 0 0 ⓪   implied zero at end
     ◄────────   scan from right to left
    ⌐⌐⌐⌐⌐──┘   make pairs
    0 –1 0   0   recoded multiplier.

Whenever multiplicand is multiplied by –1. Its 2's complement is taken as a partial result.

Example 3 : Multiply 0101(5) and 0100(4) using booth's algorithm (5 × 4).

Solution :

```
    0   1   0   0   0          multiplier with implied zero at end

   +1  -1   0   0              recoded multiplier

    0   1   0   1              multiplicand + 5

×  +1  -1   0   0              recoded multiplier
   _____

    0   0   0   0   0   0   0   0   as 8-bit product

    0   0   0   0   0   0   0   +

    1   1   1   0   1   1   +   +   multiply by -1 take 2's complement

    0   0   1   0   1   +   +   +
   _____

    0   0   0   1   0   1   0   0   final answer +20
```

When we multiply by -1 we will take 2's compliment of multiplicand and assign remaining bit to 1. Because product is negative.

Example 4 : Multiply 1011(-5) and 1100(-4) using booth's algorithm (-5 ×-4).

Solution :

```
    1   1   0   0   0          multiplier with implied zero at end

    1  -1   0   0              recoded multiplier

    1   0   1   1              multiplicand -5

×   0  -1   0   0              recoded multiplier
   _____

    0   0   0   0   0   0   0   0   as 8-bit product

    0   0   0   0   0   0   0   +

    0   0   1   0   0   1   +   +   multiply by -1 take 2's complement

    0   0   0   0   1   +   +   +
   _____

    0   0   0   1   0   1   0   0   final answer +20
```

Here 1011(-5) is 2's complement of 0101(5) so multiplying by -1 it again calculates 2's complement but already its 2's complement of 5. So we take original number 0101 (5). We get result as +20.

Example 5 : Multiply 1011(–5) and 0100(4) using booth's algorithm (–5 × 4).

Solution : Recode the multiplier 0100.

1	0	1	1	0					multiplier with implied zero at end
+1	–1	0	0						recoded multiplier
1	0	1	1						multiplicand – 5
× +1	–1	0	0						recoded multiplier
0	0	0	0	0	0	0	0		as 8-bit product
0	0	0	0	0	0	0	+		
0	0	0	1	0	1	+	+		multiply by –1 take 2's complement
1	1	0	1	1	+	+	+		
1	1	1	0	1	1	0	0		final answer – 20 (2's complement of 20)

The Booth algorithm examines adjacent pair of bits of n bit multiplier y in signed two's complement.

2. Hardware implementation booths algorithm :

- The circuit consist of n bit adder, shift add subtract control logic and four registers A, B, Q, and Q–1.

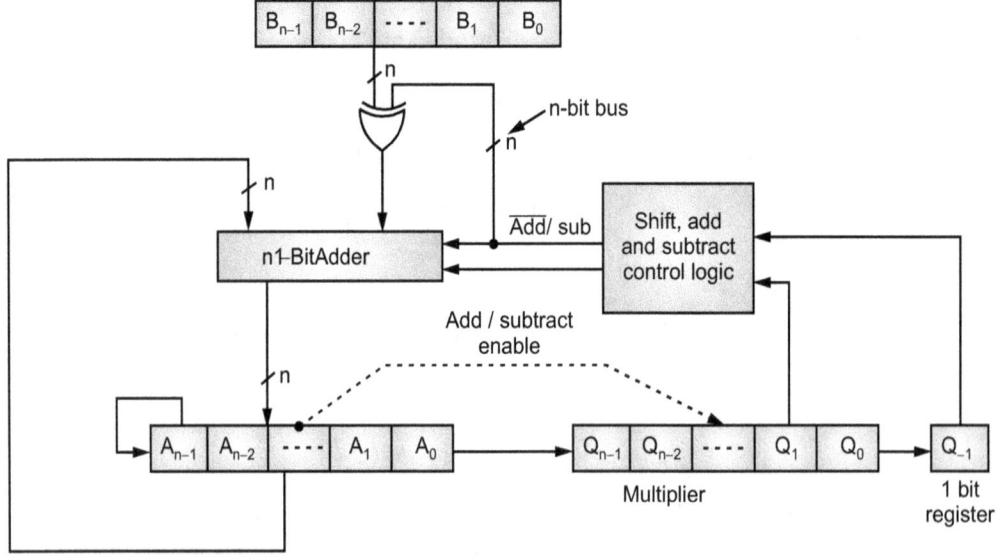

Fig. 2.5 : Hardware Implementation for Booth's algorithm

- Multiplier and multiplicand are loaded into register Q and register B respectively.

- Register A and Q–1 are initially set to 0.

- One input is A and other is multiplicand the shift, add, and subtract control logic scans bits Q and Q–1 one at a time and generate control signal. If two bits are same 1–1 or 0–0 then all of bits ofA,Q and Q–1.

(1)   The Booth's algorithm can be implemented as shown in Fig. 2.5. The circuit is similar to circuit of positive number multiplication.

(2)   It consist of n–bit adder, shift, add subtract control logic and four registers. A, B, Q and Q – 1.

(3)   The multiplier is loaded in register Q and multiplicand in A.

(4)   The n–bit adder performs addition of two inputs. One input is the A register and other input is multiplicand.

(5)   In case of addition, $\overline{\text{Add}}$ /sub line is 0, therefore cin = 0 and multiplicand is directly applied as the second input to the n–bit adder.

(6)   In case of subtraction. $\overline{\text{Add}}$ /sub line is 1, and multiplicand is complemented form is applied to the n–bit adder.

(7)   The shift, add and subtract control logic scans bits Q_0 and Q_1 and generates the signal as follows :

Q_0	Q – 1	Add/Sub	Add/subtract enable	Shift
0	0	X	0	1
0	1	0	1	1
1	0	1	1	1
1	1	X	0	1

(8)   If the two bits are (0–0 or 1–1) then all registers are shifted to right with adding or subtracting.

(9)   If the two bits are (0–1) the multiplicand is added.

(10)   If bits are (1–0) then mulplicand is subtracted.

Following Fig. 2.6 explains the sequence of events in Booths algorithm.

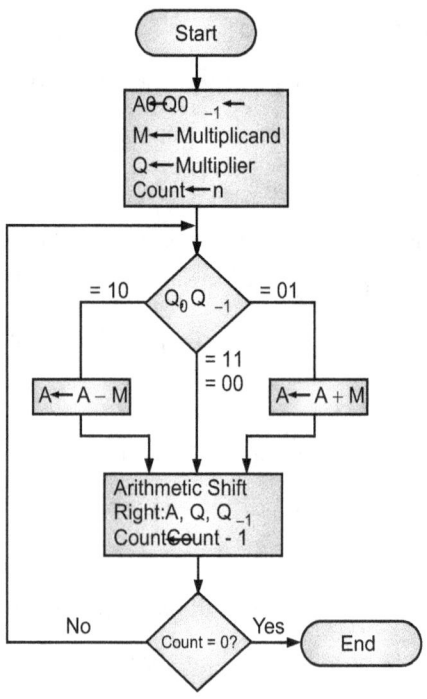

Fig 2.6 : Flowchart for booths algorithm

Examples on Booth's Algorithm :

Example 1 : Both positive numbers (5 × 4)

Multiplicand (B) = 0101 (5)   Multiplier (Q) = 0100 (4)

STEPS	A	Q	Q − 1	OPERATION
	0 0 0 0	0 1 0 0	0	Initial
Step 1	0 0 0 0	0 0 1 0	0	Arithmetic shift right
Step 2	0 0 0 0	0 0 0 1	0	Arithmetic shift right
Step 3	1 0 1 1	0 0 0 1	0	A ←A + B
	1 1 0 1	1 0 0 0	1	Arithmetic shift right
Step 4	0 0 1 0	1 0 0 0	1	A ←A + B
	0 0 0 1	0 1 0 0	0	Arithmetic shift right
Anwser : 0 0 0 1 01 00 = + 20				

Example 2 : Negative multiplier (5 × –4)

Multiplicand (B) = 0101(5)   Multiplier (Q) 1100(–4 2's complement of 4)

STEPS	A	Q	Q – 1	OPERATION
	0 0 0 0	1 1 0 0	0	Initial
Step 1	0 0 0 0	0 1 1 0	0	Arithmetic shift right
Step 2	0 0 0 0	0 0 1 1	0	Arithmetic shift right
Step 3	1 0 1 1	0 0 1 1	0	A ←A + B
	1 1 0 1	1 0 0 1	1	Arithmetic shift right
Step 4	1 1 1 0	1 1 0 0	1	Arithmetic shift right
Anwser : 1110 1100 = –20(2 complement of 20)				

Example 3 : Negative multiplicand (–5 × 4)

Multiplicand (B) = 1011(–5, 2's complement of 5)   Multiplier (Q) = 0100(4)

STEPS	A	Q	Q – 1	OPERATION
	0 0 0 0	0 1 0 0	0	Initial
Step 1	0 0 0 0	0 0 1 0	0	Arithmetic shift right
Step 2	0 0 0 0	0 0 0 1	0	Arithmetic shift right
Step 3	0 1 0 1	0 0 0 1	0	A ←A + B
	0 0 1 0	1 0 0 0	1	Arithmetic shift right
Step 4	1 1 0 1	1 0 0 0	1	A ←A + B
	1 1 1 0	1 1 0 0	0	Arithmetic shift right
Answer = 1110 1100 = –20(2 complement of 20)				

Example 4 : Both negative (–5 ×–4)

Multiplicand (B) = 1011 (–5, 2's complement of 5) Multiplier (Q) = 1100 (–4 2's complement of 4).

STEPS	A	Q	Q – 1	OPERATION
	0 0 0 0	1 1 0 0	0	Initial
Step 1	0 0 0 0	0 1 1 0	0	Arithmetic shift right
Step 2	0 0 0 0	0 0 1 1	0	Arithmetic shift right
Step 3	0 1 0 1	0 0 1 1	0	A ←A + B
	0 0 1 0	1 0 0 1	1	Arithmetic shift right
Step 4	0 0 0 1	0 1 0 0	1	Arithmetic shift right
Answer = 0001 0100 = +20				

SOLVED EXAMPLES ON BOOTH'S ALGORITHM

Example 5 : Explain Booth's Algorithm to multiply the following pair of signed two's complement numbers :

A = 110011 MultiplicandB = 101100 Multiplier

Also, implement the above using Bit–pair recording and explain how it achieves faster multiplication. **[May 05, 09, Dec. 06, Dec. 09,Dec. 10, 10 Marks]**

Solution : Both are –ve case 4 (Refer page 1–34)

Multiplicand (B)110011 (– 13)   Multiplier (Q) ←101100 (– 20)

STEPS	A	Q	Q – 1	OPERATION
	000000	101100	0	Initial
1.	000000	010110	0	Shift right
2.	000000	001011	0	Shift right
3.	001101	001011	0	A ←A + B
	000110	100101	1	Shift right
4.	000011	010010	1	Shift right
5.	110110	010010	1	A ←A + B
	111011	001001	0	Shift right
6.	001000	001001	0	A ←A – B
	000100	000100	1	Shift right

Result 000100 000100 = + 260

Check Q_0 and Q – 1 bit. It is 00 then shift right operation. If 11 then shift right.

If 10 — then perform A←A– B.

and if 01 — then perform A ←A– B.

Perform right shift operation for each step.

Implementation with bit pair recording .

Multiplier :1 100 10 1 1 00 (–20)

Booth's algorithm may need the summation at each step and number of steps required in Booth's algorithm are equal to length of multiplier in bits. The bit pair recording halves the maximum number of summations. Hence, it achieves faster multiplication.

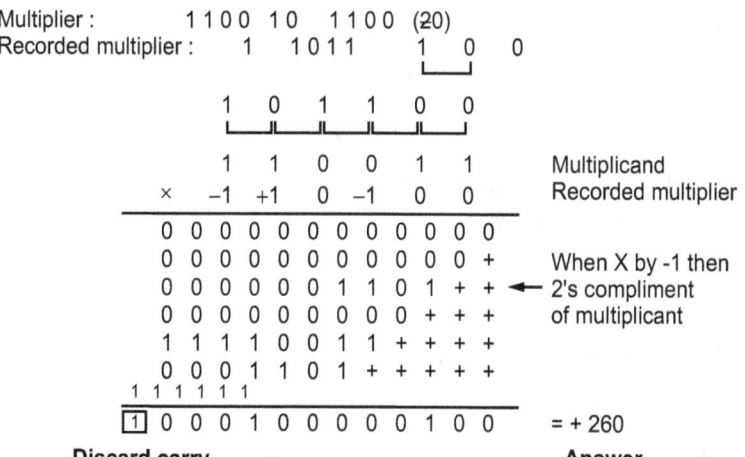

Multiplier :   1 1 0 0 1 0   1 1 0 0   (20)
Recorded multiplier :   1   1 0 1 1   1   0   0

                    1   0   1   1   0   0

                    1   1   0   0   1   1   Multiplicand
         ×   −1   +1   0   −1   0   0   Recorded multiplier
    ───
         0 0 0 0 0 0 0 0 0 0 0
         0 0 0 0 0 0 0 0 0 0 +   When X by -1 then
         0 0 0 0 0 0 1 1 0 1 + + ◄──   2's compliment
         0 0 0 0 0 0 0 0 0 + + +   of multiplicant
         1 1 1 1 0 0 1 1 + + + +
         0 0 0 1 1 0 1 + + + + +
    1 1 1 1 1 1
    ───
    ⊡ 0 0 0 1 0 0 0 0 0 1 0 0   = + 260
        Discard carry   **Answer**

Example 6 : Using Booth's algorithm multiply the following

Multiplicand = + 15

Multiplier = − 6   **[Dec. 05, 8 Marks]**

Solution : Multiplicand (B) ← 01111 multiplier (Q) ← 1010 (−6)

STEPS	A	Q	Q−1	OPERATION
	000000	1010	0	Initial
1.	000000	0101	0	Shift right
2.	10001	0101	0	A ← A − B
	11000	1010	1	Shift right
3.	00111	1010	1	A ← A + B
	00011	1101	0	Shift right
4.	10100	1101	0	A ← A − B
	11010	0110	1	Shift right

Result : 11010 0 110 = − 90 (2's complement of 90)

Example 7 : Draw the hardware implementation of Booth's Algorithm. Using Booth's Algorithm multiplicand = + 22

Multiplier = − 5   **[Dec. 07, 7 Marks]**

Solution :

Refer Fig. 2.5. For Hardware Implementation of Booth's Algorithm

Multiplicand : 22 and

Multiplier : − 5

take 2's complement of multiplier as it is −ve

111011 → 5

Recoded multiplier is

$$1 \ 1 \ 1 \ 0 \ 1 \ 0$$
$$\leftarrow\leftarrow\leftarrow\leftarrow\leftarrow\leftarrow$$
$$0 \ 0 \ -1 \ 1 \ 0 \ -1$$

When −1 is multiplied the 2's complement of the multiplicand is written and when 1 is multiplied the multiplicand is written as it is.

2's complement of 0 1 1 1 1 0→1 0 1 0 1 0

```
              0  1  0  1  1  0
      ×       0  0 -1  1  0 -1
     ─────────────────────────────────
              1  1  1  1  1  1  1  0  1  0  1  0
              0  0  0  0  0  0  0  0  0  0  0  +  When × by −1 then
              0  0  0  0  0  1  0  1  1  0  +  +  ← 2's compliment
              1  1  1  1  0  1  0  1  0  +  +  +  of multiplicand
              0  0  0  0  0  0  0  0  +  +  +  +
              0  0  0  0  0  0  0  +  +  +  +  +
              1  1  1  1  1  1  1  1
     ─────────────────────────────────
  [1]         1  1  1  1  1  0  0  1  0  1  1  0  (−110)
```

ignore

$$1 \ 1 \ 1 \ 1 \ 1 \ 0 \ 0 \ 1 \ 0 \ 0 \ 1 \ 0 \quad \text{is negative}$$

Verify the result. Take 2's complement

```
              0  0  0  0  0  1  1  0  1  1  0  1
      +                                       1
     ─────────────────────────────────
                          1  1  0  1  1  1  0  (+ 110)
```

So the result is 2's complement of + 110 i.e. − 110 is verified.

3. Modified Booth's algorithm :

Bit pair recoding is used to speed up the multiplication process in booth's algorithm. It have maximum number of summands.

In this technique, the Booth's recoded multiplier bits are grouped in the pairs. Then each pair is represented by its equivalent single bit multiplier reducing total number of multiplier bits to half. Example pair (+1 −1) is equivalent to pair (0 +1).

That is instead of adding −1 times multiplicand at shifted position i to +1 times the multiplicand at position i + 1, the same result is obtained by adding +1 times multiplicand at position i similarly (+1 0) is equivalent to (0 +2), (−1 +1) is equivalent to (0 − 1) and so on.

By replacing pairs with their equipments we can get bit pair–recoded multiplier. But instead of deriving bit pair recoded multiplier from booth recoded multiplier one can directly derive it pair recoded multiplier. The bit–pair recoding of multiplier can be directly derived from table.

Table shows the bit–pair code for all possible multiplier bit options.

Table 2.1 : Bit pair recode

Multiplier bit pair		Multiplier bit on the right	Bit pair recoded multiplier bit at position 1
$i+1$	i	$i-1$	
0	0	0	0
0	0	1	+1
0	1	0	+1
0	1	1	+2
1	0	0	−2
1	0	1	−1
1	1	0	−1
1	1	1	0

Example1: Solve following using bit pair recoding method.

Multiplicand 0 1 1 1 1

Multiplier1 0 1 1 0

2's complement of multiplicand = 10 0 0 1

Bit pair code for multiplier = sign extension

$$1\ 1\ 0\ 1\ 1\quad 0\ \textcircled{0}\quad \text{Implied zero end}$$

$$-1\quad 2\qquad -2\quad \text{Recorded multiplier}$$

By referring the table of modified booths algorithm we determine the bit pair code.

```
    0   1   1   1   1                       Multiplicand
×  -1       2      -2                       recoded multiplier
    1   1   1   1   1   0   0   0   1   0
    0   0   0   1   1   1   1   0   +   +
    0   1   0   0   0   1   +   +   +   +
 1  0   1   0   1   1   0   1   0   1   0   Final Answer
```

Modified Booth's Algorithm

Example 2 : Solve following using bit pair recoding method.

Multiplicand – 110101 (–11)

Multiplier - 011011 (27)

2's complement of multiplicand

110101

001010

+   1

___

001011   2's compliment

Bit pair code for multiplier 011010

```
        0 1 1 0 1   1  ⓪  Implied zero end
          L_JL_JL_J
         +2   –1    –1      Recorded multiplier
        110101
      + 2 – 1 – 1
      _____
        000000001011    ...2's compliment of muplicant
        0000001011++
        11101010++++
      _____
        111011010111    (–297)
```

Example on modified Booth's algorithm

Example 3 : Draw the flow chart for Booth's algorithm and solve the following using bit pair recording method.

Multiplicand 01111 Multiplier 10110   **[May 07, 8 Marks]**

Solution :

Refer Fig. 2.6 for flow chart of Booth's algorithm.

Multiplicand   0 1 1 1 1

Multiplier   101 10

2's complement of multiplicand. Refer example for modified Booth's algorithm.

2.5 DIVISIONS   **[Dec. 06, 9 Marks]**

The division is more complex than multiplication for simplicity we will see division for positive numbers. The usual algorithm for dividing positive numbers by hand. It shows examples of decimal division and binary recoded division of the same value.

49 is partial reminder. Binary division quotient bits are 0 and 1. The bits of dividend are examined from left to right until the set of bits examined represents a number greater than or equal to the divisor. This is referred to as the divisor being able to divide the number. Until

this condition occurs 0's are placed in the quotient from left to right. When condition is satisfied, a 1 is placed in the quotient and the divisor is subtracted from the partial dividend. The result is referred to as a partial remainder. From this point onwards, the division process follows repetition of steps. Each repetition cycle, additional bits from the dividend are brought down to the partial remainder until the result is greater than or equal to the divisor, and the divisor is subtracted from the result to produce a new partial remainder. The process continues until all bits of the dividend are brought down and result is still less than divisor.

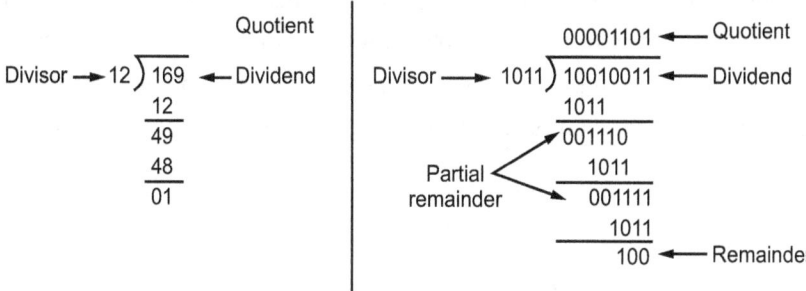

2.5.1 Restoring Division

Restoring division algorithm exist to perform division in digital designs restoring division operates on fixed point fractional number.

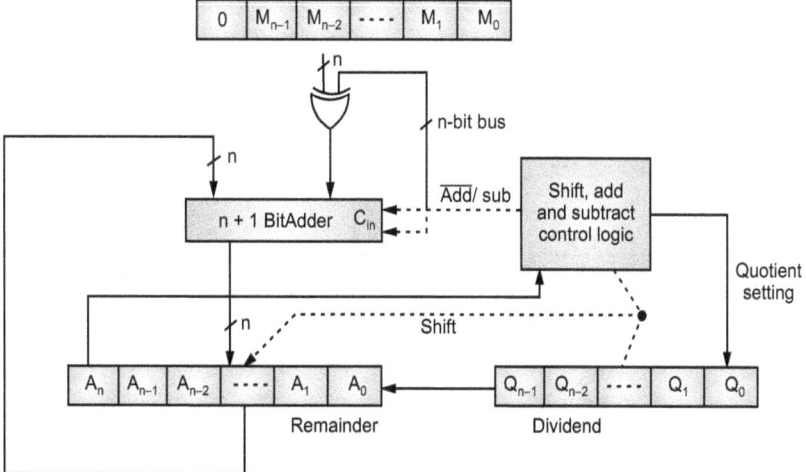

Fig 2.7 : Hardware to implement binary division.

Hardware implementation of division consist of n + 1 bit binary adder, shift, add and subtract control logic registers A, M, and Q as shown in figure divisor and dividend are loaded into register M and register Q. Register A is initially set to zero. The division operation is then carried out. After the division is complete, the n–bit quotient is in register Q and the remainder is in register A. Operation include:

1. Shift A and Q left one binary position.

2. Subtract divisor from A and place answer back in A (M–A–M).

3. If the sign bit of A is 1, set Q0 to 0 and add divisor back to A(that is restore A) otherwise, set Q0 to 1.

4. Repeat steps 1, 2 and 3 times.

The division algorithm needs restoring A, after each unsuccessful subtraction. (Subtraction is said to be unsuccessful if the result is negative) therefore it is referred to as restoring division algorithm. This algorithm is improved, giving non–restoring division algorithm. Consider the sequence of operations that takes place after the subtraction operation in the restoring algorithm.

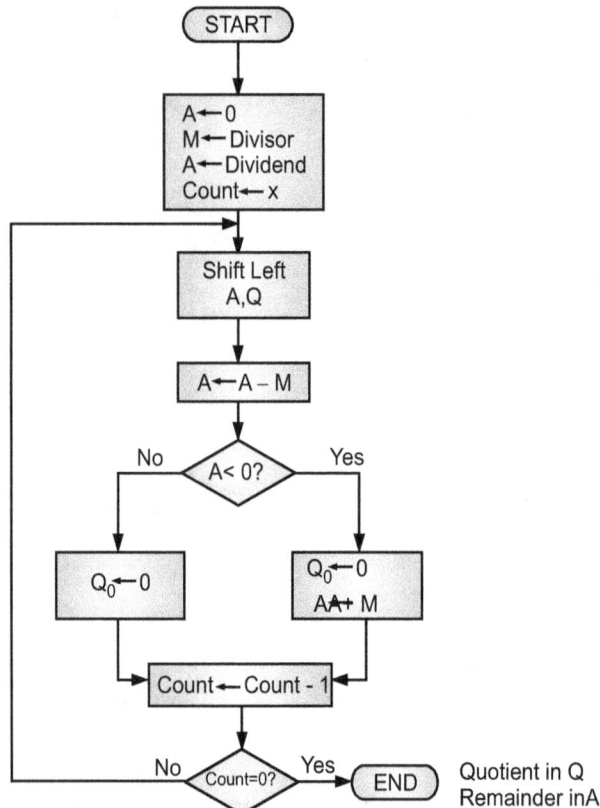

Fig. 2.8 : Flowchart for restoring division operation

Example for restoring division :

Dividend is 0 111 and divisor is 0011. Following figure shows (a), (b), (c), (d) all the four cases for signed restoring division. Where A consist of remainder and Q consist of Quotient. Consider subtract M means add M in 2's complement form.

If A is positive then shift left and subtract divisor 2A–M.

If A is negative then Restore A+M, Shift left and subtract divisor $->2(A+M)-M = 2A+M$

Consider following examples on restoring division.

A	Q	M = 0011	A	Q	M = 1101
0000	0111	Initial Value	0000	0111	Initial Value
0000	1110	Shift	0000	1110	Shift
1101		Subtract	1101		Add
0000	1110	Restore	0000	1110	Restore
0001	1100	Shift	0001	1100	Shift
1110		Subtract	1110		Add
0001	1100	Restore	0001	1100	Restore
0011	1000	Shift	0011	1000	Shift
0000		Subtract	0000		Add
0000	1001	Set $Q_0 = 1$	0000	1001	Set $Q_0 = 1$
0001	0010	Shift	0001	0010	Shift
1110		Subtract	1110		Add
0001	0010	Restore	0001	0010	Restore
(a) (7) ÷(3)			(b) (7) ÷(−3)		

A	Q	M = 0011	A	Q	M = 1101
1111	1001	Initial Value	1111	1001	Initial Value
1111	0010	Shift	1111	0010	Shift
0010		Add	0010		Subtract
1111	0010	Restore	1111	0010	Restore
1110	0100	Shift	1110	0100	Shift
0001		Add	0001		Subtract
1110	0100	Restore	1110	0100	Restore
1100	1000	Shift	1100	1000	Shift
1111		Add	1111		Subtract
1111	1001	Set $Q_0 = 1$	1111	1001	Set $Q_0 = 1$
1111	0010	Shift	1111	0010	Shift
0010		Add	0010		Subtract
1111	0010	Restore	1111	0010	Restore
(c) (−7) ÷ (3)			(d) (−7) ÷ (−3)		

2.5.2 Non-Restoring Division

Steps :

1. If the sign of A is 0,shift A and Q left one bit position and subtract divisor from A, therwise shift A and Q left and add divisor to A. if sign of A is 0,set Q_0 to 1; otherwise set Q_0 to 0.

2. Repeat steps 1 and 2 for n times.

3. If the sign of A is 1, add divisor to A.

Flowchart for non–restoring division

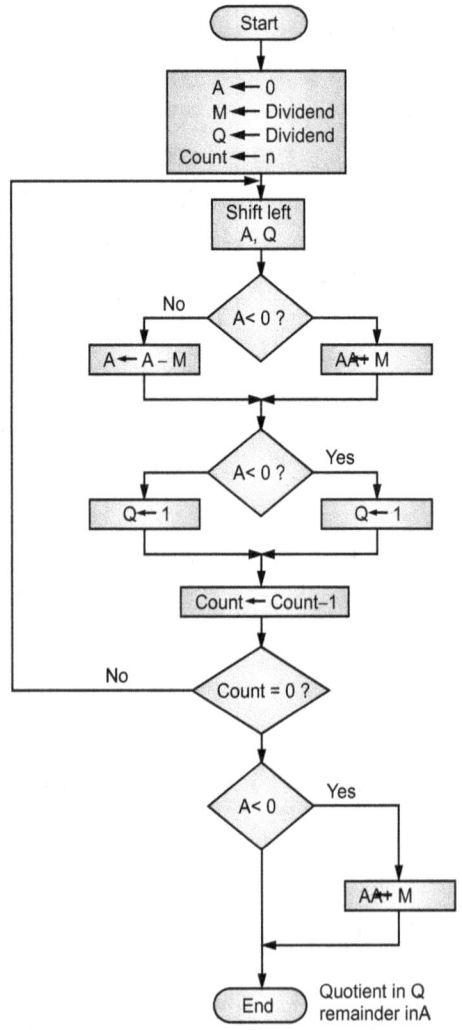

Fig 2.9 : Flowchart for non–restoring division

Step 3 is required to leave the proper positive number in A at the end of n cycles.

The hardware can also be used to perform non restoring algorithm. There is no simple algorithm for signed division. The operand is preprocessed to transform them into positive values. Then using one of the algorithm just discussed quotients and remainders are calculated. The quotient and remainders are then transformed to the correct signed values.

Example 1 : For non restoring division

Consider 4 bit dividend and 2 bit divisor

Dividend = 1010 (10)

Divisor = 0011 (3)   [May 06]

Remainder (1)   Quotient (3)

In above example after 4 register A is positive and hence step 3 is not required. Let us see another examples in which step 3 is required.

Example 2 : Dividend = 1 0 1 1 (11)

Divisor = 0 1 0 1 (5)

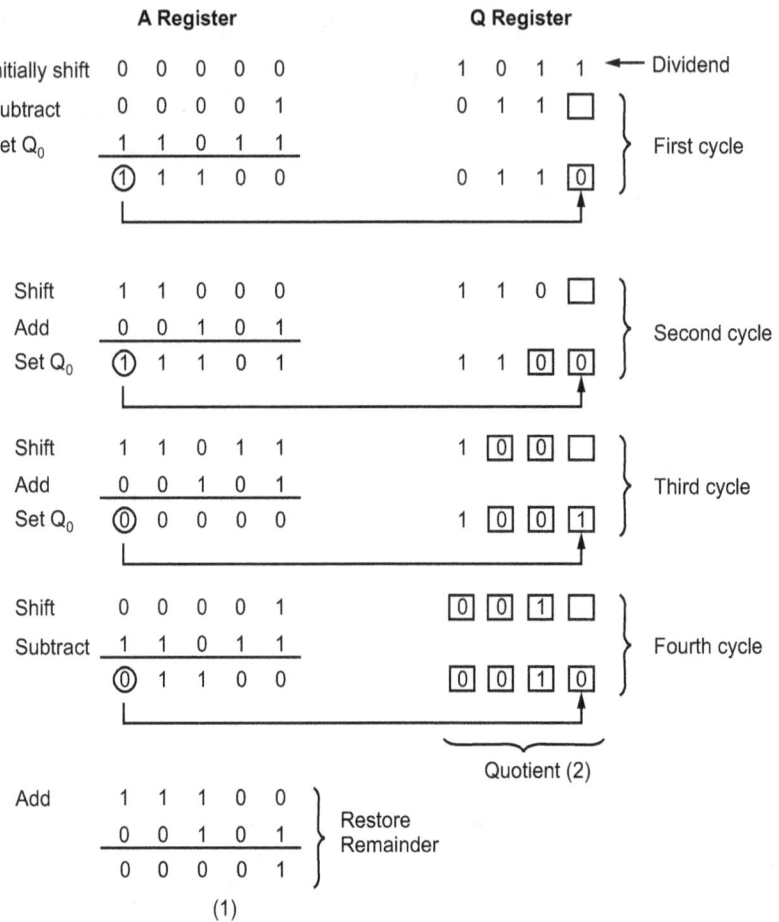

So, A consist of remainder 00001

and Quotient is 0010.

Table 2.2 : Comparison between Restoring and Non-Restoring Division Algorithm

No.	Restoring division Algorithm	Non-restoring division Algorithm
1.	Needs restoring of registers A if the result of subtraction is negative.	Does not need restoring.
2.	In such cycle content of register A is first shifted left and then divisor is subtracted from it.	In each cycle content of register A is first shifted left and then divisor is added or subtracted with the content of register A depending on the sign of A.
3.	Does not need restoring of remainder.	Needs restoring of remainder if remainder is negative.
4.	Slower algorithm.	Faster algorithm.

SOLVED QUESTIONS ON RESTORING AND NON-RESTORING DIVISION

Example 3 : Draw the flow chart for restoring division algorithm and solve the following using above algorithm.

Dividend = 17   Divisor = 03   **[Dec. 05, 09, May 10, 10 Marks]**

Solution :

Dividend = 17 = $(10001)_2 \rightarrow Q$ Divisor = 03 – $(00011)_2 \rightarrow B$

For flow chart for restoring division refer Fig. 2.8.

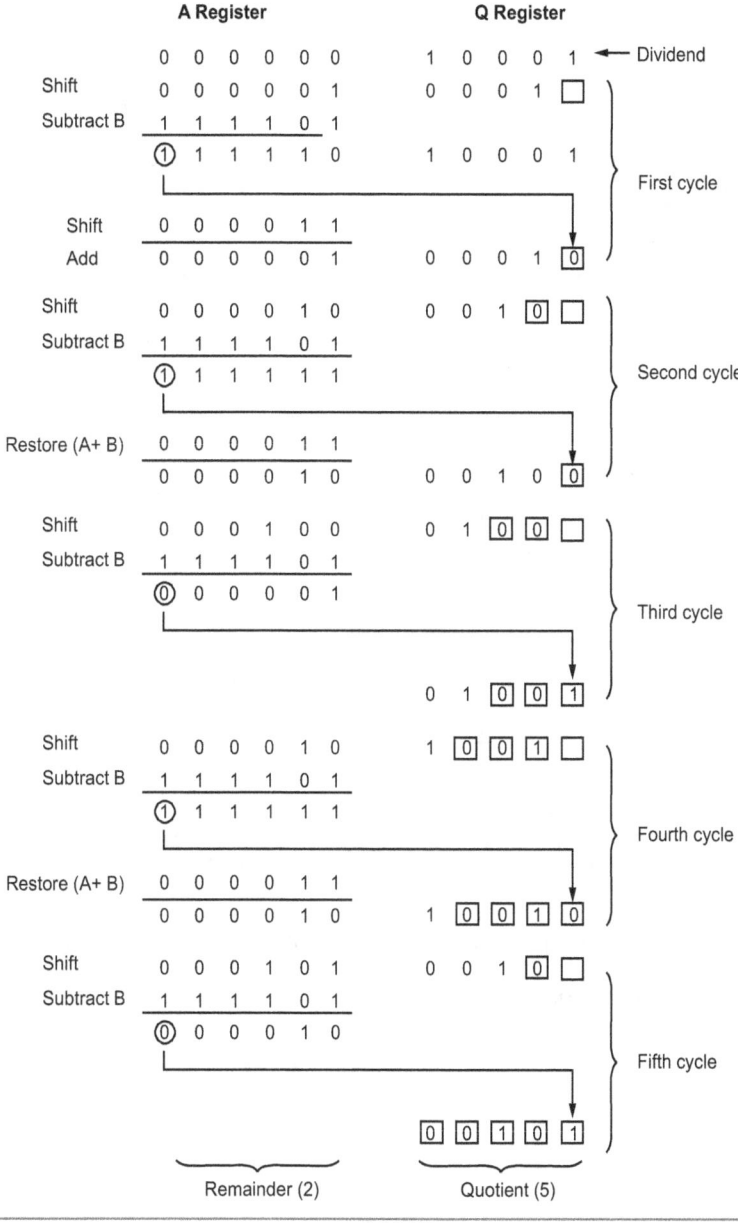

Example 4 : Draw the flow chart for non-restoring division algorithm and perform division of the following numbers using non-restoring.

Division algorithm :

    Dividend = 1011 (11)

    Divisor = 0011 (3)   **[May 06, 10, Dec. 09, 10 Marks]**

Solution : Flowchart for non-restoring division refer Fig. 2.9.

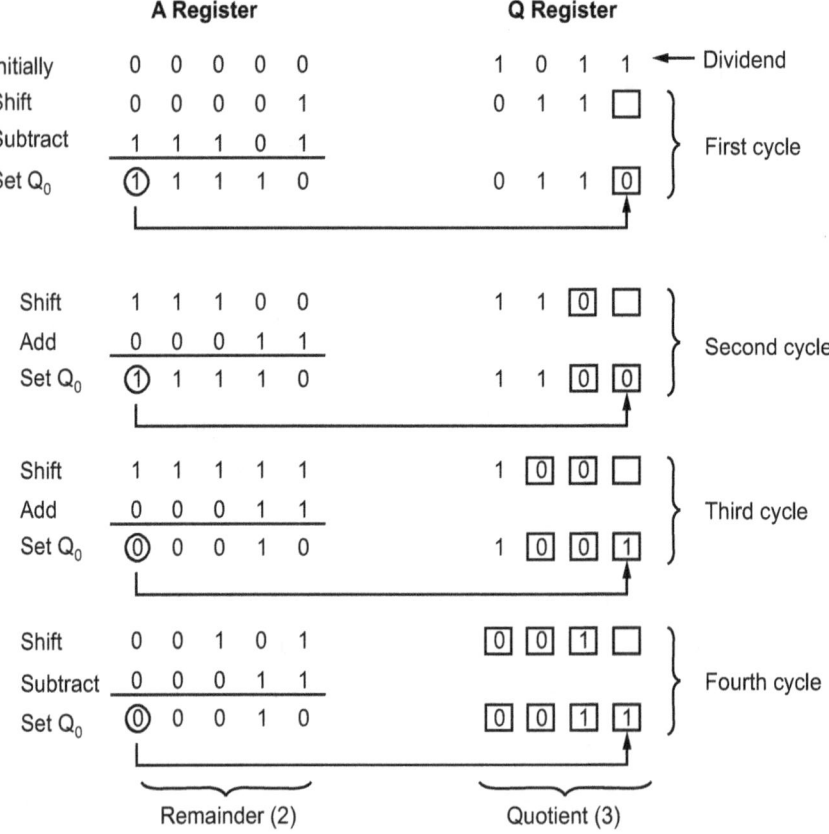

	A Register	Q Register	
Initially	0 0 0 0 0	1 0 1 1	← Dividend
Shift	0 0 0 0 1	0 1 1 ☐	
Subtract	1 1 1 0 1		First cycle
Set Q_0	① 1 1 1 0	0 1 1 ⓪	
Shift	1 1 1 0 0	1 1 ⓪ ☐	
Add	0 0 0 1 1		Second cycle
Set Q_0	① 1 1 1 0	1 1 ⓪ ⓪	
Shift	1 1 1 1 1	1 ⓪ ⓪ ☐	
Add	0 0 0 1 1		Third cycle
Set Q_0	⓪ 0 0 1 0	1 ⓪ ⓪ ①	
Shift	0 0 1 0 1	⓪ ⓪ ① ☐	
Subtract	0 0 0 1 1		Fourth cycle
Set Q_0	⓪ 0 0 1 0	⓪ ⓪ ① ①	

Remainder (2)   Quotient (3)

Example 5 : Compare restoring and non-restoring division algorithm. Perform division of the following numbers using restoring division algorithm

Division algorithm :

    Dividend = 1101 (13)

    Divisor = 11 (3)   **[Dec. 06, 10 Marks]**

Solution : For comparison refer table 2.1.

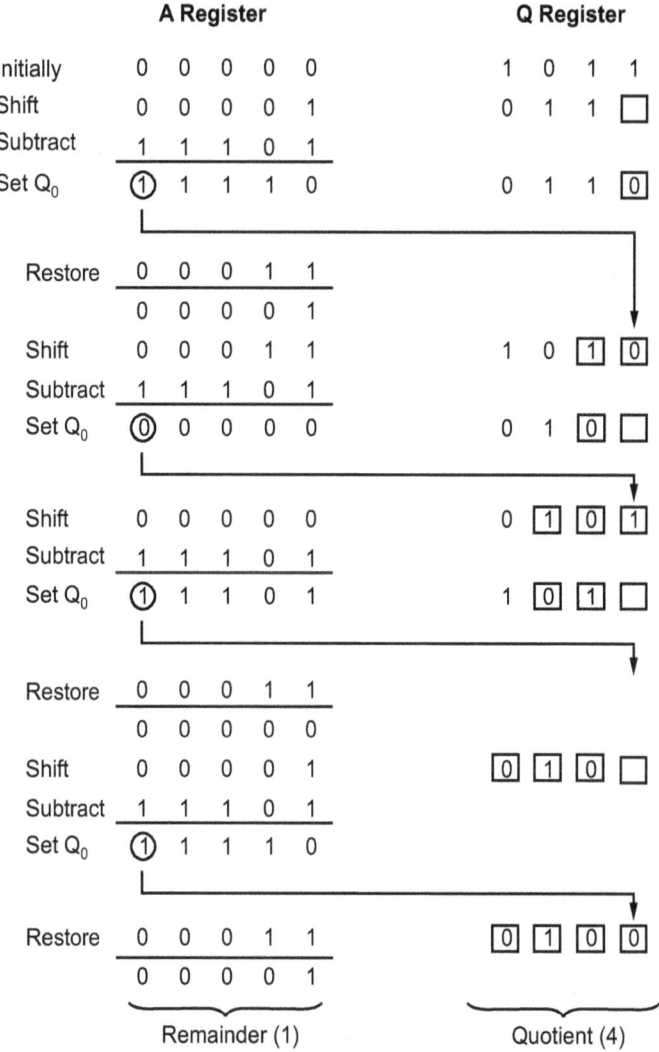

	A Register	Q Register
Initially	0 0 0 0 0	1 0 1 1
Shift	0 0 0 0 1	0 1 1 ☐
Subtract	1 1 1 0 1	
Set Q_0	① 1 1 1 0	0 1 1 ☐
Restore	0 0 0 1 1	
	0 0 0 0 1	
Shift	0 0 0 1 1	1 0 ☐ ☐
Subtract	1 1 1 0 1	
Set Q_0	⓪ 0 0 0 0	0 1 ☐ ☐
Shift	0 0 0 0 0	0 ☐ ☐ ☐
Subtract	1 1 1 0 1	
Set Q_0	① 1 1 0 1	1 ☐ ☐ ☐
Restore	0 0 0 1 1	
	0 0 0 0 0	
Shift	0 0 0 0 1	☐ ☐ ☐ ☐
Subtract	1 1 1 0 1	
Set Q_0	① 1 1 1 0	
Restore	0 0 0 1 1	☐ ☐ ☐ ☐
	0 0 0 0 1	

Remainder (1)   Quotient (4)

Example 6 : Draw flow chart for restoring division algorithm and perform division of the following numbers using restoring division algorithm.

A : 1100 (12)

B : 0100 (4)   **[May 07, 10 Marks]**

Solution : Take 2's complement of divisor (B) = 1100

	A Register					Q Register			
Initially	0	0	0	0	0	1	1	0	0
Shift	0	0	0	0	1	1	0	0	□
Subtract B	1	1	1	0	0				
Set Q_0	1	1	1	0	1	1	0	0	[0]
Restore (A+ B)	0	0	1	0	0				
	0	0	0	0	1	[1]	[0]	[0]	[0]
Shift	0	0	0	1	1	0	0	0	□
Subtract B	1	1	1	0	0				
Set Q_0	1	1	1	1	1	0	0	0	[0]
Restore	0	0	1	0	0				
	0	0	0	1	1	0	0	0	0
Shift	0	0	1	1	0	0	0	0	□
Subtract B	1	1	1	0	0				
Set Q_0	0	0	0	1	0	0	0	0	[1]
Shift	0	0	1	0	0	0	0	1	□
Subtract B	1	1	1	0	0				
Set Q_0	0	0	0	0	0	0	0	1	[1]

Remainder   Quotient (3)

Example 7 : Draw flowchart for non-restoring division operation. Perform the division of the following numbers using non-restoring division.

   Dividend = 1101 (13) Divisor = 0100 (4)   **[Dec. 07, 14 Marks]**

Solution : Refer Fig. 2.9 for flow chart

Dividend : 1101   Divisor : 0100 (2's complement of divisior)

$Q \rightarrow$ Dividend   B divisor   1100

$A \rightarrow$ 00000

	A Register					Q Register				
Initially	0	0	0	0	0	1	1	0	1	← Dividend
Shift	0	0	0	0	1	1	0	1	□	First cycle
Subtract	1	1	0	0	0					(Since sign bit ofAis
Set Q_0	①	1	0	0	1	1	0	1	[0]	'0' subtract divisor i.e. add two's comlement)

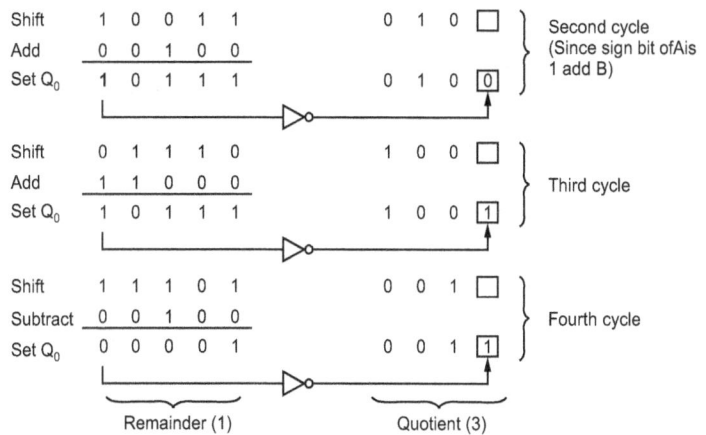

Shift	1 0 0 1 1	0 1 0 ☐	Second cycle
Add	0 0 1 0 0		(Since sign bit ofAis
Set Q_0	1 0 1 1 1	0 1 0 ⓪	1 add B)

Shift	0 1 1 1 0	1 0 0 ☐	
Add	1 1 0 0 0		Third cycle
Set Q_0	1 0 1 1 1	1 0 0 ①	

Shift	1 1 1 0 1	0 0 1 ☐	
Subtract	0 0 1 0 0		Fourth cycle
Set Q_0	0 0 0 0 1	0 0 1 ①	

Remainder (1)   Quotient (3)

Example 8 : Perform the following division using restoring and non-restoring division algorithm.

   Dividend = 1100 (12) Divisor = 0011 (3)   **[May 05, 06, 10 Marks]**

Solution : Restoring :

	A Register	Q Register
Initially	0 0 0 0 0	1 1 0 0
Shift	0 0 0 0 1	1 0 0 ☐
Subtract	1 1 1 0 1	
Set Q_0	① 1 1 1 0	
Restore	0 0 0 1 1	
	0 0 0 0 1	
Shift	0 0 0 1 1	1 0 0 ⓪
Subtract	1 1 1 0 1	
Set Q_0	⓪ 0 0 0 0	
	0 0 0 0 0	
Shift	0 0 0 0 0	0 0 ⓪ ①
Subtract	1 1 1 0 1	
Set Q_0	① 1 1 0 1	0 0 ① ⓪
Restore	0 0 0 1 1	
	0 0 0 0 0	0 0 1 ⓪
Shift	0 0 0 0 0	
Subtract	1 1 1 0 1	
Set Q_0	① 1 1 0 1	
Restore	0 0 0 1 1	
	0 0 0 0 0	⓪ ① ⓪ ⓪

Remainder (0)   Quotient (4)

Non-Restoring :

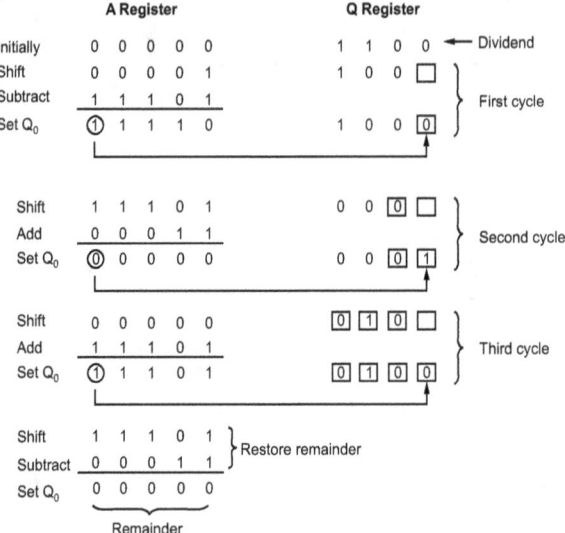

	A Register	Q Register	
Initially	0 0 0 0 0	1 1 0 0	← Dividend
Shift	0 0 0 0 1	1 0 0 ☐	
Subtract	1 1 1 0 1		First cycle
Set Q₀	① 1 1 1 0	1 0 0 0	

Shift	1 1 1 0 1	0 0 0 ☐	
Add	0 0 0 1 1		Second cycle
Set Q₀	⓪ 0 0 0 0	0 0 0 1	

Shift	0 0 0 0 0	0 1 0 ☐	
Add	1 1 1 0 1		Third cycle
Set Q₀	① 1 1 0 1	0 1 0 0	

Shift	1 1 1 0 1		
Subtract	0 0 0 1 1	Restore remainder	
Set Q₀	0 0 0 0 0		

Remainder

Example 9 : Perform the following division using restoring division algorithm :
Dividend = 1001 (9) Divisor = 0101 (5)   **[Dec. 08, 10, 08 Marks]**

Solution :

	A Register	Q Register
Initially	0 0 0 0 0	1 0 0 1
Shift	0 0 0 0 1	0 0 1 ☐
Subtract	1 1 0 1 1	
Set Q₀	① 1 1 0 0	

Restore	0 0 1 0 1	
	0 0 0 0 1	0 1 1 0
Shift	0 0 0 1 0	0 1 0 ☐
Subtract	1 1 0 1 1	
Set Q₀	① 1 1 0 1	

Restore	0 0 1 0 1	
	0 0 0 1 0	0 1 0 0
Shift	0 0 1 0 0	1 0 0 ☐
Subtract	1 1 0 1 1	
Set Q₀	① 1 1 1 1	

Restore	0 0 1 0 1	
	0 0 1 0 0	1 0 0 0
Shift	0 1 0 0 1	0 0 0 ☐
Subtract	1 1 0 1 1	
Set Q₀	⓪ 0 1 0 0	

		0 0 0 1

Remainder (4)   Quotient (1)

Example 10 : Perform the following division using restoring method :

Dividend = 1000 (8) and Divisor = 0010 (2)

Solution :

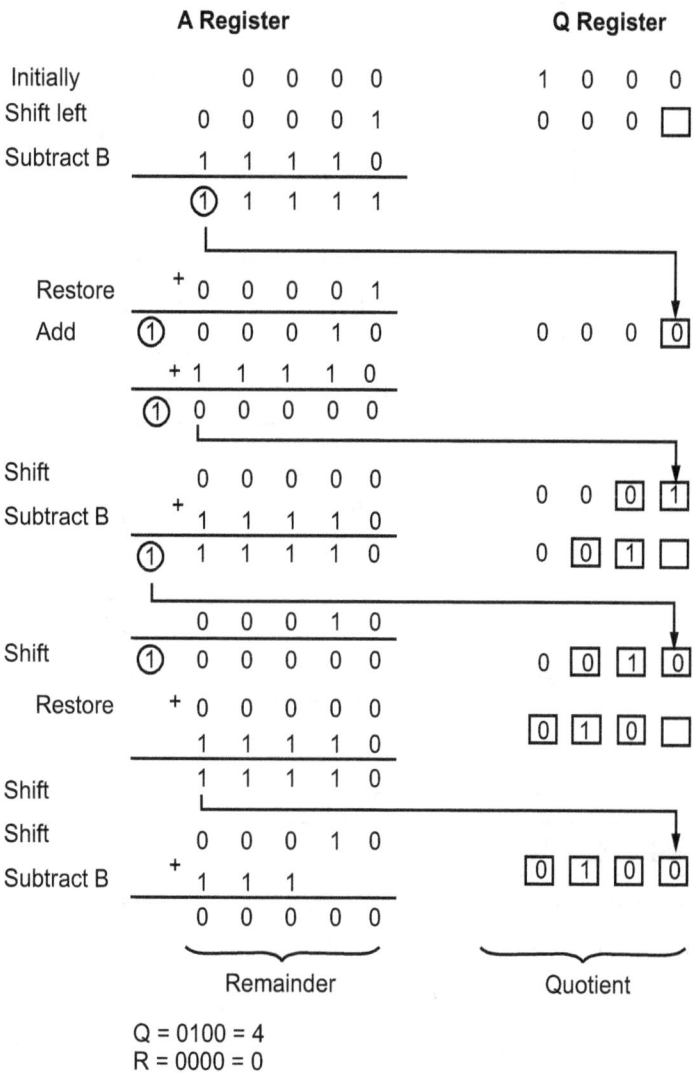

Q = 0100 = 4
R = 0000 = 0

Example 11 : Perform the following division using non-restoring method.

Dividend = 1000 (8) and Divisor = 0010 (2)

Solution :

A → 0000, B → 0010 Q → 1000

	Sign	A	Q
	0	0 0 0 0	1 0 0 0
Shift	0	0 0 0 0	0 0 0 ☐
Subtract	1	1 1 1 0	
Set Q₀	[1]	1 1 1 1	
		1 1 1 1	0 0 0 [0]
Shift left	1	1 1 1 0	0 0 [0] ☐
AddA+ B	0	0 0 1 0	
	0	0 0 0 0	
Shift	0	0 0 0 0	0 0 [0] [1]
Subtract	+ 1	1 1 1 0	0 [0] [1] ☐
	1	1 1 1 0	
Shift	1	1 1 0 0	0 0 [1] [0]
Add	0	0 0 1 0	0 [1] [0] ☐
	1	1 1 1 0	
	1	1 1 1 0	[0] [1] [0] [0]
Add	0	0 0 1 0	
	0	0 0 0 0	
		R (0)	Q (4)

2.6 FLOATING POINT REPRESENTATIONS

Integer fixed point schemes do not have the ability to represent very large or very small numbers. Need the ability to dynamically move the decimal point to a convenient location

Format : +/–M x R +/–E

Mantissas are stored in a normalized format either 1xxxxx or 0.1xxxxx, Since the 1 is required, don't need to explicitly store it in the data word insert it for calculations only. Exponents can be positive or negative values. Use biasing (Excess coding) to avoid operating on negative exponents. Bias is added to all exponent positive numbers to represent fractional binary numbers it is necessary to consider binary point. If binary point is assumed to the right of the signed bit we can represent fractional binary number as.

$$B = (b_0 \times 2^0 + b_{-1} \times 2^{-1} + b_{-2} \times 2^{-2} + \dots + b_{-[n-1]} \times 2^{(-n-1)})$$

With the fractional number system we can represent the fractional numbers in the following range.

$$2^{-(n-1)} \leq F \leq 1 - 2^{-(n-1)}$$

If n=32 then value range is approximately

$$2^{-31} \leq F \leq 1 - 2^{-31}(1 - 2.3283 \times 10^{-10})$$

This range is not sufficient for representing fractional numbers. To accommodate very large integers and very small fractions, a computer must be able to represent numbers and operate on them in such a way that the position of binary point is variable and is automatically adjusted as computation proceeds.

The floating point representation has three fields: sign, significant digits, and exponent to represent the number in floating point format first binary point is shifted to right of the first bit and the number is multiplied by the correct scaling factor to get the same value. The number is said to be in the normalized form. It is given as

$$1\ 1\ 0\ 1.1\ 0\ 0\ 0\ 1\ 1\ 0 \rightarrow 1.1\ 1\ 1\ 0\ 1\ 1\ 0\ 0\ 1\ 1\ 0 \times 2^5$$

base of scaling factor is fixed i.e. 2 and it does not need to appear explicitly in the machine representation 0 floating point number. Significant digits i.e. 2.3101100110 is known as mantissa. And exponent is 2's largest power value. i.e. 5.

2.6.1 IEEE 754 Standards for Floating Point Numbers

[May 08, 10, 11, Dec. 09, 10, 11, 8 Marks]

The standards are 32–bit s and 64–bits commonly known as single precision format and double precision format.

The 32 bit word is divided into three fields.

Field 1 is sign → it is 1 bit of length .0 signifies +ve while 1 signifies –ve number.

Field 2 is Exponent → it is 8–bit signed exponent in excess–127 representation.

Field 3 is Mantissa → it is 23–bits in length represent fractional part.

The representation of exponent is called as excess − 127 format. Where E' = E+127. The range of E' for normal values in single precision is 0 <E'<255.

Actual E is in the range − 126<=E<=127.

Double precision consists of two 32–bit words.

The 64-bit word is divided into three fields.

Field 1 is sign → it is 1–bit of length .0 signifies +ve while 1 signifies –ve number.

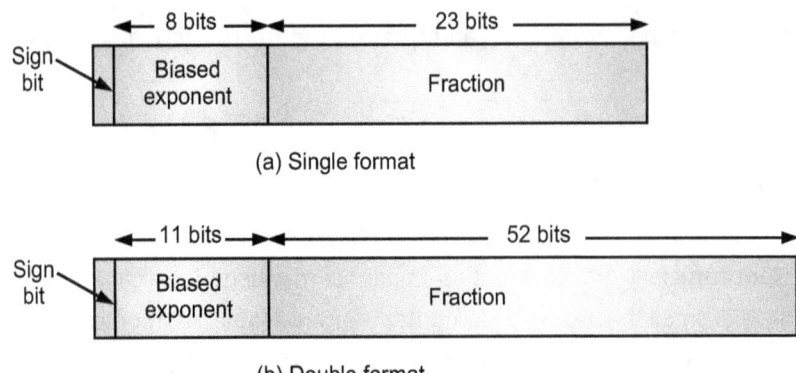

(a) Single format

(b) Double format

Fig. 2.10 : IEEE standards for floating point numbers

Field 2 is Exponent → it is 11 –bit signed exponent in excess–1023 representation.

Field 3 is Mantissa → it is 52–bits in length represent fractional part.

Here $E' = E + 1023$. The end value is in between 0 to 2047 and the range of E' is – $1022 <= E <= 1023$.

Example 1 : Represent 1259.125_{10} in single precision and double precision formats.

Solution : Step 1 : Convert decimal number in binary format.

$$
\begin{array}{r}
78 \\
16\overline{)1259} \\
112 \\
\hline
0139 \\
128 \\
\hline
011 = M
\end{array}
\qquad
\begin{array}{r}
4 \\
16\overline{)78} \\
64 \\
\hline
14 = E
\end{array}
$$

$$= 4\ EBH = \frac{100}{4} = \frac{1110}{E} = \frac{1011}{B}$$

Fractional part :

$$0.125 \times 2 = 0.25\ 0$$
$$0.25 \times 2 = 0.5\ 0$$
$$0.5 \times 2 = 1.0\ 1$$
$$0$$

$$= 0.001$$

$$\text{Binary number} = 10011101011 + 0.001$$

$$= 10011101011.001$$

Step 2 : Normalize the number

$$10011101011.001 = 1.0011101011001 \times 2^{10}$$

Now we will see the representation of the numbers in single precision and double precision formats.

Step 3 : Single precision representation for a given number S = 0. E = 10 and M = 00111 01011 001

Bias for single precision format is = 127

$$E' = E + 127 = 10 + 127 = 137_{10} = 10001001_2$$

∴ Number in double precision format is given as

0	1000 1001	0011101011001...0

Sign   Exponent   Mantissa (23 bits)

Step 4 : Double precision representation for a given number

S = 0, E = 10, and M = 0011101011001

Bias for double precision format is = 1023

$$E' = E + 1023 = 10 + 1023 = 1033_{10}$$
$$= 10000001001_2$$

∴ Number in double precision format is given as

0	1000 1001	0011101011001...0

Sign   Exponent   Mantissa (52 bits)

Example 2 : Represent–307.1875_{10} in single precision and double precision formats.

Solution : Step 1 : Convert decimal number in binary format integer part.

Integer part :

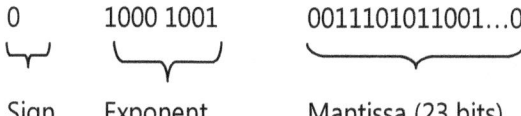

$$= 133 \ H= \frac{1}{1} = \frac{0011}{3} = \frac{0011}{3}$$

Fractional part :

$$0.1875 \times 2 = 0.3750 \quad 0$$
$$0.3750 \times 2 = 0.750 \quad 0$$
$$0.750 \times 2 = 1.5 \quad 1$$
$$0.5 \times 2 = 1.0 \quad 1$$
$$0$$
$$= 0.0011$$

$$\text{Binary number} = -100110011 + 0.0011$$
$$= -100110011.0011$$

Step 2 : Normalize the number -100110011.0011

$$= -1.001100110011 \times 2^8$$

Now we will see the representation of the numbers in single precision and double precision formats.

Step 3 : Single precision representation for a given number

$S = 1, E = 8,$ and $M = 0011\ 0011\ 0011$

Bias for single precision format is $= 127$

$$E' = E + 127 = 8 + 127 = 135_{10}$$
$$= 10000111_2$$

Number in single precision format is given as

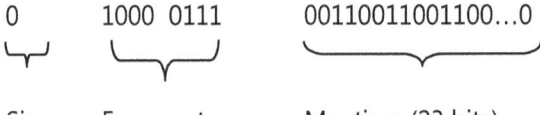

| 0 | 1000 0111 | 00110011001100...0 |

Sign   Exponent   Mantissa (23 bits)

Step 4 : Double precision representation for a given number

$S = 1, E = 8,$ andM $= 0011\ 0011\ 0011$

Bias for double precision format is $= 1023$

$$E' = E + 1023 = 8 + 1023 = 1031_{10}$$
$$= 10000100011_2$$

∴   Number in double precision format is given as

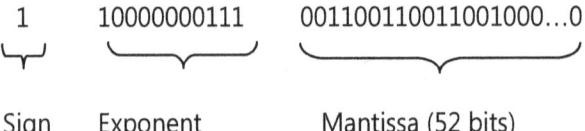

| 1 | 10000000111 | 0011001100110001000...0 |

Sign   Exponent   Mantissa (52 bits)

SOLVED QUESTIONS ON REPRESENTATIONS

Example 3 : Explain IEEE floating point number formats.   **[May 05, 4 Marks]**

Solution : Refer to page No. 1–64.

Represent $(178.1875)_{10}$ in single and double precision floating point format.

Step 1 : Convert decimal number in binary format integer part first

$$\begin{array}{r} 11 \rightarrow B \\ 16\overline{)\,178} \\ \underline{16} \\ 18 \\ \underline{16} \\ 2 \end{array}$$

$$(178)_{10} = (B2)_{16}(1\,0\,1\,1\ \ 0\,0\,1\,0)_2$$
$$\underbrace{\qquad}_{B}\ \underbrace{\qquad}_{2}$$

$$(178)_{10} = (B2)_{16} = (1\,0\,11\,0\,0\,1\,0)_2$$
$$\underbrace{\qquad}_{B}\ \ \underbrace{\qquad}_{2}$$

Fractional Part :

$$\begin{array}{ccll} 0.1875 \times 2 & = & 0.3750 & 0 \\ 0.3750 \times 2 & = & 0.750 & 0 \\ 0.750 \times 2 & = & 1.51 \\ 0.5 \times 2 & = & 1.01 \\ & & 0 \quad 0 \end{array}$$

$$= 0.0011$$

$$\text{Binary number} = 1011\,0010 + 0.0011 = 1011\,0010.0011$$

Step 2 : Normalize the number

$$1011\,0010.0011 = 1.01100100011 \times 2^7$$

Step 3 : Representation in signal precision for given number

S = 0, E = 7 and M = 011 001 000 11

Bias for single precision format is = 127

$$E' = E + 127 = 7 + 127 = 134_{10}$$
$$= 10000110_2$$

∴ Number in single precision format is given as

0   10000110   011001 000110...0

Sign   Exponent   Mantissa (23 bits)

Step 4 : Representation in double precision bias for double precision format is 1023.

$$E' = 7 + 1023 = 1030_{10}$$
$$= 100001000110_2$$

Number in double precession format

0   100001000110 01100100010...0

sign   Exponent   Mantissa (32 bits)

Example 4 : Represent the following numbers in single precision floating point format.

[May 08, Dec. 08, 5 Marks]

(a) 100.125   (b) 42.625 (c) 17.125 (d) 12.5

Solution :

(a) 100.125

Convert it into binary

$$(100)_{10} = (1100100)_2$$

Fractional part $0.125 \times 2 = 0.250$

$$0.25 \times 2 = 0.50$$

$$0.50 \times 2 = 1.00$$

$$(100.125)_{10} = (1100100.001)_2$$

To convert above number in single precession format we will convert it into the form $N \times 2^{E-127}$

$$1100100.001 = 2.20\ 100001 \times 2^6$$

$$= 2.20100001 \times 2^{133-127}$$

0 1000101   1001 100000 100000

sign E   Mantissa (B)

(b) 42.625

$$(42)_{10} = (101010)_2$$

$$0.625 \times 2 = 1.350$$

$$0.350 \times 2 = 0.70$$

$$0.70 \times 2 = 1.40$$

$$0.40 \times 2 = 0.80$$

$$0.80 \times 2 = 1.60$$

$$0.60 \times 2 = 2.4$$

$$0.20 \times 2 = 0.40$$

$$(0.625)10 = 101011001100110$$

$$42.625 = 101010.\ 101\ 0110\ 0110\ 0110$$

Convert it into $1.N \times 2^{E-127}$

$1.0101010101100110 \ldots \times 2^5 = 1.01010101\ 0110\ 0110 \times 2^{132-127}$

$\quad$ 0 $\quad\quad$ 10000100 $\quad\quad\quad$ 010 10 101 011 0110 0110 011

$\quad$ sign bit Exponent $\quad\quad\quad\quad\quad$ Mantissa

(c) 17.25

$$(17)_{10} = (10001)_2$$
$$0.125 \times 2 = 0.50$$
$$0.50 \times 2 = 1.00$$

$(17.125)_{10}\ (10001.01)_2$

Convert it into the form $(1.N) \times 2^{E-127}$

$$10001.01 = 1.000101 \times 2^4$$
$$= 1.000101 \times 2^{131-127}$$

$\quad$ 0 $\quad$ 10000011 $\quad\quad$ 0001 0100 0000 0000 0000 0000

$\quad$ sign Exponent $\quad\quad\quad\quad$ Mantissa (M)

(d) 12.5

$$(12.5)_{10} = (110.1)_2$$

Convert it into the form $1.N \times 2^{E-127}$

$$11001.1 = 2.2011 \times 2^4$$
$$= 2.2011 \times 2^{131-127}$$

$\quad$ 0 $\quad$ 10000011 1001 $\quad$ 1000 0000 0000 0000 0000

sign $\quad$ Exponent $\quad$ mantissa

Example 5 : Represent 309.1975_{10} in single precesion and double precesion formats.

2	309	1
2	154	0
2	77	1
2	38	1
2	19	1
2	9	0
2	4	0
2	2	1
2	1	
	0	

$$309 = 10011010$$

Fractional part		0.1975×2	=	0.3950
		0.3950×2	=	0.7900
		0.7900×2	=	1.58
		0.58×2	=	1.16
			=	0.0011

$$(309.1975) = 100110101.0011$$

Normalize $\dfrac{1.001101010011 \times 2^8}{M}$

$E = 8$, $S = 0$

(1) Single precesion $E' = 8 + 127 = 135_{10}$

$$= 10000111_2$$

0	10000111	001101010011

23 bit

sign   Exponent   M

(2) Double precession

$S = 0$, $E = 8$, $M = 001101010011$

Bias for double precession format is 1023

$$E' = E + 1023 = 8 + 1023$$
$$= 1031_{10} = 100001000111_2$$

0	1000000 0111	001101010011

sign   Exponentmantissa   (52 bit)

2.7 FLOATING POINT ARITHMETIC

2.7.1 Floating Point Addition and Subtraction Rules

[Dec. 10, 10 Marks]

Step 1 : Select the number with smaller exponent and shift its mantissa right, a number of steps equal to difference in exponents |e2 - e1|, for examples, if the number are 1.75×10^2 and 6.8×10^4 then the number 1.75×10^2 is selected and converted to 0.0175×10^4.

Step 2 : Set the exponent of the result equal to the larger exponent.

Step 3 : Perform addition/ subtraction on the mantissas and determine the sign of the result.

Step 4 : Normalize the result, if necessary.

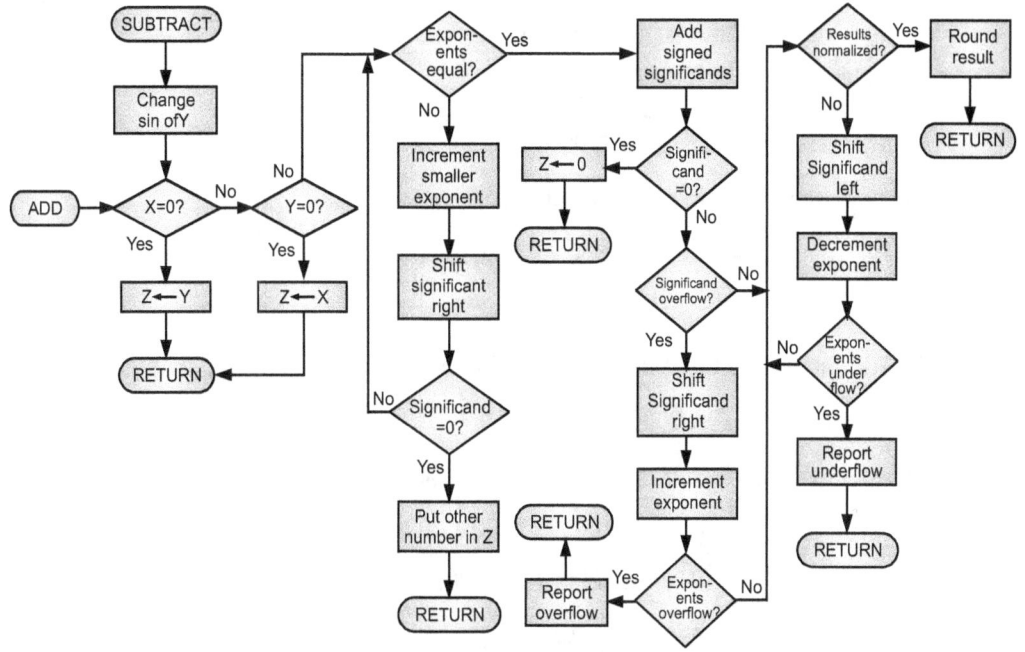

Fig. 2.11 : Floating point addition and subtraction

Example 1 : Add single precision floating point numbers A and B where

A = 44900000 H and B = 42 A 00000 H.

Solution :

Step 1 : Represent numbers in single precision format

$$A = 0\ \ 1000\ \ 1001\ \ 0010000\ \ \ \ ......0$$

$$B = 0\ 1000\ 0101\ 010000\ ......0$$

Exponent for A = 1000 1001 = 137

Actual exponent = 137 − 127 (Bias) = 10

Exponentfor B = 1000 0101 = 133

Actual exponent = 133 − 127 (Bias) = 6

Therefore, Number B has smaller exponent with difference 4. Hence its mantissa is shifted right by 4-bits as shown below.

Step 2 : Shift mantissa

Shifted mantissa of B = 00000100 0

Step 3 : Add mantissas

Mantissa of A = 001 00 000 0

Mantissa of B = 000 00 100 0

Mantissa of Result = 001 00 100 0

Both numbers are positive, sign of the result is positive

Result = 01000 1001 00100 100 0

= 44920000 H

Example 2 : Subtract single point precision floating point numbers A and B where

A = 449 00 000 H and B = 42 A 00000 H.

Solution : Step 1 : Represent numbers in single precision format

A = 0 10001001 0010000 0

B = 0 10000101 010000 0

Exponent for A = 10001001

= 137

Actual exponent = 137 – 127 (bias)

= 10

Exponent for B = 1000 0101 = 133

Actual exponent = 133 – 127 (Bias) = 6

Therefore, number B has smaller exponent with difference. Hence, its mantissa is shifted right by 4 bits as shown below.

Step 2 : Shift mantissa

Shifted mantissa of B = 0000 0 100 0

Step 3 : Subtract mantissa

Mantissa of A = 001 000 00 0

Mantissa of B = 000 001 00 0

000 111 00 0

Mantissa for A is greater than mantissa for B therefore sign of result is sign of A.

Result = 0 1000 1001 00011100 0

= 448E 0000 H

2.7.2 Hardware Implementation of Floating Point Addition and Subtraction

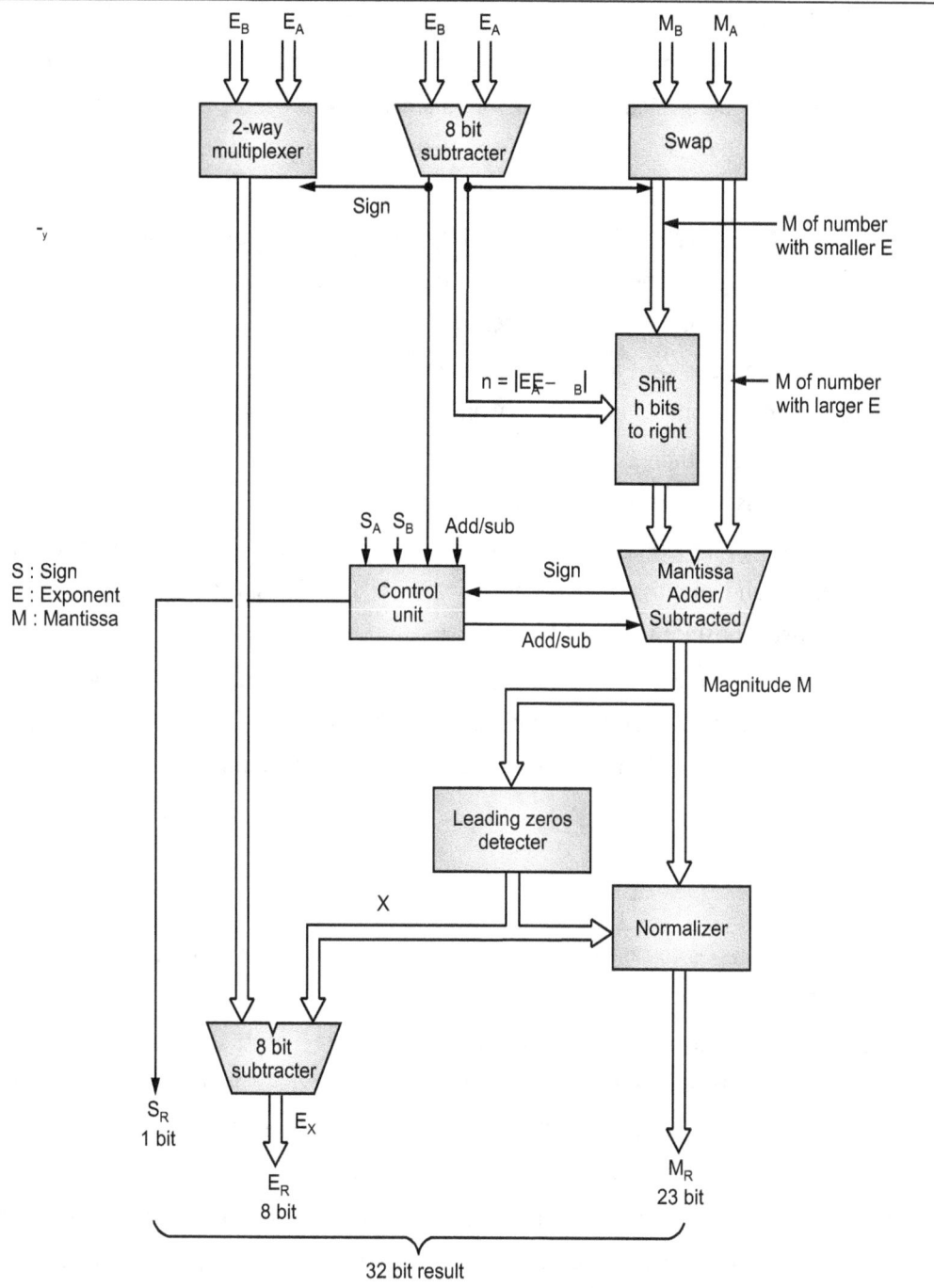

Fig. 2.12 : Hardware implementation of floating point addition and subtraction

Fig. 2.12 shows hardware implementation for the addition and subtraction of 32-bit floating point operands that have single precision format. 1 bit for sign, 8-bits for signed exponent and 23-bit for mantissa.

- As per addition or subtraction rule we have to first compare the exponents of numbers to determine a number with a smaller exponent or then to determine how for to shift the mantissa of that number so that its exponent matches with the other number.

- The shift count value n, is determined by the 8 bitsubtractor. The inputs for the 8 bit subtractor are exponent values of two numbers and the operation performed is E_A - E_B. The subtraction gives the difference n.

- This difference is sent to the shifter unit. The sign of the difference that results from comparing exponents determines which mantissa is to be shifted.

- If the sign is 0, then $E_A \geq E$. and input to SWAP network is 0. This disables swapping and mantissa M_B is sent to the shifter.

- If the sign is 1, then E_A - E_B and input to SWAP network is 1. In this cases swapping is enabled and mantissa M_A is sent to the shifter. The shifter unit shifts the given mantissa n positions to the right.

- The two way multiplexer is used to set the exponent of the result (E) equal to the larger exponent i.e. step 5. Multiplexer has two inputs E_A and E_B and its output is based on the sign of the difference resulting from comparing exponents in step 1.

- The output of multiplexer is

  $E = E_A$ if $E_A \geq E_B$

or $E = E_B$ $E_A < E_B$

- The third step is to perform addition or subtraction on the mantissas and determine the sign of the result.

- The control logic is used to determine whether the mantissas are to be added or subtracted. It decides this by checking the signs of the operands (S_A and S_B) or the operation (Add or subtract) that is to be performed on the operands. The control logic is also responsible for determining the sign of the result (S_R).

- The control logic determines the sign of the result by checking the resulted sign of mantissa adder/subtracted, sign from the exponent comparison signs of the operands and then operation to be performed.

- In step 4, the result of mantissa (M) is normalised, the normalized value is truncated to generate the 23 bit mantissa MR, of the result.

- The leading zeros detector determines the number of bits shifts, X to be applied to mantissa (M). The value X is then subtracted from the tentative resulted exponent E to generate the true result exponent, E_R.

2.7.3 Floating Point Multiplication/Division   [Dec. 10, 10 Marks]

For floating point multiplication and division first check for zero. Then add and subtract exponents.

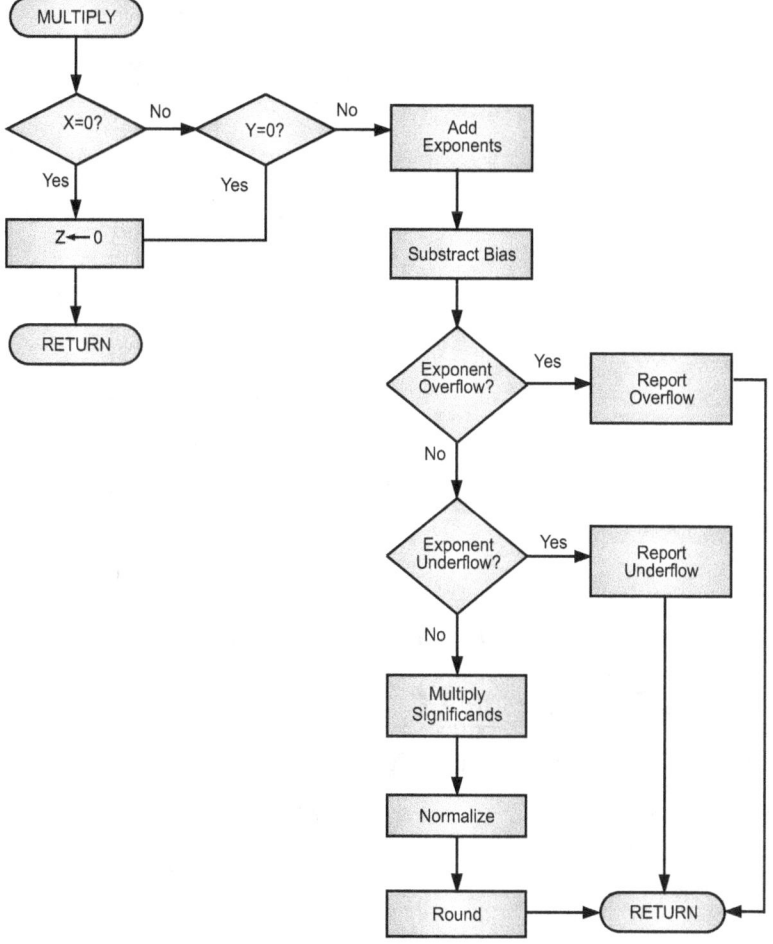

Fig. 2.13 : Floating point multiplication

Multiply or divide significant. Take care of sign of the bits. Then normalize the values. Round the values. All the intermediate results are in double length storage. Both the figures explain the steps involved in floating point multiplication and division.

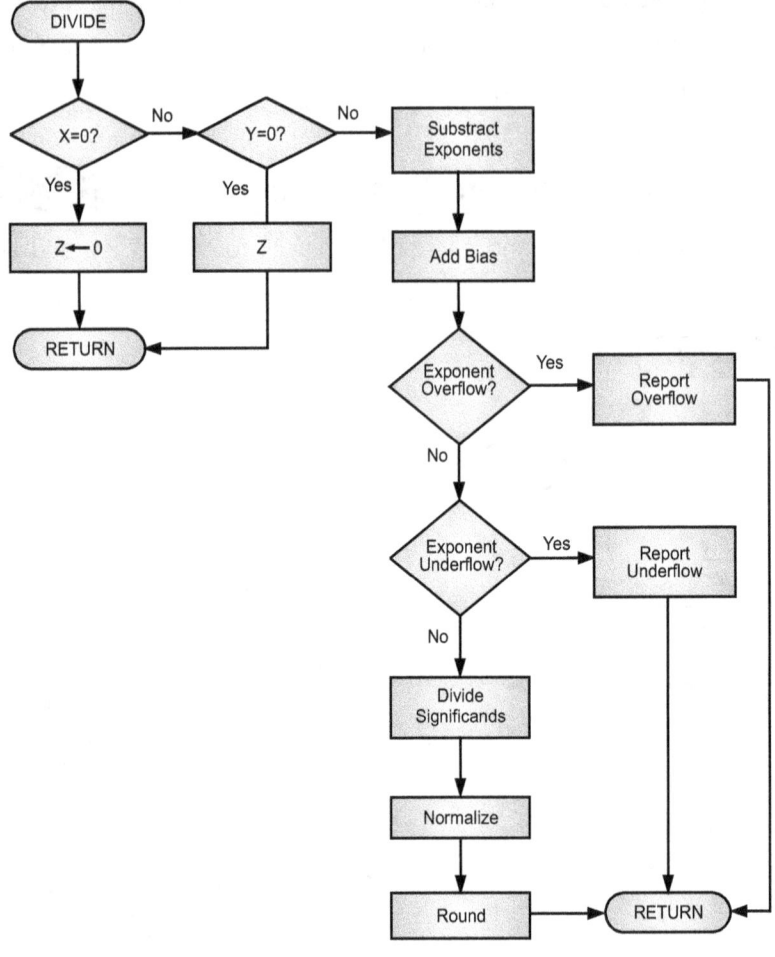

Fig. 2.14 : Floating point division

MULTIPLE CHOICE QUESTIONS (MCQs)

1. Floating point representation is used to store......

   (a) Boolean valves   (b) whole numbers

   (c) real numbers   (d) integers

2. In computers, subtraction is generally carried out by......

   (a) 9's complement   (b) 10's complement

   (c) 1's complement   (d) 2's complement'

3. The highest positive decimal number represented in signed binary numbers is ......
   the highest positive decimal number for unsigned binary numbers of a fixed number
   of bits.

   (a) Double   (b) equal

   (c) hald   (d) triple

4. 1's complement representation is nothing but bit by bit ...... operation.

   (a) OR   (b) AND   (c) Ex-OR   (d) NOT

5. Binary numbers can be used to represent

   (a) integers only   (b) fractions only

   (c) both fractions and integers   (d) none of above

6. The two's complement representation of – 10 is

   (a) 11110110   (b) 11011001

   (c) 00001010   (d) 11111100

7. 1's complement + ... = 2's complement

   (a) 1   (b) 2   (c) 3   (d) – 1

8. In 2's complement subtraction when carry is generated it is......

   (a) ignored

   (b) added to final result

   (c) subtracted from final result

   (d) ignored and 1's complement of final result is done

9. (–27)10 can be represented in a signed magnitude format and in a 1's complement
   format as

   (a) 111011 and 100100   (b) 100100 and 111011

   (c) 011011 and 100100   (d) 100100 and 011011

10. (–64)10 can be represented in a signed magnitude format as

    (a) 1101 0000   (b) 1100 0000

    (c) 1000 1100   (d) 1110 1100

11. The binary representation of 15 is

    (a) 01010   (b) 01111

    (c) 10011   (d) 00101

12. Two's complement notation is frequently used for internal representation of
   (a) fractions   (b) Integers
   (c) true and false   (d) floating point numbers

13. The ...... bit in the binary number represents sign of the number.
   (a) left most   (b) right most
   (c) both a and b   (d) none of these

14. To solve problem of representation of negative exponent in floating point numbers ...... is added to the true exponent.
   (a) packed bias valve   (b) unpacked bias valve
   (c) bias valve   (d) slating factor

15. 1's complement of (11010100) is ......
   (a) 00101011   (b) 11001011
   (c) 01010111   (d) none of these

16. 2's complement of (11000100)2 is ......
   (a) 00111100   (b) 0011011
   (c) 11001100   (d) 10111101

17. 1's complement of (01011011)2 is ......
   (a) 10100100   (b) 00111100
   (c) 10111011   (d) none of these

18. For unsigned 8 bit binary numbers the decimal range is ......
   (a) 0 to 127   (b) 255 to 127
   (c) 0 to 255   (d) none of these

19. Which is the recoded multiplier at 101100 for Booth's multiplication ?
   (a) −1 + 1 0 − 1 00   (b) 10 − 10 + 1 − 1
   (c) Both (a) and (b)   (d) None of these

20. Recoded multiplier of 011001 per Booth's multiplication is......
   (a) −1 + 1 0 − 1 0 0   (b) 1 0 − 1 0 + 1 − 1
   (c) 1 − 1 0 + 1 − 1 0   (d) none of these

21. Find the bit pair code for multiplier 11010

   (a) 0 –1 –2   (b) 2 –1 –1

   (c) –2 + 1 0   (d) none of these

22. Single procession representation occupies a single ...... word.

   (a) 16 bit   (b) 32 bit

   (c) 64 bit   (d) 8 bit

23. Double precession representation occupies a ...... word.

   (a) 16 bit   (b) 32 bit

   (c) 64 bit   (d) 8 bit

24. The 32 bit floating point system, bias value is ......

   (a) 126   (b) 1023

   (c) 127   (d) none of these

25. In 64 bit floating point system bias valve is ......

   (a) 127   (b) 1024

   (c) 1023   (d) none of these

26. Range of E' for normal values in double precision is ......

   (a) $0 < E' < 2047$ (b) $-127 < E' < 127$

   (c) $-1022 \leq E \leq 2047$ (d) none of these

27. In 2's complement subtraction of binary numbers if carry is generated then the result is ......

   (a) positive   (b) negative

   (c) zero   (d) none of these

28. In 2's complement subtraction of binary numbers if carry is not generated then the result is ......

   (a) positive   (b) negative

   (c) zero   (d) none of these

29. In Booth's algorithm , when addition is performed. Add /sub line = ... and cin = ...

   (a) 0 1   (b) 0 0

   (c) 1 0   (d) 1 1

Unit 2 | 2.51

30. In Booth's algorithm, when subtraction is performed. Add / sub line = ... and cin =......

    (a) 0 1   (b) 0 0
    (c) 1 0   (d) 1 1

31. In signed division the operands are preprocessed to transform them into ...... values.

    (a) positive   (b) negative
    (c) both (a) and (b)   (d) none of these

32. In floating point arithmetic incase of division if the dividend is zero then result is ......

    (a) one   (b) zero
    (c) ∞   (d) none of these

33. In floating point arithmetic incase of division if the divider is zero, result is ......

    (a) one   (b) zero
    (c) ∞   (d) none of these

34. In single precession format ...... bit for sign ...... bit for exponent and ...... bits for mantissa.

    (a) 1, 8, 23   (b) 8, 23, 1
    (c) 1, 1, 52   (d) none of these

35. In double precesion format ...... bit for sing, ... bit for exponent and ......bits for mantissa.

    (a) 1, 8, 52   (b) 1, 1, 52
    (c) 1, 8, 1023   (d) none of these

36. In division process of binary numbers, first bits of dividend are checked from left to right until the set of bits examined represents a number ...... the divisor.

    (a) equal to   (b) grater than or equal to
    (c) less than or equal to   (d) none of these

37. In restoring division algorithm, if the result of subtraction is ...... then it needs restering of register A.

    (a) positive   (b) negative
    (c) both (a) and (b)   (d) none of these

38. Non-restoring division algorithm needs restoring of remainder if remainder is ......

   (a)   positive   (b)   negative

   (c)   both (a) and (b)   (d)   none of these

39. A bit pair recoding technique used in Booth's algorithm ...... the multiplication process.

   (a)   speeds up   (b)   slows-down

   (c)   stops   (d)   none of these

40. Maximum positive number of sign magnitude 8 bit format is ......

   (a)   + 127   (b)   + 128

   (c)   + 255   (d)   + 256

41. Maximum negative number for sign magnitude 8 bit format is ......

   (a)   – 255   (b)   –127

   (c)   –256   (d)   – 128

42. In sign-magnitude representation of the number if MSB is 1, number is ......

   (a)   positive   (b)   negative

   (c)   integer   (d)   fraction

43. In sign-magnitude representation of number if MSB is 0, number is ......

   (a)   positive   (b)   negative

   (c)   integer   (d)   fractions

44. Techniques to represent signed integer numbers are ......

   (a)   sign magnitude representation   (b)   1's complement

   (c)   2's complement   (d)   all of these

45. IEEE 754 standard for a single pression representation includes ...... bits.

   (a)   16   (b)   32   (c)   48   (d)   64

46. IEEE 754 standard for double precesion representation includes ...... bits.

   (a)   16   (b)   32   (c)   48   (d)   64

47. ......bits are reserved for singed exponent in IEEE 754 standard for a single precesion representation of floating point numbers.

(a) 8   (b) 16   (c) 12   (d) 18

48. ......bits are reserved for signal exponent in IEEE 754 standard for a double precesion representation of floating point numbers

(a) 8   (b) 16   (c) 12   (d) 18

49. ......bits are reserved for mantissa in single precesion format of floating point.

(a) 16   (b) 20   (c) 23   (d) 32

50. ......bits are reserved for mantissa in double precesion format of floating point.

(a) 16   (b) 32   (c) 52   (d) 64

51. In integer numbers, radix point is assumed to be to the ...... of the right most digit.

(a) right   (b) left   (c) A or B   (d) none of these

52. Floating point number system allows the representation of numbers having ......

(a) integer part   (b) fractional part

(c) integer and fractional part   (d) integer or fractional part

53. (2FAOC)16 is equivalent to

(a) (195 084)10

(b) (0 0 1 0 1 1 1 1 1 0 1 0 0 0 0 0 0 1 1 0 0)2

(c) Both (a) and (b)

(d) none of these

54. A floating point number that has a 0 in the MSB of mantissa is said to have

(a) overflow   (b) underflow

(c) important   (d) underfinal

55. In signed magnitude binary division if the divided is (11100)2 2 divisior is (10011)2 then result is

(a) (00100)2   (b) (10100)2

(c) (11001)2   (d) (01100)2

ANSWERS

1.	c	2.	d	3.	c	4.	d	5.	c
6.	a	7.	a	8.	a	9.	a	10.	b
11.	b	12.	b	13.	a	14.	c	15.	a
16.	c	17.	a	18.	c	19.	a	20.	b
21.	a	22.	b	23.	c	24.	c	25.	c
26.	a	27.	a	28.	b	29.	b	30.	d
31.	a	32.	b	33.	c	34.	a	35.	b
36.	b	37.	b	38.	b	39.	a	40.	a
41.	d	42.	b	43.	a	44.	d	45.	b
46.	d	47.	a	48.	c	49.	c	50.	c
51.	a	52.	c	53.	b	54.	b	55.	b

QUESTIONS

1. Explain IEEE floating point number formats.   **[May 05, 4 Marks]**
2. Draw flow chart for floating point addition and explain.   **[May 05, 6 Marks]**
3. Explain Booth's Algorithm to multiply the following pair of signed two's complement numbers.

    A = 110011 multiplicand

    B = 101100 multiplier

    Also implement the above using bit-pair recoding k explain how it achieves faster multiplication.   **[May 05, 12 Marks]**
4. Compare restoring and non restoring division Algorithm with the help of following binary numbers.

    $1100 \div 11$ **[May 05, 12 Marks]**
5. Draw and explain von Neumann architecture.   **[Dec. 05, 6 Marks]**
6. Represent $(178.1875)_{10}$ in single and double precession format. **[Dec. 05, 8 Marks]**

7. Using Booth's algorithm multiply the following

    Multiplicand =+ 15

    Multiplier = 6   **[Dec. 05, 8 Marks]**

8. Draw the flowchart for restoring division algorithm and solve the following using above algorithm.

    Dividend = 17

    Divisor = 3   **[Dec. 05, 10 Marks]**

9. Represent $(309.1975)_{10}$ in single and double precision format.   **[May 06, 8 Marks]**

10. Draw Hardware implementation of Booth's Algorithm and explain the same

                                                                [May 06, 8 Marks]

11. Compare restoring and non-restoring division Algorithm with the help of following binary numbers. $1100 \div 11$ **[May 06, 10 Marks]**

12. Draw the flow chart for non-restoring division Algorithm and perform division of the following

    Dividend = 1011

    Divisor = 0011   **[May 06, 10 Marks]**

13. Explain IEEE floating point number formats.   **[Dec. 06, 4 Marks]**

14. Explain Booth's Algorithm to multiply the following pair of signed two's complement numbers.

    A = 110011 multiplicand

    B = 101100 multiplier

    Also implement the above using bit-pair recoding k explain how it achieves faster multiplication.   **[Dec. 06, 12 Marks]**

15. Draw flow chart for floating point subtraction.   **[Dec. 06, 6 Marks]**

16. Compare restoring and non restoring division Algorithm performs division of following numbers using restoring division Algorithm.

    Dividend = 1101

    Divisor = 11   **(12 Marks)**

17. Draw and explain Von-Neumann architecture.   **[Dec. 06, 6 Marks]**

18. Write a short note on interconnection network.   **[Dec. 06, 3 Marks]**

19. Explain IEEE floating point number formats.   **[Dec. 06, 4 Marks]**

20. Draw the flowchart for Booth's algorithm and solve the following using bit pair recoding method

    Multiplicand = 01111

    Multiplier = 10110   **[May 07, 8 Marks]**

21. Draw flow chart for restoring division Algorithm and perform division of the following numbers using restoring division Algorithm.

    A : 1100 B : 0100   **[May 07, 10 Marks]**

22. Represent $(127.1075)_{10}$ in single and double precision format.   **[Dec. 07, 4 Marks]**

23. List the rules for floating point multiplication and division.   **[Dec. 07, 6 Marks]**

24. Draw the hardware implementation of Booth's Algorithm using Booth's Algorithm multiply following

    Multiplicand = + 22

    Multiplier = 5   **[Dec. 07, 14 Marks]**

25. Draw flow chart for non-restoring division operation perform division of following number.

    Dividend = 1101

    Divisor = 0100   **[Dec. 07, 14 Marks]**

26. Draw and explain Von-Neumann architecture.   **[May 08, 6 Marks]**

27. Explain IEEE floating point number formats.   **[May 08, 4 Marks]**

28. Represent the following numbers in single precision floating point format.

    (a) 100.125   (b) 42.625   **[May 08, 6 Marks]**

29. Solve the following multiplication using Booth's algorithm and also bit-pair recoding techniques.

    Multiplicand = 1011

    Multiplier = 0011

30. Draw and explain Von-Neumann architecture.   **[Dec. 08, 6 Marks]**

31. Represent the following numbers in single precision floating point format.

    (a) 17.125   (b) 12.5   **[Dec. 08, 10 Marks]**

32. Draw a flow chart and explain the Booth's Algorithm used for signed number multiplication.   **[Dec. 08, 6 Marks]**

33. Perform the following division using restoring division Algorithm

    Dividend = 1001

    Divisor = 0101   **[Dec. 08, 13 Marks]**

34. Explain IEEE floating point number formats.   **[May 09, 4 Marks]**

35. List the rules for floating point multiplication and division.   **[May 09, 6 Marks]**

36. Explain Booth's Algorithm to multiply the following pair of signed two's complement numbers.

    A = 110011 multiplicand

    B = 101100 multiplier

    Also implement the above using bit-pair recoding k explain how it achieves faster multiplication.   **[May 09, 12 Marks]**

CONTROL UNIT

3.1 SINGLE BUS ORGANIZATION [Dec. 11]

A bus, in computer terms, is simply a channel over which information flows between two or more devices. (Technically, a bus with only two devices on it is considered as a "port" instead of a bus). A bus normally has access points, or places into which a device can tap to become part of the bus, and devices on the bus can send to, and receive information from, other devices. The bus concept is rather common, both inside the PC and outside in the real world as well. In fact, your home telephone wiring is a bus : information flows through the wiring that goes through your house, and you can tap into the "bus" by installing a phone jack, plugging in the phone and picking it up. All the phones can share the "information" (voice) on the bus.

Data and Address Buses :

Every bus is composed of two distinct parts: the data bus and the address bus. The data bus is what most people refer to when talking about a bus; these are the lines that actually carry the data being transferred. The address bus is the set of lines that carry information about where in memory the data is to be transferred to or from.

Control Bus :

In addition, there are a number of control lines that, control how the bus functions, and allow users of the bus to signal when data is available. These are sometimes referred to as the control bus, though often they are simply not mentioned. It contains control and timing information

-   Memory read/write signal
-   Interrupt request
-   Clock signals

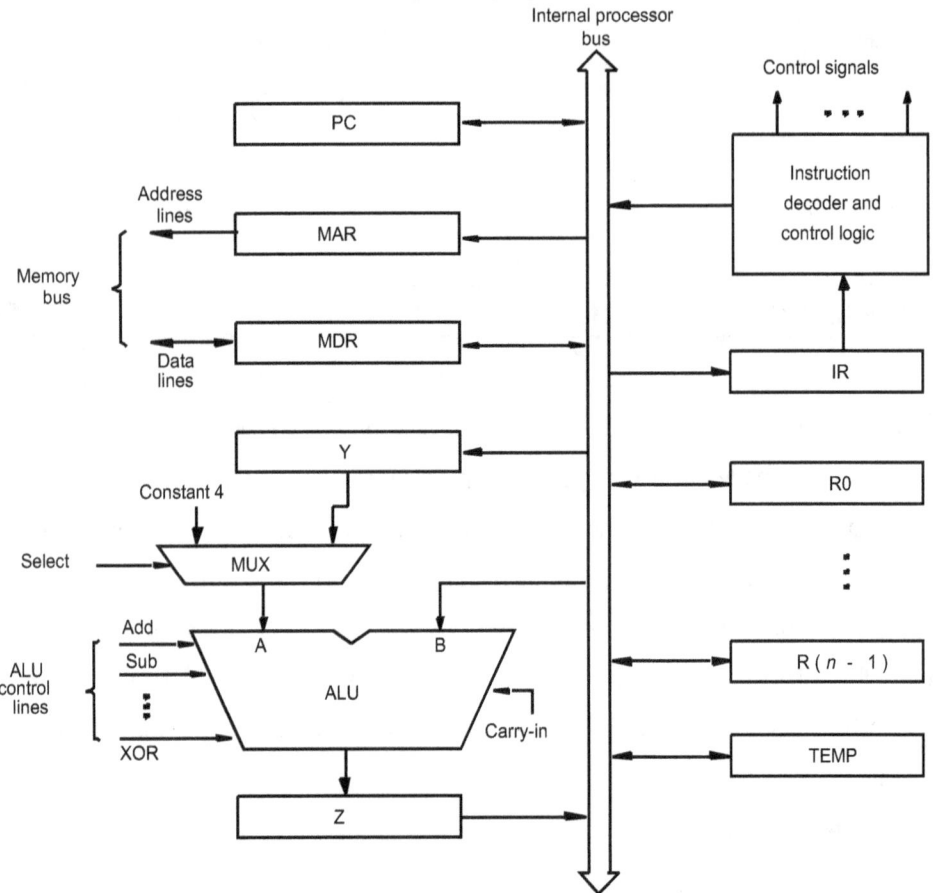

Fig. 3.1 : Single Bus Organization

Fig. 3.1 shows single bus organization of processor. It shows that ALU and all CPU registers are connected through a single common bus. It also shows that external memory bus connected to memory address register (MAR) and data register (MDR). The registers Y, Z and TEMP are used only by CPU unit for temporary storage during the execution of some instructions. These registers are never used for storing data generated by one instruction for later used by another instruction. The programmer can not access these registers. The IR and instruction decoder are integral parts of the control circuitry in the CPU unit. All other registers and the ALU are used for storing and manipulating data.

The registers R_0 through $P_{(n-1)}$ are the CPU registers. These registers include general purpose registers and special purpose registers such as stack pointer, index registers and pointers.

There are two options provided for A input of the ALU. The multiplexer is used to select one of the two inputs. It selects either output of Y register or a constant number as A input for the ALU according to the status of select input. It selects output of Y when select input is 1 and it selects a constant number when select input is 0. The constant number is used to increment the contents of the programmed counter.

For the executions of various instructions CPU has to perform one or more of the following basic operations.

- Transfer a word of data from one CPU register to another or the ALU.
- Perform the arithmetic or logic operations on the data from the CPU registers and store the result in CPU register.
- Fetch word or data from specified memory location and load them into a CPU register.
- Store the word of data from CPU register into a specified memory location.

Use of registers in single bus organization :

Y, Z, Temp – Not used for data storage but for temporary storage during execution of some instructions.

PC, MAR, MDR, IR – Storing and manipulation of data.

Ro through $R_{(n-1)}$ – It includes general purpose and special purpose registers.

Single Bus Problems :

Lots of devices on one bus leads to :

- Propagation delays.
- Long data paths mean that co–ordination of bus use can adversely affect performance.
- Data transfer approaches bus capacity.

To overcome these problems, most systems use multiple buses.

3.1.1 Four Categories of Micro-operations in Digital Computers

1. Register transfer micro-operations transfer binary information from one register to another.
2. Arithmetic micro-operations perform arithmetic operations on numbers stored in registers.
3. Logic micro-operations perform bit manipulation operations on non–numeric data stored in registers.
4. Shift micro-operations perform shift operations on contents of registers.
   - 1s' category doesn't change the contents of registers.
   - 2nd, 3rd, and 4th categories change the contents of registers.

3.1.1.1 Register Transfer   [Dec. 11, May 13]

Basic symbols for register transfers

- Copying the contents of one register to another is a register transfer.

- A register transfer is indicated as

    $R_2 \leftarrow R_1$

    - In this case, the contents of register R_1 are copied (loaded) into register R_2.

    - Simultaneous transfers of all bits from the source R_1 to the destination register R_2, during one clock pulse.

3.1.1.2 Memory Transfer Micro-operation

Two basic memory operations are

(a) Memory read

(b) Memory write

(a) Memory read :

1. Put memory address in memory register (MAR). This can be done by generating the control signal MAR_{in}.

2. Read the data of memory. Put MAR data on address bus along with a memory read control signal on the control bus.

3. The result of memory read operation is put on data bus, which in turn stores data in Memory Data Register (MDR).

    $MDR \leftarrow M (MAR)$

Sequence of control signals for read operation

1st cycle : MAR_{in}

2nd cycle : MAR_{out}, RAM_{out}, $MDR_{in, system}$

(b) Memory write :

1. Put memory address in memory register (MAR).

2. Put the data to be written in MDR.

3. Write the data in memory address supplied by MAR.

    $M (MAR) \leftarrow MDR$

Sequence of control signals for read operation

1st cycle : MAR_{in}

2nd cycle : $MDR_{in, local}$

3rd cycle : MAR_{out}, $MDR_{out, system}$, RAM_{in}

3.1.1.3 Arithmetic Micro-operations

The basic arithmetic micro-operations are :

- Addition

- Subtraction

- Increment

- Decrement

The additional arithmetic micro-operations are :

- Add with carry

- Subtract with borrow

- Transfer/Load etc.

Table 3.1 : Summary of Typical Arithmetic Micro-Operations

$R_3 \leftarrow R_1 + R_2$	Contents of R_1 plus R_2 transferred to R_3
$R_3 \leftarrow R_1 - R_2$	Contents of R_1 minus R_2 transferred to R_3
$R_2 \leftarrow R_{2'}$	Complement the contents of R_2
$R_2 \leftarrow R_2 . + 1$	2's complement the contents of R_2 (negative)
$R_3 \leftarrow R_1 + R_2 . + 1$	Subtraction
$R_1 \leftarrow R_1 + 1$	Increment
$R_1 \leftarrow R_1 - 1$	Decrement

For example : $R_3 \leftarrow R_1 + R_2$

Step 1 : Store contents of R_1 in X,

Control signal : R_{1out}, X_{in}

Step 2 : Send contents of R_2 and X to ALU and control signal ADD is applied to ALU.

Control signals : R_{2out}, ALU_{in}, ADD.

Store Result in Z.

Step 3 : Transfer contents of Z to CPU register R_4.

Control signals : Z_{out}, R_{3in} .

Steps :

Step	Operation	Control Signals
1	$X \leftarrow R_1$	$R_{i\ out}, X_{in}$
2	$Z \leftarrow X + R_1$	$R_{2\ out}, ALU_{in}, ADD$
3	$R_3 \leftarrow Z$	$Z_{out}, R_{3\ in}$

(1) Sub (R₃), R₄ where R₃ is source and R₄ is destination register :

Step	Operation	Control Signals
Instruction Fetch		
1	MAR $\leftarrow$ PC	PC_{out}, MAR_{in}
2	MDR $\leftarrow$ M (MAR)	$MAR_{out}, RAM_{out}, MDR_{in,\ system}$
3	$PC_3 \leftarrow$ PC + 1	$PC_{out}, MAR_{in}, Z_{out}, PC_{in}$
4	IR $\leftarrow$ Opcode	$MDR_{out,\ Opcode}, IR_{in}$
Opernad Fetch		
1	MAR $\leftarrow R_3$	$MAR_{in}, R_{3\ out}$
2	MDR $\leftarrow$ M(MAR)	$MAR_{out}, RAM_{out}, MDR_{in,\ system}$
Execute Cycle		
1	Y $\leftarrow$ MDR	$MDR_{out,\ local}, Y_{in}$
2	$Z \leftarrow R_4 - Y$	$R_{4\ out}, Z_{in}, ALU_{in}, SUB$
3	$R_4 \leftarrow Z$	$Z_{out}, R_{4\ in}$

(2) Sub (R₃), R₂. R₃ is source and R₂ is destination register :

Step	Operation	Control Signals
Instruction Fetch		
1	MAR $\leftarrow$ PC	PC_{out}, MAR_{in}
2	MDR $\leftarrow$ M (MAR)	$MAR_{out}, RAM_{out}, MDR_{in,\ system}$
3	PC $\leftarrow$ PC + 1	$PC_{out}, MAR_{in}, Z_{out}, PC_{in}$
4	IR $\leftarrow$ Opcode	$MDR_{out,\ Opcode}, IR_{in}$
Opernad Fetch		
1	MAR $\leftarrow R_3$	$MAR_{in}, R_{3\ out}$
2	MDR $\leftarrow$ M(MAR)	$MAR_{out}, RAM_{out}, MDR_{in,\ system}$

Execute Cycle		
1	$Y \leftarrow MDR$	$MDR_{out, \, local}, Y_{in}$
2	$Z \leftarrow R_2 - Y$	$R_{2 \, out}, Z_{in}, ALU_{in}, SUB$
3	$R_2 \leftarrow Z$	$Z_{out}, R_{2 \, in}$

(3) SUB R_1, (R_2) + :

$R_4 \leftarrow R_1 - R_2$

$R_2 \leftarrow R_2 + 1$

Step	Operation	Control Signals
Instruction Fetch		
1	$MAR \leftarrow PC$	PC_{out}, MAR_{in}
2	$MDR \leftarrow M (MAR)$	$MAR_{out}, RAM_{out}, MDR_{in, \, system}$
3	$PC \leftarrow PC + 1$	$PC_{out}, MAR_{in}, Z_{out}, PC_{in}$
4	$IR \leftarrow Opcode$	$MDR_{out, \, Opcode}, IR_{in}$
Opernad Fetch		
1	$MAR \leftarrow R_2$	$MAR_{in}, R_{2 \, out}$
2	$MDR \leftarrow M(MAR)$	$MAR_{out}, RAM_{out}, MDR_{in, \, system}$
Execute Cycle		
1	$Y \leftarrow R_1$	$Y_{in}, R_{1 \, out}$
2	$Z \leftarrow Y - MDR$	$MDR_{out, \, local}, Z_{in}, ALU_{in}, SUB$
3	$R_1 \leftarrow Z$	$Z_{out}, R_{1 \, in}$
4	$R_2 \leftarrow R_2 + 1$	$Z_{out}, R_{2 \, in}$

(4) Add (R_1), R_2 :

Step	Operation	Control Signals
Instruction Fetch		
1	$MAR \leftarrow PC$	PC_{out}, MAR_{in}
2	$MDR \leftarrow M (MAR)$	$MAR_{out}, RAM_{out}, MDR_{in, \, system}$
3	$PC \leftarrow PC + 1$	$PC_{out}, MAR_{in}, Z_{out}, PC_{in}$
4	$IR \leftarrow Opcode$	$MDR_{out, \, Opcode}, IR_{in}$

Opernad Fetch		
1	MAR ← R_1	MAR_{in}, $R_{1\ out}$
2	MDR ← M(MAR)	$MAR_{out,\ opcode}$, RAM_{out}, $MDR_{in,\ system}$
Execute Cycle		
1	Y ← MDR	$MDR_{out,\ local}$, Y_{in}
2	Z ← R_2 + Y	$R_{2\ out}$, Z_{in}, ALU_{in}, SUB
3	R_1 ← Z	Z_{out}, $R_{1\ in}$

(5) ADD (RS_{rc}) + Rd_{st} :

Step	Operation	Control Signals
Instruction Fetch		
1	MAR ← PC	PC_{out}, MAR_{in}
2	MDR ← M (MAR)	MAR_{out}, RAM_{out}, $MDR_{in,\ system}$
3	PC ← PC + 1	PC_{out}, MAR_{in}, Z_{out}, PC_{in}
4	IR ← Opcode	$MDR_{out,\ Opcode}$, IR_{in}
Opernad Fetch		
1	MAR ← R_{1st}	MAR_{in}, R_{1stout}
2	MDR ← M(MAR)	$MAR_{out,}$, RAM_{out}, $MDR_{in,\ system}$
Execute Cycle		
1	Y ← MDR	$MDR_{out,\ local}$, Y_{in}
2	Z ← RSrc + Y	$RS_{r\ out,}$ Z_{in}, ALU_{in}, SUB
3	RSrc ← Z	Z_{out}, $RS_{rc\ in}$

(6) ADD (R_3) + R_1 :

Step	Operation	Control Signals
Instruction Fetch		
1	MAR ← PC	PC_{out}, MAR_{in}
2	MDR ← M (MAR)	MAR_{out}, RAM_{out}, $MDR_{in,\ system}$
3	PC ← PC + 1	PC_{out}, MAR_{in}, Z_{out}, PC_{in}
4	IR ← Opcode	$MDR_{out,\ Opcode}$, IR_{in}

Opernad Fetch		
1	MAR ← R_1	MAR_{in}, $R_{1\ out}$
2	MDR ← M(MAR)	MAR_{out}, RAM_{out}, $MDR_{in,\ system}$
Execute Cycle		
1	Y ← MDR	$MDR_{out,\ local}$, Y_{in}
2	Z ← R_3 + Y	$R_{3\ out}$, Z_{in}, ALU_{in}, SUB
3	R_3 ← Z	Z_{out}, $R_{3\ in}$

3.1.1.4 Logic Micro-operations

Specify binary operations on the strings of bits in registers.

- Logic micro-operations are bit–wise operations, i.e., they work on the individual bits of data.

- Useful for bit manipulations on binary data.

- Useful for making logical decisions based on the bit value.

However, most systems only implement four of these

- AND (^), OR (v), XOR ⊕, Complement/NOT

3.1.1.5 Logical Shift Micro-operations

In a Register Transfer Language, the following notation is used

- shl for a logical shift left

- shr for a logical shift right

- Examples :

R_2 ← shr R_2

R_3 ← shl R_3

3.1.1.6 Branch Instructions

Loads the branch target address in PC so that PC will fetch next instruction. Two types of branching :

(a) **Unconditional :** Transfer the control of program to some another routine, so PC will start execution of another routine.

Unconditional branch instruction :

Step	Operation	Control Signals
Instruction Fetch		
1	MAR ← PC	PC_{out}, MAR_{in}
2	MDR ← M (MAR)	MAR_{out}, RAM_{out}, $MDR_{in, system}$
3	PC ← PC + 1	PC_{out}, MAR_{in}, Z_{out}, PC_{in}
4	IR ← MDR (opcode)	$MDR_{out, Opcode}$, IR_{in}
Opernad Fetch		
Operand not required		
Execute Cycle		
1	PC ← (MDR)	$MDR_{out, adr}$, PC_{in}

CALL SUB 1 :

Step	Operation	Control Signals
Instruction Fetch		
1	MAR ← PC	PC_{out}, MAR_{in}
2	MDR ← M (MAR)	MAR_{out}, RAM_{out}, $MDR_{in, system}$
3	PC ← PC + 1	PC_{out}, MAR_{in}, Z_{out}, PC_{in}
4	IR ← MDR (opcode)	$MDR_{out, Opcode}$, IR_{in}
Opernad Fetch		
Not required		
Execute Cycle		
1	Temp ← MDR	$MDR_{out, operand}$, $Temp_{in}$
2	MDR ← PC	PC_{out}, $MDR_{in. local}$
3	MAR ← Temp	$Temp_{out}$, MAR_{in}, ALU_{in}, INC
4	PC ← Temp	$Temp_{out}$, PC_{in}
5	M (MAR) ← MDR	$MDR_{out, system}$, RAM_{in}, MAR_{in}
6	PC ← PC + 1	PC_{out}, MAR_{in}, Z_{out}, PC_{in}

(b) Conditional : Depending upon the condition specified transfer the control of program to specified routine, so PC will start execution of that routine.

Conditional branch instruction Branch on negative :

Step	Operation	Control Signals
Instruction Fetch		
1	MAR ← PC	PC_{out}, MAR_{in}
2	MDR ← M (MAR)	MAR_{out}, RAM_{out}, $MDR_{in, system}$
3	PC ← PC + 1	PC_{out}, MAR_{in}, Z_{out}, PC_{in}
4	IR ← MDR (opcode)	$MDR_{out, Opcode}$, IR_{in}
Opernad Fetch		
Not required		
Execute Cycle		
1	If negative flag is set then PC ← (MDR)	$MDR_{out, add}$, PC_{in}

3.1.2 Execution of Machine Instruction by Single Bus CPU

[May 11, Dec. 11, May 12, 13]

- A computer executes a program of instructions (or instruction cycles). Each instruction cycle has a number to steps or phases:
  - **Fetch,**
  - **Indirect** (if specified),
  - **Execute,**
  - **Interrupt** (if requested)

- Each of these steps are, in turn, made up of a smaller series of steps called micro-operations.

- Micro-operation execution: Each micro-operation is initiated and controlled based on the use of control signals/lines coming from the control unit.

Micro-operations are the functional, or atomic, operations of a processor. In this section, we will examine micro-operations to gain an understanding of how the events of any instruction cycle can be described as a sequence of such micro-operations.

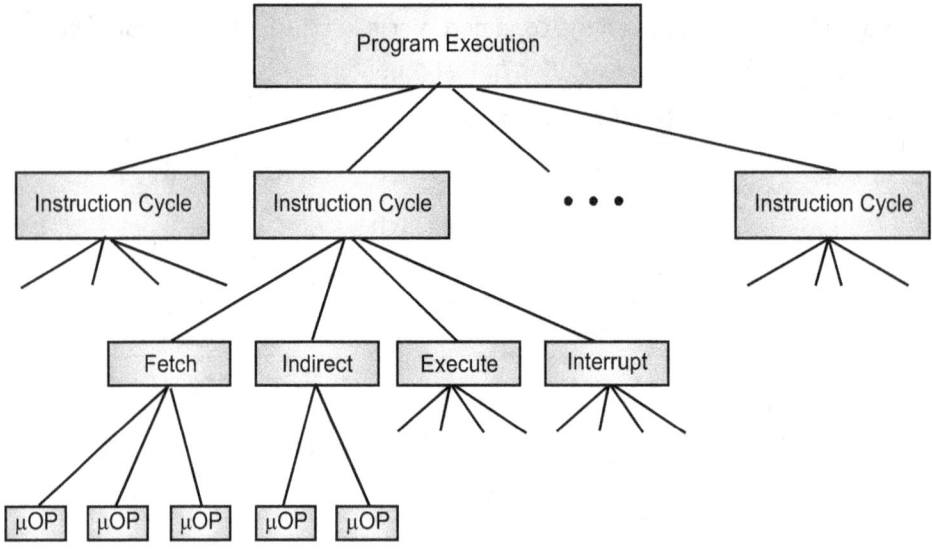

Fig. 3.2 : Constituent Elements of Program Execution

1. The Fetch Cycle :

We begin by looking at the fetch cycle, which occurs at the beginning of each instruction cycle and causes an instruction to be fetched from memory. Four registers are involved :

- Memory address register (MAR) : It is connected to the address lines of the system bus. It specifies the address in memory for a read or write operation.

- Memory buffer register (MBR) : It is connected to the data lines of the system bus. It contains the value to be stored in memory or the last value read from memory.

- Program counter (PC) : Holds the address of the next instruction to be fetched.

- Instruction register (IR) : Holds the last instruction fetched.

Let us look at the sequence of events for the fetch cycle from the point of view of its effect on the processor registers. An example appears in Fig. 3.3.

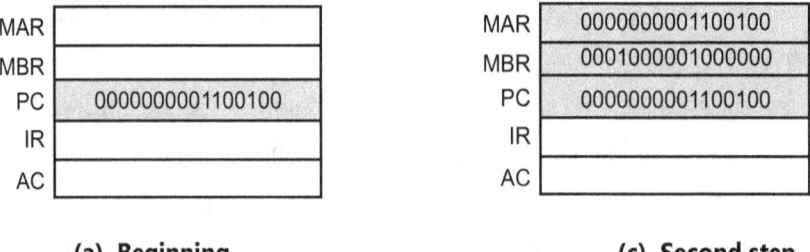

        (a) Beginning   **(c) Second step**

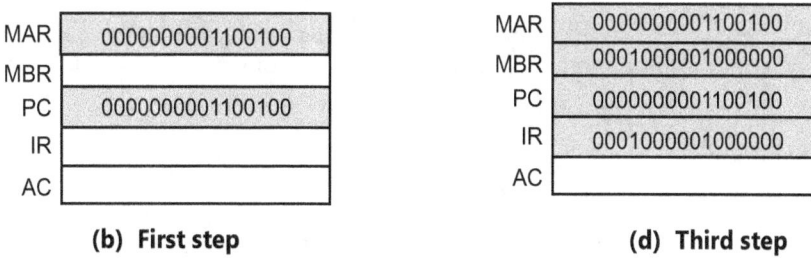

(b) First step   **(d) Third step**

Fig. 3.3 : Sequence of Events, Fetch Cycle

- At the beginning of the fetch cycle, the address of the next instruction to be executed is in the program counter (PC); in this case, the address is 1100 100.

- The first step is to move that address to the memory address register (MAR) because this is the only register connected to the address lines of the system bus.

- The second step is to bring in the instruction. The desired address (in the MAR) is placed on the address bus, the control unit issues a READ command on the control bus, and the result appears on the data bus and is copied into the memory buffer register (MBR). We also need to increment the PC by 1 to get ready for the next instruction. Because these two actions (read word from memory, add 1 to PC) do not interfere with each other, we can do them simultaneously to save time.

- The third step is to move the contents of the MBR to the instruction register (IR). This frees up the MBR for use during a possible indirect cycle.

Thus, the simple fetch cycle actually consists of three steps and four micro-operations. Each micro-operation involves the movement of data into or out of a register. So long as these movements do not interfere with one another, several of them can take place during one step, saving lime. Symbolically, we can write this sequence of events as follows :

t1 : MAR <= (PC)

t2 : MBR <= Memory

     PC <= (PC) + 1

t3 : IR <= (MBR)

Where 1 is the instruction length.

Instruction which is to be executed is fetched from memory to CPU.

Steps of instruction fetch cycle :

Step 1 : Instruction address is transferred from PC to MAR.

       MAR ← PC

       Control Signals : PC_{out}, MAR_{in}

Step 2 : Contents of MAR are put on the address bus for selection of control word of main data memory, control unit generates a memory read control signal. Data read from memory is put on data bus where it is accepted in Memory Data Register (MDR).

MDR ← M (MAR)

Control Signals : MAR_{out}, RAM_{out}, $MDR_{in, system}$

Step 3 : PC incremented by 1 with the help of ALU, to fetch next instruction.

PC ← PC + 1

Control Signals :1st step – PC_{out}, MAR_{in}

2nd step – Z_{out}, PC_{in}

Step 4 : Opcode of fetched instruction is transferred to IR.

Control Signals : $MDR_{out,OPcode}$, IR_{in}

Control Signals for Fetch Cycle :

Table 3.2 : Control Signals for Fetch Cycle

Step No.	Operation	Control Signals
1.	MAR ← PC	PC_{out} MAR_{in}
2.	MDR ← M (MAR)	MAR_{out}, RAM_{out}, $MDR_{in, system}$
3.	PC ← PC+1	PC_{out} MAR_{in}, Z_{out}, PC_{in}
4.	IR ← Opcode	$MDR_{out, OPcode}$, IR_{in}

2. Operand Fetch Cycle :

Once an instruction is fetched, the next step is to fetch source operands.

1.   If operand is present in CPU then operand fetch is not required.

2.   If operand is an immediate data operand fetch is not required

3.   If operand is present at some address operand fetch is required.

Continuing our simple example, let us assume a one-address instruction format, with direct and indirect addressing allowed. If the instruction specifies an indirect address, then an indirect cycle must precede the execute cycle. The data flow includes the following micro-operations

t1 : MAR <= (IR (Address))

t2 : MBR <= Memory

t3 : IR(Address) <= (MBR(Address))

The address field of the instruction is transferred to the MAR. This is then used to fetch the address of the operand.

Steps of operand fetch cycle :

Step 1 : Get address of operand from MDR and store in MAR.

$MAR \leftarrow MDR$

Control Signals : $MDR_{out, .addr,} MAR_{in}$

Step 2 : Memory read is performed to read data from memory.

$MDR \leftarrow M (MAR)$

Control Signals : $MAR_{out,} RAM_{out,} MDR_{in. system}$

Case 1 : Memory Indirect :

Control signals for memory indirect fetch cycle :

e.g.: ADD $R_{1,X}$

Table 3.3 : Control Signals for Memory Indirect operation

Step No.	Operation	Control Signals
1.	$MAR \leftarrow MDR$	$MDR_{out, adr,} MAR_{in}$
2.	$MDR \leftarrow M (MAR)$	$MAR_{out,} RAM_{out,} MDR_{in, system}$
3.	$MAR \leftarrow MDR$	$MAR_{in,} MDR_{out, local}$
4.	$MDR \leftarrow M (MAR)$	$MAR_{out,} RAM_{out,} MDR_{in, system}$

Case 2 : Register Indirect :

Control signals for register indirect fetch cycle.

e.g. : ADD $R_1, (R_2)$

Table 3.4 : Control Signals for Register Indirect operation

Step No.	Operation	Control Signals
1.	$MAR \leftarrow R_2$	$MAR_{in} R_{2\ out}$
2.	$MDR \leftarrow M (MAR)$	$MAR_{out,} RAM_{out,} MDR_{in, system}$

Case 3 : Execute Cycle :

The fetch, indirect, and interrupt cycles are simple and predictable. Each involves a small, fixed sequence of micro-operations and, in each ease, the same micro-operations are repeated each time around. This is not true of the execute cycle. For a machine with N different opcodes, there are N different sequences of micro-operations that can occur.

Control signals for execute cycle :

For example : ADD R_1, X.

One of the register say X is stored in temporary register (Y) of ALU.

Table 3.5 : Control Signals for Execute operation

Step No.	Operation	Control Signals
1.	Y← MDR	MDR$_{out, local}$ Y$_{in}$
2.	Z ← R$_1$ + Y	R$_{1\ out}$, ALU$_{in}$, ADD
3.	R$_1$ ← Z	Z$_{out}$, R$_1$ in

Case 4 : The Interrupt Cycle :

At the completion of the execute cycle, a test is made to determine whether any enabled interrupts have occurred. If so, the interrupt cycle occurs. The nature of this cycle varies greatly from one machine to another. We present a very simple sequence of events, we have

t1 : MBR <= (PC)

t2 : MAR <= Save Addres

PC <= Routine Addres

t3 : Memory <= (MBR)

In the first step, the contents of the PC are transferred to the MBR, so that they can be saved for return from the interrupt. Then the MAR is loaded with the address at which the contents of the PC are to be saved, and the PC is loaded with the address of the start of the interrupt–processing routine. These two actions may each be a single micro-operation.

However, because most processors provide multiple types and/or levels of interrupts, it may take one or more additional micro-operations to obtain the save address and the routine address before they can be transferred to the MAR and PC, respectively. In any case, once this is done, the final step is to store the MBR, which contains the old value of the PC, into memory. The processor is now ready to begin the next instruction cycle.

Case 5 : The Instruction Cycle :

We have seen that each phase of the instruction cycle can be decomposed into a sequence of elementary micro-operations. There is one sequence each for the fetch, indirect, and interrupt cycles, and, for the execute cycle; there is one sequence of micro-operations for each opcode. To complete the picture, we need to tie sequences of micro-operations together, and this is done in Fig 3.4.

1.   Instruction fetch IR = (PC) and PC increment PC = PC + 1.

2.   Execute the instruction in IR. May require several cycles

(i)   Decode instruction.

(ii) Fetch any additional instruction words.

(iii) Fetch any operands.

(iv) Perform operation.

(v) Store result.

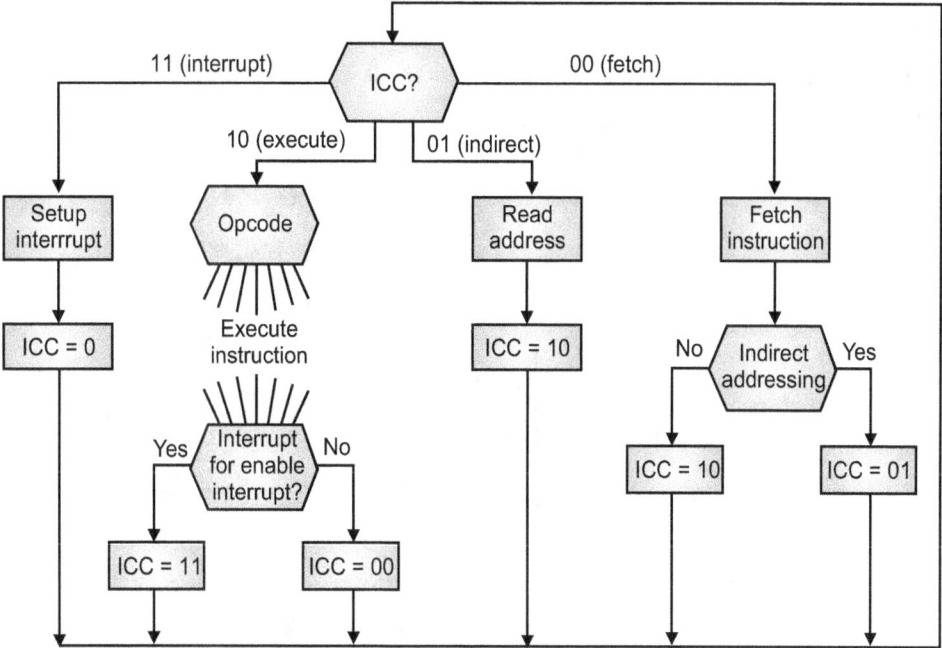

Fig. 3.4 : Flowchart for Instruction Cycle

Once an instruction is fetched, the next step is to fetch source operands with direct and indirect addressing allowed. If the instruction specifies an indirect address, then an indirect cycle must precede the execute cycle. If an indirect addressing had not been used, and it is ready for the execute cycle. We skip that cycle for a moment, to consider the interrupt cycle.

Z_{in} and END Signal Generation :

With the help of circuit diagram, see how Z_{in} and END signals are generated. To draw the circuit diagram, to generate Z_{in}, and END signal. Let us take example of the instruction ADD R_1, R_2.

In this instruction content of R_2 is added with contents of R_1 and result is stored in R_1. ALU performs the ADD operation.

1. R_{1out}, Z_{in}

2. R_{2out} selects Y, Add Z_{in},

3. Z_{out}, R_{1in} END

According to the control step sequences, the encoder circuit implements the logic function to generate Z_{in}.

$$Z_{in} = T_1 + T_5 . ADD + T_4 \text{ Branch} + \ldots\ldots$$

The Z_{in} signal is asserted during time internal T_1 for all instructions, during T_5 for an ADD instruction, during T_4 for an unconditional branch instruction and so on.

Now, suppose signal is asserted during the time intervals T_2 of all instructions, for ADD R_1, R_2. When result is stored in the R_1 the END is there.

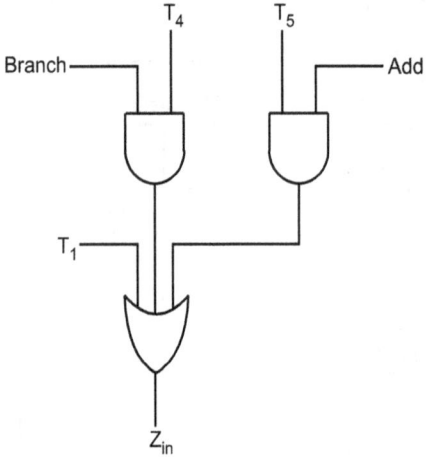

Fig. 3.5 : Generation of Z_{in} control signal

Suppose during time period T_1 for an ADD instruction and during T_6, for an unconditional for branch instructions and so on.

Step 1 :

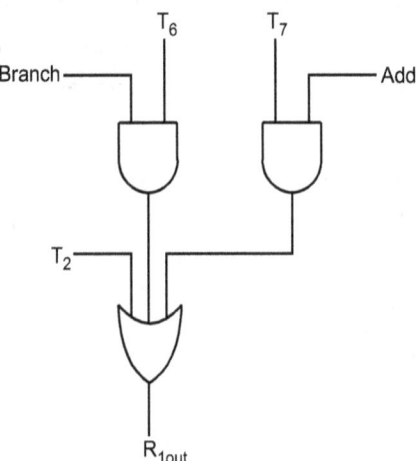

Fig. 3.6 : Generation of Z_{in} control signal

Step 2 : END signal with the help of sequence counter.

There are two possibilities if the

    (1)   END pin of Modulo–3 sequence counter is high and

    (2)   When signal Q_3 of sequence counter and one output of flip–flop is 1 which are the inputs for AND Gate 1.

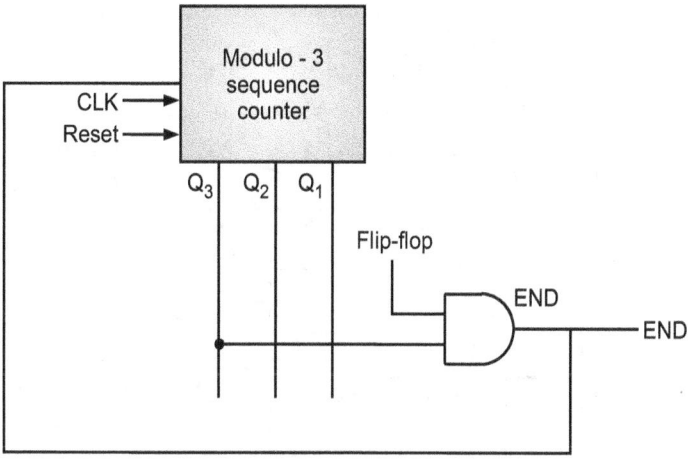

Fig. 3.7 : Generation of END signal

3.1.3 Multi-Bus Organization   [May 11, Dec. 11, 12, May 13]

Multi-Bus organization supports execution of several micro-operations in parallel.

Consider a three-operand instruction:

SUB R_{scr1}, R_{scr2}, R_{dst}

Contents of two R_{scr2} are subtracted from R_{scr1} and result is placed in destination register R_{dst}. The three buses A, B, C can be used simultaneously. Buses A and B can be used for R_{scr1} and R_{scr2} respectively. Bus C can used for destination register R_{dst}.

The number and type of buses used strongly affect the machine's overall speed. Simple computer designs move data on a single bus; multiple buses, however, vastly improve performance. In a multiple-bus architecture, each pathway is suited to handle a particular kind of information.

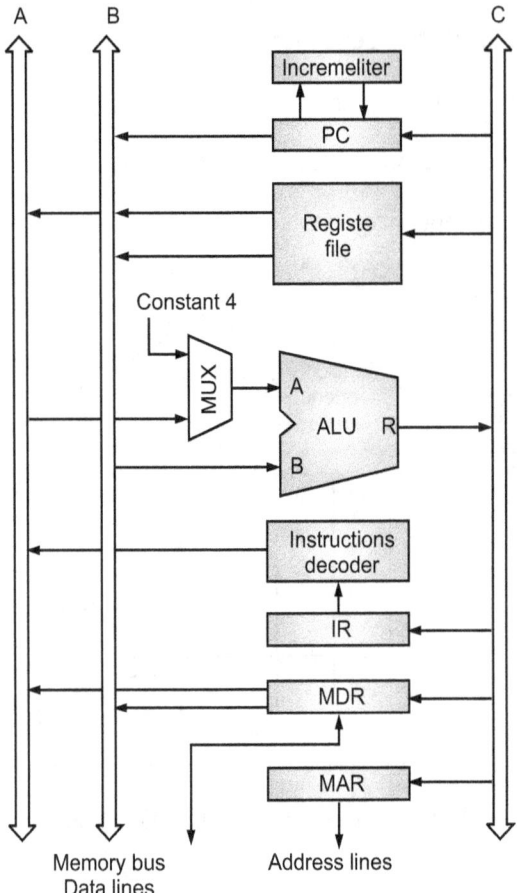

Fig.3.8 : Multi-Bus Organization

Speed and Efficiency :

In a single-bus architecture, all components including the central processing unit, memory and peripherals share a common bus. When many devices need the bus at the same time, this creates a state of conflict called bus contention; some wait for the bus while another has control of it. The waiting wastes time, slowing the computer down. Multiple buses permit several devices to work simultaneously, reducing time spent waiting and improving the computer's speed. Performance improvements are the main reason for having multiple buses in a computer design.

Expansion :

Having multiple different buses available gives you more choices for connecting devices to your computer, as hardware makers may offer the same component for more than one bus type. For example, most desktop PCs use the Serial Advanced Technology Attachment interface for internal hard drives, but many external hard drives and flash drives connect via

USB. If your computer's SATA connections are all used, the USB interface lets you connect additional storage devices.

Compatibility :

As with all of a computer's components, bus designs evolve, with new types being introduced every few years. For example, the PCI bus that supports video, network and other expansion cards predates the newer PCIe interface, and USB has undergone several major revisions. Having multiple buses that support equipment from different eras lets you keep legacy equipment such as printers and older hard drives and add newer devices as well.

Multi-core :

A single central processing unit places heavy demands on the bus that carries memory data and peripheral traffic for hard drives, networks and printers; since the mid-2000s, however, most computers have adopted a multi-core model that require additional buses. To keep each core busy and productive, the new bus designs ferry increased amounts of information in and out of the microprocessor, keeping wait times to a minimum.

3.2   DESIGN OF HARDWIRED CONTROL UNIT   [May 13]

To execute instructions, a computer's processor must generate the control signals used to perform the processor's actions in the proper sequence. This sequence of actions can either be executed by another processor's software or in hardware. Hardware methods falls into two categories : the processor's hardware signals are generated either by **hardwired control**, in which the instruction bits directly generate the signals, or by **microprogrammed control** in which a dedicated microcontroller executes a microprogram to generate the signals.

Before microprocessors, hardwired control was usually implemented using discrete components, flip–chips, or even rotating discs or drums. This can be generally done by two methods.

Method 1 : The classical method of sequential circuit design. It attempts to minimize the amount of hardwire, in particular, by using only log2p flip–flops to realize a p state circuit.

Method 2 : An approach that uses one flip-flop per state and is known as one hot method. While expensive in terms of flip-flops, this method simplifies controller unit design and debugging.

Hardwired control unit has a processor that generates signals or instructions to be implemented in correct sequence. This was the older method of control that works through the use of distinct components, drums, a sequential circuit design, or flip chips.

In the hardwired control, the instruction decoder decodes the instructions loaded in the IR. If IR is an 8 bit register then instruction decoder generates 2^8 i.e. 256 lines; one for each instructions. According to code in the IR, only one line amongst all output lines of decoder goes to high. The step generator/counter provides a separate signal line for each step, or time slot, in the control sequence. The encoder gets the input from instruction decoder, step generator, status and condition codes. From this it generates individual control signals.

The major goal of hardwired control scheme is to minimize cost of the circuit while achieving higher efficiency in terms of operation speed.

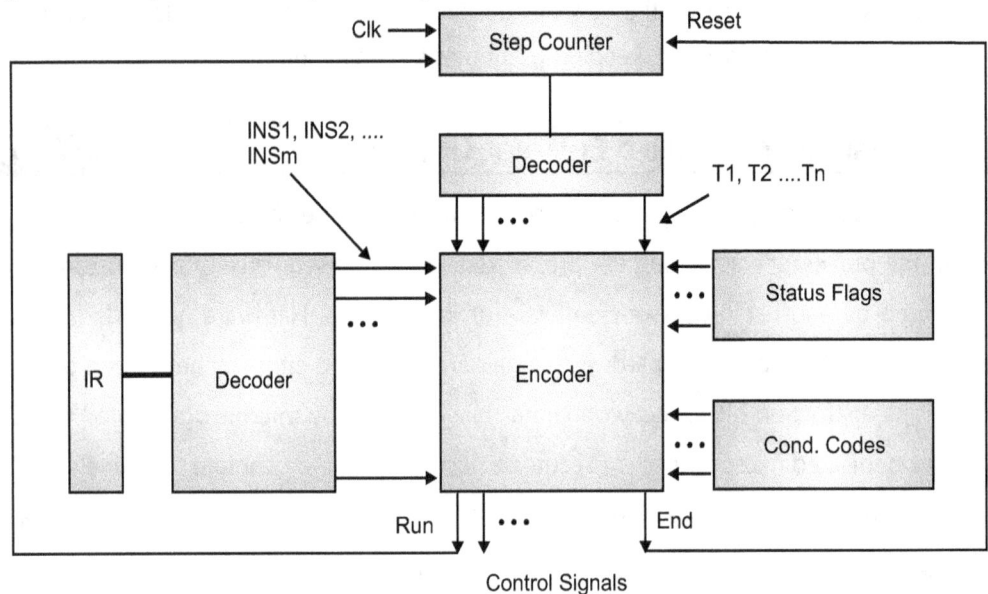

Fig. 3.9 : Block diagram of hardwired control

Design Methods :

1. **State table method :** This scheme employs the traditional algorithmic approach to sequential circuit design using classical state table method.

2. **Sequence counter method :** This is the most popular method conveniently employed for design of controller of moderate complexity. It uses counter for timing purposes.

3. **Delay element method :** This method depends on the use of clocked delay elements for generating the sequence of control signals.

4. **PLA method :** It uses programmable logic array.

Under the control of a set of programmed instructions I_1, I_2, ..., I_{i+1}, ... the CPU changes states (say) S_1, S_2, S_1, S_{i+1}. Fetching and executing any instruction. Then it is changes the state of CPU in a specified sequence say S_{i1}, S_{i2},...S_{ij}, $S_{i(j+1)}$. While the CPU is in state S_{ij}, a set of micro-operations are executed whereby CPU changes state to $S_{i(j+1)}$. The controller generates the control signals associated with the set of micro-operations causing the state change of CPU.

Hence, the flowchart specifying the sequence of micro-operations associated with fetch and execution cycles of an instruction provides directly the controller specification.

To generate the control signals C_{01}, (C_{02},C_{03}), C_{04}, C_{05} in the specified order on accepting the external start signal S = 1.

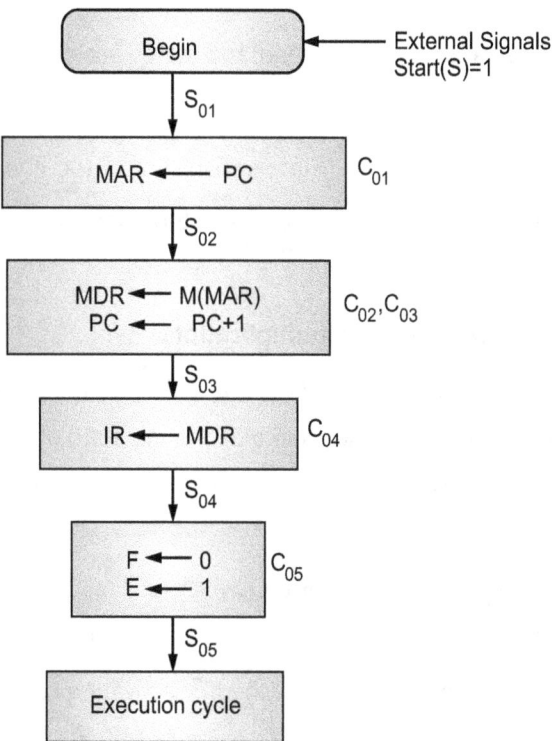

Fig. 3.10 : Controller Specification for fetch cycle

3.2.1 State Table Method   [Dec. 12]

In the flowcharts shown in Fig. 3.11, state has been marked above each block of the flowchart. This can be viewed as the state of the controller which generates the control signals to control the microoperations. A controller in state S_i on receiving the primary input signals I_j switched over to state S_i while generating the output signals C_i. The set of output signals executes the micro-instructions.

The control structure realizing the behaviour noted in the flowchart can be designed by executing the following steps :

1. **State Assignment :** States are assigned as shown in the flowchart. Each such state specifics a particular state of the controller at the specific time.

2. **State minimization :** A set of states $(S_1, S_2,... S_n,)$ can be merged to a single state S' if that states are compatible.

3. **State encoding :** State variables are defined and states are encoded in terms of state variables.

Next flip–flops are selected to realize the state variables and the combinational circuit is designed to implement the state transition and the output signals as specified in the state transition table.

Example : Flowchart for 2's complement multiplication.

We can associate a state with every micro-instruction block, as shown in Fig. 3.11. Giving 9 states labelled S_0 through S_8. State represents idle or waiting state of the control unit. There are 4 primary input signals BEGIN, COUNT and Q_{-1}. So there are 16 possible input combinations.

Table 3.6 shows a state table for the control unit which is directly derived from flowchart. Each entry indicates the next state followed by a list of control signals that are activated.

For example, for S_1, the next state is S_2 and is reached by activating control signals C_0 and C_2. So state table entry is S_2, C_0, and C_2.

Certain state and input signal combinations should not occur during normal operation, so the corresponding table entries are left blank.

For example, BEGIN signal should assume the 1 value only when the control unit is in the idle state So. Similarly, COUNT (which becomes 1 when counter count = 0) is never 1 in state S_2, since counter is loaded with count n in the preceding state S_1.

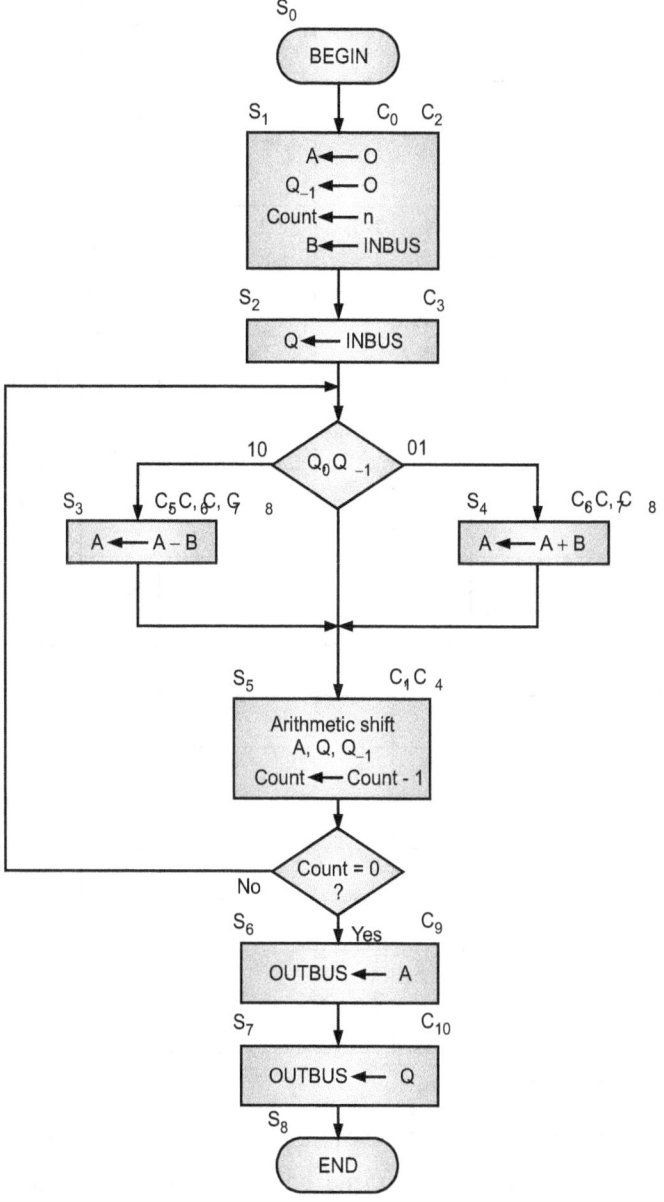

Fig. 3.11 : Flowchart for 2's complement multiplication

Table 3.6 : State Table

BEGIN	COUNT	Q_0	Q_{-1}	S_0	S_1	S_2	S_3	S_4	S_5	S_6	S_7	S_8
0	0	0	0	S_0	$S_2, C_0,$ C_2	S_5, C_3			$S_5, C_1,$ $C_4,$			
0	0	0	1	S_0	$S_2, C_0,$ C_2	S_4, C_3		$S_5, C_6,$ C_7, C_8	$S_4, C_1,$ C_4			
0	0	1	0	S_0	$S_2, C_0,$ C_2	S_3, C_3	$S_5, C_5,$ $C_6, C_7,$ C_6		$S_3, C_1,$ C_4			
0	0	1	1	S_0	$S_2, C_0,$ C_2	S_2, C_3			$S_5, C_1,$ C_4			
0	1	0	0	S_0	$S_2, C_0,$ C_2				$S_6, C_1,$ C_4	S_7, C_9	S_8, C_{10}	$S_{10},$ END
0	1	0	1	S_0	$S_2, C_0,$ C_2				$S_6, C_1,$ C_4	S_7, C_9	S_8, C_{10}	$S_{10},$ END
0	1	1	0	S_0	$S_2, C_0,$ C_2				$S_6, C_1,$ C_4	S_7, C_9	S_8, C_{10}	$S_{10},$ END
0	1	1	1	S_0	$S_2, C_0,$ C_2				$S_6, C_1,$ C_4	S_7, C_9	S_8, C_{10}	$S_{10},$ END
1	0	0	0	S_1								
1	0	0	1	S_1								
1	0	1	0	S_1								
1	0	1	1	S_1								
1	1	0	0	S_1								
1	1	0	1	S_1								
1	1	1	1	S_1								
1	1	1	1	S_1								

Disadvantages of state table method :

1. The manual design process for the state table method based controller design becomes extremely difficult. Also, the computation time to automate the design process grows exponentially.

2. High design cost and time.

3.2.2 Sequence Counter Method

Step 1 : Identify the distinct phases in the flowchart.

Step 2 : Identify maximum number of sequential micro-operations (say k) in each of the phases.

Step 3 : Execute these k number of sequential operations with the help of Mod counter.

Step 4 : The counter output can be decoded and used to generate k control signals in a sequence to execute k micro-operations.

Step 5 : At the end, counter can be reset with E (execution) and F (fetch) being set to '1' and '0' respectively to start execution phase.

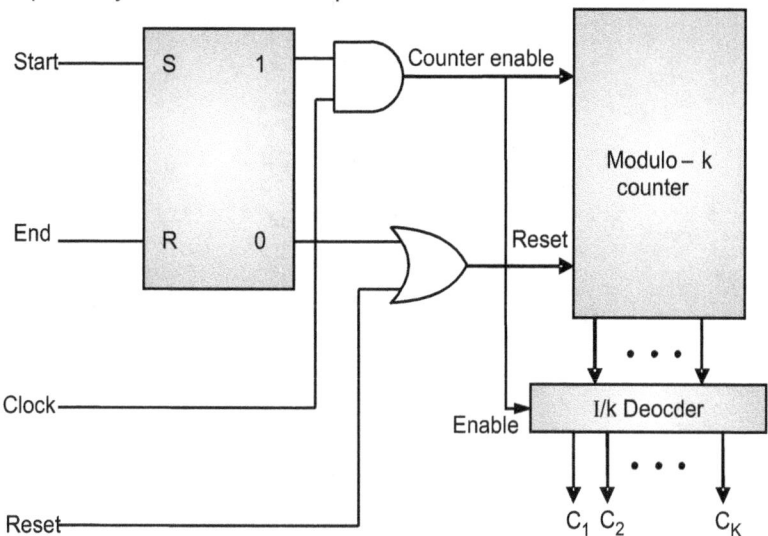

Fig. 3.12 : Modulo k sequence counter

3.2.3 Delay Element Method   [Dec. 12]

It is simplified form the scheme is illustrated in Fig. 3.13 for designing a controller .

The ith block in the flowchart is replaced be delay element D_i having a delay of d_i unit. The control signals necessary to execute the micro-operations noted in the ith block are generate directly from line input to D_i. The time span t_i is the time elapsed from the beginning to the point while executions of the micro-operation(s) associate with the ith block of the flowchart get completed. Then

$$t_i - t_{i-1} = d_i$$

i.e. the delay block D_i introduces a delay of d_i after which the control signals associated with the $(i+1)^{th}$ block may be generated.

The control signals or groups of control signals from the control unit are activated in a proper sequence. There is specific time delay between activation of two contiguous control signals. To ensure synchronous operation, the delay elements are implemented by D flip–flops and controlled by a common clock signal.

A control unit using delay elements can be constructed directly from flowchart that specifies required control signal sequences. There are some rules to drive control circuit from flowchart :

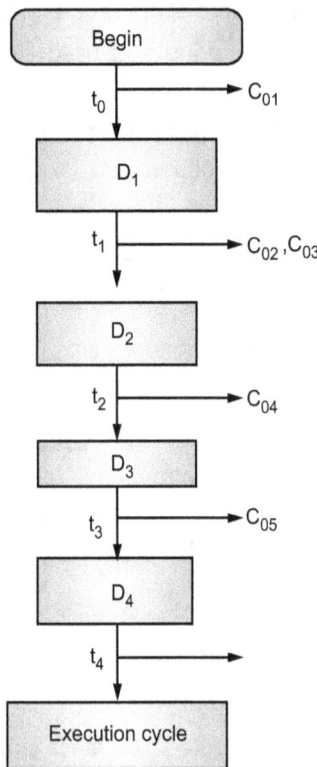

Fig. 3.13 : Control unit based on delay element method for fetch cycle

Rule 1 : Each sequence of two successive micro-operations requires a delay element. The signals that activate the control lines are taken directly from the input and output lines of the delay element as shown in Fig. 3.14 (a). The signals that are intended to activate same control line are logically ORed to get one common output signal as shown in Fig. 3.14 (b).

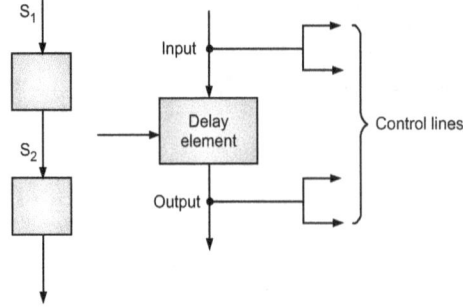

Fig. 3.14 (a)

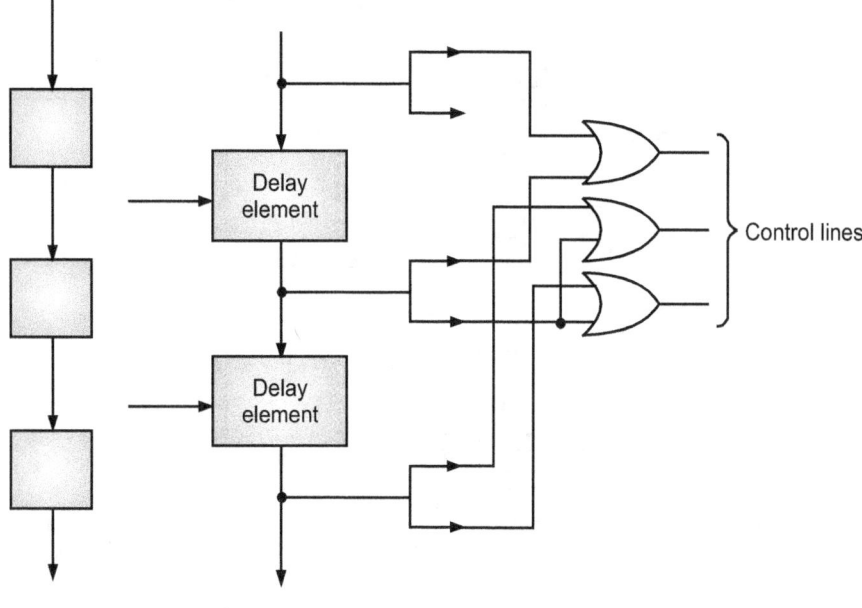

Fig. 3.14 (b)

Rule 2 : In lines in the flowchart merge to a common Ilne are transformed into input OR gate, as shown in Fig. 3.15.

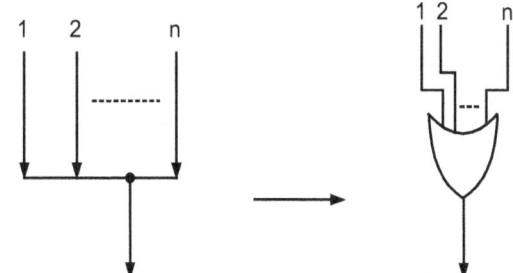

Fig. 3.15

Rule 3 : A decision box can be implemented by two AND gates, as shown in Fig. 3.16.

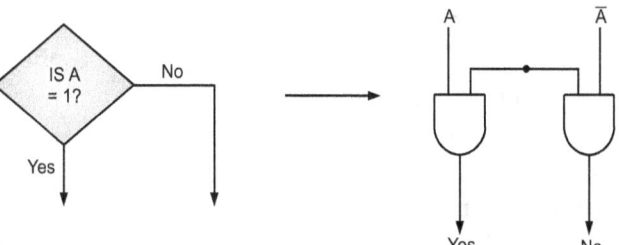

Fig. 3.16

Fig. 3.17 shows final circuit.

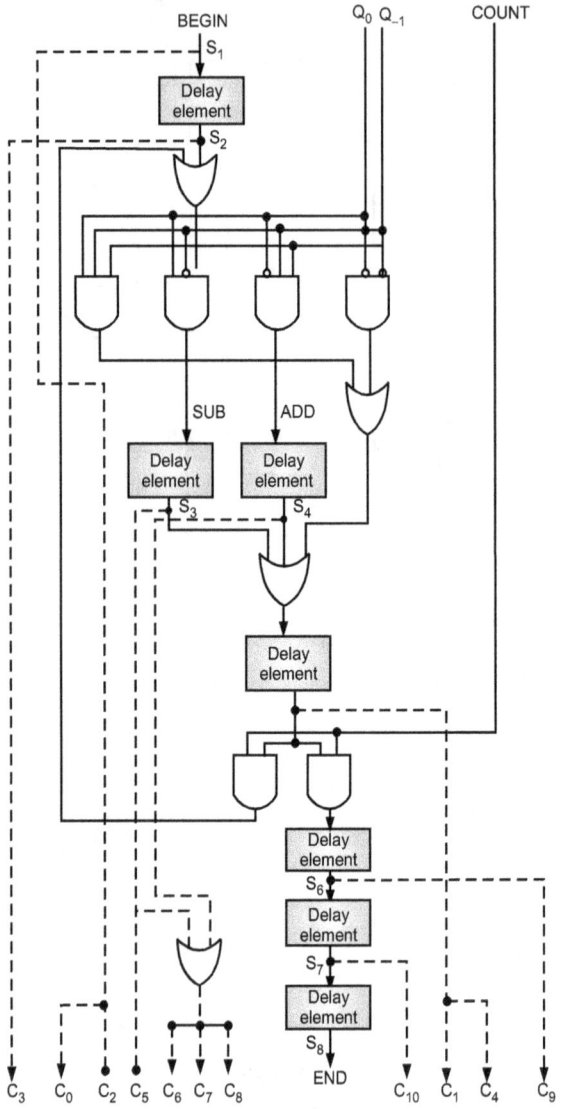

Fig 3.17 : Multiplier control unit using delay elements

Advantages of Delay element method :

1. Simple design since there is no encoding and decoding of control unit states.
2. Less number of combinational logic elements.
3. Minimum design turnaround time, since there is direct correspondence of the controller structure.

Disadvantages of Delay element method :

1. For an n state controller while the sequence counter method needs login flip–flops, the delay element method needs n number of delay elements each having one or more flip–flops.
2. Synchronization of widely distributed delay elements is often difficult to achieve.

3.2.4 PLA Method

The control unit designed methods discussed so far are suitable only for small control units due to their size and complexity. In modern computer VLSI technology based circuitry is used for the design of control unit. One such structure PLA is discussed here.

AND and OR both arrays can be programmed to implement combinational logic functions. As shown in Fig. 3.18 (a) X_i, X_2, X_3 are input signals and f_1, f_2, f_3 are combinations of input signals as outputs.

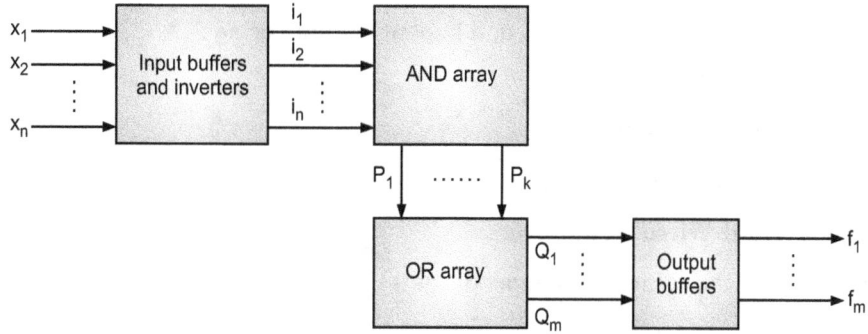

Fig. 3.18 (a) : Block diagram of PLA

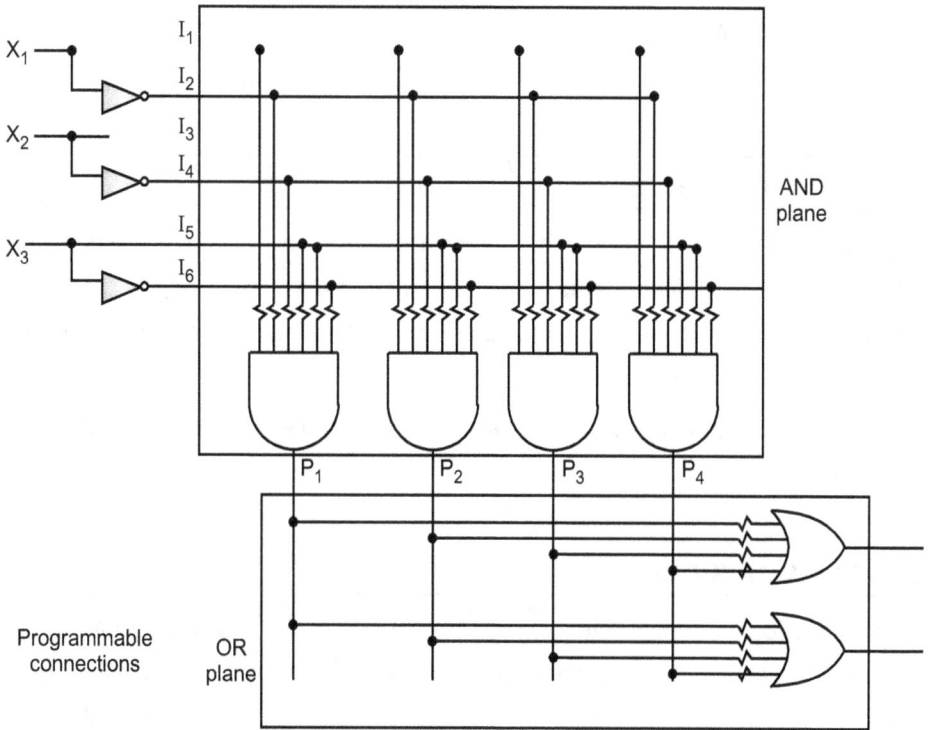

Fig. 3.18 (b) : Function structure of PLA

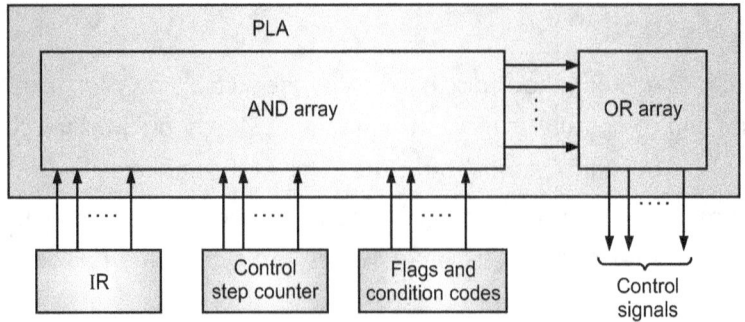

Fig. 3.19 : Control unit implementation using PLA

Advantages of hardwired design :

- A higher speed operation.

- The smaller implementations.

Problems with Hard-Wired Design :

- Sequencing and micro-operation logic gets complex.

- Difficult to design, prototype, and test.

- Resultant design is inflexible, and difficult to build upon (Pipeline, multiple computation units etc.).

- Adding new instructions requires major design and adds complexity quickly.

3.3   DESIGN OF MICROPROGRAMMED CONTROL UNIT

A microprogrammed control unit on the other hand makes use of a micro-sequencer from which instruction bits are decoded to be implemented. It acts as the device supervisor that controls the rest of the subsystems including arithmetic and logic units, registers, instruction registers, off-chip input/output, and buses.

Microprogrammed control in which a dedicated microcontroller executes a microprogram to generate the signals.

3.3.1 Basic Concepts

- **Micro-operations :** We have already seen that the programs are executed as a sequence of instructions, each instruction consists of a series of steps that make up the instruction cycle fetch, decode etc. Each of these steps are, in turn, made up of a smaller series of steps called micro-operations.

- **Micro-operation execution :** Each step of the instruction cycle can be decomposed into micro-operation primitives that are performed in a precise time sequence. Each micro-operation is initiated and controlled based on the use of control signals/lines coming from the control unit.

- **Micro-instruction :** Each instruction of the processor is translated into a sequence of lower level micro-instructions. The process of translation and execution are to as microprogramming.

- **Microprogramming :** A microprogram consists of a sequence of micro-instructions in a microprogramming.

- **Microprogrammed Control Unit :** It is a relatively logic circuit that is capable of sequencing through micro-instructions and generating control signal to execute each micro-instruction.

- **Control Unit :** The control Unit is an important portion of the processor.

The control unit issues control signals external to the processor to cause data exchange with memory and 1/0 unit. The control Unit issues also control signals internal to the processor to move data between registers, to perform the ALU and other internal operations in processor. In a hardwired control unit, the control signals are generated by a micro-instruction are used to controller register transfers and ALU operations. Control Unit design is then the collection and the implementation of all of the needed control signals for the micro-instruction executions.

3.3.2 Basic Layout of a Micro-programmed Control Unit   [Dec. 12]

The control unit Functions as follows :

1. To execute an instruction the sequencing logic unit issues a READ command to the control memory.

2. The word whose address is specified in the control address register is read into control buffer register.

3. The content of the control buffer register generates the control signal and next address information for sequencing logic unit.

4. The sequencing logic unit loads a new address into the control address register based on the next address information from the control buffer register and the ALU flags. All this happens during one clock pulse.

The last step just listed needs elaboration. At the conclusion of each micro-instruction, the sequencing logic unit loads a new address into the control address register. Depending on the value of the ALU flags and the control buffer register, one of three decisions is made :

- **Get the next instruction :** Add 1 to control address register.

- **Jump to a new routine based on a Jump micro-instruction :** Load the address field of the control buffer register into the control address register.

- **Jump to a machine instruction routine :** Load the control address register based on the opcode in the IR.

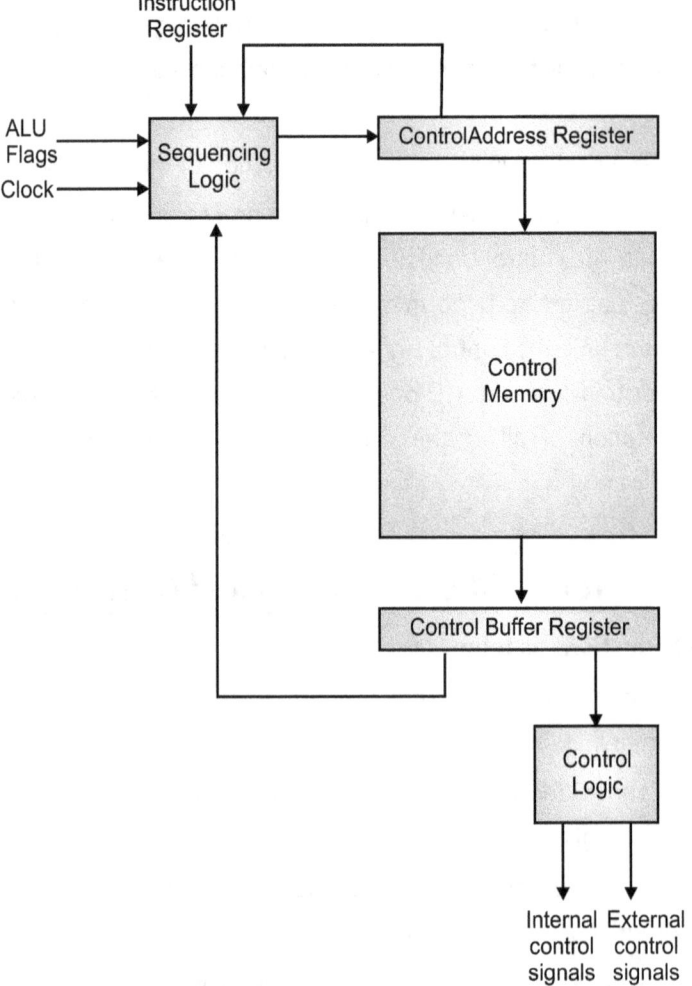

Fig. 3.20 : Functioning of micro-programmed control unit

3.3.3 Microprogramming Advantages

1. It simplifies the design of control unit.
2. It is cheaper and less error prone to implement.
3. Control functions are implemented in software rather than hardware.
4. The design process is orderly and systematic.
5. More flexible, adapt to changes in any organization, at any time.
6. Complex function can be realized efficiently.
7. Very powerful instruction sets.
8. Generality : Multiple instruction sets on same machine.
9. Compatibility.
   - Easy to be backward compatible in one family.
   - Many organizations, same instruction set.
10. Improvement in performance.
11. A high degree of parallelism in data paths e.g., multiple bit micro-instructions are performed in one cycle.

3.3.4 Microprogramming Disadvantages

1. Costly to implement.
2. Microprogrammed control slower than hardwired control unit because of the following reasons :
   - Micro-instruction interpreted at execution time.
   - Interpretation is internal to CPU.
   - Interpret one instruction at a time.

3.3.5 Hardwired Control Versus Micro-programmed Control

[May 11, 12]

Hardwired control is a control mechanism to generate control signals by using appropriate finite state machine (FSM). Microprogrammed control is a control mechanism to generate control signals by using a memory called control storage (CS), which contains the control signals. Although microprogrammed control seems to be advantageous to CISC machines, since CISC requires systematic development of sophisticated control signals, there is no intrinsic difference between these two control mechanisms.

The pair of "micro-instruction-register" and "control storage address register" call be regarded as a "state register" for the hardwired control. Note that the control storage can be regarded as a kind of combinational logic circuit. We can assign any 0, 1 values to each output corresponding to each address, which can be regarded as the input for a combinational logic circuit.

Table 3.7 : Difference between Hardwired and Microprogrammed control

Attribute	Hardwired control	Microprogrammed control
Speed	Fast	Slow
Control functions	Implemented in hardware.	Implemented in software.
Flexibility	Not flexible to accommodate new system specifications or new instructions.	More flexible to accommodate new system specifications or new, instructions, redesign is required.
Ability to handle large/complex instruction sets	Somewhat difficult.	Easier
Ability to support operating systems and diagnostic features	Very difficult (unless anticipated during design).	Easy.
Design process	Somewhat complicated.	Orderly and systematic.
Applications	Mostly RISC microprocessors.	Mainframes, some micro-processors
Instruction set size	Usually under 100 instructions	Usually over under 100 instructions
ROM size	...	2 K to 10 K by 20-400 bit micro-instructions
Chip area efficiency	Uses least area	Uses more area.
Generation of signals	By using appropriate finite state machine (FSM).	By using a memory called control storage.

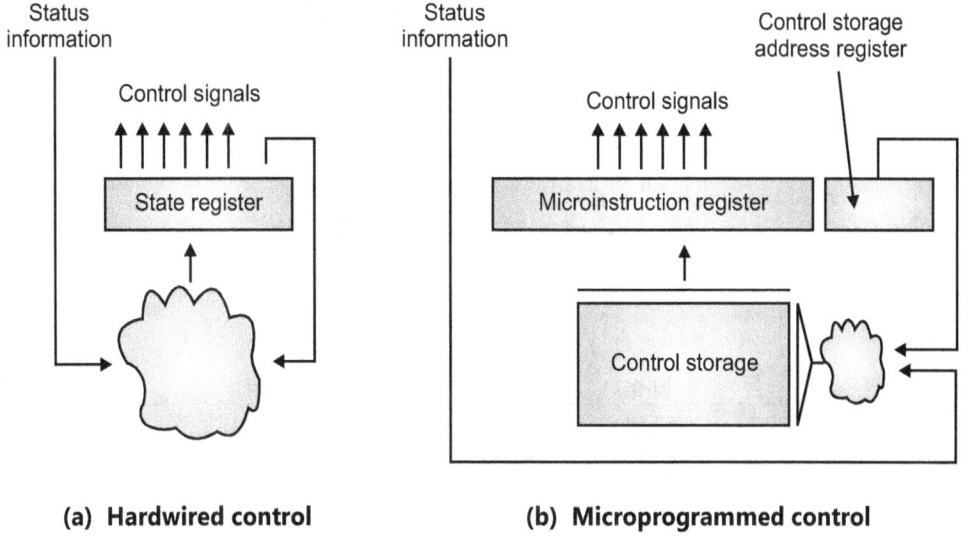

(a) **Hardwired control**   (b) **Microprogrammed control**

Fig. 3.21 : Difference between Hardwired control and microprogrammed control

3.3.6 Branch Address Modification using bit-ORing and Wide-Branch Addressing

In a microprogram to reduce complexity of branching, how to do branch address modification using bit-ORing and wide-branch addressing.

Bit–ORing : In this technique, the branch address is determined by ORing particular bit or bits with the current address of the micro-instruction.

For example, if the current address is 170, and branch address is 172, then the branch address can be generated by ORing 02 (bit 1), with the current address.

Wide-Branch Addressing : Generating branch addresses becomes more difficult as the number of branch addresses increases. In such situations programmable logic array (PLA) can be used to generate the required branch address. This simple and inexpensive way of generating branch addresses is known as wide-branch addressing.

Here, the opcode of a machine instruction is translated into the starting address of the corresponding micro-routine. This is achieved by connecting the opcode bits of the instruction register as inputs to the PLA, which acts as a decoder. The output of PLA is the address of the desired micro-routine.

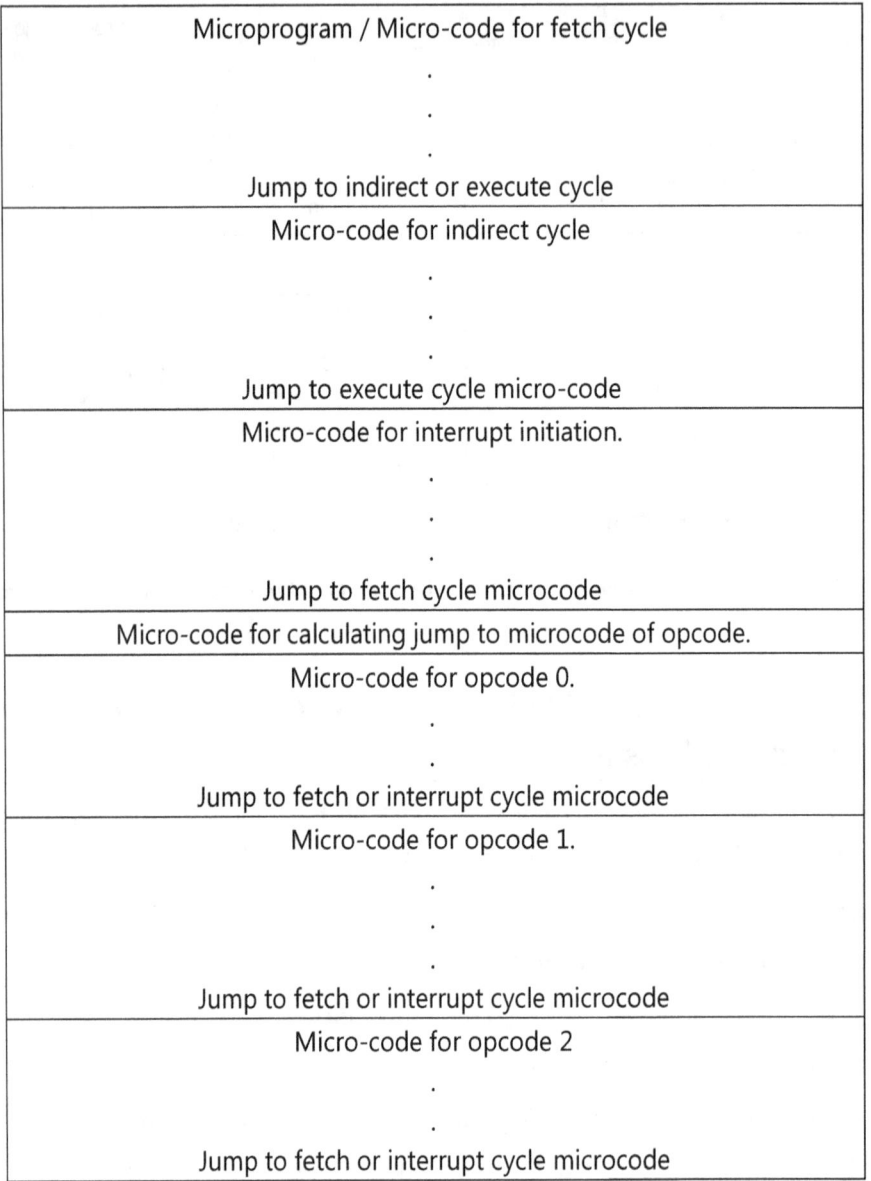

Microprogram / Micro-code for fetch cycle
.
.
.
Jump to indirect or execute cycle
Micro-code for indirect cycle
.
.
.
Jump to execute cycle micro-code
Micro-code for interrupt initiation.
.
.
.
Jump to fetch cycle microcode
Micro-code for calculating jump to microcode of opcode.
Micro-code for opcode 0.
.
.
Jump to fetch or interrupt cycle microcode
Micro-code for opcode 1.
.
.
.
Jump to fetch or interrupt cycle microcode
Micro-code for opcode 2
.
.
Jump to fetch or interrupt cycle microcode

Fig. 3.22 : Instruction execution steps

3.3.7 Grouping of Control Signals in Microprogrammed Control

A simple way to structure micro-instructions is to assign one bit position to each control signal required in the CPU. However, this scheme has one drawback, i.e. assigning individual bits to each control signal results in long micro-instructions, because the number of required signals is usually large. Moreover, only a few bits are used in any given instruction.

The solution of this problem is to group the control signals.

Grouping of control signals : Grouping technique is used to reduce the number of bits in the micro-instruction.

Let us consider single bus CPU having different control signals, as shown in Fig. 3.23.

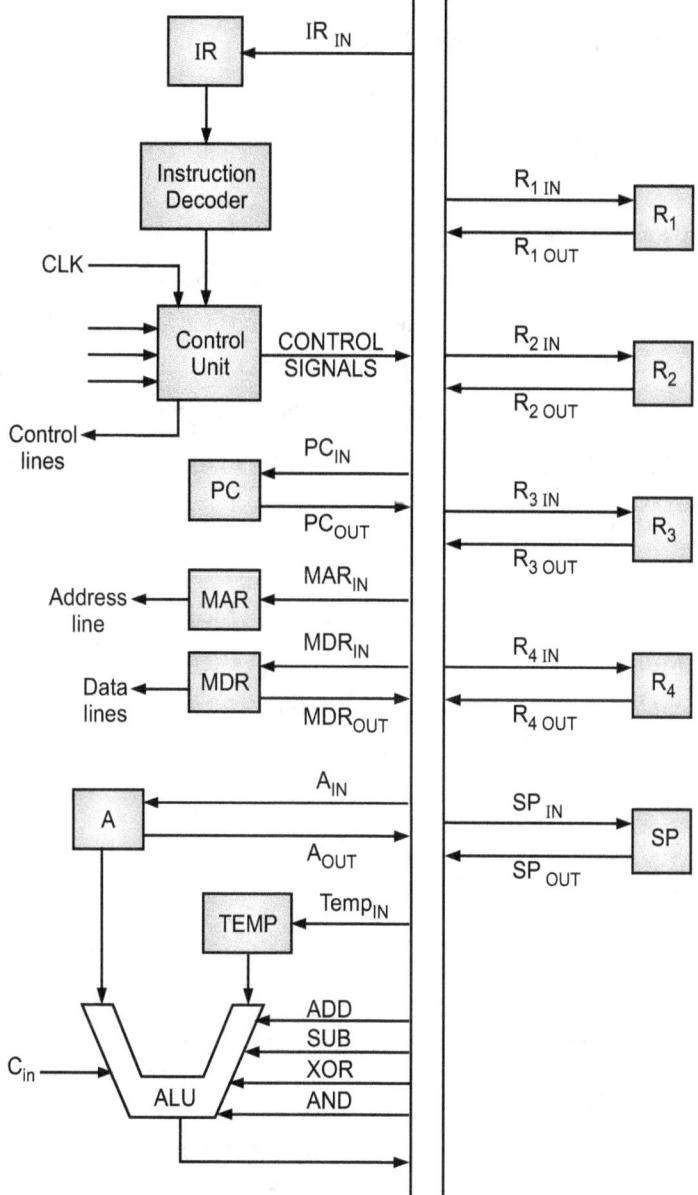

Fig. 3.23 : Single Bus CPU structure with control signals

Gating Signals : IN and OUT signals.

Control Signals : Read, Write, Clear A, set carry in, continue operation, end etc.

ALU Signals : Add, Sub etc.

There are total 39 signals and hence each micro-instruction will have 39 bits. It is not necessary to use all 39 bits for every micro-instruction because by using grouping of control signals we minimize number of bits for micro-instruction.

Ways to reduce number of bits in micro-instruction :

1. Most signals not needed simultaneously.

2. Many signals are mutually exclusive e.g. only one function of ALU can be activated at a time.

3. A source for data transfers must be unique which means that it should not be possible to get the contents of two different registers on to the bus at the same time.

4. Read and write signals to the memory can't be activated simultaneously. So with these suggestions 39 control signals can be grouped in 8 different group.

Table 3.8 : Groups of Control Signals

G_1 (4–Bits) : IN grouping		G2 (4–Bits) OUT grouping	
0000	No Transfer	0000	No Transfer
0001	IR_{IN}	0001	PC_{OUT}
0010	PC_{IN}	0010	MDR_{out}
0011	MDR_{IN}	0011	$R_{1\ OUT}$
0100	MAR_{IN}	0100	R_{2OUT}
0101	A_{IN}	0101	R_{3OUT}
0110	$TEMP_{IN}$	0110	R_{4OUT}
0111	R_{1IN}	0111	SP_{OUT}
1001	R_{2IN}		
1010	R_{3IN}		
1011	SP_{IN}		
G_3 (4 – bits) : ALU Functions		**G_4 (2 – Bits) : RD/WR Control Signals**	
0000	ADD ⎫		
0001	SUB ⎪	00	No Action
..	⎬ 16 ALU	01	Read
..	⎪ Function	10	Write
1111	XOR ⎭		

G5 (1–Bit) : A Register		G_6(1-Bit) : Carry	
0	No Action	0	Carry in to ALU = 0
1	Clear A	1	Carry in to ALU = 1
G_7 (1 – Bit)		G_8 (1 – Bit) : Operation	
0	No Action	0	Continue operation
1	WMFC	1	End

The total numbers of grouping bits are 18. So, we minimized 39–bits micro-instruction to 18-bit micro-instruction. Grouping results in small increase in the required hardware as it becomes necessary to use decoding circuits to translate bit patterns of each group into actual control signals.

3.4   MICRO-INSTRUCTION

Definition of Micro-instruction

An instruction that controls data flow and instruction–execution sequencing in a processor at a more fundamental level than machine instructions.

The control unit seems reasonably simple device. Nevertheless to implement a control unit as an interconnection of basic logic elements is no easy task. The design must include logic for sequencing through micro-operations, for executing micro-operations, for interpreting opcodes and for staking decisions based on ALU flags. It is difficult to design and test such a piece of hardware. Furthermore, the design is relatively inflexible. For example, it is difficult to change the design if one wishes to add a new machine instruction.

3.4.1 Classification of Micro-instructions

Micro-instructions can be classified as vertical and horizontal :

1. Horizontal Micro-instruction :

Individual bits of micro-instructions correspond to individual control lines. A horizontal micro-instruction has the following attributes :

1. Long format.
2. Horizontal micro-instructions are long and allow maximum parallelism since each bit controls a single control line.
3. No decoding is needed in horizontal micro-instructions

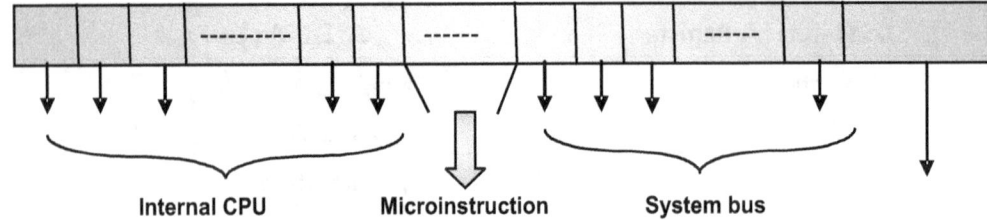

Fig. 3.24 : Horizontal Micro-instruction

Format of horizontal micro-instructions is as follows :

1. There is one-bit for each internal control line.
2. There is one-bit for each system bus control line.
3. There is condition field for each condition for conditional branching.
4. Address field stores the address field of the micro-instructions to be executed next when a branch is taken.

Horizontal Micro-instructions Advantages :

1. It can control a variety of components operating in parallel. So efficient hardware utilization.
2. Horizontal control unit is faster.

Horizontal Micro-instructions Disadvantages :

1. Each bit directly controls each micro-operation
2. Control word bits are not fully utilized.
3. CS becomes large so, Costly.

2. Vertical Micro-instruction :

It allows encoding of control information.

A vertical micro-instruction has following attributes :

1. Short format. Because of the encoding vertical micro-instructions are much shorter than horizontal ones.
2. In vertical micro-instructions control lines are coded into specific fields within a micro-instruction.
3. Decoders are needed to map fields of k bits to possible 2k bits possible combinations of control lines.

    E.g. 3–bit fields in a micro-instruction could be used to specify any one of eight possible lines.
4. Control lines encoded in the same field cannot be activated simultaneously. Therefore, vertical micro-instructions allow only limited parallelism.

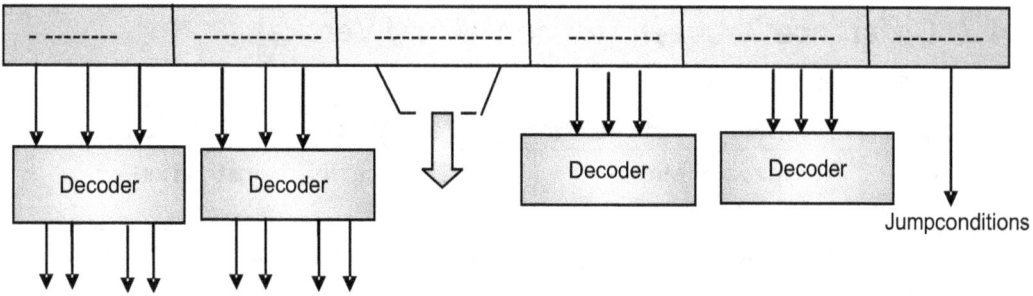

Fig. 3.25 : Vertical micro-instruction

As the CPU may need hundreds of control signals, the control word will be inevitably long. To reduce the length of the control word, groups of control signals that are mutually exclusive (only one of them need be asserted at a time) can be encoded to form shorter fields. This shorter form of control word is called vertical organization.

For example, if only 1 of a group of 8 signals is needed at any time, they can be encoded into a field of $\log_2 8 = 3$ bits, instead of 8 bits. The price to pay is the time delay needed for decoding the encoded field.

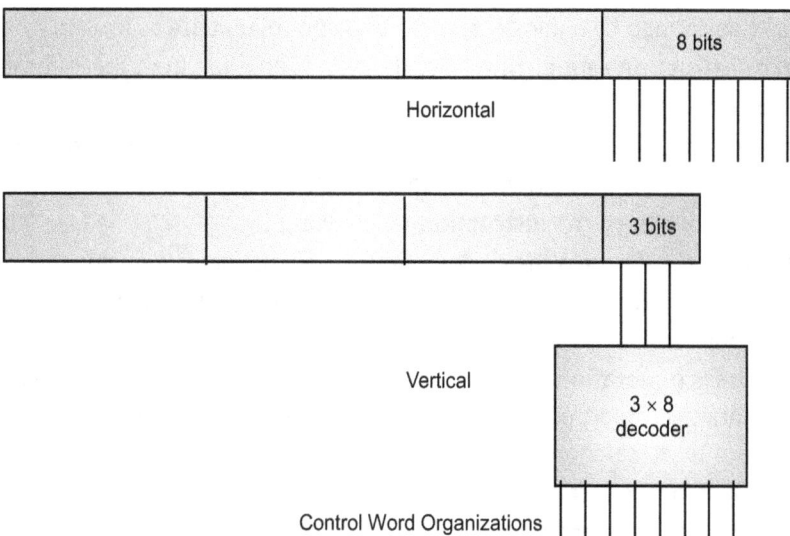

Fig. 3.26 : Control word organizations in horizontal and vertical micro-instruction

Vertical Micro-instructions Advantage :

Vertical implies a short micro-instruction word.

Vertical Micro-instructions Disadvantages :

1. Decoders are required because of encoded micro-instruction fields.
2. It allows only limited parallelism.

3.4.2 Difference Between Horizontal and Vertical Micro-instruction

Table 3.9 : Difference between Horizontal and Vertical micro-instruction

Sr. No.	Horizontal Micro-instruction	Vertical micro-instruction
1	In this each bit of units represents a control signal.	It allows encoding of control information.
2	Decoders are not needed.	Because of higher degree of encoding complex decoders are needed.
3	Long format	Short format.
4	High degree of parallelism.	Allows limited parallelism.
5	Limited encoding.	Considerable encoding of the control information.

3.4.3 Micro-Instruction Sequencing

Two basic tasks performed by a micro-programmed control unit are as follows :

1. **Micro-instruction sequencing :** Get the next instruction from the control memory.
2. **Micro-instruction execution :** Generate the control signals needed for execution.

In designing a control unit, these tasks must be considered together, because both affect the format of the micro-instruction and the timing of the control unit.

Design considerations in micro-instruction sequencing :

Two concerns are involved in the design of micro-instruction sequencing technique :

1. **The size of micro-instruction :** Minimizing size of control unit reduces the cost of component.
2. **The address generation time :** To execute micro-instructions as fast as possible. In Executing a microprogram, the address of the next micro-instruction to be executed is in one of these categories.
   - Determined by instruction register
   - Next sequential address
   - Branch

The first category occurs only once per instruction cycle, just after an instruction is fetched. The second category is the most common in most designs. However, the design cannot be optimized just for sequential access. Branches, both conditional and unconditional, are a necessary part of a microprogram.

Sequencing Techniques :

Based on the current micro-instruction, condition flags, and the content of the instruction register, the Control memory address must be generated for the next micro-instruction. A wide variety of techniques have been used. We can group there into three general categories.

Three general categories for a control memory address are as follows –

- Two address fields
- Single address field
- Variable format

1. Two Address Field :

In Fig. 3.27, the branch control logic with a two address field is illustrated.

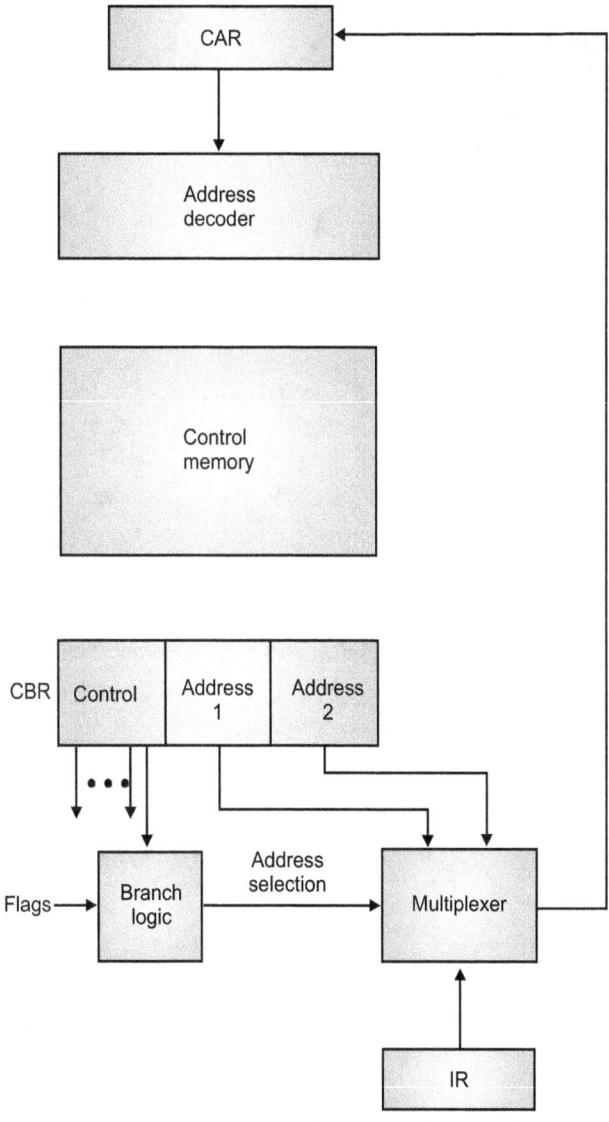

Fig. 3.27 : Branch Control Logic two address fields

This is the simplest approach. A multiplexer is provided that serves as it destination for both address fields plus the instruction register. Based on an address–selection input, the multiplexer transmits either the opcode or one of the two addresses to the control address register (CAR). The CAR is sub–sequently decoded to produce the next micro-instruction address. The address–selection signals are provided by a branch logic module whose input consists of control unit flags plus bits front the control portion of the micro-instruction.

Although the two-address approach is simple. It requires more bits in the micro-instruction than other approaches.

2. **Single Address Field :**

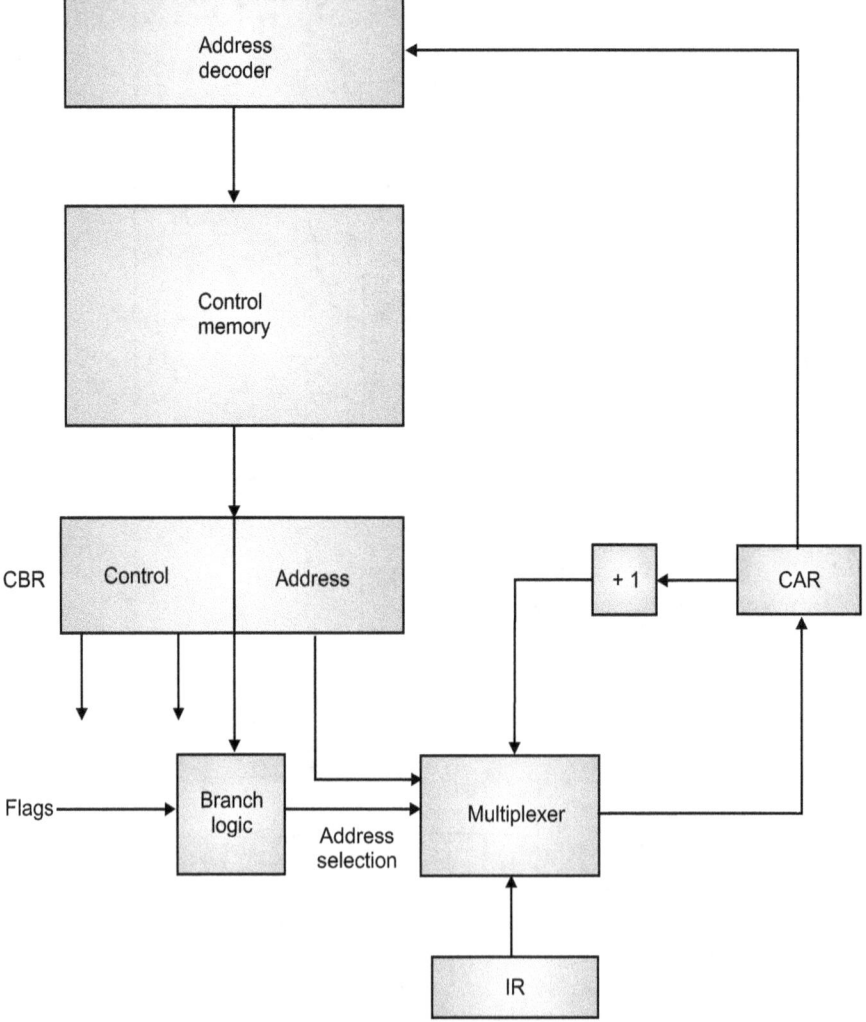

Fig. 3.28 : Branch control logic single address field

A common approach is to have a single address field (Fig. 3.28). With this approach, the options for next address are as follows :

A single address field present in the micro-instruction with the following options for next address :

1.   Address field

2.   Based on OPcode I instruction register.

3.   Next sequential address.

The address selection signals determine which option is selected. This approach reduces number of address field to one. In case of sequential execution address field not used. So, micro-instruction encoding does not efficiently utilize entire micro-instruction.

Advantages of single address field format :

Reduces number of address field to one.

Disadvantages of single address field format :

In case of sequential execution address field not used. So, micro-instruction encoding does not efficiently utilize entire micro-instruction

3. Variable Format Addressing :

In this approach, there are two entirely different micro-instruction formats. One–bit designates which format is being used. In the first format, the remaining bits are used to activate control signals. In the second format, some bits drive the branch logic module, and the remaining bits provide the address. With the first format, the next address is either the next sequential address or an address derived from the instruction register. With the second format either a conditional or unconditional branch is specified.

Disadvantages of variable format :

One entire cycle is consumed with each branch micro-instruction. With other approaches, address generation occurs as part of the same cycle as control signal generation, minimizing control memory access.

These all approaches described are general. Specific implementation will often involve a combination of these techniques.

The next micro-instruction address is determined in one of five ways :

1. Next sequential address : The control unit's control address register is incremented by 1.

2. **OPcode mapping :** At the beginning of each instruction cycle, the next micro-instruction address is determined by the opcode.

3. **Subroutine facility :** The address of subroutine is loaded in control address register and executes subroutine.

4. **Interrupt testing :** Certain micro-instructions specify a test for interrupts. If an interrupt has occurred, this determines the next micro-instruction address.

5. **Branch :** Conditional and Unconditional branch micro-instructions are used.

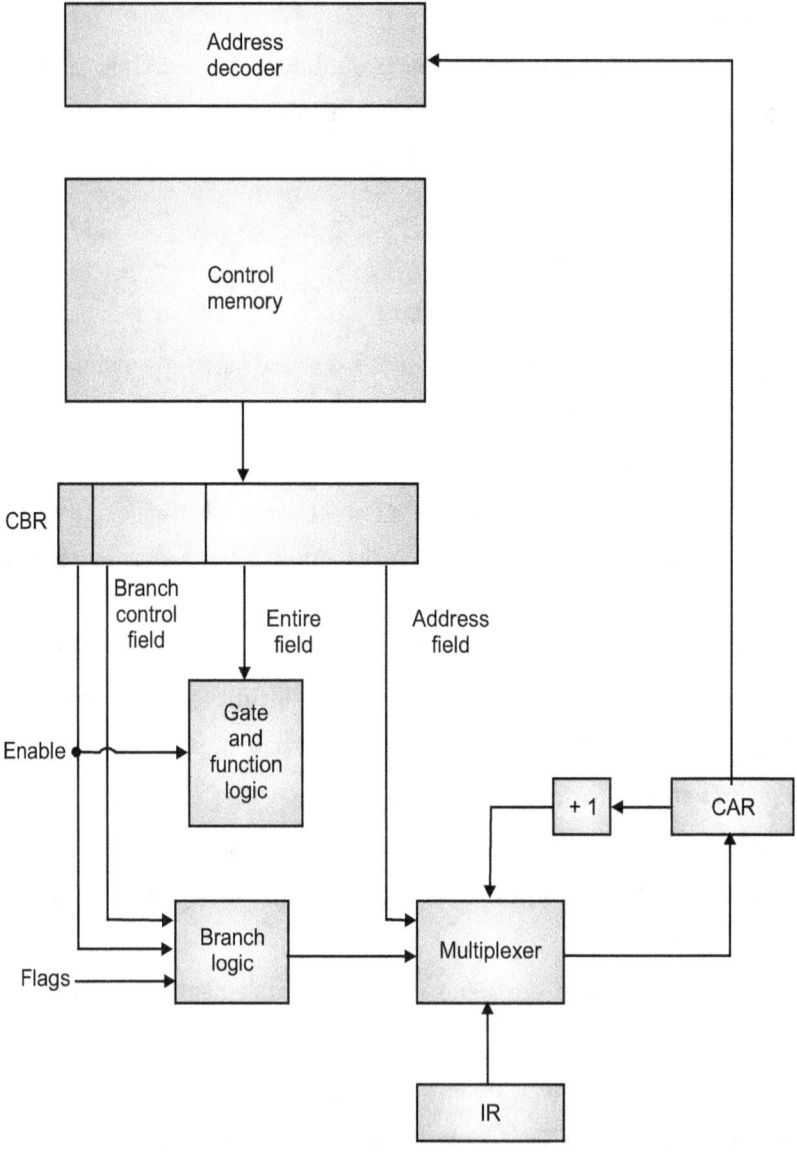

Fig. 3.29 : Branch control logic, variable format

3.4.4 Micro-Instruction Encoding

Microprogrammed control units are not designed using a pure encoding or horizontal micro-instruction format. At least some degree of encoding is used to reduce control memory width and to simplify the task of microprogramming.

Two aspects of encoding are :

    1.   Direct Encoding   2. Indirect Encoding

1. Direct Encoding :

The basic technique for encoding is illustrated in Fig. 3.30. The micro-instruction is organized as set of fields. Each field contains a code, which upon decoding activates one or more control signals.

When the micro-instruction is executed, every field is decoded and generates control signals. So, with N fields N simultaneous actions are specified. Generally, but not always we want to design the format so that each control signal is activated by no more than one field.

Now consider the individual field. A field consisting of L bits can contain one of 2L codes, each of which can be encoded to a different control signal.

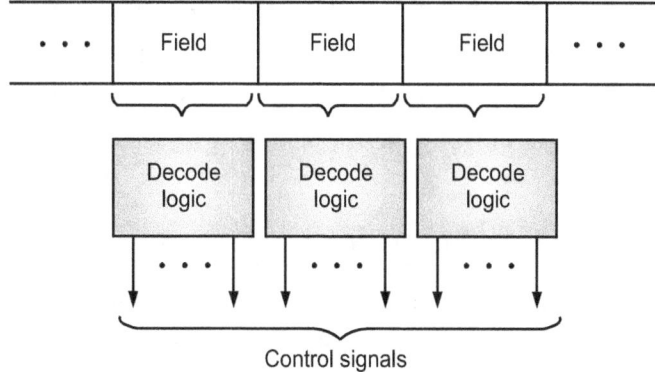

Control signals

Fig. 3.30 : Direct encoding

Two approaches can be taken to organizing the encoded micro-instructions into fields :

Functional and Resource Encoding :

(i) The functional encoding method identifies functions within the machine and designates fields by function type. For example, if various sources can be used for transferring data to the accumulator, one field can be designated for this purpose, with each code specifying a different resource.

(ii) Resource encoding views the machine as consisting of a set of independent resources and devotes one field to each (e.g. I/O, memory, ALU).

2. Indirect Encoding :

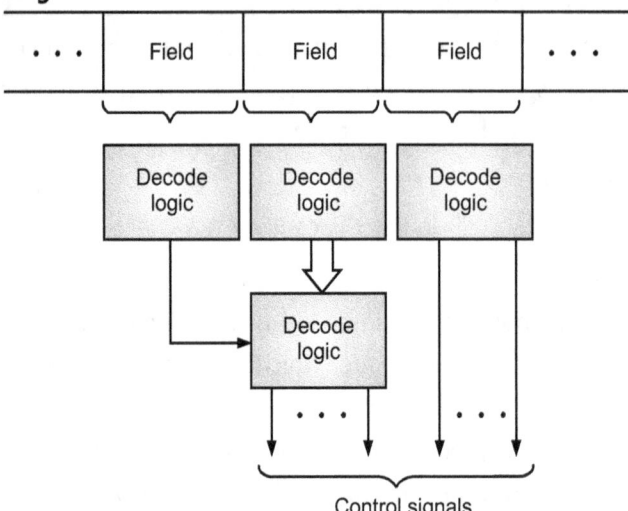

Fig. 3.31 : Indirect encoding

The indirect technique is illustrated in Fig. 3.31 One field is used to determine the interpretation of another field. For example, consider an ALU that is capable of performing eight different arithmetic operations and eight different shift operations. A 1–bit field could be used to indicate whether a shift or arithmetic operation is to be used; a 3–bit field would indicate the operation. This technique generally implies two levels of decoding.

3.4.5 Micro-Instruction Execution

The micro-instruction cycle is the basic event on a microprogrammed processor. Each cycle is made up the two parts : fetch and execute. This section deals with the execution of micro-instruction.

A microprogrammed computer has two distinct levels of control :

(i) Instruction level and (ii) Micro-instruction level

(i) Instruction level : Here CPU continuously executes instruction cycles that involves following steps

1. By using PC, CPU fetches an instruction fro main memory.

2. The opcode part of instruction is stored in IR, the operation specified by IR is then decoded and executed.

3. PC is altered to point to the next instruction to be fetched from memory.

(ii) Micro-instruction level : Control unit continuously executes micro-instruction cycles as follows :

1. The addressing portion of the control unit fetches a micro-instruction MI from control memory CM, whose address is stored in the microprogram counter.

2. MI is loaded into the micro- instruction register MIR and is decoded to produce the required control signals.

3. Micro PC is altered to point to the next instruction to be fetched from CM.

A micro-instruction cycle can be executed faster than an instruction cycle, since micro-instructions are stored within CPU, whereas instructions must be fetched from an external memory.

3.5 APPLICATIONS OF MICROPROGRAMMING

1. Input Output Processing :

An area of application of microprogramming which is developing rapidly is input/output processing, characterized by communications processing and control of peripheral devices. Examples of input/output processing can include polling, multiplexing, routing and addressing messages, generating transmission codes, error detection and correction, data compression, as well as more sophisticated processes such as editing and source data automation.

2. Real Time Data Processing :

Real–time data processing includes the processing of data which is collected at frequent intervals and referred to as real–time data. Examples of real–time data are signals, whether from radars, acoustic or optical devices. Examples of real–time data processing are multi–sensor correlation, spectral analysis, pattern recognition, and filtering of digital signals.

3. Airbone Systems :

An airborne system which uses a digital computer has many of the requirements found in input/output processing and real-time data processing. Additional requirements of airborne computer systems are very high reliability, compact size, and minimized weight. The hardware technology of microprogrammed machines, particularly with LSI components, should make them more compact and more reliable than their hard–wired logic counterparts.

4. Data Management Systems :

Through microprogramming reduce the implementation and performance problems of data management systems and to make it easier to instrument system software for debugging and performance analysis. The DMS usually offers data management services consisting, at a minimum, of file creation, updating, retrieval, and report generation.

5. Security :

Protection must be provided against accidental or overt destruction of processes and data as well as illegal access. The solution to the security problem in information processing will probably involve a combination of hardware and software techniques.

6. Software Production :

A notable attempt to improve programmer productivity and software reliability was the development of high-order programming. Microprogramming can be used to improve the effectiveness of HOLs (High–Order Programming Languages) in the software production process.

7. Emulation :

Emulation is the combined software/ hardware interpretation of the machine instruction of one machine by another. Target's machine architecture is mapped onto the host machine.

Programs written in the machine language of one processor can then be run by another processor. This is known as emulation. If P_1 can execute instructions of P_2 then we can say that P_1 emulates P_2.

Advantages of Emulation :

1. Emulation allows us **to replace** obsolete equipment with more up–to–date machines. The replacement of computer fully emulates the original one so no software changes have to be made to run existing programs.

2. Emulation is usually used **to test and debug the hardware and software** of an external system such as the prototype of a microprocessor–based instrument. The hardware part of an emulator consists of multiware cable which connects the host system to the system being developed. A connector at the end of the cable is plugged into the prototype system in place of its microprocessor. This connection is used to download your object code program into RAM in the system being tested and run with the help of software of emulator.

3. Like a debugger, an emulator allows you to load and run programs, **test and change** the contents of registers, test and change the contents of memory location and insert breakpoints in the program

4. The emulator also stores block of data containing the contents of registers, activity on the address bus and data bus, and the state of the flags as each instruction executes. This is known as **trace data**. The emulator allows this trace data to print so that it is possible to see the results of the program on the step–by–step basic.

8. Micro Diagnostics :

Microprogramming diagnostic routines have allowed refinements and increased the speed of detecting and localizing faults, including error detection and correction of micro-storage itself.

(a) Software diagnostics

(b) Hardware diagnostics (Test Generation Methods)

(c) Micro-diagnostics

9. Special-Purpose Devices :

Special processors for data communication, data acquisition, and device controllers can be designed through microprogramming.

10. Dynamic Microprogramming :

This allows routines to be easily microprogrammed. Computer can be restructured to represent any instruction vocabulary by use of writable control memory (WCM). It allows the instruction set of the machine to be changed and be TAILORED to specific applications.

3.6   PREFETCHING MICROINSTRUCTIONS

The disadvantage of micro-programmed control is that it results slower operating speed because of the time it takes to fetch microinstructions from the control store. This problem can be solved by prefetching the next microinstruction while the current one is being executed .In this technique, the execution time can be overlapped with the fetch time .

Sometimes the address of next microinstruction is determined from the status flags and from the result of the currently executed microinstructions. In such cases   prefetching of microinstruction occasionally prefetches a wrong microinstruction. So in such cases, the fetch must be repeated with correct address, which requires more complex hardware. Eventhough this difficulty, the prefetching technique is oftenly used to increase instruction execution speed.

MULTIPLE CHOICE QUESTIONS (MSQS)

1. Which of the following registers in a single bus organization of processor are inaccessible to the programmer ?

(a) Temp   (b) Y

(c) Z   (d) all of these

2. ...... coordinates the input and output devices of a computer system.

(a) Processor   (b) ALU

(c) Control Unit   (d) None of these

3. Which registers are used as temporary register ?

(a) Y   (b) Z

(c) a and b   (d) none of these

4. The ...... bus is set of lines that carry information about where in memory data is to be transferred to or form.

    (a) data   (b) address

    (c) control   (d) all of these

5. The ...... bus are the lines that actually carry data being transferred.

    (a) address   (b) control

    (c) data   (d) none of these

6. The ...... bus control how bus functions and allow users of bus to signal when data is available.

    (a) control   (b) data

    (c) address   (d) single

7. The control unit of a computer ......

    (a) accepts input data

    (b) generates control signals to execute an instruction

    (c) stores data in the memory

    (d) all of above

8. The programmer can not access following registers......

    (a) IR   (b) MAR and MDR

    (c) Y, Z and Temp   (d) PC

9. Which of following are special purpose registers ?

    (a) stack pointer   (b) index registers

    (c) pointers   (d) all of these

10. ALU, data registers and interconnecting bus combinely form ......

    (a) data path   (b) address path

    (c) control path   (d) all of these

11. In a single bus organization ...... data ...... can be transferred over the bus in a clock cycle.

    (a) single, word   (b) double, word

    (c) signel, byte   (d) double, byte

12. Instructions written in a proper sequence to execute a particular task is called ......
    (a) algorithm   (b) program
    (c) function   (d) procedure

13. After branching...... is fetched for execution.
    (a) first instruction of program
    (b) instruction following branch instruction in program
    (c) last instruction of program
    (d) instruction of target address

14. JB is next is ......
    (a) condition branch   (b) unconditional branch
    (c) loop   (d) none of these

15. CALL NEXT, is ......
    (a) conditional branch   (b) unconditional branch
    (c) loop   (d) none of these

16. After execution of instruction, PC = ...
    (a) PC + 1   (b) PC + 2
    (c) PC + size of current instruction   (d) PC + Size of next instruction

17. The ...... is used to select of the two inputs.
    (a) multiplex   (b) demultiplexer
    (c) encoder   (d) decoder

18. Registers Ro through R (n −1) includes ......
    (a) general purpose register   (b) special purpose register
    (c) both (a) and (b)   (d) none of these

19. Job of programmer to select and write appropriate instructions one after the other in a proper sequence is called as ......
    (a) programming   (b) instruction sequencing
    (c) algrothim   (d) instruction routing

20. Once an instruction is executed, then next will be executed is described as ......
    (a) straight line execution   (b) branching
    (c) instruction decoding   (d) instruction fetching

21. ...... register is used to fetch address of next instruction to be executed.

(a) MAR   (b) PC

(c) MDR   (d) IR

22. Depending upon the condition specifies transfer the control of program of specified routine is called ......

(a) instruction sequencing   (b) looping

(c) unconditional branches   (d) conditional branching

23. Without checking any condition, transfer program control to some another loop is called......

(a) conditional branching   (b) unconditional branching

(c) looping   (d) instruction sequencing

24. Each instruction cycle has the following steps......

(a) execute, fetch, indirect, corrupt   (b) indirect, execute, interrupt fetch

(c) fetch, indirect, execute, interrupt   (d) none of these

25. ...... cycle occurs at beginning of each instruction cycle.

(a) execute   (b) fetch

(c) interrupt   (d) indirect

26. ...... is connected to address lines of the system bus.

(a) MAR   (b) MBR

(c) PC   (d) IR

27. ...... is connected to data lines of the system bus.

(a) MAR   (b) MBR

(c) PC   (d) Ir

28. ...... holds the last instruction fetched.

(a) PC   (b) IR

(c) MAR   (d) MBR

29. In which of the following cases operand fetch is required.

(a) If operand is present in CPU

(b) If operand is an immediate data

(c) If operand is present at some address

(d) None of these

30. Which cycle does not involves a small, fixed sequence of micro-instructions and same micro-operations are not repeated each time around.

    (a) fetch   (b) Indirect

    (c) interrupt   (d) execute

31. Execution of an instruction requires the following cycles......

    (a) Fetch operand, decode instruction

    (b) Decode instruction, fetch operands, perform operation, store result

    (c) Perform operation , decode instruction

    (d) decode instruction, perform operation, store result

32. ...... micro-operations transfer binary information from one register to another.

    (a) Register transfer   (b) Arithmetic micro-operations

    (c) Logic micro-operation   (d) Shift micro-operations

33. In branch instructions new address is loaded into......

    (a) stack register   (b) memory address register

    (c) memory data register   (d) program counter

34. ...... micro-operations perform arithmetic operations on numbers stored in registers.

    (a) Register transfer   (b) Arithmetic

    (c) Logic   (d) Shirt

35. ...... micro-operations perform bit manipulation operations on non-numeric data stored in registers.

    (a) Register transfer   (b) Arithmetic

    (c) Logic   (d) Shift

36. ...... micro-operations perform shift operations on contents of register.

    (a) Register transfer   (b) Arithmetic

    (c) Logic   (d) Shift

37. ...... micro-operation doesn't change contents of registers.

    (a) Register transfer   (b) Arithmetic

    (c) Logic   (d) Shift

38. In ...... instruction bits directly generate the signals.

    (a) hardwired control   (b) microprogrammed control

    (c) micro-instruction sequencing   (d) none of these

39. In ...... a dedicted microcontroller executes a microprogram to generate signals.

    (a) hardwired control   (b) micro-programmed control

    (c) microinstruction sequencing   (d) all of these

40. There is specific time delay between activation of two contiguous control signals in ......method.

    (a) sequence counter   (b) state table

    (c) PLA   (d) delay element method

41. Each instruction consists of a series of steps that, in turn, made up of a smaller series of steps called as ......

    (a) micro-operations   (b) micro-controller

    (c) micro-processor   (d) instructions

42. A ...... consists of a sequence of micro-instructions in a micro-pragramming.

    (a) program   (b) algorithm

    (c) microprogram   (d) micro-instruction

43. An instruction that controls data flow and instruction execution sequencing in a processor at more fundamental level than machine instructions is called as ......

    (a) micro-program   (b) conditional instruction

    (c) micro-instruction   (d) none of these

44. PLA means ......

    (a) programmable logic analysis   (b) programmable logic array

    (c) programmable logical addressing (d) programmable logic algorithm

45. Horizontal micro-instruction has ...... format.

    (a) long   (b) short   (c) double

46. Vertical micro-instruction has ...... format.

    (a) long   (b) short   (c) double

47. No decoding is needed in ...... micro-instructions.

    (a) vertical   (b) horizontal

48. Decodes are required in ...... mico-instruction

    (a) horizontal   (b) vertical

49. Hardwired control is implemented in ......
   (a) software   (b) hardware

50. Microprogrammed control is implemed in ......
   (a) hardware   (b) software

51. Speed of hardwired control is ...... than microprogrammed control.
   (a) slow   (b) same as   (c) fast

52. The number of bits required in horizontal microinstruction are ...... compared to vertical microinstruction.
   (a) less   (b) same as
   (c) more   (d) none of these

53. Sequence counter, Delay-elements, state-table, PLA are the methods for design of ...... control unit.
   (a) microprogrammed   (b) hardwired
   (c) (a) and (b)   (d) (a) or (b)

54. If IR is an 8-bit register, then instruction decoder generates ...... signals one for each instruction.
   (a) 16   (b) 32   (c) 64   (d) 256

55. A microprogrammed control unit ......
   (a) implemented in hardware
   (b) contains instruction set size usually under 100 instructions
   (c) faster than hardware wired unit
   (d) facilitates easy of new instructions

56. The microinstruction MAR ← PC is executed to ......
   (a) Fetch operand from memory   (b) Fetch an instruction
   (c) stores result in memory   (d) To fetch register value

57. MDR ← M (MAR) is executed to ......
   (a) Data from memory put to data bus
   (b) Data from memory is put on address bus
   (c) Data from memory is put on control bus
   (d) None of above

58. M (MAR) ← MDR operations is ......
   (a) memory read   (b) memory write
   (c) data read   (d) data write

59. To transfer contents of memory location Z into register R_2 use the following instruction ......

    (a) $Z \leftarrow R_2$ (b) $R_2 \leftarrow Z$

    (c) $R_1 \leftarrow Z$ (d) $Z \leftarrow R1$

60. To transfer contents of register R_2 into register R_1 use following instruction ......

    (a) $R_2 \leftrightarrow R_1$ (b) $X \leftarrow R_2$

    (c) $R_2 \leftarrow R_1$ (d) $R_1 \leftarrow R_2$

61. To transfer contents of register R2 into memory location Y......

    (a) $R_2 \leftarrow R_1$ (b) $X \leftarrow R_2$

    (c) $Y \leftarrow R_2$ (d) $R_2 \leftarrow Y$

62. ...... means contents of R_1 plus R_2 transferred to R_3.

    (a) $X \leftarrow R_1 + R_2$ (b) $R_3 \leftarrow R_1 + R_2$

    (c) $R_3 \leftarrow R_1 + 1$ (d) $R_3 \leftarrow R_2 + 1$

63. ...... means contents of R1 minus R2 transferred to R3.

    (a) $X \leftarrow R_1 - {}_{R2}$ (b) $R_1 - R_2 \leftarrow X$

    (c) $R_1 - R_2 \leftarrow R_3$ (d) $R_3 \leftarrow R_1 - R_2$

64. ...... means contents of register R1 and memory location X is added and result is stored in memory location Z.

    (a) $R_1 + X \leftarrow Z$ (b) $Z \leftarrow R_1 + X$

    (c) $X \leftarrow R_1 + Z$ (d) $Z \leftarrow R_1 + 1$

65. ......means contents of memory locations Z is substracted from register R1 and result is stored in memory location Y.

    (a) $Y \leftarrow R_1 - Z$ (b) $Y \leftarrow Z - R_1$

    (c) $Y \leftarrow R_1 + Z$ (d) $Y \leftarrow R_1 + R_2$

66. shl instruction is for a ......

    (a) logical shift left   (b) logical shift right

    (c) logical shift left and right   (d) logical shift right and then left

67. shr instruction is for ......

    (a) logical shift right   (b) logical shift left

    (c) logical shift right and then left   (d) logical shift left and then right

68. Negative flag will have value '1' when result is ......

    (a) greater than 0   (b) less than 0

    (c) 1   (d)borrow or carry is generated

69. Zero flag is set to '1' when result is ......

   (a) greater than 0   (b) less than 0

   (c) 0   (d) 1

70. Overflow flag will have value '1' when result ......

   (a) is one   (b) is negative

   (c) is zero   (d) has arithmetic overflow

71. Carry flag will have value '1' when result

   (a) is one   (b) is zero

   (c) borrow or carry is generate   (d) has arithmetic overflow

72. An instruction may contain ...... address(es).

   (a) 0 or 1   (b) 2

   (c) 3   (d) any of above

73. The instruction Add is ...... address instruction.

   (a) 0   (b) 1   (c) 2   (d) 3

74. The instruction Add Y is ...... address instruction.

   (a) 0   (b) 1   (c) 2   (d) 3

75. The instruction Add Y, Z is ...... address instruction.

   (a) 0   (b) 1   (c) 2   (d) 3

76. The instruction Add X, Y, Z is ...... address instruction.

   (a) 0   (b) 1   (c) 2   (d) 3

77. Memory transfer operations ...... register contains the address an address bus.

   (a) MAR   (b) MDR

   (c) IR   (d) All of these

78. In memory transfer operations ...... register contains the data an data bus.

   (a) MAR   (b) MDR

   (c) IR   (d) All of these

79. The control signals generated for operation MAR ← PC are ......

   (a) PCin, MARin   (b) PCin, MARout

   (c) PCout, MARin   (d) PCout, MARout

80. The control signals generated for operation MDR ← M (MAR) are ......

    (a) MARin, RAMout, MDRin system   (b) MARout, RAMout, MDRin system

    (c) MARout, RAMin, MDRin system   (d) MARout, RAMout, MDRout system

81. The control signals generated for operation PC ← PC + 1 are ......

    (a) PCout, MARin, Zin, PCin   (b) PCout, MARout, Zin, PCin

    (c) PCin, MARin, Zout, PCin   (d) PCout, MARin, Zout, PCin

82. The control signals generated for IR← MDR (opcode) are ......

    (a) MDRout, opcode, IRout   (b) MDRout, opcode, IRin

    (c) MDRin, opcode, IRin   (d) MDRin, opcode, IRout

83. The delay elements are implemented by ...... and controlled by a common clock signal.

    (a) T flip-flops   (b) D flip-flops

    (c) SR flip-flops   (d) JK flip-flops

84. In delay element method, the signal that activate same control signals are ...... to get one common output signal.

    (a) Anded   (b) ORed

    (c) XORed   (d) XNoRed

85. In delay element method, a decision box can be implemented by two ...... gates.

    (a) AND   (b) OR

    (c) XOR   (d) NOR

86. We can associated a state with every micro-instruction block in ......

    (a) Delay element method   (b) State table method

    (c) PLA method   (d) Sequence counter method

87. In ...... control memory is organized as a program logic array.

    (a) Sequence counter method   (b) Delay element method

    (c) Wilkes control method   (d)State table method

88. In ...... control unit, control memory is used.

    (a) microprogrammed control unit   (b) Hardwired control unit

    (c) (a) and (b)   (d) None of these

89. In ...... control unit, control memory is absent,

    (a) microprogrammed control unit   (b) hardwired control unit

    (c) (a) and (b)   (d) none of these

90. The hardwired control unit based system contains ...... instructions.

    (a) smaller   (b) larger

    (c) both (a) and (b)   (d) None of these

91. The microprogrammed control unit based system contains ...... instructions.

    (a) smaller   (b) larger

    (c) both (a) and (b)   (d) None of these

92. The hardwired control units find more applications in ...... processors.

    (a) CISC   (b) RISC

93. The microprogrammed control units find more applications in ...... processors.

    (a) CISC   (b) RISC

94. ...... control unit required less chip area.

    (a) Hardwired   (b) Microprogrammed

95. ...... control unit required more chip area.

    (a) Hardwired   (b) Microprogrammed

96. ...... control unit generates signals using appropriate finite state machine (FSM).

    (a) Hardwired   (b) Microprogrammed

97. The ...... is sub-sequently decoded to produce next micro-instruction address.

    (a) memory address register   (b) control address register

    (c) program counter   (d)memory data register

98. The ......encoding method identifies functions within the machine and designates fields by function type.

    (a) Functional Encoding   (b) Resource Encoding

    (c) Indirect encoding   (d) All of these

99. The ...... encoding views the machine as consisting of set of independent resources and devoted one filed to each.

    (a) Functional encoding   (b) Resource Encoding

    (c) Indirect encoding   (d) All of these

100. Microprogramming can be used for Data management system.

    (a) False   (b) True

101. Microprogramming can be used for real time data.

    (a) False   (b) True

102. Microprogramming can be used for emulation.

    (a) True   (b) False

103. Special processors can be designed through microprogramming.

    (a) True   (b) False

104. Microprogramming can be used for ......

    (a) software diagnostics   (b) hardware diagnostics

    (c) Micro-diagnostics   (d) All of these

105. Microprogramming allow instruction set of machine to be changed and be TAILORED to specific applications.

    (a) True   (b) False

106. Microprogramming can be used to improve effectiveness of higher order programming languages.

    (a) True   (b) False

107. Security can be provided against illegal access using microprogramming.

    (a) True   (b) False

108. Microprogramming can be used in airbone system.

    (a) True   (b) False

109. Microprogramming can be used in input output processing.

    (a) True   (b) False

ANSWERS

1.	d	2.	c	3.	c	4.	b	5.	c
6.	a	7.	b	8.	c	9.	d	10.	a
11.	a	12.	b	13.	d	14.	a	15.	b
16.	c	17.	a	18.	c	19.	b	20.	a
21.	b	22.	d	23.	b	24.	c	25.	b

26.	a	27.	b	28.	b	29.	c	30.	d
31.	b	32.	a	33.	d	34.	b	35.	c
36.	d	37.	a	38.	a	39.	b	40.	d
41.	a	42.	c	43.	c	44.	b	45.	a
46.	b	47.	b	48.	b	49.	b	50.	b
51.	c	52.	c	53.	b	54.	d	55.	d
56.	b	57.	a	58.	b	59.	b	60.	d
61.	c	62.	b	63.	d	64.	b	65.	a
66.	a	67.	a	68.	b	69.	c	70.	d
71.	c	72.	d	73.	a	74.	b	75.	c
76.	d	77.	a	78.	b	79.	c	80.	b
81.	d	82.	b	83.	b	84.	b	85.	a
86.	b	87.	c	88.	a	89.	b	90.	a
91.	b	92.	b	93.	a	94.	a	95.	b
96.	a	97.	b	98.	a	99.	b	100.	b
101.	b	102.	a	103.	a	104.	d	105.	a
106.	a	107.	a	108.	a	109.	a		

QUESTIONS

1. Draw a neat diagram of single bus organization of a CPU showing ALU, all types of registers and the data paths among them.

2. Write a microprogram of micro-instructions for the following instruction ADD(R_3), R_1

3. Explain the design of multiplier control unit using delay element method.

4. Explain briefly : Emulation

5. Compare hardwired control over microprogrammed control unit.

6. Draw the single bus organization of the CPU and write the control sequence for the following instructions

    (i) SUB (R_3), R_4 and   (ii) Branch–on–negative

    Where, R_3 is source register and R_4 is destination register.

7. In microprogrammed control what is the necessity of the grouping of control signals? Also explain the procedure of grouping of control signals with the help of suitable example.

8. What is micro-program sequencing ? Explain with the help of suitable diagram the technique used to solve the problem due to several branch instructions microprogram sequencing.

9. Write control sequence for an unconditional branch instruction.

10. What are the different design methods for hardwired control units ? Explain any one.

11. Write a control sequence for the execution of the following instruction. SUB R_1, (R_2), R_1.

12. Draw the diagram of micro-programmed control unit and give the advantages and disadvantages.

13. Write a microprogram of micro-instructions for the following instructions ADD (R_3) + R_1.

14. Draw the block diagram of hardwired control unit and compare it with the microprogram control unit.

15. Write a micro-program of micro-instruction for the following, also draw flowchart : ADD (RSrc)+, Rdst.

16. List the application of micro-programming.

17. With the help of circuit diagram, explain how Z_{in} and End signals are generated.

18. Compare horizontal and vertical micro-instruction representation.

19. Write a control sequence for execution of the instruction add (R_i), R_2 for single Bus architecture.

20. In a microprogram, to reduce complexity of branching, how do you do branch address modification using Bit–Oring and wide–branch addressing.

21. Explain with suitable example how the size of control words can be reduced in order to obtain small control store.

22. Write the control sequence for the following instruction considering single bus organization of the CPU SUB (R_3), R_2 Where, R_3 is source register and R_2 is destination register.

UNIT IV

INPUT / OUTPUT ORGANIZATION

4.1 INTRODUCTION

The important components of any computer system are processor, memory and I/O devices. The processor fetches instruction processes the data stores result in memory. The major component or computer system we can call as Input and output system. The main function of computer system is to transfer the information between processor or memory and the outside world. The I/O devices or other peripherals cannot connect directly to the system bus. It is necessary to use a module in between system bus and peripheral called as I/O module or I/O system.

The computer system's I/O architecture provides an interface to the outside world. Input/output systems or I/O provides the communication between computer and the outside world. Inputs are the signals or data sent to the system, and outputs are the signals or data sent by the system to the outside world.

The most common input devices used by the computer are the keyboard and mouse. The keyboard allows the entry of textual information while the mouse allows the selection of a point on the screen by moving a screen cursor to the point and pressing a mouse button. Input devices include keyboard, mouse, trackball, joystick, and pen and microphones. They also include sensors, optical laser scanner.

The most common output devices are monitors and speakers. Output equipment includes video display terminals (either cathode-ray tubes or liquid crystal displays), ink-jet and laser printers, loudspeakers.

Other examples include magnetic tapes, magnetic disk drives, and certain types of optical compact discs.

4.2 INPUT / OUTPUT SYSTEM

The input / output system interfaces the processor and memory via system bus and one or more I/O devices by data bus input and output systems are not simply connectors for connecting different devices it contains some logic for communication between the I/O devices and the bus.

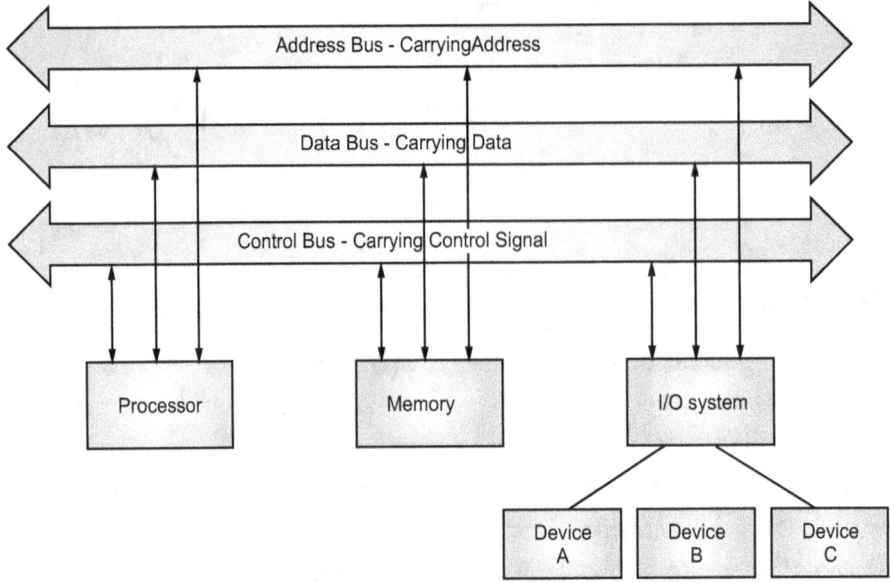

Fig. 4.1 : Computer system

The input/output system must have an internal and external interface.

4.2.1 Input / Output Interface

The I/O system is nothing but the hardware required to connect an I/O device to the bus which is called as I/O interface.

A number of peripheral devices may be connected to the I/O interface. The I/O interface controls the communication of each peripheral with processor. So it must recognize one unique address for each peripheral connected to it. The I/O interface must able to perform device communication which involves commands, status information and data.

The I/O interface is also responsible for error detection and for reporting errors to the processor.

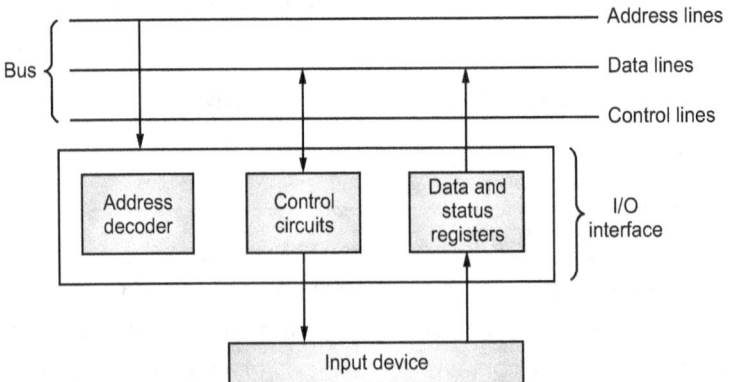

Fig. 4.2 (a) : I/O interface for Input device

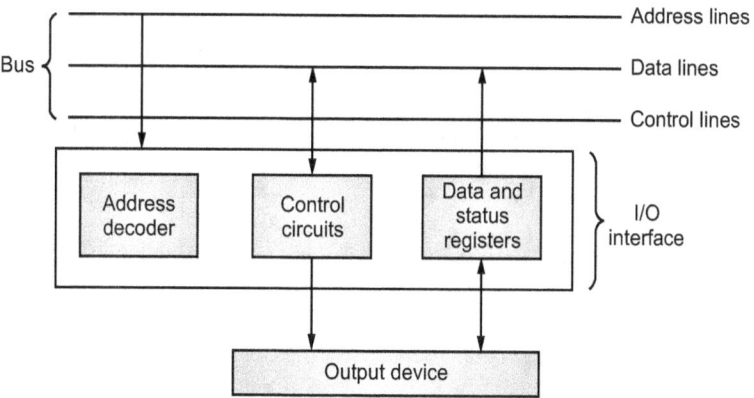

Fig. 4.2 (b) : I/O Interface for output device

The Address decoder enables the device when its address appears on the address lines. The data register holds the data being transferred to or form the processor.

The status register contains information relevant to the operation of the I/O device. Both the data and status registers are assigned with unique addresses and they are connected to the data bus.

4.2.2 I/O Interfacing Techniques

The most of the processors support isolated I/O system. It partitions memory from I/O via software, by having instructions that specifically access memory and others that specifically access I/O. When these instructions are decoded by the processor an appropriate control signal is generated to activate either memory or I/O operation. I/O devices can be interfaced to a computer system in two ways, which are called interfacing techniques.

1.   Memory mapped I/O

2.   I/O mapped I/O

1.   Memory mapped I/O :

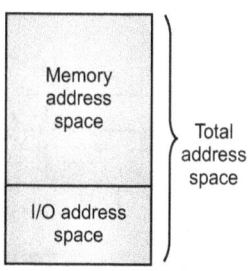

Fig. 4.3 : Address space

In this technique, the total memory address space is partitioned. When this technique is used, a memory reference instruction automatically becomes an I/O instruction if that address is made the address of an I/O part. The usual memory related instruction are used for I/O related operations. The special I/O instructions are required.

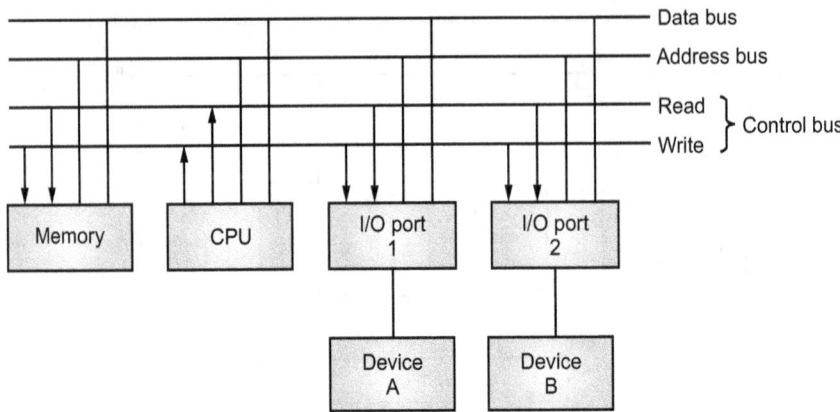

Fig. 4.4 : Programmed I/O with memory mapped I/O

2. **I/O mapped I/O :** Different I/O address space apart from the total memory space is used for instructions and operations which is called as I/O mapped I/P.

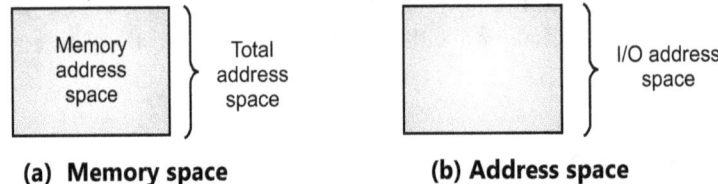

(a) Memory space   **(b) Address space**

Fig. 4.5 : Address space

The advantage is that the full memory address space is available but the memory related instructions do not work therefore, processor can only use this mode if it has special instructions for I/O related operations such as I/O read, I/O write.

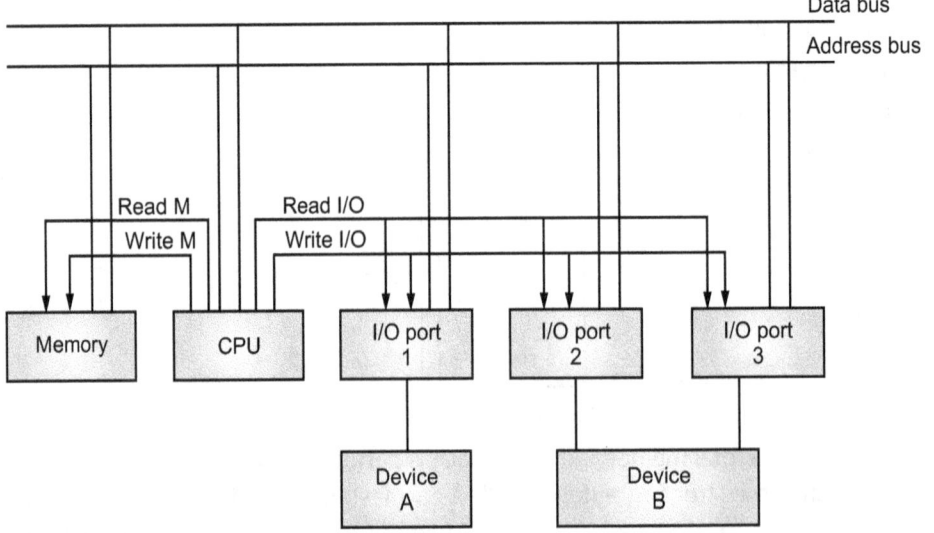

Fig. 4.6 : Programmed I/O with I/O mapped I/O

Difference between memory mapped I/O and I/O mapped I/O

Sr. No.	Memory Mapped I/O	I/O Mapped I/O
1.	Memory and I/O share the entire memory of processor.	Processor provides separate address range for memory and I/O devices.
2.	Usually processor provides more add lines for accessing memory so more decoding is required.	Usually processor provides less add lines for accessing I/O. So less decoding is required.
3.	Memory control signals are used to control read and write I/O operations.	I/O control signals are used to control read and write I/O operations.

There are several reasons why an I/O device or peripheral device is not directly connected to the system bus. Some of them are as follows :

- There are a wide variety of peripherals with various methods of operation. It would be impractical to include the necessary logic within the processor to control several devices.
- The data transfer rate of peripherals is often much slower than that of the memory or processor. Thus, it is impractical to use the high-speed system bus to communicate directly with a peripheral.
- Peripherals often use different data formats and word lengths than the computer to which they are attached.

Thus, an I/O module is required. Various standards for connecting peripherals to computers exist. For example, Integrated Drive Electronics (IDE) and Enhanced Integrated Drive Electronics (EIDE) are common interfaces, or buses, for magnetic disk drives. A bus (also known as a port) can be either serial or parallel, depending on whether the data path carries one bit at a time (serial) or many at once (parallel). Serial connections, which use relatively few wires, are generally simpler and slower than parallel connections. Universal Serial Bus (USB) is a common serial bus. A common example of a parallel bus is the Small Computer Systems Interface (SCSI) bus.

4.3   INPUT/OUTPUT MODULES

The major functions of an I/O module are categorized as follows :

- Control and timing
- Processor Communication
- Device Communication
- Data Buffering
- Error Detection

During any period of time, the processor may communicate with one or more external devices in unpredictable manner, depending on the program's need for I/O.

The internal resources, such as main memory and the system bus, must be shared among a number of activities, including data I/O.

(a) Control and timings :

The I/O function includes a control and timing requirement to co-ordinate the flow of traffic between internal resources and external devices.

For example, the control of the transfer of data from an external device to the processor might involve the following sequence of steps :

1. The processor interacts with the I/O module to check the status of the attached device.
2. The I/O module returns the device status.
3. If the device is operational and ready to transmit, the processor requests the transfer of data, by means of a command to the I/O module.
4. The I/O module obtains a unit of data from external device.
5. The data are transferred from the I/O module to the processor.

If the system employs a bus, then each of the interactions between the processor and the I/O module involves one or more bus arbitrations.

(b) Processor and Device Communication :

During the I/O operation, the I/O module must communicate with the processor and with the external device.

Processor communication involves the following :

1. **Command decoding :** The I/O module accepts command from the processor, typically sent as signals on control bus.
2. **Data :** Data are exchanged betweeen the processor and the I/O module over the data bus.
3. **Status Reporting :** Because peripherals are so slow, it is important to know the status of the I/O module. For example, if an I/O module is asked to send data to the processor(read), it may not be ready to do so because it is still working on the previous I/O command. This fact can be reported with a status signal. Common status signals are BUSY and READY.
4. **Address Recognition :** Just as each word of memory has an address, each of the I/O devices has an unique address. Thus, an I/O module must recognize one unique address for each peripheral it controls.

On the other hand, the I/O must be able to perform device communication. This communication involves command, status information and data.

(c) Data Buffering :

An essential task of an I/O module is data buffering. The data buffering is required due to the mismatch of the speed of CPU, memory and other peripheral devices. In general, the speed of CPU is higher than the speed of the other peripheral devices. So, the I/O modules store the data in a data buffer and regulate the transfer of data as per the speed of the devices.

In the opposite direction, data are buffered so as not to tie up the memory in a slow transfer operation. Thus the I/O module must be able to operate at both device and memory speed.

(d) Error Detection :

Another task of I/O module is error detection and for subsequently reporting error to the processor. One class or error includes mechanical and electrical malfunctions reported by the device (e.g. paper jam). Another class consists of unintentional changes to the bit pattern as it is transmitted from devices to the I/O module.

Block diagram of I/O Module as shown in the Fig. 4.7.

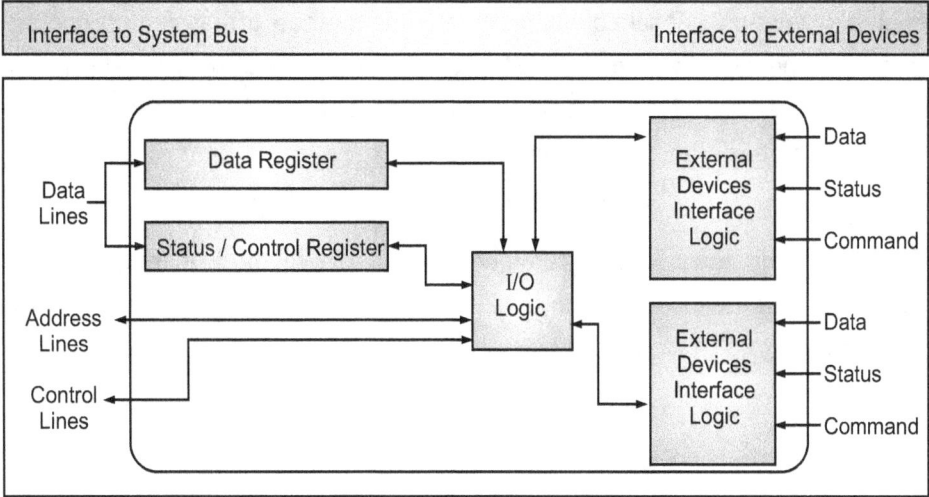

Fig. 4.7 : Block diagram of I/O Module

There will be many I/O devices connected through I/O modules to the system. Each device will be identified by a unique address.

When the processor issues an I/O command, the command contains the address of the device that is used by the command. The I/O module must interpret the address lines to check if the command is for itself.

Generally in most of the processors, the processor, main memory and I/O share a common bus (data address and control bus).

4.3.1 Modes of Data Transfer

Data can be transferred from one device to other device either in serial or parallel way.

Following Fig. 4.8 shows different data transfer modes.

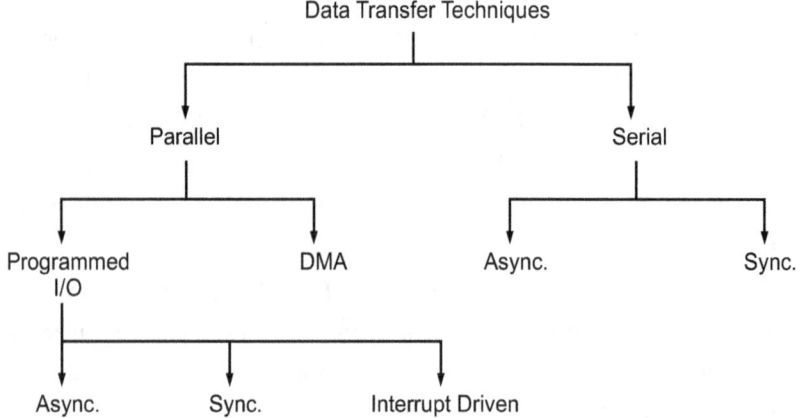

Fig. 4.8 : Data transfer modes

1. Serial transmission : Serial communication is the method of transferring one bit at a time through a medium. Serial data transfer refers to the type of data transfer in which a group of data bits are transferred one bit at a time. The amount of data transferred serially is less than the data transferred parallelly per second.

0   1   0   0   0   0   1   0

2. Parallel transmission : Parallel communication is the method of transferring blocks, e.g. bytes of data at the same time. In parallel data transfer a group of bits are transferred simultaneously

0
1
0
0
0
0
1
0

As parallel communication is faster than serial. For this reason, the internal connections in a computer, i.e. the busses, are linked together to allow parallel communication.

The serial and parallel transmission may synchronous or asynchronous.

3. Synchronous transmission : The term synchronous is used to describe a continuous and consistent timed transfer of data blocks.

- Synchronous transmission is a data transfer method in which a continuous stream of data signals is accompanied by timing signals (generated by an electronic clock) to ensure that the transmitter and the receiver are in step (synchronized with one another).

- The data is sent in blocks (called frames or packets) spaced by fixed time intervals.

- Synchronous transmission modes are used when large amounts of data must be transferred very quickly from one location to the other. The speed of the synchronous connection is attained by transferring data in large blocks instead of individual characters.

- Synchronous transmission synchronizes transmission speeds at both the receiving and sending end of the transmission using clock signals built into each component. A continual stream of data is then sent between the two nodes.

- The data blocks are grouped and spaced in regular intervals and are preceded by special characters called "syn" or synchronous idle characters. See the following illustration.

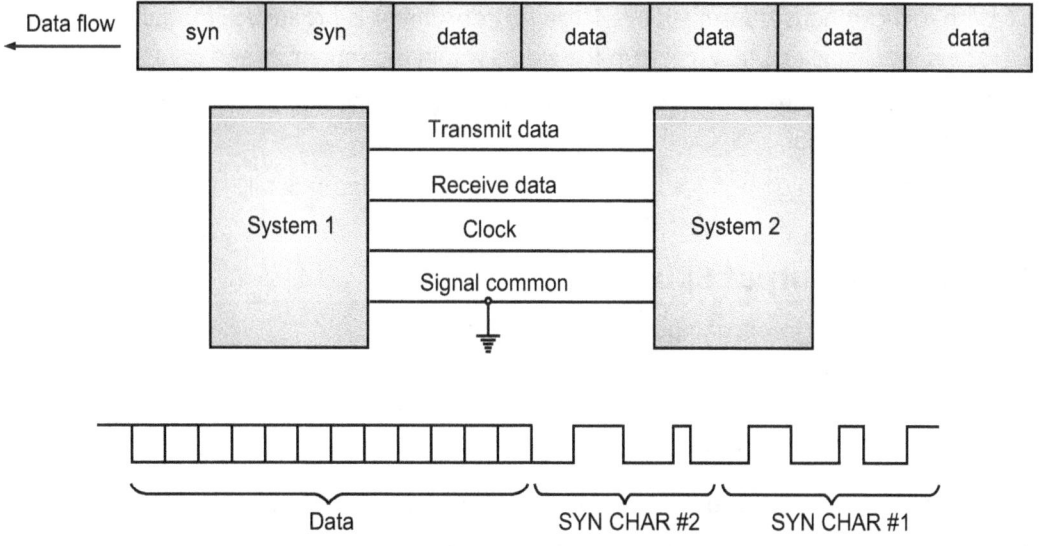

Fig. 4.9 : **Synchronous data transmission**

- After the "syn" characters are received by the remote device, they are decoded and used to synchronize the connection. After the connection is correctly synchronized, data transmission may begin.

- An analogy of synchronous transmission would be the transmission of a large text document. Before the document is transferred across the synchronous line, it is first broken into blocks of sentences or paragraphs. The blocks are then sent over the communication link to the remote site.

- The timing needed for synchronous connections is obtained from the devices located on the communication link. All devices on the synchronous link must be set to the same clocking.

4. Asynchronous transmission : Asynchronous transmission inserts a start bit before each data character and a stop bit at its termination to inform the receiver where it begins and ends.

- The term asynchronous is used to describe the process where transmitted data is encoded with start and stop bits, specifying the beginning and end of each character.

- An example of synchronous transmission is shown in the following Fig. 4.9.

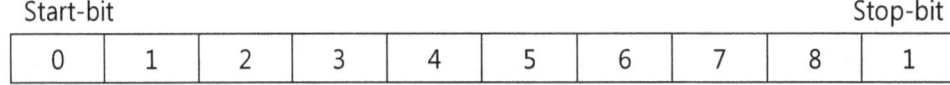

Start-bit   Stop-bit

0	1	2	3	4	5	6	7	8	1

Fig. 4.10 : Asynchronous transmission

- These additional bits provide the timing or synchronization for the connection by indicating when a complete character has been sent or received. Thus, timing for each character begins with the start bit and ends with the stop bit.

- With asynchronous transmission, a large text document is organized into long strings of letters (or characters) that make up the words within the sentences and paragraphs.

- These characters are sent over the communication link one at a time and reassembled at the remote location.

In this chapter, we are going to learn these data transfer modes in detail.

4.3.2 Input / Output Subsystem

There are three basic forms of input and output systems :

- Programmed I/O
- Interrupt driven I/O
- Direct Memory Access(DMA)

With programmed I/O, the processor executes a program that gives its direct control of the I/O operation, including sensing device status, sending a read or write command, and transferring the data.

With interrupt driven I/O, the processor issues an I/O command, continues to execute other instructions, and is interrupted by the I/O module when the I/O module completes its work.

In Direct Memory Access (DMA), the I/O module and main memory exchange data directly without processor involvement.

With both programmed I/O and Interrupt driven I/O, the processor is responsible for extracting data from main memory for output operation and storing data in main memory for input operation.

To send data to an output device, the CPU simply moves that data to a special memory location in the I/O address space if I/O mapped input/output is used or to an address in the memory address space if memory mapped I/O is used.

To read data from an input device, the CPU simply moves data from the address (I/O or memory) of that device into the CPU.

4.3.3 Input/Output Operation

The input and output operation looks very similar to a memory read or write operation except it usually takes more time since peripheral devices are slow in speed than main memory modules.

The working principle of the three methods for input of a block of data as shown in the Fig. 4.11.

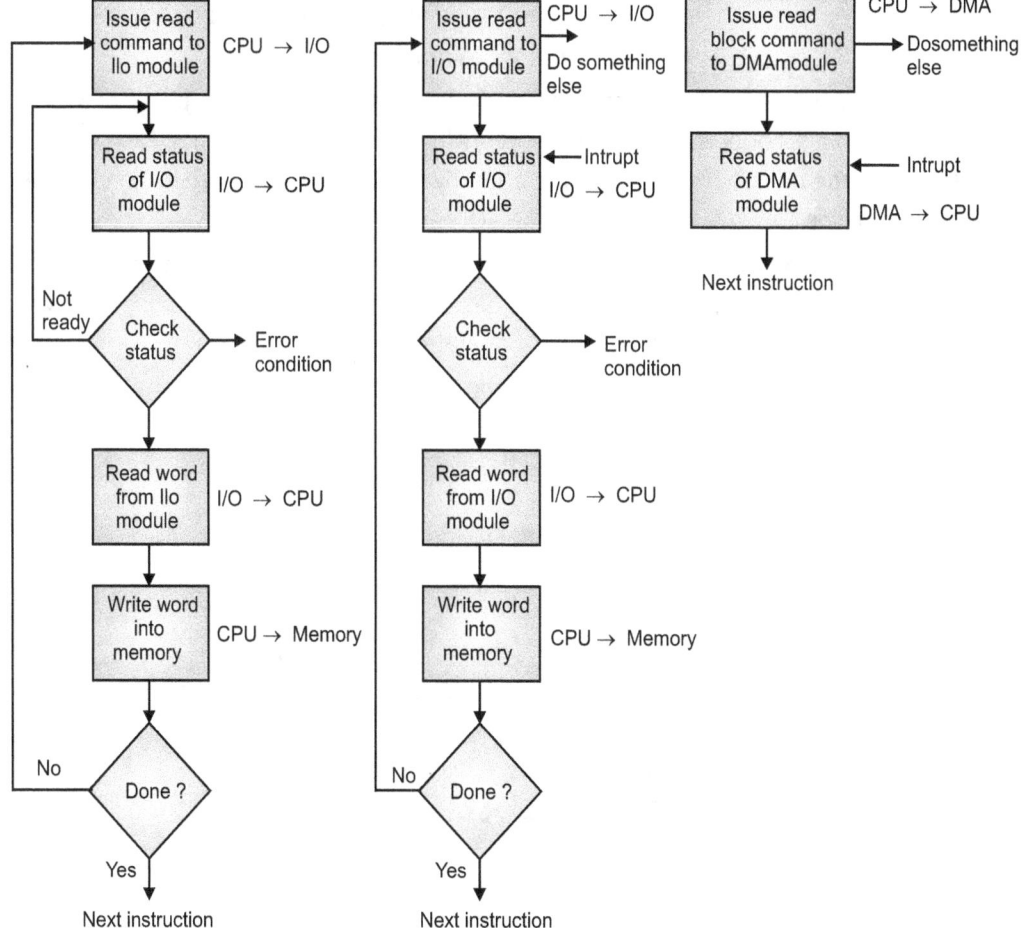

Fig. 4.11 : Working of three techniques for input of block of data

4.3.4 Input/Output Port

An I/O port is a device that looks like a memory cell to the computer but contains connection to the outside world. An I/O port typically uses a latch. When the CPU writes to the address associated with the latch, the latch device captures the data and makes it available on a set of wires external to the CPU and memory system.

The I/O ports can be read-only, write-only, or read/write. The write-only port is shown in the Fig. 4.12.

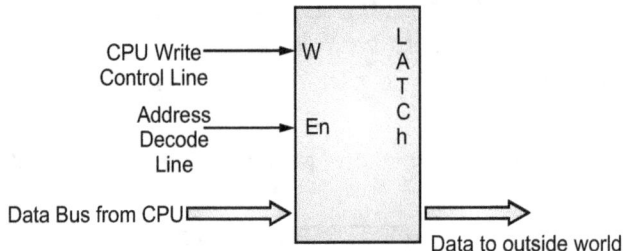

Fig. 4.12 : The write only port

- First, the CPU will place the address of the device on the I/O address bus and with the help of address decoder a signal is generated which will enable the latch. Next, the CPU will indicate the operation is a write operation by putting the appropriate signal in CPU write control line.

- Then the data to be transferred will be placed in the CPU bus, which will be stored in the latch for the onward transmission to the device. Both the address decode and write control lines must be active for the latch to operate.

The read/write or input/output port is shown in the Fig. 4.13.

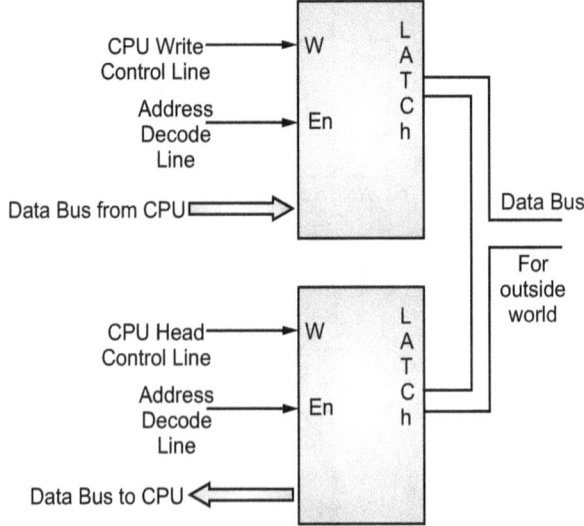

Fig. 4.13 : Read / Write port

- The device is identified by putting the appropriate address in the I/O address lines. The address decoder will generate the signal for the address decode lines.

- According to the operation, read or write, it will select either of the latch. If it is a write operation, then data will be placed in the latch from CPU for onward transmission to the output device.

If it is in a read operation, the data that are already stored in the latch will be transferred to the CPU.

4.4 PROGRAMMED I/O

With Programmed I/O data is exchanged between the processor and the I/O module. When the processor is executing a program and encounters an I/O instruction, it issues a command to the appropriate I/O module and gives control of the I/O operation.

The CPU issues a command then waits for I/O operations to be complete. As the CPU is faster than the I/O module, the problem with programmed I/O is that the CPU has to wait a long time. The CPU, while waiting, must repeatedly check the status of the I/O module, and this process is known as Polling. As a result, the level of the performance of the entire system is severely degraded.

With programmed I/O, the I/O module will perform the requested operation and then sets the I/O status register. The I/O module doesn't take any action to tell the processor that I/O operation is completed. It doesn't interrupt the processor. Thus, it is the responsibility of processor to check the status of the I/O module periodically until it finds that the operation is completed.

Programmed I/O basically works in these ways:

- CPU requests I/O operation
- I/O module performs operation
- I/O module sets status bits
- CPU checks status bits periodically
- I/O module does not inform CPU directly
- I/O module does not interrupt CPU
- CPU may wait or come back later

4.4.1 I/O Commands

There are four types of I/O commands that an I/O module may receive when it is addressed by a processor:

1. **Control Commands :** Used to activate a peripheral device and instruct it what to do. For example, a magnetic tape unit may be instructed to rewind or to move forward one record. These commands are specific to a particular type of peripheral device.

2. **Test Commands :** Used to test various status conditions associated with an I/O module and its peripherals. The processor will want to know if the most recent I/O operation is completed or any error has occurred.

3. **Read Commands :** Causes the I/O module to obtain an item of data from the peripheral and place it in an internal buffer (READ operation).

4. **Write Commands :** Causes the I/O module to take an item of data (byte or word from the data bus and subsequently transmit that data item to the peripheral (WRITE operation).

4.5 INTERRUPT DRIVEN I/O

The problem with programmed I/O is that the processor has to wait a long time for the I/O module of concern to be ready for either reception or transmission of data. The processor, while waiting, must repeatedly interrogate the status of the I/O module.

This type of I/O operation, where the CPU constantly tests a part to see if data is available, is polling, that is, the CPU Polls (asks) the port if it has data available or if it is capable of accepting data. Polled I/O is inherently inefficient.

The solution to this problem is to provide an interrupt mechanism. In this approach, the processor issues an I/O command to a module and then go on to do some other useful work. The I/O module then interrupt the processor to request service when it is ready to exchange data with the processor. The processor then executes the data transfer. Once the data transfer is over, the processor then resumes its former processing.

Working of Interrupt driven I/O:

(a) From the point of view of the I/O module :

For input, the I/O module services a READ command from the processor.

- The I/O module then proceeds to read data from an associated peripheral device.

- Once the data are in the modules data register, the module issues an interrupt to the processor over a control line.

- The module then waits until its data are requested by the processor.

- When the request is made, the module places its data on the data bus and is then ready for another I/O operation.

(b) From the processor point of view; the action for an input is as follows :

The processor issues a READ command.

It then does something else (e.g. the processor may be working on several different programs at the same time).

At the end of each instruction cycle, the processor checks for interrupts.

When the interrupt from an I/O module occurs, the processor saves the context (e.g. program counter and processor registers) of the current program and processes the interrupt.

In this case, the processor reads the word of data from the I/O module and stores it in memory.

It then restores the context of the program it was working on and resumes execution.

4.5.1 Interrupt Processing

The occurrence of an interrupt triggers a number of events, both in the processor hardware and in software.

When an I/O device completes an I/O operation, the following sequences of hardware events occurs :

1. The device issues an interrupt signal to the processor.
2. The processor finishes execution of the current instruction before responding to the interrupt.
3. The processor tests for the interrupt; if there is one interrupt pending, then the processor sends an acknowledgement signal to the device which issued the interrupt. After getting acknowledgement, the device removes its interrupt signals.
4. The processor now needs to prepare to transfer control to the interrupt routine. It needs to save the information needed to resume the current program at the point of interrupt. The minimum information required to save is the Processor Status Word (PSW) and the location of the next instruction to be executed which is nothing but the contents of program counter. These can be pushed into the system control stack.
5. The processor now loads the program counter with the entry location of the interrupt handling program that will respond to the interrupt.
    *   An interrupt occurs when the processor is executing the instruction of location N.
    *   At that point, the value of program counter is N+1.
    *   Processor services the interrupt after completion of current instruction execution.
    *   First, it moves the content of general registers to system stack.
    *   Then it moves the program counter value to the system stack.

- Top of the system stack is maintained by stack pointer.
- The value of stack pointer is modified to point to the top of the stack.
- If M elements are moved to the system stack, the value of stack pointer is changed from T to T-M.
- Next, the program counter is loaded with the starting address of the interrupt service routine.
- Processor starts executing the interrupt service routine.
- Next, the program counter is loaded with the starting address of the interrupt service routine.
- Processor starts executing the interrupt service routine.

The data changes of memory and registers during interrupt service is shown in the Fig. 4.14.

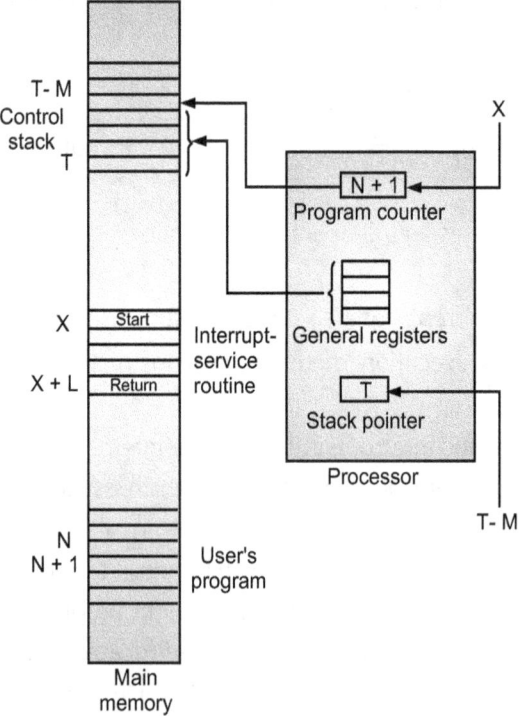

Fig. 4.14 : Changes of memory and register for an interrupt

4.5.2 Return from Interrupt

- Interrupt service routine starts at location X and the return instruction is in location X + L.
- After fetching the return instruction, the value of program counter becomes X + L+ 1.
- While returning to user's program, processor must restore the earlier values.

- From control stack, it restores the value of program counter and the general registers.
- Accordingly it sets the value of the top of the stack and accordingly stack pointer is updated.
- Now the processor starts execution of the user's program (interrupted program) from memory location N + 1.

The data changes of memory and registers during return from and interrupt is shown in the Fig. 4.15.

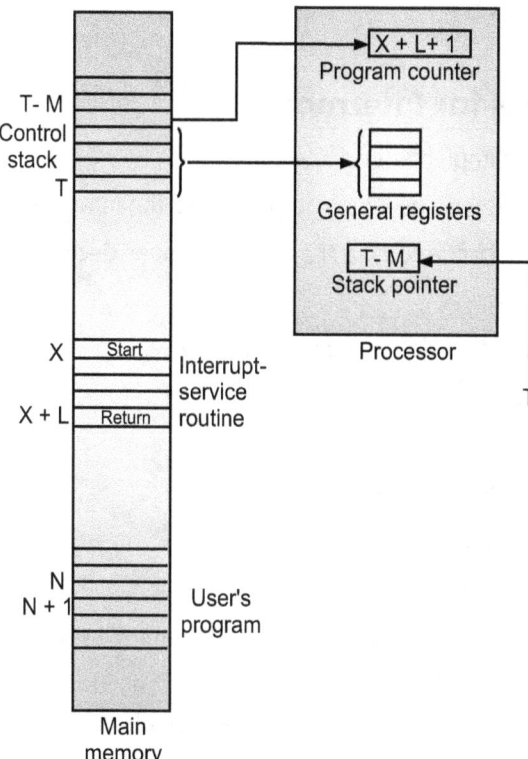

Fig. 4.15 : Return from interrupt

Once the program counter has been loaded, the processor proceeds to the next instruction cycle, which begins with an interrupt fetch. The control will transfer to interrupt handler routine for the current interrupt.

The following operations are performed at this point :

1. At the point, the program counter and PSW relating to the interrupted program have been saved on the system stack. In addition to that some more information must be saved related to the current processor state which includes the control of the processor registers, because these registers may be used by the interrupt handler. Typically, the interrupt handler will begin by saving the contents of all registers on stack.

2. The interrupt handles next processes the interrupt. This includes an examination of status information relating to the I/O operation or, other event that caused an interrupt.

3. When interrupt processing is complete, the saved register values are retrieved from the stack and restored to the registers.

4. The final act is to restore the PSW and program counter values from the stack. As a result, the next instruction to be executed will be from the previously interrupted program.

4.5.3 Design Issues for Interrupt

Two design issues arise in implementing interrupt I/O.

How does the processor determine which device issued the interrupt?

If multiple interrupts have occurred how the processor does decide which one to process?

(a) Device Identification

Four general categories of techniques are in common use:

- Multiple interrupt lines
- Software poll
- Daisy chain (hardware poll, vectored)
- Bus arbitration (vectored)
- Multiple Interrupts Lines:
- The most straight forward approach is to provide multiple interrupt lines between the processor and the I/O modules.
- It is impractical to dedicate more than a few bus lines or processor pins to interrupt lines.
- Thus, though multiple interrupt lines are used, it is most likely that each line will have multiple I/O modules attached to it. Thus one of the other three techniques must be used on each line.

Software Poll :

- When the processor detects an interrupt, it branches to an interrupt service routine whose job is to poll each I/O module to determine which module caused the interrupt.
- The poll could be implemented with the help of a separate command line (e.g. TEST I/O). In this case, the processor raises TEST I/O and place the address of a particular

I/O module on the address lines. The I/O module responds positively if it set the interrupt.

- Alternatively, each I/O module could contain an addressable status register. The processor then reads the status register of each I/O module to identify the interrupting module.

- Once the correct module is identified, the processor branches to a device service routine specific to that device.

- The main disadvantage of software poll is that it is time consuming. Processor has to check the status of each I/O module and in the worst case it is equal to the number of I/O modules.

Daisy Chain :

- In this method for interrupts all I/O modules share a common interrupt request lines. However the interrupt acknowledge line is connected in a daisy chain fashion. When the processor senses an interrupt, it sends out an interrupt acknowledgement.

- The interrupt acknowledge signal propagates through a series of I/O module until it gets to a requesting module.

- The requesting module typically responds by placing a word on the data lines. This word is referred to as a vector and is either the address of the I/O module or some other unique identification.

- In either case, the processor uses the vector as a pointer to the appropriate device service routine. This avoids the need to execute a general interrupt service routine first. This technique is referred to as a vectored interrupt. The daisy chain arrangement is shown in the Fig. 4.16.

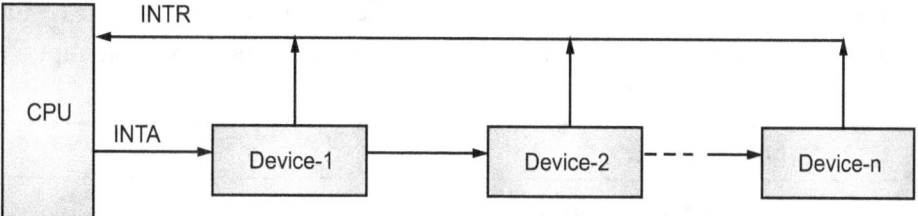

Fig. 4.16 : Daisy chain arrangement

Bus Arbitration :

In bus arbitration method, an I/O module must first gain control of the bus before it can raise the interrupt request line. Thus, only one module can raise the interrupt line at a time. When the processor detects the interrupt, it responds on the interrupt acknowledge line. The requesting module then places it vector on the data line.

(b) Handling multiple interrupts

There are several techniques to identify the requesting I/O module. These techniques also provide a way of assigning priorities when more than one device is requesting interrupt service. With multiple lines, the processor just picks the interrupt line with highest priority. During the processor design phase itself priorities may be assigned to each interrupt lines. With of polling, the order in which modules are polled determines their priority. In case of daisy chain configuration, the priority of a module is determined by the position of the module in the daisy chain. The module nearer to the processor in the chain has got higher priority, because this is the first module to receive the acknowledge signal that is generated by the processor.

In case of bus arbitration method, more than one module may need control of the bus. Since only one module at a time can successfully transmit over the bus, some method of arbitration is needed. The various methods can be classified into two group – centralized and distributed.

In a centralized scheme, a single hardware device, referred to as a bus controller or arbiter is responsible for allocating time on the bus. The device may be a separate module or part of the processor.

In distributed scheme, there is no central controller. Each module contains access control logic and all modules shares the bus.

Interrupt Nesting :

The arrival of an interrupt request from an external device causes the processor to suspend the execution of one program and starts the execution of another. The execution of this another program is nothing but the interrupt service routine for that specified device. Interrupt may arrive at any time. So during the execution of an interrupt service routine, another interrupt may arrive. This kind of interrupts are known as nesting of interrupt.

4.6   DIRECT MEMORY ACCESS

DMA Stands for "Direct Memory Access"

To transfer large block of data at high speed, a special control unit provided to allow transfer of a block of data directly between an external device and the main memory, without continuous intervention by the processor. This approach is called direct memory access or DMA.

- DMA is a method of transferring data from the computer's RAM to another part of the computer without processing it using the CPU.

- While most data that is input or output from your computer is processed by the CPU, some data does not require processing, or can be processed by another device.
- In these situations, DMA can save processing time and is a more efficient way to move data from the computer's memory to other devices.
- DMA is an essential feature of all modern computers, as it allows devices to transfer data without subjecting the CPU to a heavy overhead. Otherwise, the CPU would have to copy each piece of data from the source to the destination, making it unavailable for other tasks. Direct Memory Access is system that can control the memory system without using the CPU.
- DMA transfers are performed by a control circuit associated with the I/O device and this circuit is referred as DMA controller. The DMA controller allows direct data transfer between the device and the main memory without involving the processor.
- A DMA transfer copies a block of memory from one device to another.
- While the CPU initiates the transfer by issuing a DMA command, it does not execute it. To transfer data between memory and I/O devices, DMA controller takes control of the system from the processor and transfer of data take place over the system bus.
- For this purpose, the DMA controller must use the bus only when the processor does not need it, or it must force the processor to suspend operation temporarily.
- The later technique is more common and is referred to as cycle stealing, because the DMA module in effect steals a bus cycle.
- The typical block diagram of a DMA controller is shown in the Fig. 4.17. which consist of Registers, data count and control logic.

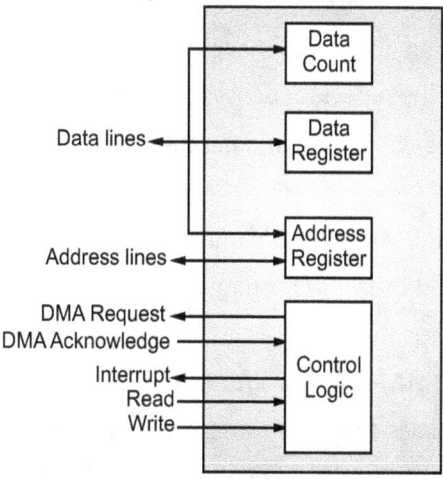

Fig. 4.17 : Typical DMA block diagram

When the processor wishes to read or write a block of data, it issues a command to the DMA module, by sending to the following information.

o   Whether a read or write is requested, using the read or write control line between the processor and the DMA module.

o   The address of the I/O device involved, communicated on the data lines.

o   The starting location in the memory to read from or write to, communicated on data lines and stored by the DMA module in its address register.

The number of words to be read or written again communicated via the data lines and stored in the data count register.

•   The processor then continues with other works. It has delegated this I/O operation to the DMA module. The DMA module checks the status of the I/O device whose address is communicated to DMA controller by the processor.

•   If the specified I/O device is ready for data transfer, then DMA module generates the DMA request to the processor. Then the processor indicates the release of the system bus through DMA acknowledge.

•   The DMA module transfers the entire block of data, one word at a time, directly to or from memory, without going through the processor.

•   When the transfer is completed, the DMA module sends an interrupt signal to the processor. After receiving the interrupt signal, processor takes over the system bus.

•   Thus the processor is involved only at the beginning and end of the transfer. During that time the processor is suspended. When the processor is suspended, then the DMA module transfer one word and return control to the processor.

•   Note that, this is not an interrupt, the processor does not save a context and do something else. Rather, the processor pauses for one bus cycle.

The DMA mechanism can be configured in different ways. The most common amongst them are:

(a) Single bus, detached DMA - I/O configuration.

(b) Single bus, Integrated DMA - I/O configuration.

(c) Using separate I/O bus.

(a) Single bus, detached DMA - I/O configuration

In this organization, all modules share the same system bus. The DMA module here acts as a surrogate processor. This method uses programmed I/O to exchange data between memory and an I/O module through the DMA module.

- For each transfer it uses the bus twice. The first one is when transferring the data between I/O and DMA and the second one is when transferring the data between DMA and memory. Since the bus is used twice while transferring data, so the bus will be suspended twice. The transfer consumes two bus cycle.

The interconnection organization is shown in the Fig. 4.18.

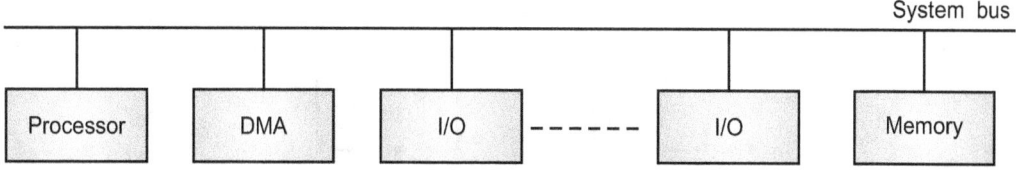

Fig. 4.18 : Single bus arrangement for DMA transfer

(b) Single bus, Integrated DMA - I/O configuration

By integrating the DMA and I/O function the number of required bus cycle can be reduced. In this configuration, the DMA module and one or more I/O modules are integrated together in such a way that the system bus is not involved.

- The system bus is not involved when transferring data between DMA and I/O device, so processor is not suspended. Processor is suspended when data is transferred between DMA and memory. The configuration is shown in the Fig. 4.19.

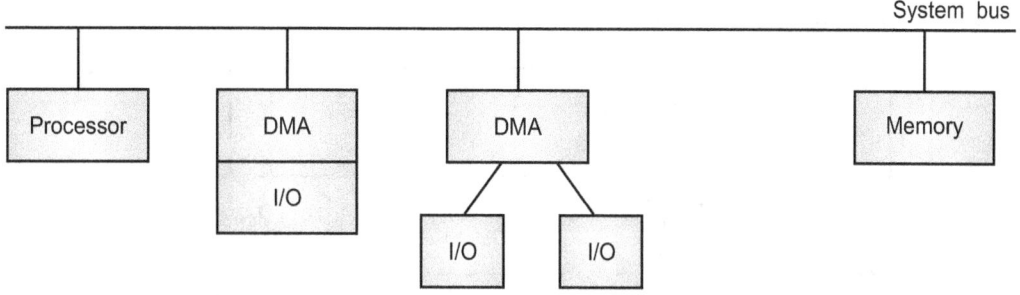

Fig. 4.19 : Single bus integrated DMA transfer

(c) Using separate I/O bus

In this configuration the I/O modules are connected to the DMA through another I/O bus. In this case the DMA module is reduced to one.

- Transfer of data between I/O module and DMA module is carried out through this I/O bus. In this transfer, system bus is not in use and so it is not needed to suspend the processor.

- There is another transfer phase between DMA module and memory. In this time system bus is needed for transfer and processor will be suspended for one bus cycle. The configuration is shown in the Fig. 4.20.

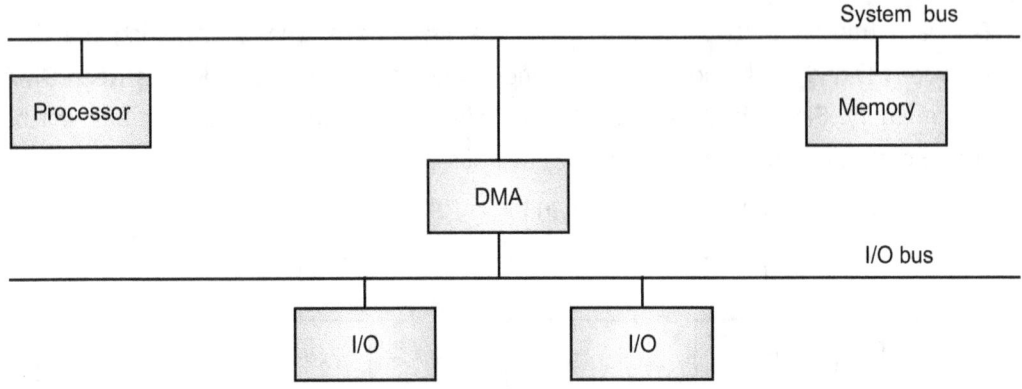

Fig. 4.20 : Seperate I/O bus for DMA transfer

4.7   BUSES AND STANDARD INTERFACES

4.7.1 Types of Interfaces

Interfaces are of type :

(i)   Parallel interface

(ii)   Serial interface

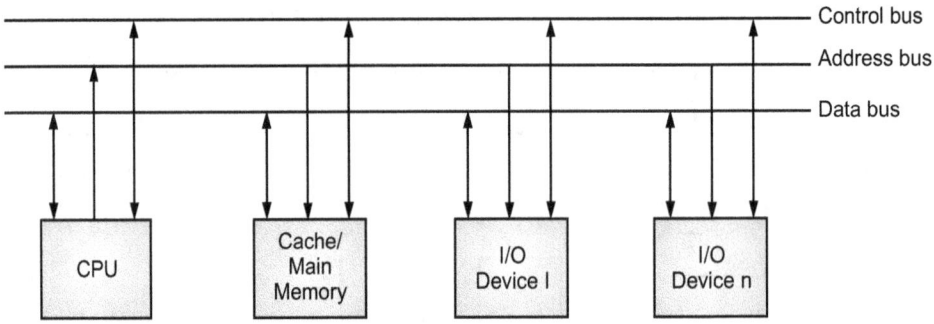

Fig. 4.21 : Communication via single shared Bus

I/O module contains internal buffer that can store data being passed between the peripheral and the rest of the system.

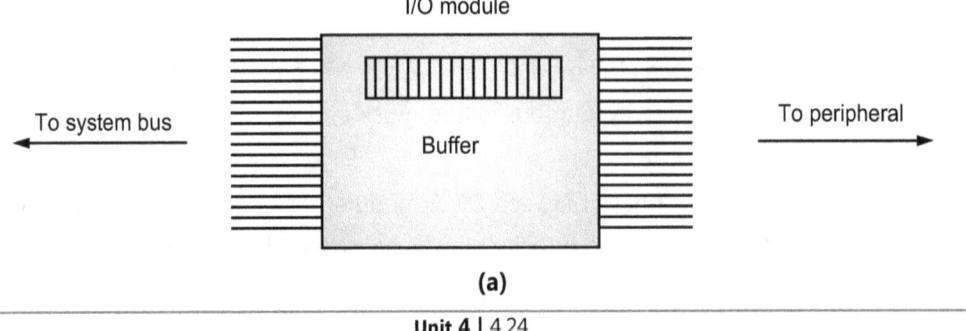

(a)

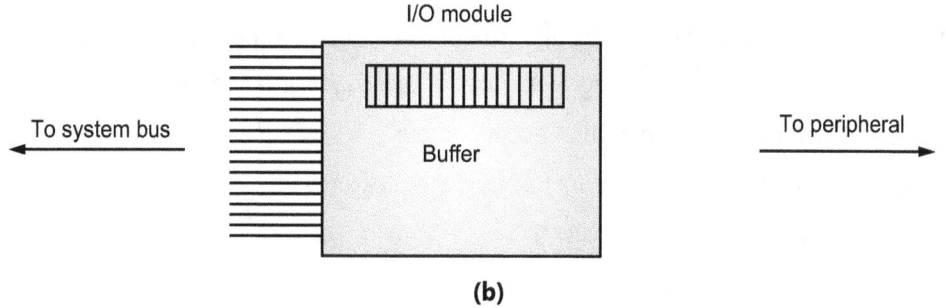

(b)

Fig. 4.22 : Parallel and Serial I/O

4.7.2 Buses

- A bus is a common electrical pathway between multiple devices.
- Can be internal to the CPU to transport data to and from the ALU.
- Can be external to the CPU, to connect it to memory or to I/O devices.
- Early PCs had a single external bus or system bus.
- Modern PCs have a special-purpose bus between the CPU and memory and (at least) one other bus for the I/O devices.
- Some devices that attach to a bus are active and can initiate bus transfers. They are called masters.
- Some devices are passive and wait for requests. They are called slaves.
- Some devices may act as slaves at some times and masters at others.
- Memory can never be a master device.
- Most bus masters are connected to the bus by a chip called a bus driver which is essentially a digital amplifier.
- Most slaves are connected to the bus by a bus receiver.
- A bus has address, data, and control lines.
- The more address lines a bus has, the more memory the CPU can address directly.
- If a bus has n address lines, then the CPU can use it to address 2n different memory locations.
- Buses can be divided up into two categories depending on their clocking.

4.7.2.1 Synchronous Bus

In the synchronous bus occurrence of events on the bus is determined by a clock. A single high-low transmission is called a clock cycle. A time slot is defined by a clock cycle. All devices on the bus can read the clock line, and all events start at the beginning of clock cycle.

- A synchronous bus has a line driven by a crystal oscillator.

- The signal on this line consists of a square wave with a frequency of 5 - 100 MHz.
- All bus activities take an integral number of these cycles, called bus cycles.

- **Timing Diagram :** Co-ordination of events on bus

In Synchronous bus the timing diagram has following features :

(i) Events determined by clock signals

(ii) Control Bus includes clock line

(iii) A single 1-0 is a bus cycle

(iv) All devices can read clock line

(v) Usually sync on leading edge

(vi) Usually a single cycle for an event

Following Fig. 4.23 shows a typical timing diagram for synchronous read operation.

(a) Read operation :

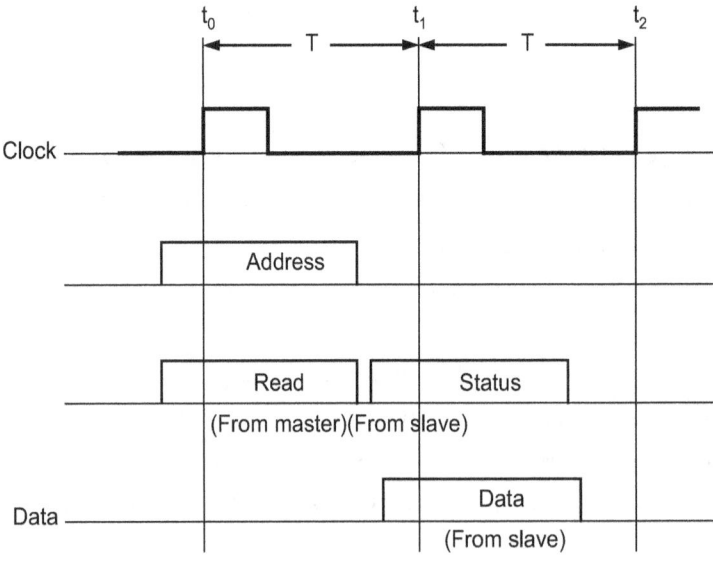

Fig. 4.23 : Timing diagram for read synchronous bus

Sequence of events in synchronous read :

1. Processor places the device-address at time t_0.
2. Processor Activates the Read Control signal to indicate an input operation, at time to. The clock pulse with t_1-t_0 should be larger than the maximum propogation delay on the bus.

3. The addressed device, recognizing that an input operation has been requested, places its input data on data bus t_1, addressed device can place its status information at time t_1.

4. At the end of clock cycle, that is, at time t_2, the processor reads the data lines and loads the data into its buffer register.

(b) Write Operation :

Write operation is similar to read operation. In write operation, slave is the data source. Timing diagram for write operation is shown in Fig. 4.24.

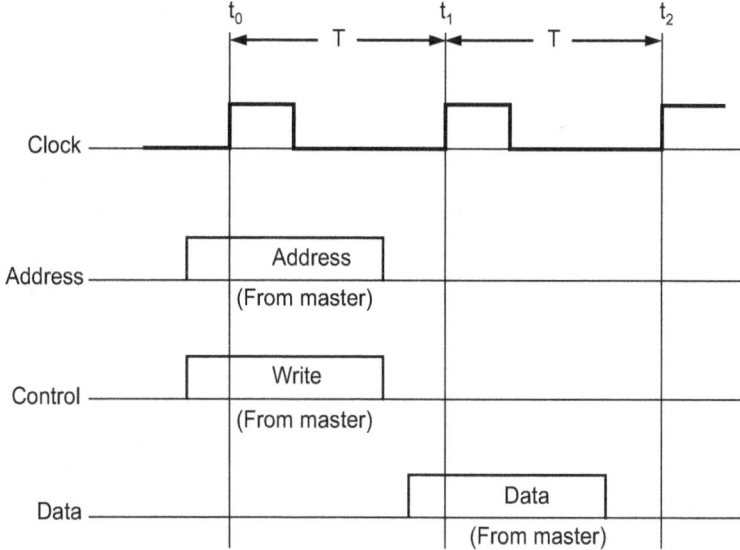

Fig. 4.24 : Timing diagram for write synchronous bus

Sequence of events in synchronous write :

1. Processor places the device-address at time t_0.

2. Processor Activates the Write Control signal to indicate an output operation, at time t_0. The clock pulse with t_1-t_0 should be larger than the maximum propagation delay on the bus.

3. The address device, recognizing that an output operation has been requested, memory module responds to write operation by copying the data from data lines. This is done during the t_2-t_1 time interval.

4. Master then deactivates the write signal.

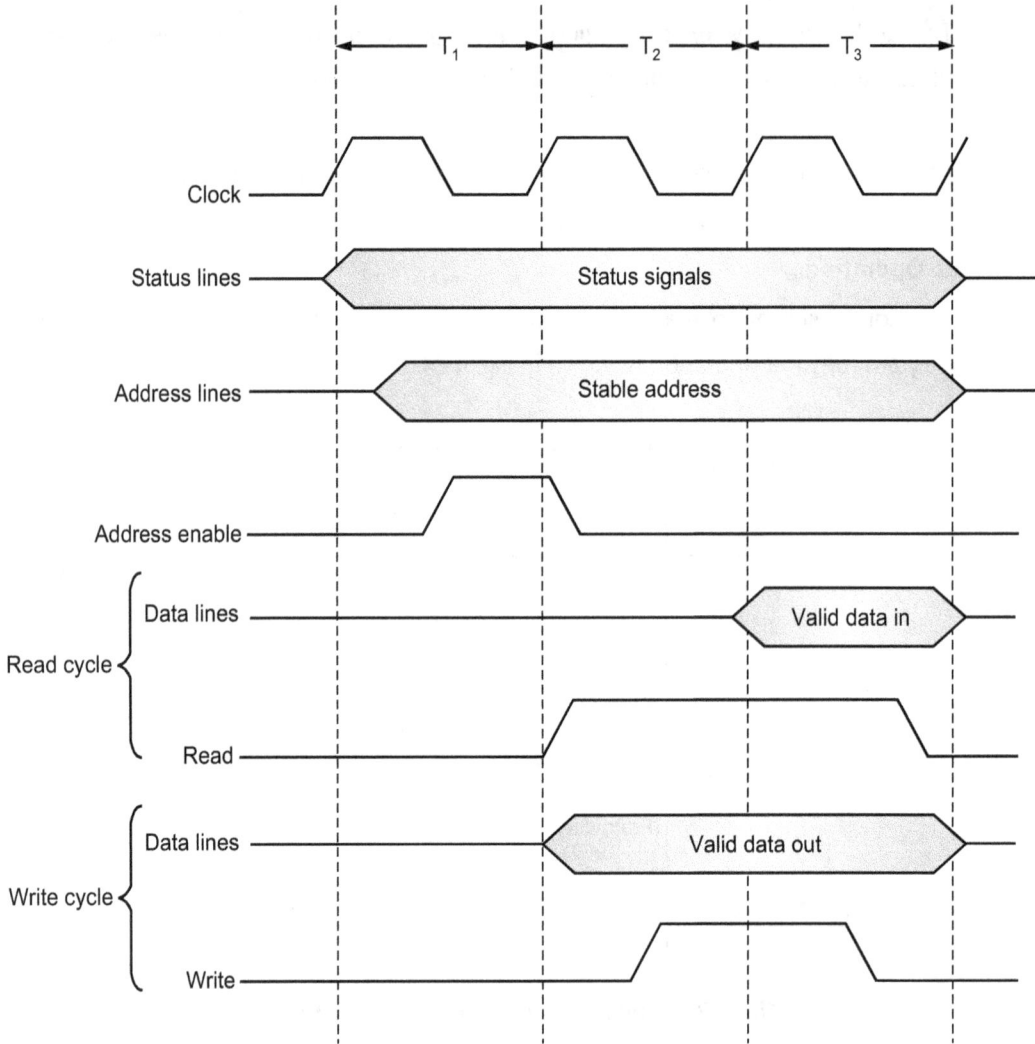

Fig. 4.25 : Synchronous read and write timing diagram

Advantages and Disadvantages of Synchronous Bus

1. Synchronous scheme is simple to implement.

2. It is simple to design device interface for synchronous bus.

3. Difficult to detect a malfunctioning device as a malfunctioning device does not respond.

4. Speed of system bus is determined by the slowest device on the bus. Very slow devices are never put directly on the system bus. They are connected on local Input/Output bus.

4.7.2.2 Asynchronous Bus

There is no common clock in Asynchronous Bus. Control of data transfer is based on use of handshake between the processor and the device selected for input/output.

- The asynchronous bus does not have a master clock. Bus cycles can be of any length required and need not be the same.
- Consider a synchronous bus with a 40 MHz clock, which gives a clock cycle of 25 nsec.
- Assume reading from memory takes 40 nsec from the time the address is stable.
- It takes three bus cycles to read a word.
- MREQ' indicates that memory is being accessed. RD' is asserted for reads and negated for writes. WAIT' inserts wait states (extra bus cycles) until the memory is finished.

The clock line is replaced by two timing control lines:

1. Ready
2. Accept

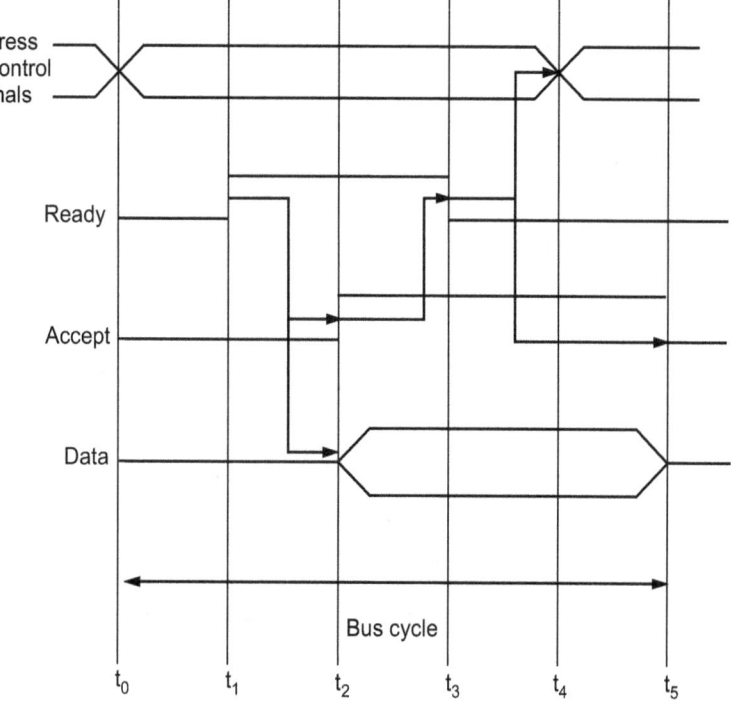

Fig. 4.26 : Timing diagram for read asynchronous bus

Ready and accept lines are used to implement handshake protocol. The processor places the address and activates the required control signals (Read/Write). When the addressed device receives the ready signal, it performs the required operation and then informs by activating the accept line. The processor waits for the Accept signal before removing its signal from the bus. Synchronous Bus has advantage of handling both slow and fast devices on the same.

Device interface is comparatively more complex for Asynchronous Bus.

(a) Read operation :

- Sequence of events in asynchronous read:
  1. Processor places the device-address at time t_0.
  2. Processor Activates the Read Control signal to indicate an input operation, at time t_0.
  3. The processor sets the ready line to 1 to inform input/output devices that address and control signals are on the bus at time t_1.
  4. The addressed device receives the ready signal and seeing the read control signal it knows there is an input operation. It sends its data on data lines and sets the accept signal to 1 at t_2.

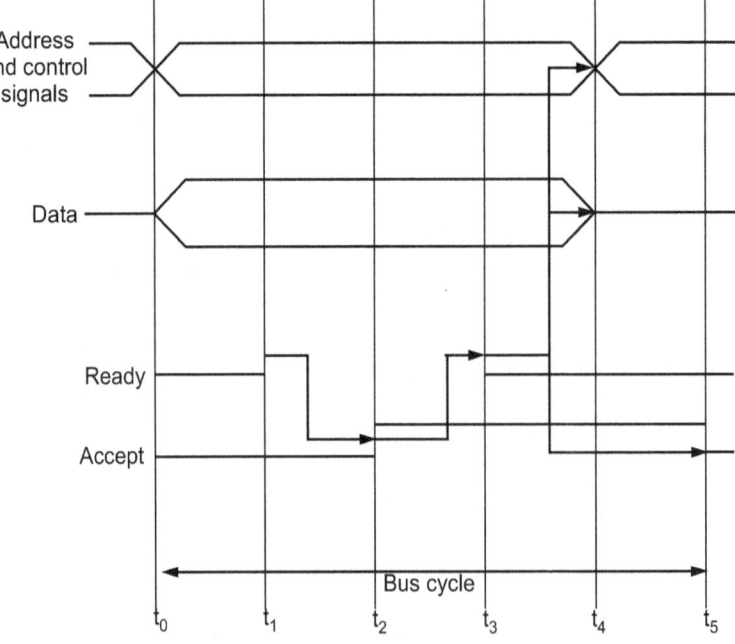

Fig. 4.27 : Timing diagram for write asynchronous bus

  5. The accept signal arrives at the processor, indicating that the input data are available on the bus. The processor stores the data into its input buffer and also deactivates the ready signal, indicating that it has received the data at t_3.

6. The processor removes the address and control signals from the bus. At t_4.

7. When the device receives 1 to 0 transition of the ready signal, it removes the data and the Accept signal from the bus at t_5.

(b) Write Operation :

- Sequence of events in asynchronous write :

    1. Processor places the device-address at time t_0.

    2. Processor activates the write Control signal to indicate an input operation, at time t_0.

    3. The processor sets the ready line to 1 to inform input/output devices that address and control signals are on the bus at time t_1.

    4. The addressed device receives the ready signal and seeing the write control signal it knows there is an output operation. The device stores the data into its input buffer and indicates that by seting the Accept signal to 1 at cycle t_2.

    5. Cycle's t_3 and t_4 are same as read operation.

4.8 PCI

- A bus is a channel or path between the components in a computer. Bus connects components to the computer's processor which include hard disks, memory, sound systems, and video systems and so on.

PCI bus is known as the Peripheral Component Interconnect (PCI).

4.8.1 System Bus versus PCI Bus

Few years ago, the processors were so slow. The bus ran at the same speed as the processor, and there was one bus in the machine. Today, the processors run so fast as most computers have two or more buses. Each bus specializes in a certain type of traffic. A typical desktop PC today has two main buses :

- The first one, known as the system bus or local bus, connects the microprocessor (central processing unit) and the system memory. This is the fastest bus in the system.

- The second one is a slower bus for communicating with things like hard disks and sound cards. One very common bus of this type is known as the PCI bus. These slower buses connect to the system bus through a bridge, which is a part of the computer's chipset and acts as a traffic cop, integrating the data from the other buses to the system bus.

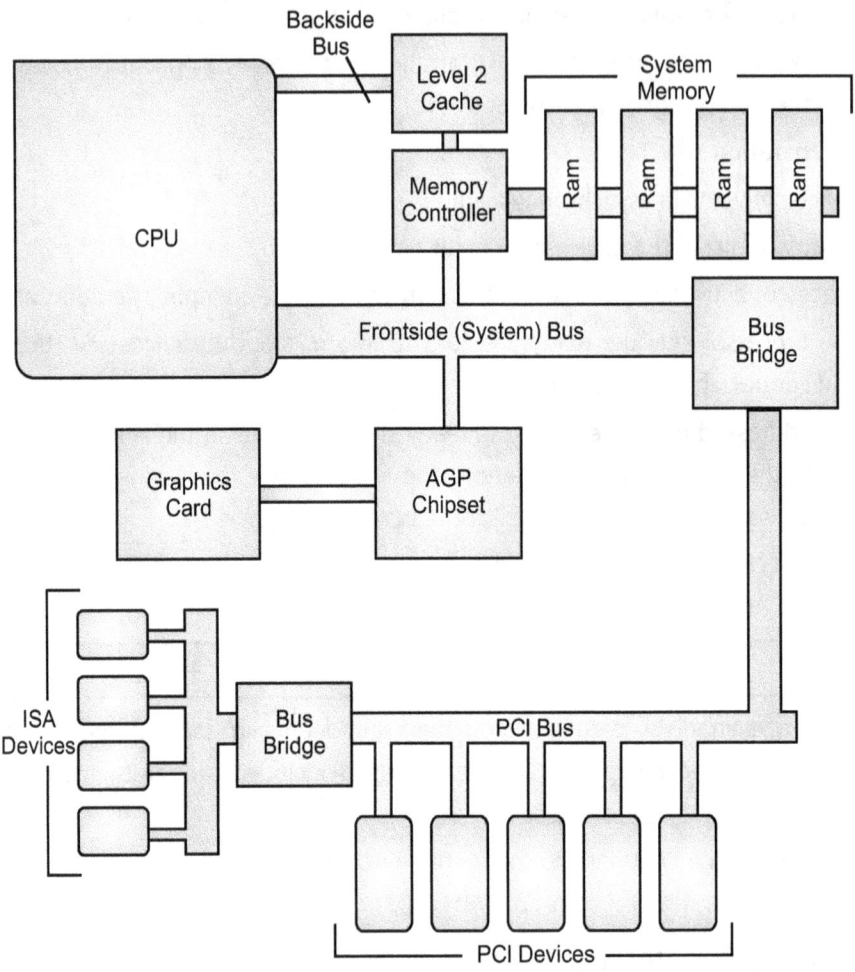

Fig. 4.28 : various buses connected to the CPU

4.8.2 PCI History

During the early 1990s, Intel introduced a new bus standard for consideration, the Peripheral Component Interconnect (PCI) bus. It provides direct access to system memory for connected devices, but uses a bridge to connect to the front side bus and therefore to the CPU. Basically, this means that it is capable of even higher performance than VL-Bus while eliminating the potential for interference with the CPU.

4.8.3 PCI Cards Use 47 Pins

- PCI cards use 47 pins to connect.
- PCI is synchronous bus architecture with all data transfers being performed relative to a system clock (CLK).
- In PCI terminology, data is transferred between an initiator which is the bus master, and a target which is the bus slave.
- A PCI bus transfer consists of one address phase and any number of data phases.
- PCI provides separate memory and I/O port address spaces for the x86 processor family, 64 and 32 bits, respectively. Addresses in these address spaces are assigned by software.
- A third address space, called the PCI Configuration Space, which uses a fixed addressing scheme.
- It allows software to determine the amount of memory and I/O address space needed by each device.

4.8.4 PCI Command Codes/Bus Cycles

- There are 16 possible 4-bit command codes, and 12 of them are assigned. the least significant bit of the command code indicates whether the following data phases are a read (data sent from target to initiator) or a write (data sent from an initiator to target).
- PCI targets must examine the command code as well as the address and not respond to address phases which specify an unsupported command code.

C/BE	Command Type
0000	Interrupt Acknowledge
0001	Special Cycle
0010	I/O Read
0011	I/O Write
0100	Reserved
0101	Reserved
0110	Memory Read
0111	Memory Write
1000	Reserved
1001	Reserved

1010	Configuration Read
1011	Configuration Write
1100	Multiple Memory Read
1101	Dual Address Cycle
1110	Memory-Read Line
1111	Memory Write and Invalidate

➤ **0000 : Interrupt Acknowledge**

This is a special form of read cycle implicitly addressed to the interrupt controller, which returns an interrupt vector. The 32-bit address field is ignored. Generates an interrupt acknowledge cycle on an ISA bus using a PCI/ISA bus bridge.

➤ **0001 : Special Cycle**

The address field of a special cycle is ignored, but it is followed by a data phase containing a payload message. The currently defined messages announce that the processor is stopping for some reason (e.g. to save power). No device ever responds to this cycle; it is always terminated with a master abort after leaving the data on the bus for at least 4 cycles.

0 x 0000	Processor Shutdown
0×0000	Processor Shutdown
0×0001	Processor Halt
0×0002	x86 Specific Code
0×0003 to $0 \times$ FFFF	Reserved

➤ **0010 : I/O Read**

This performs a read from I/O space. All 32 bits of the read address are provided; so that a device can (for compatibility reasons) implement less than 4 bytes worth of I/O registers. If the bytes enabled request data not within the address range supported by the PCI device, it must be terminated with a target abort. Multiple data cycles are permitted.

➤ **0011 : I/O Write**

This performs a write to I/O space.

➤ **010x : Reserved**

A PCI device must not respond to an address cycle with these command codes.

➢ **0110 : Memory Read**

This performs a read cycle from memory space. Because the smallest memory space a PCI device is permitted to implement is 16 bytes, the two least significant bits of the address are not needed; equivalent information will arrive in the form of byte select signals. They instead specify the order in which burst data must be returned. If a device does not support the requested order, it must provide the first word and then disconnect.

If a memory space is marked as "prefetchable", then the target device must ignore the byte select signals on a memory read and always return 32 valid bits.

➢ **0110 : Memory Write**

This operates similarly to a memory read. The byte select signals are more important in a write, as unselected bytes must not be written to memory.

Generally, PCI writes are faster than PCI reads, because a device can buffer the incoming write data and release the bus faster. For a read, it must delay the data phase until the data has been fetched.

➢ **100x : Reserved**

A PCI device must not respond to an address cycle with these command codes.

➢ **1010 : Configuration Read**

This is similar to an I/O read, but reads from PCI configuration space. A device must respond only if the low 11 bits of the address specify a function and register that it implements, and if the special IDSEL signal is asserted. It must ignore the high 21 bits. Burst reads are permitted in PCI configuration space.

Unlike I/O space, standard PCI configuration registers are defined so that reads never disturb the state of the device.

➢ **1011 : Configuration Write**

This operates analogously to a configuration read.

➢ **1100 : Memory Read Multiple**

This command is identical to a generic memory read, but includes the hint that a long read burst will continue beyond the end of the current cache line, and the target should internally prefetch a large amount of data. A target is always permitted to consider this a synonym for a generic memory read.

➢ **1101 : Dual Address Cycle**

When accessing a memory address that requires more than 32 bits to represent, the address phase begins with this command and the high 32 bits of the address, followed by a second cycle with the actual command and the low 32 bits of the address.

➢ **1110 : Memory Read Line**

This command is identical to a generic memory read, but includes the hint that the read will continue to the end of the cache line. A target is always permitted to consider this a synonym for a generic memory read.

➢ **1111 : Memory Write and Invalidate**

This command is identical to a generic memory write, but comes with the guarantee that one or more whole cache line will be written, with all byte selects enabled. This is an optimization for write-back caches snooping the bus. If the write is performed using this command, the data to be written back is guaranteed to be irrelevant, and can simply be invalidated in the write-back cache.

4.8.5 PCI Timing Diagrams

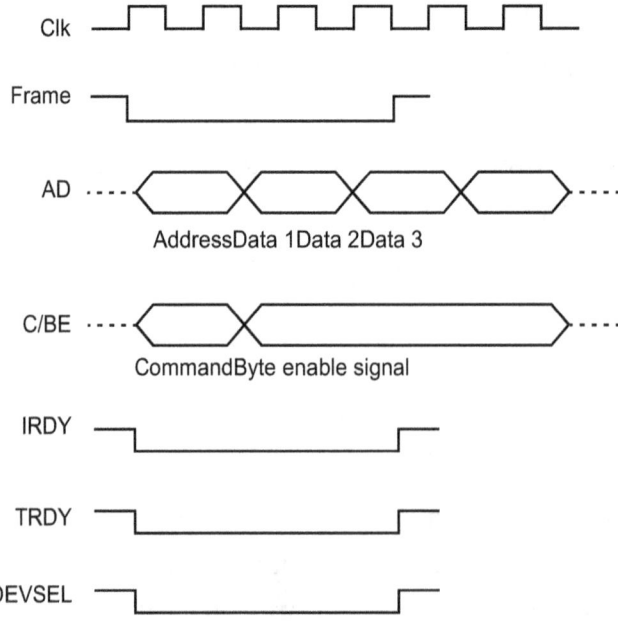

Fig. 4.29 : PCI timing diagrams

PCI transfer cycle, with wait states. Data is transferred on the rising edge of CLK at points labeled A, B, and C.

Signal timing

- All PCI bus signals are sampled on the rising edge of the clock. Signals nominally change on the falling edge of the clock, giving each PCI device approximately one half a clock cycles to decide how to respond to the signals it observed on the rising edge, and one half a clock cycle to transmit its response to the other device.

- The PCI bus requires that every time the device driving a PCI bus signal changes, one turnaround cycle must elapse between the time the one device stops driving the signal and the other device starts. The combination of this turnaround cycle and the requirement to drive a control line high for one cycle before ceasing to drive it means that each of the main control lines must be high for a minimum of 2 cycles when changing owners is it necessary to insert additional delay to meet this requirement.

Arbitration

- Any device on a PCI bus that is capable of acting as a bus master may initiate a transaction with any other device. To ensure that only one transaction is initiated at a time, each master must first wait for a bus grant signal, GNT#, from an arbiter located on the motherboard. Each device has a separate request line REQ# that requests the bus, but the arbiter may "park" the bus grant signal at any device if there are no current requests.

- The arbiter may remove GNT# at any time. A device which loses GNT# may complete its current transaction, but may not start one (by asserting FRAME#) unless it observes GNT# asserted the cycle before it begins.

- The arbiter may also provide GNT# at any time, including during another master's transaction. During a transaction, either FRAME# or IRDY# or both are asserted; when both are disserted, the bus is idle. A device may initiate a transaction at any time that GNT# is asserted and the bus is idle.

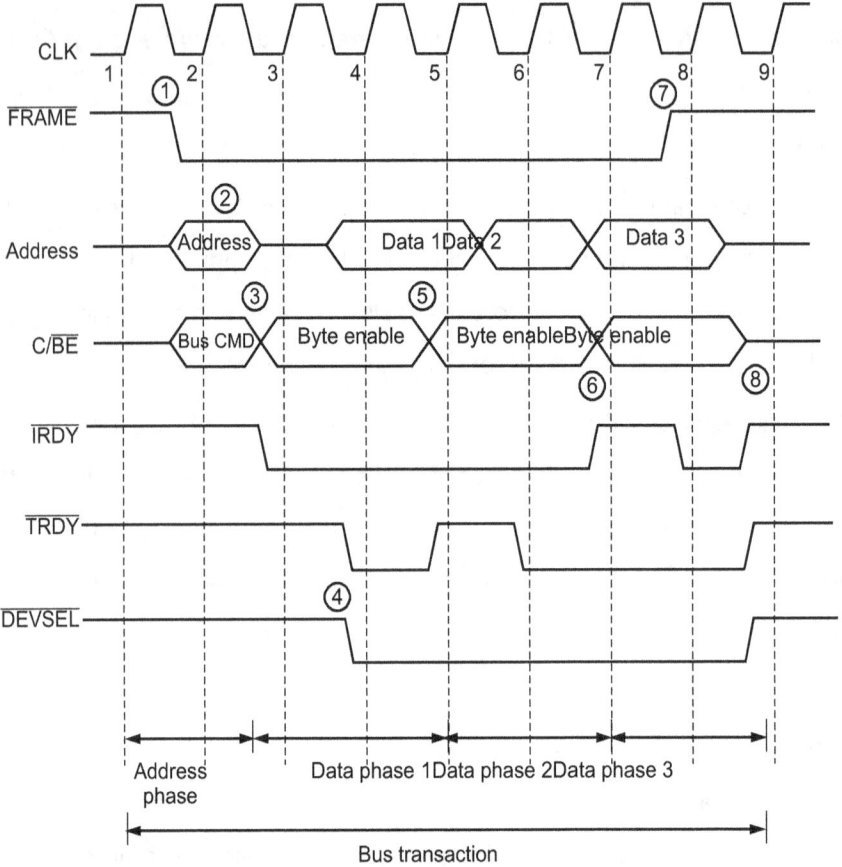

Fig. 4.30 : Address Phase and timing diagram

4.9 SCSI

A computer is full of busses or highways that take information and power from one place to another.

- For example, when you plug an MP3 player or digital camera into your computer, you are probably using a universal serial bus (USB) port.

- Your USB port is good at carrying the data and electricity required for small electronic devices that do things like create and store pictures and music files. But that bus isn't big enough to support a whole computer, a server or lots of devices simultaneously.

For that, we need SCSI.

- Small Computer System Interface, or SCSI is a set of standards for physically connecting and transferring data between computers and peripheral devices. The SCSI standards define commands, protocols, and electrical and optical interfaces. The Small Computer System Interface (SCSI) is a parallel I/O bus and protocol that permits the connection of a variety of peripherals including disk drives, tape drives, modems, printers, scanners, optical devices, test equipment, and medical devices to a host computer.

- It's a fast bus that can connect lots of devices to a computer at the same time, including hard drives, scanners, CD-ROM/RW drives, printers and tape drives. The SCSI bus connects all parts of a computer system so that they can communicate with each other.

- SCSI is an intelligent interface: it hides the complexity of physical format. Every device attaches to the SCSI bus in a similar manner.

- SCSI is a peripheral interface: up to 8 or 16 devices can be attached to a single bus. There can be any number of hosts and peripheral devices but there should be at least one host.

- SCSI is a buffered interface: it uses hand shake signals between devices, SCSI-1, SCSI-2 have the option of parity error checking. Starting with SCSI-U160 (part of SCSI-3) all commands and data are error checked by a CRC32 checksum.

- SCSI is a peer to peer interface: the SCSI protocol defines communication from host to host, host to a peripheral device, and peripheral device to a peripheral device.

4.9.1 SCSI Types

SCSI has three basic specifications:

1. **SCSI-1 :** The original specification developed in 1986, SCSI-1 is now obsolete. It featured a bus width of 8 bits and clock speed of 5 MHz.

2. **SCSI-2 :** Adopted in 1994, this specification included the Common Command Set (CCS) 18 commands considered an absolute necessity for support of any SCSI device. It also had the option to double the clock speed to 10 MHz (Fast), double the bus width from to 16 bits and increase the number of devices to 15 (Wide), or do both (Fast/Wide). SCSI-2 also added command queuing, allowing devices to store and prioritize commands from the host computer.

3. **SCSI-3 :** This specification debuted in 1995 and included a series of smaller standards within its overall scope. A set of standards involving the SCSI Parallel Interface (SPI), which is the way that SCSI devices communicate with each other, has continued to evolve within SCSI-3. Most SCSI-3 specifications begin with the term Ultra, such as Ultra for SPI variations, Ultra2 for SPI-2 variations and Ultra3 for SPI-3 variations. The Fast and Wide designations work just like their SCSI-2 counterparts. SCSI-3 is the standard currently in use.

4.9.2 Controllers, Devices and Cables

- A SCSI controller coordinates between all of the other devices on the SCSI bus and the computer. The controller can be a card that you plug into an available slot or it can be built into the motherboard. The SCSI BIOS is also on the controller. This is a small ROM or Flash memory chip that contains the software needed to access and control the devices on the bus.

- Each SCSI device must have a unique identifier (ID) in order for it to work properly.

- Internal devices connect to a SCSI controller with a ribbon cable. External SCSI devices attach to the controller in a daisy chain using a thick, round cable. (Serial Attached SCSI devices use SATA cables.)

The cable itself typically consists of three layers:

➢ Inner layer: The most protected layer, this contains the actual data being sent.

➢ Media layer: Contains the wires that send control commands to the device.

➢ Outer layer: Includes wires that carry parity information, which ensures that the data is correct.

- When two devices communicate on the bus, one device initiates the communication to the target, and the target performs the task. SCSI devices usually have a fixed role as an initiator or a target, although some devices can perform both roles.

- Fig. 4.31 shows a typical SCSI configuration.

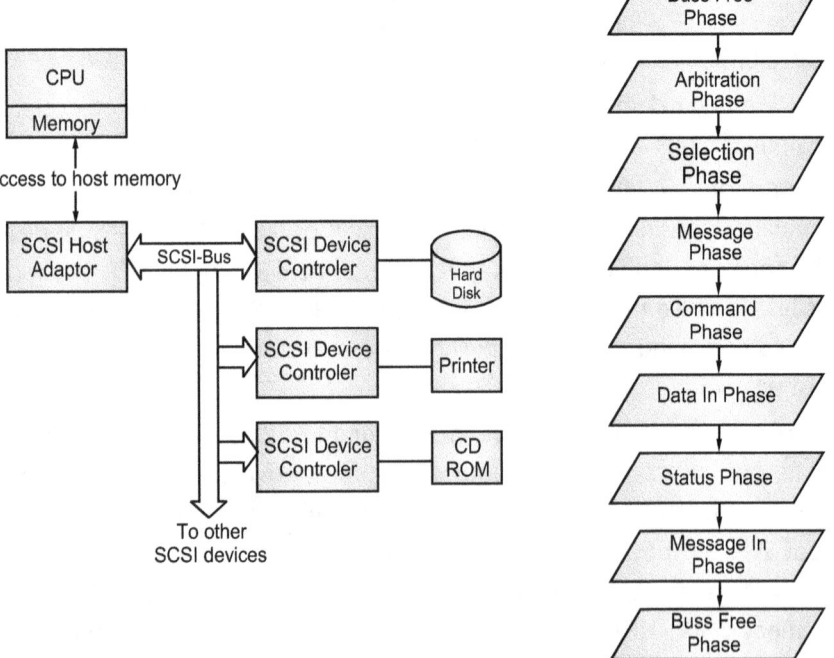

Fig. 4.31 : SCSI Configuration   **Fig. 4.32 : SCSI Bus Phases**

4.9.3 SCSI Bus signals

The SCSI bus uses eighteen signals. Nine are control signals used to develop logical bus phases, and nine are data signals, including parity, for messages, commands, status, and data.

The state of the SEL, BSY, and I/O signals and the sequence of the phases determine when the Bus Free, Arbitration, Selection, and Reselection phases are entered.

Table 4.1 describes the nine control signals.

- The Selection or Reselection phase can be entered only from the Arbitration phase.
- The Arbitration phase can be entered only from the Bus Free phase.
- The Bus Free phase can be entered from any of the other phases (although some transitions are caused by errors).

I/O determine the current phase, you need to know information about the previous phase and the state of the signals. The initiator and target drive these signals to change from one phase to another phase.

Table 4.1 : SCSI Bus Signals

Signal	Description
BSY(BUSY)	An 'OR-tied signal which indicates that the bus is being used.
SEL(SELECT)	A signal used by an initiator to select a target or by a target to reselect an initiator.
C/D (CONTROL/DATA)	A signal driven by a target to indicate whether or not control or data information is on the data bus. True indicates control.
I/O (INPUT/OUTPUT)	A signal driven by a target to control the direction of data movement on the data bus. True indicates input to the initiator. This signal is also used to distinguish between selection and reselection phases.
MSG (MESSAGE)	A signal driven by a target during the Message phase.
REQ (REQUEST)	A signal driven by a target to request a REQ/ACK data transfer handshake.
ACK (ACKNOWLEDGE)	A signal driven by an initiator to acknowledge a REQ/ACK data transfer.

ATN (ATTENTION)	A signal driven by an initiator to indicate the condition (initiator has a message for the target).
RST (RESET)	An 'OR-tied' signal and hard Reset condition.
DB (7-0,P) (DATA BUS)	Eight data-bit (DB) signals, plus a parity-bit signal that form a Data Bus. DB (7) is the most significant bit and has the highest during the Arbitration phase. Bit number, significance, and priority decreases downward to DB (0). A data bit is defined as one when the signal value is true, and defined as zero when the signal value is false. Data parity DB (P) shall be odd, but parity is undefined during the Arbitration phase.

A SCSI device usually has a fixed role as an initiator or target, but some devices are able to assume either role. In most cases, the host is the initiator and the device is the target.

An initiator may address up to eight peripheral devices that are connected to a target. These are called Logical Units Numbers (LUNs). Digital devices currently only support a single LUN per device.

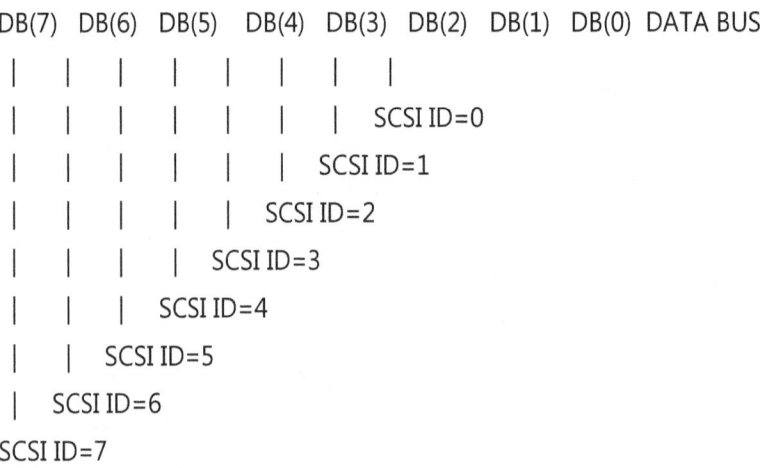

Fig. 4.33 : SCSI ID Bits

4.9.4 SCSI Bus Phases

- The Small Computer System Interface bus can be time-shared, which results in greater usage of bus bandwidth. This is how it works: while one device is using the bus, other devices may be active and performing internal activities.

- System performance is significantly increased when devices disconnect and reconnect to the bus. During the bus phases devices must first contend for access to the bus.

- Then a physical path is established between the initiator and target. The SCSI bus cannot be in more than one phase at a same time.

The SCSI architecture includes eight distinct phases:

- Bus free phase
- Arbitration phase
- Selection phase
- Reselection phase.
- Command phase
- Data phase
- Message phase
- Status phase.

- The SCSI bus can never be in more than one phase at any given time. Unless otherwise noted in the following description, signals that are not mentioned shall not be asserted.

Bus Free Phase

- The Bus Free Phase is used to indicate that no SCSI device is actively using the SCSI bus and that it is available for subsequent users. SCSI devices shall detect the Bus Free Phase after SEL and BSY are both false for at least a bus settles delay. SCSI devices shall release all SCSI bus signals has a bus clear delay after BSY and SEI, become continuously false for a bus settle delay.

- If a SCSI device requires more than a bus settle delay to detect the Bus Free Phase then it releases all SCSI bus signals within a bus clear delay minus the excess time to detect the Bus Free Phase.

- The total time to clear the SCSI bus does not exceed a bus settle delay plus a bus clear delay. Initiators normally do not expect Bus Free Phase to begin because of the target's release of BSY except after one of the following occurrences:

- After a Reset condition is detected.
- After an Abort message is successfully received by a target.
- After a Bus Device Reset message is successfully received by a target.
- After a Disconnect message is successfully transmitted from a target.
- After a Command Complete message is successfully transmitted from a target.
- After- a Release Recovery message is successfully received by a target.

The Bus Free Phase may also be entered after an unsuccessful selection or reselection of SEL rather than the release of BSY that first although in this case it is the established the Bus Free Phase.

- If an initiator detects the release of BSY by the target at other times, the target is indicating an error condition to the initiator. The target may perform this transition to the Bus Free Phase independent of the state of the ATN signal. The initiator manages this condition as an unsuccessful I/O process termination.

- The target terminates the I/O process by clearing all pending data and status information for the affected logical unit or process.

- The target may optionally prepare sense bytes that could be read by a Request Sense command.

- When an initiator detects an unexpected Bus Free condition it is normal that a Request Sense command is attempted to obtain any valid sense information that may be available. If the error that caused the Bus Free termination of the I/O process is still present, the Request Sense command may not be successful.

Arbitration Phase :

The Arbitration Phase allows one SCSI device to gain control of the SCSI bus so that it can assume the role of an initiator or target. The procedure for an SCSI device to obtain control of the SCSI bus is as follows:

1. The SCSI device shall first wait for the Bus Free Phase to occur. The Bus Free Phase is detected whenever both BSY and SEL are simultaneously and continuously false for a minimum of a bus settle delay

2. The SCSI device waits a minimum of a bus free delay alter detection of the Bus Free Phase (that is after BSY and SEL are both false for a bus settles delay) before driving any signal

3. Following the bus free delay in step (2), the SCSI device may arbitrate for the SCSI bus by asserting both BSY and its own SCST ID, however the SCSI device does not arbitrate (that is assert BSY and its SCSI I(D) if more than a bus settle delay has passed since the Bus Free Phase was last observed

4. After waiting at least an arbitration delay (measured from its assertion of BSY) the SCSI device examines the Data Bus if a higher priority SCSI ID bit is true on the DATA BUS (DB(7) is the highest), then the SCSI device has lost the arbitration and the SCSI device releases its' signals and returns to step (1). If no higher priority SCSI ID bit is

true on the Data Bus, then the SCSI device has won the arbitration and it asserts SEL. Any other SCSI device that is participating in the Arbitration Phase has lost the arbitration and releases BSY and its SCSI ID bit within a bus clear delay after SEL becomes true. A SCSI device that loses arbitration returns to step (1).

5.   The SCSI device that wins arbitration shall wait at least a bus clear delay plus a bus settle delay after asserting SEL before changing any signals.

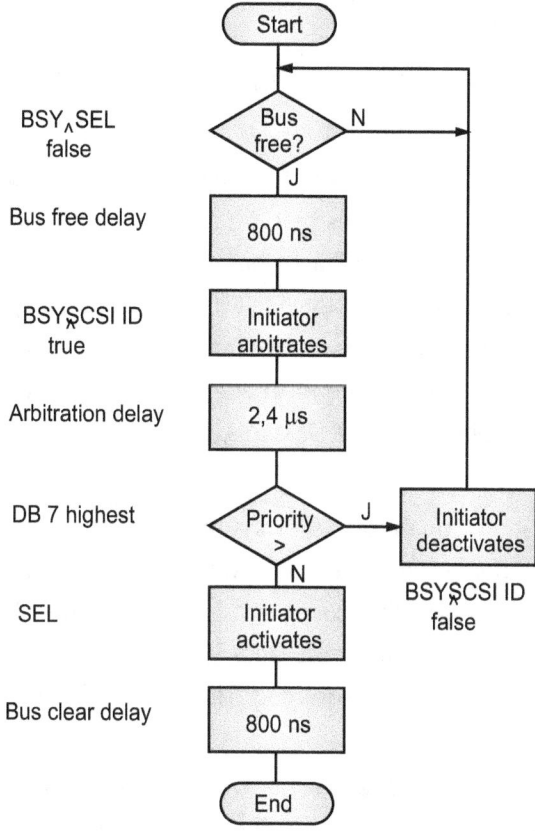

Fig. 4.34 : SCSI Arbitration

Selection Phase :

The Selection Phase allows an initiator to select a target for the purpose of initiating some target function, for example, the Read or Write command.

During the Selection Phase the I/O signal is negated so that this phase can be distinguished from the Reselection Phase.

- The SCSI device that won the arbitration has both BSY and SEL asserted and has delayed at least a bus clear delay plus a bus settle delay before ending the Arbitration Phase. The SCSI device that won the arbitration becomes an initiator by not asserting the I/O signal. The initiator sets the Data Bus to a value which is the OR of its SCSI ID bit and the target's SCSI ID bit. The initiator then waits at least two deskew delays and releases BSY. The initiator then waits at least a bus settle delay before looking for a response from the target.

Selection Phase

DB(0)	DB(1)	DB(2)	DB(3)	DB(4)	DB(5)	DB(6)	DB(7)
1	0	0	0	0	0	1	0

- In this example, SCSI ID 6 (host) has asserted both its own SCSI ID (DB (6)) and that of a device (DB (0)). The target determines that it is selected when SEL and its SCSI ID bit are true and BSY and I/O are false for at least a bus settle delay. The selected target examines the data Bus in order to determine the SCSI ID of the selecting initiator. The selected target is BSY within a selection; this is required for correct operation of the time-out procedure. The target shall not respond to a selection if bad parity is detected. Also, if more than two SCSI ID bits are on the Data Bus, the target does not respond to selection.

Reselection Phase :

- Reselection is an optional phase that allows a target to reconnect to an initiator for the purpose of continuing some operation that was previously started by the initiator but was suspended by the target. For example, a host system may have requested a Read from a disk. The disk can disconnect and Reconnect if the Read involves a time consuming seek operation to be performed. This is one of the optimization features of SCSI.

- The initiator determines that it is reselected when SEL, I/O and its SCSI ID bit are true and BSY is false for at least a bus settle delay. The reselected initiator may examine the Data Bus in order to determine the SCSI ID of the reselecting target. The reselected initiator then asserts BSY within a selection abort time of its most recent detection of being reselected; this is required for correct operation of the time-out procedure. The initiator does not respond to a Reselection Phase if bad party is detected. Also, the initiator may not respond to a Reselection Phase if other than two SCSI ID bits are on the Data Bus.

- After the target detects BSY, it also asserts BSY and wait at least two deskew delays and then release SEL. The target may then change the I/O signal and the Data Bus. After the reselected initiator detects SEL false, it releases BSY. The target continues asserting BSY until it relinquishes the SCSI bus.

Information Transfer Phases :

The Command, Data, Status, and Message Phases are all grouped together as the Information Transfer Phases because they are all used to transfer data or control information via the Data Bus.

- The C/D, I/O, and MSG signals are used to distinguish between the different Information Tansfer Phases. The target drives these three signals and therefore controls all changes from one phase to another.

- The initiator can request a Message out Phase by asserting ATN, while the target can cause the Bus Free Phase by releasing MSG, C/D, I/O and BSY. The Information Tansfer Phases use one or more REQ/ACK handshakes to control the information transfer.

- Each REQ/ACK handshake allows the transfer of one byte of information. During the information transfer phases BSY remains true and SEL remains false.

- The target shall continuously envelope the REQ/ACK handshake(s).

Signal

MSG	C/D	I/O		Phase Name	Direction of Transfer	Comment
0 0	0	Data out		Initiator to Target	Data	
0 0	1	Data in		Initiator from Target	Phase	
0 1	0	Command		Initiator to Target		
0 1	1	Status		Initiator from Target		
1 0	0	*				
1 0	1	*				
1 1	0	Message Out	Initiator To Target		Message	
1 1	1	Message In	Initiator From Target		Phase	

Key : 0 = False

1 = True

* = Reserved for future specification

Asynchronous Information Transfer

- The target controls the direction of information transfer by means of the I/O signals. When I/O are true, information is transferred from the target to the initiator. When I/O is false, information is transferred from the initiator to the target.

- If I/O is true (transfer to the initiator),

- If I/O is false (transfer to the target)
- When ACK becomes true at the target, the target reads DB(7-0,P) then negates REQ. When REQ becomes false at the initiator, the initiator may change or release DB(7-0,P) and negates ACK. The target may continue the transfer by asserting REQ, as described above.

Synchronous Data Transfer :

- Synchronous data transfer is only used in data phases.
- The REQ/ACK offset specifies the Maximum number of REQ pulses.
- If the number of REQ pulses exceeds the number of ACK pulses by the REQ/ACK offset, the target shall not assert REQ until alter the leading edge of the next ACK pulse is received.
- The target asserts the REQ signal for a minimum of an assertion period. The target shall wait at least a transfer period from the last transition of REQ to false before asserting the REQ signal.
- The initiator sends one pulse on the ACK signal for each REQ pulse received. The ACK signal may be asserted as soon as the leading edge of the corresponding REQ pulse has been received.
- The initiator asserts the ACK signal for a minimum of an assertion period.
- If I/O is true (transfer to the initiator), the target first drives DB(7-0,P) to their desired values, waits at least one deskskew delay plus one cable skew delay, then assert REQ. DB(7-0,P) shall be held valid for a minimum of one deskew delay plus one cable skew delay plus one hold time after the assertion of REQ. The target asserts REQ for a minimum of an assertion period.
- The target may then negate REQ and change or release DB(7-0,P). The initiator reads the value on DB(7-0,P) within one hold tirne of the transition of REQ to true. The initiator then responds with an ACK pulse.

Command Phase :

The Command Phase allows the target to request command information from the initiator.The target shall assert the C/D signal and negate the I/O and MSG during the REQ/ACK handshake(s) of this phase.

- **Data Phase**

The Data Phase is a term that encompasses both the Data In Phase and the Data Out Phase.

(a) Data In Phase

The Data In Phase allows the target to request that data be sent to the initiator from the target. The target asserts the I/O signal and negate the C/D and MSG signals during the REQ/ACK handshake(s) of this phase.

(b) Data Out Phase

The Data Out Phase allows the target to request that data be sent from the initiator to the target. The target negates the C/D, I/O, and MSG signals during the REQ/ACK handshake(s) of this phase.

(c) Status Phase

The Status Phase allows the target to request that status information be sent from the target to the initiator. The target asserts C/D and I/O and negates the MSG signal during the REQ/ACK handshake of this phase.

(d) Message Phase

The Message Phase is a term that references either a Message In, or a Message Out Phase. Multiple messages may be sent during either phase. The first byte transferred in either of these phases is either a single-byte message or the first byte of a multiple-byte message. Multiple-byte messages are wholly contained within a single message phase.

(e) Message In Phase

The Message In Phase allows the target to request that message(s) be sent to the initiator from the target.

The target asserts C/D, I/O, and MSG during the REQ/ACK handshake(s) of this phase.

(f) Message Out Phase

The Message Out Phase allows the target to request that message(s) be sent from the initiator to the target. The target invokes this phase in response to the Attention condition created by the initiator.

4.9.5 SCSI Bus Conditions

The SCSI bus has two asynchronous conditions; the Attention condition and the Reset condition. These conditions cause the SCSI device to perform certain actions and can alter the phase sequence.

1. **Attention Condition**

    - The Attention condition allows an initiator to inform a target that the initiator has a message ready. The target may get this message by performing a Message Out Phase.

    - The initiator creates the Attention condition by asserting ATN at any time except during the Arbitration or Bus Free Phases.

    - The initiator asserts the ATN signal before negating ACK for the last byte transferred in a bus phase.

    - The initiator negates ATN before asserting ACK when transferring the last byte of the messages.

    - If the target detects that the initiator failed to meet this requirement, then the target goes to Bus Free Phase.

2. **Reset Condition**

    - The Reset condition is used to immediately clear all SCSI devices from the bus.

    - All SCSI devices release all SCSI bus signals (except RST) within a bus clear delay of the transition of RST to true. The Bus Free Phase always follows the Reset condition

4.9.6 SCSI Bus Phase Sequences

- The order in which phases are used on the SCSI bus follows a prescribed sequence.

  The Reset condition can abort any phase and is always followed by the Bus Free Phase.

- Also any other phase can be followed by the Bus Free Phase but many such instances are error conditions.

- The normal Progression is from the Bus Free Phase to Arbitration, from Arbitration to Selection or Reselection, and from Selection or Reselection to one or more of the Information Transfer Phases (Command, Data, Status, or Message).

- Normally, the final Information Humanster Phase is Message In Phase where a Disconnect, Command Complete, or Linked Command Complete message is transferred, followed by Bus Free phase.

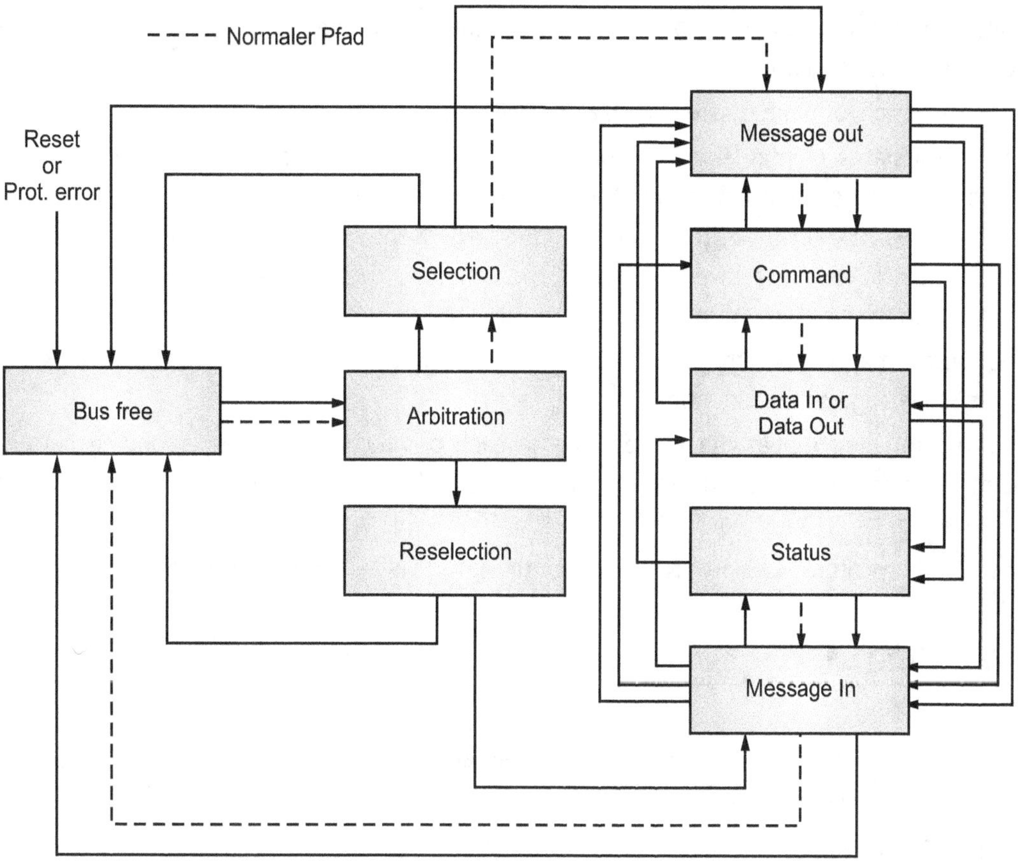

- - - - Normaler Pfad

Reset
or
Prot. error

Message out

Selection

Command

Bus free

Arbitration

Data In or
Data Out

Reselection

Status

Message In

Fig. 4.35 : SCSI phase sequences

4.9.7 SCSI Pointers

Consider the system shown in Fig. 4.36 in which an initiator and target communicate on the SCSI bus in order to execute an I/0 operation.

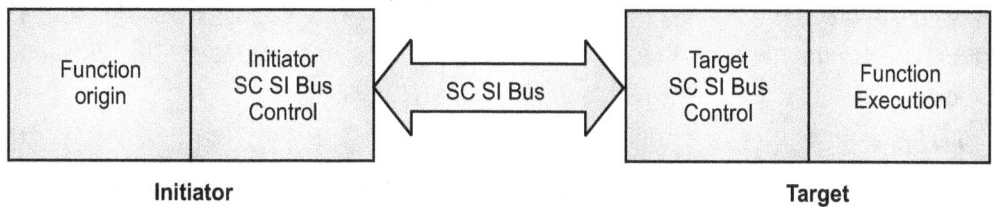

| Function origin | Initiator SC SI Bus Control | SC SI Bus | Target SC SI Bus Control | Function Execution |

Initiator **Target**

Fig. 4.36 : Simplified I/O Operation

The SCSI architecture provides for two sets of three pointers within each initiator. The first sets of pointers are known as the current (or active) pointers. These pointers are used to represent the state of the interface and point to the next command, data, or status byte to be transferred between the initiator's memory and the target. There is only one set of current pointers in each initiator.

The second sets of pointers are known as the saved pointers.

The saved status pointer always points to the start of the status area for the current PO process. At the beginning of each I/O processes, the saved data pointer points to the start of the data area. It remains at this value until the target sends a Save Data Pointer message to the initiator. In response to this message, the initiator stores the value of the current data pointer into the saved data pointer.

The Target may restore the current pointers to their saved values by sending a Restore Pointers message to the initiator.

The initiator then moves the saved value of each pointer into the corresponding current pointer. Whenever an SCSI device disconnects from the bus, only the saved pointer values are retained.

The current pointer values are restored from the saved values upon the next reconnection.

4.9.8 SCSI Messages

* **Abort**

This message is sent from the initiator to the target to clear the present I/0 process plus any queued I/O process for the I-T-x nexus.

* **Bus Device Reset**

This message is sent from an initiator to direct a target to clear all current I/0 processes on that SCSI device.

* **Command Complete**

This message is sent from a target to an initiator to indicate that the execution of a command has terminated and that valid status has been sent to the initiator. After successfully sending this message, the target enters the Bus Free Phase by releasing BSY. The target considers the message transmission to be successful when it detects the negation of ACK for the Command Complete message with the ATN signal false.

* **Disconnect**

This message is sent from a target to inform an initiator that the present connection is going to be broken (the target plans to disconnect by releasing BSY), but that a later reconnect will be required in order to complete the current I/O process.

This message may also be sent from an initiator to a target to instruct the target to disconnect from the SCSI bus.

- **Identify**

The Identify message is sent by either the initiator or the target to establish an I-T-L nexus or an I-T-R nexus. Fig. 4.37 shows an example of the SCSI signals, its sequence and the timing.

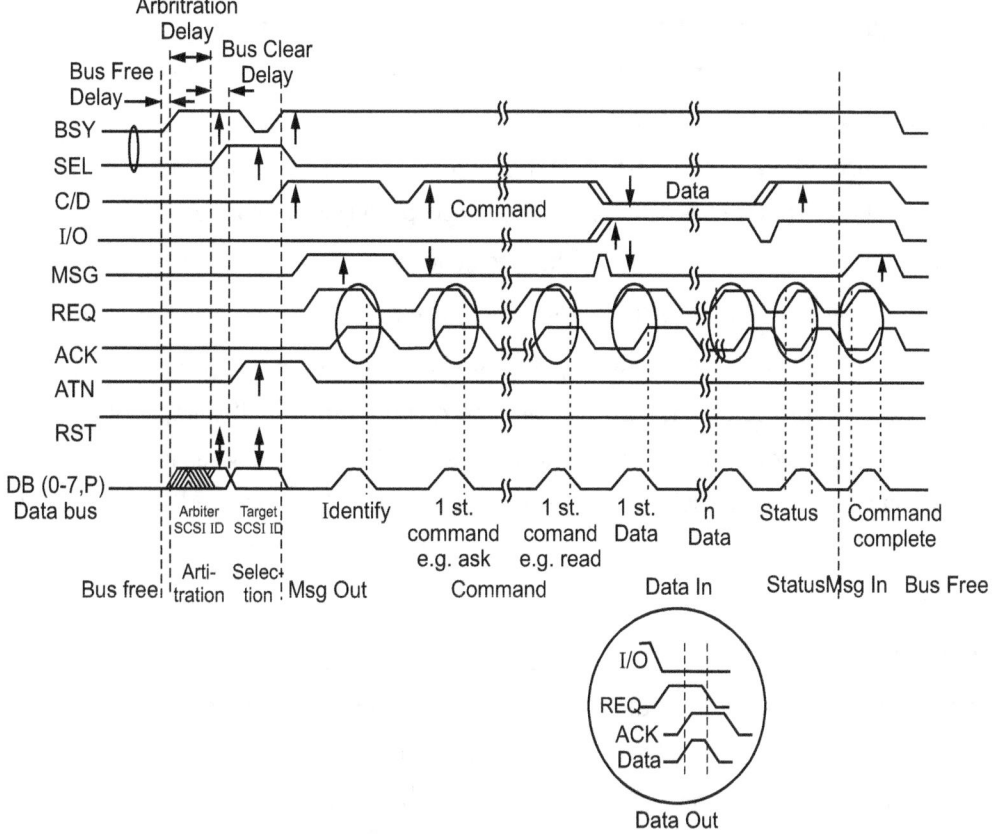

Fig. 4.37 : SCSI timing diagram

4.10 USB PORTS

USB is short form of Universal Serial Bus, an external bus standard that supports data transfer rates of 12 Mbps. A single USB port can be used to connect up to 127 peripheral devices, such as mice, modems, and keyboards. USB also supports Plug-and-Play installation and hot plugging. the USB system is so flexible and is able to support so many devices so easily. The Universal Serial Bus gives a single, standardized, easy-to-use way to connect up to 127 devices to a computer.

4.10.1 USB Cables and Connectors

Connecting a USB device to a computer is simple. You find the USB connector on the back of your machine and plug the USB connector into it.

If it is a new device, the operating system auto-detects it and asks for the driver disk. If the device has already been installed, the computer activates it and starts talking to it. USB devices can be connected and disconnected at any time.

Many USB devices come with their own built-in cable, and the cable has an "A" connection on it. If not, then the device has a socket on it that accepts a USB "B" connector.

The USB standard uses "A" and "B" connectors to avoid confusion:

- "A" connectors head "upstream" toward the computer.
- "B" connectors head "downstream" and connect to individual devices.

By using different connectors on the upstream and downstream end, it is impossible to ever get confused. If you connect any USB cable's "B" connector into a device, you know that it will work. Similarly, you can plug any "A" connector into any "A" socket and know that it will work.

4.10.2 USB Hubs

Most computers for example, on the computer that I am typing on right now, I have a USB printer, a USB scanner, a USB Webcam and a USB network connection. My computer has only one USB connector on it, so the obvious question is, "How do you hook up all the devices?"

The easy solution to the problem is to buy an inexpensive USB hub. The USB standard supports up to 127 devices, and USB hubs are a part of the standard.

A hub typically has four new ports. You plug the hub into your computer, and then plug your devices into the hub. By connecting hubs together, you can build up dozens of available USB ports on a single computer.

Hubs can be powered or unpowered. If you have self-powered devices (like printers and scanners), then your hub does not need to be powered the computer can handle it. If you have lots of unpowered devices like mice and cameras, you probably need a powered hub. The hub has its own transformer and it supplies power to the bus so that the devices do not overload the computer's supply.

4.10.3 The USB Process

When the host powers up, it queries all of the devices connected to the bus and assigns each one an address. This process is called enumeration devices are also enumerated when they connect to the bus. The host also finds out from each device what type of data transfer it wishes to perform:

- **Interrupt :** A device like a mouse or a keyboard, which will be sending very little data, would choose the interrupt mode.

- **Bulk :** A device like a printer, which receives data in one big packet, uses the bulk transfer mode. A block of data is sent to the printer (in 64-byte chunks) and verified to make sure it is correct.

- **Isochronous :** A streaming device (such as speakers) uses the isochronous mode. Data streams between the device and the host in real-time, and there is no error correction.

The host can also send commands or query parameters with control packets.

The Universal Serial Bus divides the available bandwidth into frames, and the host controls the frames. Frames contain 1,500 bytes, and a new frame starts every millisecond. During a frame, isochronous and interrupt devices get a slot so they are guaranteed the bandwidth they need. Bulk and control transfers use whatever space is left.

4.10.4 USB Features

The Universal Serial Bus has the following features:

1. The computer acts as the host.

2. Up to 127 devices can connect to the host, either directly or by way of USB hubs.

3. Individual USB cables can run as long as 5 meters; with hubs, devices can be up to 30 metres (six cables' worth) away from the host.

3. With USB 2.0,the bus has a maximum data rate of 480 megabits per second.

4. A USB cable has two wires for power (+5 volts and ground and a twisted pair of wires to carry the data.

5. On the power wires, the computer can supply up to 500 milliamps of power at 5 volts.

6. Low-power devices (such as mice) can draw their power directly from the bus. High-power devices (such as printers) have their own power supplies and draw minimal power from the bus. Hubs can have their own power supplies to provide power to devices connected to the hub.

USB devices are hot-swappable, meaning you can plug them into the bus and unplug them any time.

Many USB devices can be put to sleep by the host computer when the computer enters a power-saving mode.

The devices connected to a USB port rely on the USB cable to carry power and data.

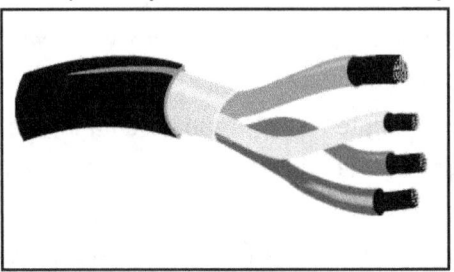

Fig. 4.38 : Inside a USB cable: There are two wires for power +5 volts (red and ground (brown) and a twisted pair (yellow and blue) of wires to carry the data. The cable is also shielded

MULTIPLE CHOICE QUESTIONS (MCQS)

1. A collection of lines that connects several devices is called ....
   (a) bus
   (b) peripheral connection wires
   (c) both (a) and (b)
   (d) internal wires

2. A complete microcomputer system consist of ....
   (a) microprocessor
   (b) memory
   (c) peripheral equipment
   (d) all of the these

3. PC Program Counter is also called ....
   (a) instruction pointer
   (b) memory pointer
   (c) data counter
   (d) file pointer

4. In a single byte how many bits will be there?
   (a) 8
   (b) 16
   (c) 4
   (d) 32

5. CPU does not perform the operation ....
   (a) data transfer
   (b) logic operation
   (c) arithmetic operation
   (d) all of these

6. The access time of memory is .... the time required for performing any single CPU operation.

   (a) longer than   (b) shorter than

   (c) negligible than   (d) same as

7. Memory address refers to the successive memory words and the machine is called as ....

   (a) word addressable   (b) byte addressable

   (c) bit addressable   (d) tera byte addressable

8. A microprogram written as string of 0's and 1's is a ....

   (a) symbolic microinstruction   (b) binary microinstruction

   (c) symbolic microprogram   (d) binary microprogram

9. A pipeline is like ....

   (a) an automobile assembly line   (b) house pipeline

   (c) both (a) and (b)   (d) a gas line

10. Data hazards occur when ....

   (a) greater performance loss

   (b) pipeline changes the order of read/write access to operands

   (c) some functional unit is not fully pipelined

   (d) machine size is limited

11. Computers use addressing mode techniques for ....

   (a) giving programming versatility to the user by providing facilities as pointers to memory counters for loop control

   (b) to reduce number of bits in the field of instruction

   (c) specifying rules for modifying or interpreting address field of the instruction

   (d) all the above

12. ....register keeps track of the instructions stored in program stored in memory.

   (a) AR (Address Register)   (b) XR (Index Register)

   (c) PC (Program Counter)   (d) AC (Accumulator)

13. The addressing mode used in an instruction of the form ADD X Y, is

    (a) absolute   (b) indirect

    (c) index   (d) none of thes

14. In a vectored interrupt.

    (a) the branch address is assigned to a fixed location in memory.

    (b) the interrupting source supplies the branch information to the processor
        through an interrupt vector.

    (c) the branch address is obtained from a register in the processor

    (d) none of the above

15. The circuit used to store one bit of data is known as

    (a) Encoder   (b) OR gate

    (c) Flip Flop   (d) Decoder

16. In a program using subroutine call instruction, it is necessary

    (a) initialise program counter   (b) clear the accumulator

    (c) reset the microprocessor   (d) clear the instruction register

17. A Stack-organised Computer uses instruction of

    (a) Indirect addressing   (b) Two-addressing

    (c) Zero addressing   (d) Index addressing

18. An n-bit microprocessor has

    (a) n-bit program counter   (b) n-bit address register

    (c) n-bit ALU   (d) n-bit instruction register

19. A group of bits that tell the computer to perform a specific operation is known as

    (a) Instruction code   (b) Micro-operation

    (c) Accumulator   (d) Register

20. A binary digit is called a

    (a) Bit   (b) Byte

    (c) Number   (d) Character

21. Self-contained sequence of instructions that performs a given computational task called

    (a) Function   (b) Procedure

    (c) Subroutine   (d) Routine

22. Status bit is also called

    (a) Binary bit   (b) Flag bit

    (c) Signed bit   (d) Unsigned bit

23. An address in main memory is called

    (a) Physical address   (b) Logical address

    (c) Memory address   (d) Word address

24. If the value V(x) of the target operand is contained in the address field itself, the addressing mode is

    (a) immediate   (b) direct

    (c) indirect   (d) implied

25. The instructions which copy information from one location to another either in the processor's internal register set or in the external main memory are called......

    (a) Data transfer instructions   (b) Program control instructions

    (c) Input-output instructions   (d) Logical instructions

26. A device/circuit that goes through a predefined sequence of states upon the application of input pulses is called......

    (a) register   (b) flip-flop

    (c) transistor   (d) counter

27. Content of the program counter is added to the address part of the instruction in order toobtain the effective address is called.

    (a) relative address mode   (b) index addressing mode

    (c) register mode   (d) implied mode

28. A register capable of shifting its binary information either to the right or the left is called a......

    (a) parallel register   (b) serial register

    (c) shift register   (d) storage register

29. State True or False A byte is a group of 16 bits.

    (a) True   (b) False

30. A nibble is a group of 16 bits.

    (a) True   (b) False

31. In an operation performed by the ALU, carry bit is set to 1 if the end carry C8 is .... It is cleared to 0 (zero) if the carry is.....................

    (a) One, two   (b) Zero, one

32. A stack organized computer has

    (a) Three-address Instruction   (b) Two-address Instruction

    (c) One-address Instruction   (d) Zero-address Instruction

33. A system program that translates and executes an instruction simultaneously is

    (a) Compiler   (b) Interpreter

    (c) Assembler   (d) Operating system

34. A 32-bit address bus allows access to a memory of capacity......

    (a) 64 Mb   (b) 16 Mb

    (c) 1Gb   (d) 4 Gb

35. Which processor structure is pipelined?

    (a) all x80 processors   (b) all x85 processors

    (c) all x86 processors

36. In 8086 microprocessor one of the following statements is not true.

    (a) Coprocessor is interfaced in MAX mode

    (b) Coprocessor is interfaced in MIN mode

    (c) I/O can be interfaced in MAX / MIN mode

    (d) Supports pipelining

37. The ....ensures that only one IC is active at a time to avoid a bus conflict caused by two ICs writing different data to the same bus.

    (a) control bus   (b) control instructions

    (c) address decoder   (d) CPU

38. The necessary steps carried out to perform the operation of accessing either memory or I/O Device, constitute a ....

    (a) fetch operation   (b) execute operation

    (c) machine cycle   (d) instruction cycle

39. Interfacing devices for DMA controller, programmable interval timer are respectively......

    (a) 8257, 8253   (b) 8253, 8257

    (c) 8257, 8251   (d) 8251, 8257

40. Feature of fetching the next instruction while current instruction is executing called

    (a) Fetching   (b) Executing

    (c) Pipelining   (d) Decoding

41. The process of fetching of next instruction when the current instruction has been executed is called ....

    (a) execution   (b) decoding

    (c) fetching   (d) pipelining

42. A complete transfer operation over the BUS, involving the address and a burst of data is called ....

    (a) Transaction   (b) Transfer

    (c) Move   (d) Procedure

43. The device connected to the BUS are given addresses of..................bit.

    (a) 24   (b) 64   (c) 32   (d) 16

Explanation : Each of the devices connected to the BUS will be allocated an address during the initialisation phase.

44. The PCI BUS has ....interrupt request lines.

    (a) 6   (b) 1   (c) 4   (d) 3

Explanation : The interrupt request lines are used by the devices connected to raise the interrupts.

45. ....signal is sent by the initiator to indicate the duration of the transaction.

    (a) FRAME#   (b) IRDY#

    (c) TMY#   (d) SELD#

Explanation : The FRAME signal is used to indicate the time required by the device.

46.   ....signal is used enable commands.

    (a)   FRAME#   (b)   IRDY#

    (c)   TMY#   (d)   c/BE#

Explanation : The signal is used to enable a 4 command lines.

47. IRDY# signal is used for

    (a)   Selecting the interrupt line

    (b)   Sending an interrupt

    (c)   Saying that the initiator is ready

    (d)   None of the above

Explanation : The initiator transmits this signal to tell the target that it is ready.

48. The signal used to indicate that the slave is ready is....................

    (a)   SLRY#   (b)   TRDY#

    (c)   DSDY#   (d)   None of the above

49. DEVSEL# signal is used

    (a)   To select the device

    (b)   To list all the devices connected

    (c)   By the device to indicate that it is ready for transaction

    (d)   None of the above

Explanation : This is signal is activated by the device after it as recognised the address and commands put on the BUS.

50. The signal used to initiate device select ....

    (a)   IRDY#   (b)   S/BE

    (c)   DEVSEL#   (d)   IDSEL#

Explanation : This signal is used to initialisation of device select.

51. The PCi BUS allowsus to connect ....I/O devices.

    · (a)   21   (b)   13   (c)   9   (d)   11

Explanation : The PCI BUS allows only 21 devices to be connected as only the higher order 21 bits of the 32 bit address space is used to specify the device

52. The PCI follows a set of standards primarily used in ....PC's.

   (a) Intel   (b) Motorola

   (c) IBM   (d) SUN

Explanation : The PCI BUS has a closer resemblance to IBM architecture.

53. The ....is the BUS used in Macintosh PCs.

   (a) NuBUS   (b) EISA

   (c) PCI   (d) None of these

Explanation : The NuBUS is an extension of the processor BUS in Macintosh PC's.

54. The key feature of the PCI BUS is

   (a) Low cost connectivity   (b) Plug and Play capability

   (c) Expansion of Bandwidth   (d) Both (a) and (c)

Explanation : The PCI BUS was the first to introduce plug and play interface for I/O devices.

55. PCI stands for

   (a) Peripheral Component Interconnect

   (b) Peripheral Computer Internet

   (c) Processor Computer Interconnect

   (d) Processor Cable Interconnect

Explanation : The PCI BUS is used as an extension for the processor BUS.

56. The PCI BUS supports ....address space/s.

   (a) I/O   (b) Memory

   (c) Configuration   (d) All of these

Explantion : The PCI BUS is mainly built to provide a wide range of connectivity for devices.

57. ....address space gives the PCI its plug and play capability.

   (a) Configuration   (b) I/O

   (c) Memory   (d) All of these

Explanation : The coniguration address space is used to store the details of the connected device.

58. ....provides a seperate physical connection to the memory.

    (a) PCI BUS   (b) PCI interface

    (c) PCI bridge   (d) Switch circuit

Explanation : The PCI bridge is circuit that acts as a bridge between the BUS and the memory.

59. When transfering data over the PCI BUS, the master as to hold the address till the completion of transfer to the slave.

    (a) True   (b) False

Explanation : The address is stored by the slave in a buffer and hence it is not required by the master to hold it.

60. The master is also called as ....in PCI terminology.

    (a) Initiator   (b) Commander

    (c) Chief   (d) Starter

Explanation : The Master is also called as initiator in PCI terminology as it is the one that initiates a data transfer.

61. Signals whose names end in ....are asserted in the low voltage state.

    (a) $ (b) #

    (c) *   (d) !

62. What is SCSI?

    (a) Small Computer Simple Interface

    (b) System Computer Select Interface

    (c) Small Computer System Interface

    (d) Small Computer System Interconnect

63. Nexus is a relation between

    (a) Initiator and Target

    (b) Initiator, Target and Logical Unit

    (c) Initiator, Target, Logical Unit and Task

    (d) Any of the above

64. Task can constitute

    (a) One command only

    (b) One or more commands

    (c) A single command or group of linked commands

    (d) Linked Commands Only

65. Task manager

    (a) Manages the devices   (b) Manages tasks

    (c) Both (a) and (b)   (d) None of the above

66. Untagged task is represented by

    (a) I-T nexus   (b) I-T-L nexus

    (c) I-T-L-Q nexus   (d) None of these

67. Which is not the main phase of I/O?

    (a) Data   (b) Command

    (c) Status   (d) Control

68. Which of the following is false?

    (a) CDB has a operation code   (b) CDB has a control byte

    (c) Both (a) and (b)   (d) None of the above

69. What is incorrect about Command Descriptor block?

    (a) It has SCSI command

    (b) Has fixed length of 6, 10, 12 or 16 bytes

    (c) Target fetches CDB from initiator

    (d) The CDB is sent during Data Phase

70. What is a Logical Unit?

    (a) subset of Target device   (b) subset of Initiator

    (c) Subset of Device Server   (d) Component of Interface

71. Which of them is not a valid SCSI command?

    (a) Bus Reset   (b) Inquiry

    (c) Mode Sense   (d) Read_10

Unit 4 | 4.65

72. SCSI stands for

    (a)   Small Computer System Interface.

    (b)   Switch Computer system Interface.

    (c)   Small Component System Interface.

    (d)   None of the above.

Explanation : The SCSI BUS is one of the expansion BUSes used in a system.

73. ANSI stands for

    (a)   American National System Interface.

    (b)   ASCII National Standard Interface.

    (c)   American Network System Interface.

    (d)   American National Standard Institute.

Explanation : This a standard for designing BUSes and other system components.

74. A narrow SCSI BUS has ....data lines.

    (a)   6   (b)   8   (c)   16   (d)   4

Explanation : The SCSI BUS which is narrow is capable of transfering 8 bits of data at a time.

75. Single ended transmission means

    (a)   That all the signals have a similar bit pattern.

    (b)   That the signals have a common source.

    (c)   That the signals have a common ground return.

    (d)   That the signals have a similar voltage signature.

Explanation : These type of signals are a common feature of the SCSI BUS.

76. HVD stands for

    (a)   High Voltage Differential   (b)   High Voltage Density

    (c)   High Video Definition   (d)   None of the above

Explanation : This is a type of signaling which uses 5v of current.

77. For better transfer rates on the SCSI BUS the length of the cable is limited to ....
    (a)   2 m   (b)   4 m   (c)   1.3 m   (d)   1.6 m

Explanation : To increase the transmission rate in SCSI in SE mode of transfer the wire length is restricted to 1.6 m.

78. The maximum number of devices that can be connected to SCSI BUS is ....

    (a) 12   (b) 10   (c) 16   (d) 8

79. THe SCSI BUS is connected to the processor through ....

    (a) SCSI Controller   (b) Bridge

    (c) Switch   (d) None of these

Explanation : This is used to co-ordinate and monitor the data transfer over the BUS.

80. The mode of data transfer used by the controller is ....

    (a) Interrupt   (b) DMA

    (c) Asynchronous   (d) Synchronous

81. The data is stored on the disk in the form of blocks called ....

    (a) Pages   (b) Frames

    (c) Sectors   (d) Tables

Explanation: The data is stored on the disk in the form of a collection of blocks called as sectors.

82. The key features of the SCSI BUS is

    (a) The cost effective connective media.

    (b) The ability overlap data transfer requests.

    (c) The highly effecient data transmission.

    (d) None of the above.

Explanation: The SCSI BUS can overlap various data transfer requests by the devices.

83. In a data transfer operatioon involving SCSI BUS, the control is with _____.

    (a) Initiator   (b) Target

    (c) SCSI controller   (d) Target Controller

Explanation : The initiator involves in arbitration process and after winning the BUS it will handover the control to the target controller.

84. In SCSI transfers the processor is not aware of the data being transfered.

    (a) True   (b) False

Explanation: The processor or the controller is unaware of the data being transfered.

85. The DB(P) line means ......

    (a) That the data line is carrying the device information.

    (b) That the data line is carrying the parity information.

    (c) That the data line is partly closed.

    (d) That the data line is temporarily occupied.

86. The BSY signal signifies

    (a) The BUs is busy   (b) The controller is busy

    (c) The initiator is busy   (d) The target is Busy

Explanation : This signal is generally initiated when the BUS is currently occupied in an operation.

87. The SEL signal signifies

    (a) The initiator is selected.

    (b) The device for BUS control is selected.

    (c) That the target is being selected.

    (d) None of the above.

Explanation : This signal is usually asserted during the selection or reselection process.

88. ....signal is asserted when the initiator wishes to send a message to the target.

    (a) MSG   (b) APP
    (c) SMS   (d) ATN

Explanation: The ATN signal is short for attention, which is used to initimate the target that the initiator sent a message to it.

89. The MSG signal is used

    (a) To send a message to the target.

    (b) To recieve a message from the mailbox.

    (c) To tell that the information being sent is a message.

    (d) None of these.

90. ....is used to reset all the device controls to their startup state.
    (a) SRT   (b) RST
    (c) ATN   (d) None of the above

91. The SCSI BUS uses _____ arbitration.

(a) Distributed   (b) Centralised

(c) Daisy chain   (d) Hybrid

Explanation : The SCSI uses distributed arbitration to select the device to give the BUS control.

92. How many ports a computer may have ?

(a) 256   (b) 128   (c) 65535   (d) 1024

93. Which is the type of port ?

(a) Serial   (b) Parallel

(c) AGP   (d) All of these

94. Parallel port can transfer ....bits of data at a time.

(a) 2   (b) 4   (c) 8   (d) 16

95. Parallel Port can not connect......

(a) Printers   (b) Scanners

(c) Telephones   (d) Monitors

96. In computer which range is in registered ports ?

(a) 0 to 1023   (b) 1024 to 49151

(c) 49151 to 65535   (d) None of these

97. USB stands for:

(a) United Serial Bus   (b) Universal Serial By-Pass

(c) Universal System Bus   (d) Universal Serial Bus

98. Which is the fastest port for data transfer ?

(a) USB   (b) Serial

(c) Parallel   (d) FireWire

99. An interface that provides a method for transferring binary information between internal storage and external devices is called

(a) I/O interface   (b) Input interface

(c) Output interface   (d) I/O bus

100. An address in main memory is called DC-04 COMPUTER ORGANIZATION.

    (a) Physical address   (b) Logical address

    (c) Memory address   (d) Word address

101. The instructions which copy information from one location to another either in the processor's internal register set or in the external main memory are called

    (a) Data transfer instructions   (b) Program control instructions

    (c) Input-output instructions   (d) Logical instructions

102. A device/circuit that goes through a predefined sequence of states upon the application of input pulses is called

    (a) register   (b) flip-flop

    (c) transistor   (d) counter

103. An interface that provides I/O transfer of data directly to and form the memory unit and peripheral is termed as

    (a) DD (A)   (b) Serial interface.

    (c) BR.   (d) DM (A)

104. Buffering is done to ......

    (a) cope with device speed mismatch

    (b) cope with device transfer size mismatch

    (c) maintain copy semantics

    (d) all of these

105. Caching is _____ spooling.

    (a) same as   (b) not the same as   (c) none of these

106. Caching : (choose all that apply)

    (a) holds a copy of the data   (b) is fast memory

    (c) holds the only copy of the data   (d) holds output for a device

107. The ...... keeps state information about the use of I/O components.

    (a) CPU   (b) OS

    (c) kernel   (d) shell

108. The kernel data structures include ......

(a)   process table   (b)   open file table

(c)   close file table   (d)   All of these

109. Windows NT uses a ....implementation for I/O.........

(a)   message – passing   (b)   draft – passing

(c)   secondary memory   (d)   cache

110. A ....is a full duplex connection between a device driver and a user level process.

(a)   bus   (b)   I/O operation

(c)   stream   (d)   flow

111. I/O is a ....in system performance.

(a)   major factor   (b)   minor factor

(c)   does not matter   (d)   none of these

112. If the number of cycles spent busy – waiting is not excessive, then :

(a)   interrupt driven I/O is more efficient than programmed I/O

(b)   programmed I/O is more efficient than interrupt driven I/O

(c)   both programmed and interrupt driven I/O are equally efficient

(d)   none of these

113. Which is an important data transfer technique :

(a)   CPU   (b)   DMA

(c)   CAD   (d)   None of these

114. Which device can be thought of as transducers which can sense physical effects and convert them into machine-tractable data ?

(a)   Storage devices   (b)   Peripheral devices

(c)   Both   (d)   None

115. Which devices are usually designed on the complex electromechanical principle ?

(a)   Storage devices   (b)   Peripheral devices

(c)   Input devices   (d)   All of these

116. NAND type flash memory data storage devices integrated with a ....interface.

(a)   ATM   (b)   LAN

(c)   USB   (d)   DBMS

117. The human-interactive I/O devices can be further categorized as___:

    (a) Direct   (b) Indirect

    (c) Both   (d) None

118. I/O devices are categorized in 2 parts are ......

    (a) Character devices   (b) Block devices

    (c) Numeral devices   (d) Both (a) and (b)

119. Which are following pointing devices ?

    (a) Light pen   (b) Joystick

    (c) Mouse   (d) All of these

120. _____interface is an entity that controls data transfer from external device, main memory and or CPU registers.

    (a) I/O interface   (b) CPU interface

    (c) Input interface   (d) Output interface

121. The operating mode of I/O devices is.........for different device.

    (a) Same   (b) Different

    (c) Optimum   (d) Medium

122. To resolve problems of I/O devices there is a special hardware component between CPU and.........to supervise and synchronize all input output transfers.

    (a) Software   (b) Hardware

    (c) Peripheral   (d) None of these

123. I/O modules are designed with aims to

    (a) Achieve device independence

    (b) Handle errors

    (c) Speed up transfer of data

    (d) Handle deadlocks

    (e) Enable multi-user systems to use dedicated device

    (f) All of these

124. IDE is a_____ controller.

    (a) Disk   (b) Floppy

    (c) Hard   (d) None of these

125. In devices, controller is used for.........

    (a) Buffering the data   (b) Manipulate the data

    (c) Calculate the data   (d) Input the data

126. By which signal flow of traffic between internal and external devices is done.........

    (a) Only control signal   (b) Only timing signal

    (c) Control and timing signal   (d) None of these

127. In devices 2 status reporting signals are ....

    (a) BUSY   (b) READY

    (c) Both (a) and (b)   (d) None of these

128. I/O module must recognize a.........address for each peripheral it controls:

    (a) Long   (b) Same

    (c) Unique   (d) Bigger

129. Each interaction between CPU and I/O module involves:

    (a) Bus arbitration   (b) Bus revolution

    (c) Data bus   (d) Control signals

130. Which are four types of commands received by an interface:

    (a) Control, status, data output, data input

    (b) Only data input

    (c) Control, flag, data output, address arbitration

    (d) Data input, data output, status bit, decoder

131. Two ways in which computer buses can communicate with memory in case of I/O devices by using:

    (a) Separate buses for memory and I/O device

    (b) Common bus for memory and I/O device

    (c) both (a) and (b)

    (d) none of these

132. There are two ways in which addressing can be done in memory and I/O device:

    (a) Isolated I/O   (b) Memory-mapped I/O

    (c) Both (a) and (b)   (d) None of these

133. Advantages of isolated I/O are:

   (a) Commonly usable   (b) Small number of I/O instructions

   (c) Both (a) and (b)   (d) None of these

134. In _____ addressing technique separate address space is used for both memory and I/O device:

   (a) Memory-mapped I/O   (b) Isolated I/O

   (c) Both (a) and (b)   (d) None of these

135. _____is a single address space for storing both memory and I/O devices:

   (a) Memory-mapped I/O   (b) Isolated I/O

   (c) Separate I/O   (d) Optimum I/O

136. Following are the disadvantages of memory-mapped I/O are:

   (a) Valuable memory address space used up

   (b) I/O module register treated as memory addresses

   (c) Same machine intersection used to access both memory and I/O device

   (d) All of these

137. Who determine the address of I/O interface:

   (a) Register select   (b) Chip select

   (c) Both (a) and (b)   (d) None of these

138. Two control lines in I/O interface is ......

   (a) RD, WR   (b) RD,DATA

   (c) WR, DATA   (d) RD, MEMORY

139. In I/O interface RS1 and RS0 are used for selecting ?

   (a) Memory   (b) Register

   (c) CPU   (d) Buffer

140. If CPU and I/O interface share a common bus than transfer of data b/w 2 units is said to be......

   (a) Synchronous   (b) Asynchronous

   (c) Clock dependent   (d) Decoder independent

141. All the operations in a digital system are synchronized by a clock that is generated by ......

    (a) Clock   (b) Pulse

    (c) Pulse generator   (d) Bus

142. Asynchronous means:

    (a) Not in step with the elapse of address

    (b) Not in step with the elapse of control

    (c) Not in step with the elapse of data

    (d) Not in step with the elapse of time

143. _____is a single control line that informs destination unit that a valid is available on the bus.

    (a) Strobe   (b) Handshaking

    (c) Synchronous   (d) Asynchronous

144. Which refers the execution of various software process concurrently ?

    (a) Multiprocessor   (b) Serial communication

    (c) DCP   (d) IOP

145. What is disadvantage of strobe scheme ?

    (a) No surety that destination received data before source removes it

    (b) Destination unit transfer without knowing whether source placed data on data bus

    (c) Can not said

    (d) Both (a) and (b)

146. In......technique has 1 or more control signal for acknowledgement that is used for intimation.

    (a) Handshaking   (b) Strobe

    (c) Both (a) and (b)   (d) None of these

147. The keyboard has a......asynchronous transfer mode.

    (a) Parallel   (b) Serial

    (c) Optimum   (d) None

148. In ......transfer each bit is sent one after the another in a sequence of event and requires just one line.

    (a) Serial   (b) Parallel

    (c) Both (a) and (b)   (d) None of these

149. Modes of transfer between computer and I/O device are:

    (a) Programmed I/O

    (b) Interrupt-initiated I/O

    (c) DMA

    (d) Dedicated processor such as IOP and DCP

    (e) All of these

150. ......operations are the results of I/O operations that are written in the computer program.

    (a) Programmed I/O   (b) DMA

    (c) Handshaking   (d) Strobe

151. ......is a dedicated processor that combines interface unit and DMA as one unit.

    (a) Input-Output Processor   (b) Only input processor

    (c) Only output processor   (d) None of these

152. ......is a special purpose dedicated processor that is designed specially designed for data transfer in network.

    (a) Data Processor   (b) Data Communication Processor

    (c) DMA Processor   (d) Interrupt Processor

153. ......processor has to check continuously till device becomes ready for transferring the data.

    (a) Interrupt-initiated I/O   (b) DMA

    (c) IOP   (d) DCP

154. Interrupt-driven I/O data transfer technique is based on......concept.

    (a) On demand processing   (b) Off demand processing

    (c) Both (a) and (b)   (d) None of these

155. Which technique helps processor to run a program concurrently with I/O operations?

   (a) Interrupt driven I/O   (b) DMA

   (c) IOP   (d) DCP

156. Three types of exceptions are ......

   (a) Interrupts   (b) Traps

   (c) System calls   (d) All of these

157. Which exception is also called software interrupt ?

   (a) Interrupt   (b) System calls

   (c) Traps   (d) All of these

158. User programs interact with I/O devices through ......

   (a) Operating system   (b) Hardware

   (c) CPU   (d) Microprocessor

159. Which table handle store address of interrupt handling subroutine ?

   (a) Interrupt vector table   (b) Vector table

   (c) Symbol link table   (d) None of these

160. Which technique is used that identifies the highest priority resource by means of software ?

   (a) Daisy chaining   (b) Polling

   (c) Priority   (d) Chaining

161. ......interrupt establishes a priority over the various sources to determine which request should be entertained first.

   (a) Priority interrupt   (b) Polling

   (c) Daisy chaining   (d) None of these

162. ......method is used to establish priority by serially connecting all devices that request an interrupt.

   (a) Polling   (b) Daisy chaining

   (c) Priority   (d) None of these

163. In daisy chaining device 0 will pass signal only if it has:

   (a) Interrupt request   (b) No interrupt request

   (c) Both (a) and (b)   (d) None of these

164. VAD stands for

    (a) Vector address   (b) Symbol address

    (c) Link address   (d) None of these

165. ......interrupt method uses a register whose bits are set separately by interrupt signal for each device:

    (a) Parallel priority interrupt   (b) Serial priority interrupt

    (c) Both (a) and (b)   (d) None of these

166. ......register is used whose purpose is to control status of each interrupt request in parallel priority interrupt.

    (a) Mass   (b) Mark

    (c) Make   (d) Mask

167. Data communication with a remote device a special data communication is used......

    (a) Multiprocessor   (b) Serial communication

    (c) DCP   (d) IOP

168. Which is commonly used in high speed devices to realize full efficiency of communication link ?

    (a) Transmission   (b) Synchronous communication

    (c) Multiprocessor   (d) All of these

169. Multiprocessor use ......than two CPUs assembled in single system unit.

    (a) One or More   (b) Two or More

    (c) One or two   (d) Two or three

ANSWERS

1.	a	2.	d	3.	a	4.	a	5.	a
6.	a	7.	a	8.	d	9.	a	10.	b
11.	d	12.	c	13.	c	14.	b	15.	c
16.	d	17.	c	18.	d	19.	a	20.	a
21.	a	22.	b	23.	a	24.	b	25.	a
26.	d	27.	a	28.	c	29.	b	30.	b

31.	a	32.	d	33.	c	34.	d	35.	c
36.	b	37.	c	38.	c	39.	a	40.	c
41.	d	42.	a	43.	b	44.	c	45.	a
46.	d	47.	c	48.	b	49.	c	50.	d
51.	a	52.	c	53.	a	54.	b	55.	a
56.	d	57.	a	58.	c	59.	b	60.	a
61.	b	62.	c	63.	d	64.	c	65.	b
66.	b	67.	d	68.	d	69.	d	70.	a
71.	a	72.	a	73.	d	74.	b	75.	c
76.	a	77.	d	78.	c	79.	a	80.	b
81.	c	82.	b	83.	d	84.	a	85.	b
86.	a	87.	b	88.	d	89.	c	90.	b
91.	a	92.	c	93.	d	94.	c	95.	d
96.	b	97.	d	98.	d	99.	a	100.	a
101.	a	102.	d	103.	d	104.	d	105.	b
106.	a, b	107.	c	108.	b	109.	a	110.	c
111.	a	112.	b	113.	b	114.	b	115.	c
116.	c	117.	c	118.	d	119.	d	120.	a
121.	b	122.	c	123.	f	124.	a	125.	a
126.	c	127.	c	128.	c	129.	a	130.	a
131.	c	132.	c	133.	c	134.	b	135.	a
136.	d	137.	c	138.	a	139.	b	140.	a
141.	c	142.	d	143.	a	144.	a	145.	d
146.	a	147.	b	148.	a	149.	e	150.	a
151.	a	152.	b	153.	a	154.	a	155.	a
156.	d	157.	b	158.	a	159.	a	160.	b
161.	a	162.	b	163.	b	164.	a	165.	a
166.	d	167.	b	168.	b	169.	b		

Questions

1. Compare programmed Input/output and Interrupt driven Input/output.

   [May 05, 6 Marks]

2. What is an interrupt? How does CPU recognize an interrupt? What is the response of the CPU after recognition of the interrupt? **[May 05, 6 Marks]**

3. What is the difference between subroutine and interrupt service routine ?

   [May 05, 4 Marks]

4. Explain asynchronous bus in an input operation with timing diagram.

   [May 05, 8 Marks]

5. Draw and explain typical DMA block diagram and explain cycle stealing.

   [May 05, 8 Marks]

6. Discuss with suitable example programmed Input/output and interrupt driven Input/output. **[Dec 05, 6 Marks]**

7. What is an Input/output channel? Explain with suitable diagram three types of Input/output channel. **[Dec 05, 10 Marks]**

8. Discuss with suitable diagram how DMA is used to transfer a block of data From FDO to main memory. **[Dec 05, 8 Marks]**

9. Discuss in detail methods used for Input/output addressing. **[Dec 05, 8 Marks]**

10. What is DMA? Explain DMA operation with diagram. What is single transfer mode and block transfer mode? **[May 06, 10 Marks]**

11. Explain PCI bus with a diagram. **[May 06, 6 Marks]**

12. Explain the synchronous bus in an input operation with timing diagram.

    [May 06, 8 Marks]

13. Compare programmed Input/output and interrupt driven Input/output. Which is advantageous and why? **[May 06, 8 Marks]**

14. Explain the synchronous bus in an output operation with timing diagram.

    [Dec 06, 8 Marks]

15. Explain the feature of USB. Also give details of USB connector with the Diagram.

[Dec 06, 8 Marks]

16. Explain DMA operation with diagram. Also explain data transfer modes in DMA.

[Dec 06, 8 Marks]

17. What are the three types of Input/Output channels? Explain with a suitable Example.

[Dec 06, 8 Marks]

18. What is an Input/Output channel? Explain with suitable diagram types of Input / output channels.   **[May 07, 10 Marks]**

19. Explain PCI bus with a diagram.   **[May 07, 6 Marks]**

20. Compare programmed Input/Output and interrupt driven Input/Output.

[May 07, 6 Marks]

21. Explain synchronous and asynchronous bus in an input operation with timing diagram.   **[May 07, 10 Marks]**

22. Explain the synchronous bus in an output operation with timing diagram.

[Dec 07, 8 Marks]

23. Explain the encoding method used by the USB. Also give any four USB Commands.

[Dec 07, 8 Marks]

24. Compare programmed I/O and interrupt I/O. What is advantageous ? Explain.

[Dec 07, 8 Marks]

25. Discuss the following terms:
    (i) Programmed I/O   **[May 08, 4 Marks]**
    (ii) Interrupt I/O   **[May 08, 4 Marks]**

26. Explain briefly the following bus standards.
    (i) PCI   **[May 08, 4 Marks]**
    (ii) SCSI   **[May 08, 4 Marks]**

27. Explain with suitable diagram types of I/O channels.   **[May 08, 8 Marks]**

28. What are the different bus standards used in computers ? Explain any one in brief.

[Dec 08, 8 Marks]

29. What is DMA? With a neat block schematic explain how it is used for Data transfer.

[Dec 08, 8 Marks]

30. Write a short note on interrupt driven Input/output.   **[Dec 08, 8 Marks]**

31. Explain synchronous and asynchronous bus in an input operation with timing diagram.   **[May 09, 10 Marks]**

32. Compare programmed I/O and interrupt driven I/O.   **[May 09, 6 Marks]**

33. Explain with suitable diagram types of I/O channel.   **[May 09, 8 Marks]**

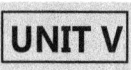
MEMORY ORGANIZATION

5.1 CHARACTERISTICS OF MEMORY SYSTEMS [Dec. 06]

5.1.1 Hierarchy of Storage

Primary storage, presently known as **memory**, is the only one directly accessible to the CPU. The CPU continuously reads instructions stored there and executes them as required. Any data actively operated on is also stored there in uniform manner.

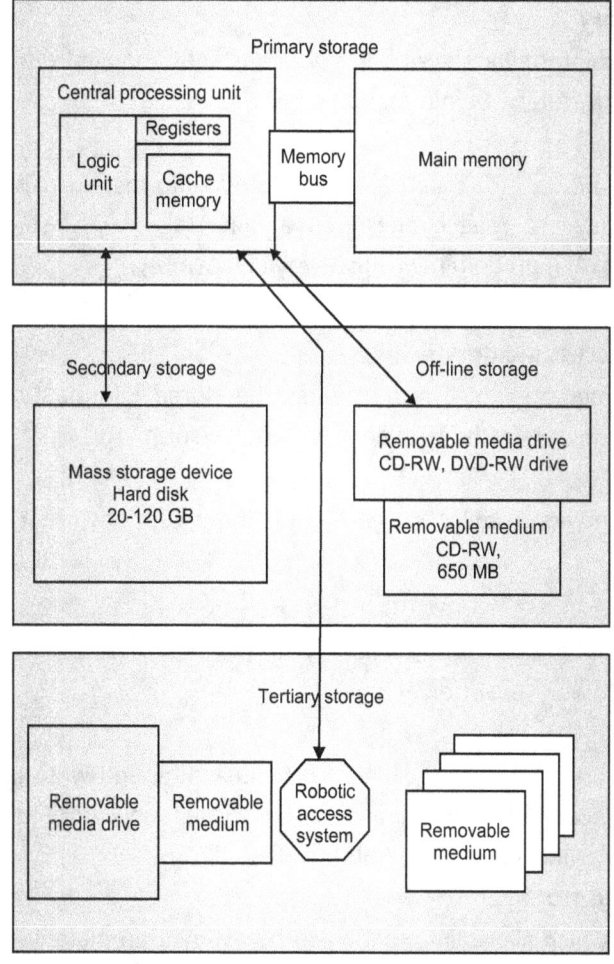

Fig. 5.1 : Computer storage types

Secondary storage in popular usage differs from primary storage in that it is not directly accessible by the CPU. The computer usually uses its input/output channels to access secondary storage and transfers the desired data using intermediate area in primary storage. Secondary storage does not lose the data when the device is powered down, it is non-volatile.

Tertiary storage : Typically, it involves a robotic mechanism which will mount (insert) and dismount removable mass storage media into a storage device according to the system's demands; this data is often copied to secondary storage before use. Off line storage contains CD-RW, DVD-RW drive.

5.1.2 Characteristics of Storage

➢ **Volatility**

Non-volatile memory

Will retain the stored information even if it is not constantly supplied with electric power. It is suitable for long-term storage of information.

Volatile memory

Requires constant power to maintain the stored information. The fastest memory technologies of today are volatile ones (not a universal rule). Since primary storage is required to be very fast, it predominantly uses volatile memory.

➢ **Differentiation**

Dynamic random access memory

A form of volatile memory which also requires the stored information to be periodically re-read and re-written, or refreshed, otherwise it would vanish.

Static memory

A form of volatile memory similar to DRAM with the exception that it never needs to be refreshed.

➢ **Mutability**

Read/write storage or mutable storage.

Allows information to be overwritten at any time.

Read Only Storage

Retains the information stored at the time of manufacture, and write once storage (Write Once Read Many) allows the information to be written only once at some point after manufacture. Examples include CD-ROM and CD-R.

Slow write, fast read storage

Read/write storage which allows information to be overwritten multiple times, but with the write operation being much slower than the read operation.

Examples include CD-RW and flash memory.

> **Accessibility**

Random access : Any location in storage can be accessed at any moment in approximately the same amount of time. Such characteristic is well suited for primary and secondary storage.

Sequential access : The accessing of pieces of information will be in a serial order, therefore the time to access a particular piece of information depends upon which piece of information was last accessed.

> **Addressability**

Location-addressable

Each individually accessible unit of information in storage is selected with its numerical memory address.

File addressable

Information is divided into files of variable length, and a particular file is selected with human-readable directory and file names.

Content-addressable

Each individually accessible unit of information is selected with a hash value, or a short identifier with a number pertaining to the memory address the information is stored on.

> **Capacity**

Raw capacity

The total amount of stored information that a storage device or medium can hold. It is expressed as a quantity of bits or bytes (e.g. 10.4 mega bytes).

> **Performance**

Latency

The time it takes to access a particular location in storage. Throughput

The rate at which information can be read from or written to the storage. In computer data storage, throughput is usually expressed in terms of megabytes per second or MB/s.

> **Environmental Impact**

The impact of a storage device on the environment.

Energy

Storage devices that reduce fan usage, automatically shut-down during inactivity, and low power hard drives can reduce energy consumption 90 per cent.

> **Manufacturing**

- The amount of raw materials (metals, aluminum, plastics, lead) used to manufacture the device.
- Chemicals used in manufacturing.
- Shipping distance for the device itself and parts.
- Amount of packaging materials and if they are recyclable.

5.1.3 Characteristics of Main/Internal Memory

- Closely connected to the processor.
- Holds the programs and data the processor is actively using.
- Interacts with processor millions of times per second.
- Contents are easily changed.
- Relatively low capacity.
- Fast access.

5.1.4 How Memory Works ?

Programs and data files are stored as binary numbers. Binary is made up of just 0's or 1's.

To **store** the **0**'s and **1**'s while the computer is running you need a memory chip. This is made up of millions of tiny electrical switches called transistors. They can store a **0** or a **1** by the 'switch' being either **open** or **closed**. This **0** or **1** is the simplest unit of memory and is called a **'bit'** (Binary Digit).

Bits are arranged in units of eight to make a **byte**. One byte can therefore store eight **0**'s or **1**'s in **256** different combinations

One byte is a very small amount of memory and it is more usual to refer to **kilobytes (kB)**, **megabytes (MB)** and **gigabytes (GB)**.

$$1 \text{ kB} = 1024 \text{ bytes (approximately 1 thousand bytes)}$$
$$1 \text{ MB} = 1024 \text{ KB (approximately 1 million bytes)}$$
$$1 \text{ GB} = 1024 \text{ MB (approximately 1 thousand million bytes)}$$

5.2 INTERNAL MEMORY

All computers have **main/internal memory** chips to store programs and data while the computer is running.

Semiconductor Main Memory :

The basic element of a semiconductor memory is the memory cell.

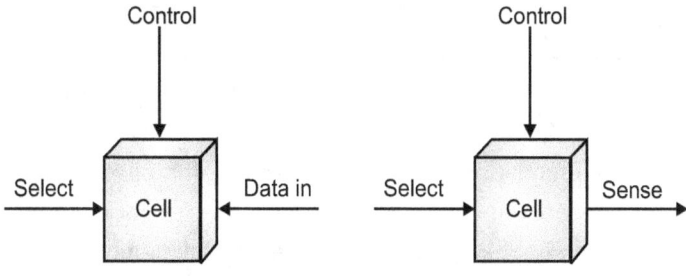

Fig. 5.2 : Memory cell operation

Fig. 5.2 shows the operation of a memory cell. The cell has three functional terminals capable of carrying an electrical signal. The select terminal selects a memory cell for a read or writes operation. The control terminal indicates a read or writes.

For writing third terminal (data in) provides an electrical signal that sets the state of cell 1 or 0. For reading, third terminal (sense) is used for output of the cells state. There are a lot of semiconductor memory types shown in table 5.1

Table 5.1 : Semiconductor Memory Types

Memory Type	Category	Erasure	Write Mechanism	Volatility
Random Access Memory (RAM)	Read-write memory	Electrically byte level	Electrically	Volatile
Read Only Memory (ROM)	Read-only memory	Not possible	Masks	
Programmable ROM (PROM)				
Erasable PROM (EPROM)		UV light chip level		
Electrically Erasable, PROM (EEPROM)	Read-mostly memory	Electrically byte level	Electrically	Non-volatile
Flash memory		Electrically, block level		

Two Types of Internal Memory : 1. RAM 2. ROM.

5.3 EXTERNAL MEMORY

External memory which is sometimes called backing store or secondary memory, allows the permanent storage of large quantities of data.

Magnetic discs are the foundation of external memory for all computer systems. RAID (Redundant array of independent discs) also works as an external memory. An increasingly important component of computer systems is external optical memory.

5.4 TYPES OF MEMORIES

5.4.1 ROM Internal Memory

ROM (**R**ead **O**nly **M**emory) chips are described as non-volatile, the contents cannot be changed by a program or user and are **not lost** when the computer is switched-off. They are used to store the programs used to start the hardware running (an example is the BIOS chip which permanently stores the software needed to start a computer's hardware and operating system). There are several types of ROM that can be written for read, erased and written to with new data.

ROM is the memory which is available to the user only for the purpose of reading information from it. One cannot write quite often into ROM. ROM contains special software, often called the BIOS (Basic Input Output System) that manages the communication between hardware and other critical information you need to start and use your computer. Unlike a computers random access memory (RAM), the data in ROM is not lost when the computer power is turned-off. ROM is referred to as being non-volatile, whereas RAM is volatile. The information in ROM is coded by the computer manufacturer and you cannot easily change it. The ROM is sustained by a small long-life battery in your computer.

ROM chips are used not only in computers. In addition, ROMs are used extensively in calculators and peripheral devices such as laser printers.

- **ROM for program storage :**
  1. Most home computers of the 1980s stored a BASIC interpreter or operating system in ROM as other forms of non-volatile storage such as magnetic disk drives were too expensive.
  2. In modern PCs, "ROM" (or Flash) is used to store the basic bootstrapping firmware for the main processor, as well as the various firmware needed to internally control self contained devices such as graphic cards, hard disks, DVD drives, TFT screens etc, in the system.
  3. ROM is also useful for binary storage of cryptographic data, as it makes them difficult to replace, which may be desirable in order to enhance information security.

- **ROM for data storage :**

Since ROM (at least in hard-wired mask form) cannot be modified, it is really only suitable for storing data which is not expected to need modification for the life of the device. To that end, ROM has been used in many computers to store look-up tables for the evaluation of mathematical and logical functions. This was especially effective when CPUs were slow and ROM was cheap compared to RAM.

The use of ROM to store such small amounts of data has disappeared almost completely in modern general-purpose computers. However, Flash ROM has taken over a new role as a medium for mass storage or secondary storage of files.

- **Speed of ROMs**

Reading speed :

RAM chips can be read faster than most ROMs. For this reason, ROM content is sometimes copied to RAM before its first use, and subsequently read from RAM.

Writing speed :

For those types of ROM that can be electrically modified, writing speed is always much slower than reading speed, and it may require unusually high voltage Modern NAND Flash achieves the highest write speeds of any rewritable ROM technology.

- **How ROM Works ?**

Similar to RAM, ROM chips contain a grid of columns and rows. But where the columns and rows intersect, ROM chips are fundamentally different from RAM chips. While RAM uses transistors to turn on or off access to a capacitor at each intersection,

ROM uses a **diode** to connect the lines if the value is 1. If the value is 0, then the lines are not connected at all.

A diode normally allows current to flow in only one direction and has a certain threshold, known as the forward break over, that determines how much current is required before the diode will pass it on. In silicon-based items such as processors and memory chips, the forward break over voltage is approximately 0.6 volts. By taking advantage of the unique properties of a diode, a ROM chip can send a charge that is above the forward break over down the appropriate column with the selected row grounded to connect at a specific cell. If a diode is present at that cell, the charge will be conducted through to the ground, and, under the binary system, the cell will be read as being "on" (a value of 1). The neat part of ROM is that if the cell's value is 0, there is no diode at that intersection to connect the column and row. So the charge on the column does not get transferred to the row.

As you can see, the way a ROM chip works necessitates the programming of perfect and complete data when the chip is created. You cannot reprogram or rewrite a standard ROM chip. If it is incorrect, or the data needs to be updated, you have to throw it away and start over.

Once the template is completed, the actual chips can cost as little as a few cents each. They use very little power, are extremely reliable and, in the case of most small electronic devices, contain all the necessary programming to control the device.

- **Types of ROMs**

Each type has unique characteristics, but they are all types of memory with two things in common :

Data stored in these chips is non-volatile - it is not lost when power is removed.

Data stored in these chips is either unchangeable or requires a special operation to change (Unlike RAM, which can be changed as easily as it is read).

This means that removing the power source from the chip will not cause it to lose any data.

5.4.1.1 PROM

Programmable Read-Only Memory (PROM), or **One-Time programmable ROM** (OTP), (allowed users to program its contents exactly once by physically altering its structure) can be written to or **programmed** via a special device called a PROM **programmer**. Typically, this device uses high voltages to permanently destroy or create internal links within the chip. Consequently, a PROM can only be programmed once.

This addressed problems, since a company can simply order a large batch of fresh PROM chips and program them with the desired contents at its designer's convenience.

Creating ROM chips totally from scratch is time consuming and very expensive in small quantities. For this reason, mainly, developers created a type of ROM known as programmable read only memory (PROM). Blank PROM chips can be bought inexpensively and coded by anyone with a special tool called a programmer.

PROM chips have a grid of columns and rows just as ordinary ROMs.

The difference is that every intersection of a column and row in a PROM chip has a fuse connecting them. A change sent through a column will pass through the fuse in a cell to a grounded row indicating a value of 1. Since all the cells have a fuse, the initial (blank) state of a PROM chip is all 1 s. Since all these value of a cell to 0, you use a programmer to send a specific amount of current to the cell. The higher voltage breaks the connection between the column and row by burning out the fuse. This process is known as burning the PROM.

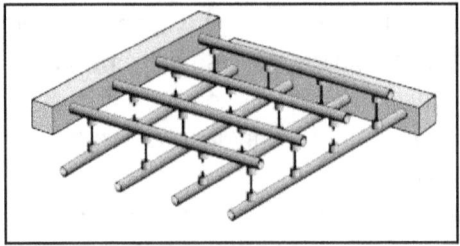

Fig. 5.3 : PROM

Advantages :

- Reliability.
- Stores data permanently.
- Moderate price.
- Built using integrated circuits, rather than discrete components.
- Fast : reading is between 35 ns and 60 ns.

Disadvantages :

- PROM can only be programmed once.
- Uses high voltages to permanently destroy

5.4.1.2 EPROM (Erasable Programmable Read-Only Memory)

Working with ROMs and PROMs can be a wasteful business. Even though they are inexpensive per chip, the cost can add up over time. **Erasable Programmable Read-Only Memory** (EPROM) addresses this issue. EPROM chips can be rewritten many times. To write an EPROM, you must first erase it. Erasing an EPROM requires a special tool that emits a certain frequency of ultraviolet (UV) light. EPROMs are configured using an EPROM programmer that provides voltage at specified levels depending on the type of EPROM used. Repeated exposure to UV light will eventually wear out an EPROM.

An EPROM eraser is not selective; it will erase the entire EPROM. The EPROM must be removed from the device it is in and placed under the UV light of the EPROM eraser for several minutes. An EPROM that is left under too long can become **over-erased**.

However, more modern types such as EPROM and flash EEPROM can be erased and re-programmed multiple times; they are still described as "read-only memory" (ROM) because the reprogramming process is generally infrequent, comparatively slow, and often does not permit random access writes to individual memory locations.

Once again we have a grid of columns and rows. In an EPROM, the cell at each intersection has two transistors. The two transistors are separated from each other by a thin oxide layer. One of the transistors is known as the floating gate and the other as the control gate. The floating gate's only link to the row (word line) is through the control gate. As long as this link is in place, the cell has a value of 1. To change the value to 0 requires a curious process called Fowler-Nordheim tunneling. Tunneling is used to alter the placement of electrons in the floating gate. An electrical charge, usually 10 to 13 volts, is applied to the floating gate. The charge comes from the column (bitline), enters the floating gate and drains to a ground.

This charge causes the floating-gate transistor to act like an electron gun. The excited electrons are pushed through and trapped on the other side of the thin oxide layer, giving it a negative charge. These negatively charged electrons act as a barrier between the control gate and the floating gate. A device called a cell sensor monitors the level of the charge passing through the floating gate. If the flow through the gate is greater than 50 percent of the charge, it has a value of 1. When the charge passing through drops below the 50 percent threshold, the value changes to 0. A blank EPROM has all of the gates fully open, giving each cell a value of 1. The write under each address bit the logic level that must be on that line to address the first location in the first EPROM.

Advantages :

1. It is Erasable PROM .
2. It can be rewritten after erasing.

Disadvantages :

1. EPROM eraser is not selective.
2. To erase, you must supply a high frequency of UV light.
3. Repeated exposure to UV light will eventually wear out an EPROM,
4. Reprogramming process is generally infrequent, comparatively slow, and often does not permit random access writes to individual memory locations.
5. They still require dedicated equipment and a labor-intensive process to remove and reinstall them each time a change is necessary.

5.4.1.3 EEPROM (Electrically Erasable Programmable Read-Only Memory)

It is based on a similar semiconductor structure to EPROM, but allows its entire contents (or selected banks) to be electrically erased, then rewritten electrically, so that they need not be removed from the computer (or camera, MP3 player etc.). Writing or flashing an EEPROM is much slower than reading from a ROM or writing to a RAM.

Electrically erasable programmable read-only-memory chips remove the biggest drawbacks of EPROMs.

In EEPROMs:

- The chip does not have to removed to be rewritten.
- The entire chip does not have to be completely erased to change a specific portion of it.
- Changing the contents does not require additional dedicated equipment.

Instead of using UV light, you can return the electrons in the cells of an EEPROM to normal with the localized application of an electric field to each cell.

This erases the targeted cells of the EEPROM, which can then be rewritten. EEPROMs are changed 1 byte at a time, which makes them versatile but slow. In fact, EEPROM chips are too slow to use in many products that make quick changes to the data stored on the chip.

EEPROM's are realized as arrays of floating-gate transistors.

Advantages of EEPROM :
1. It is selective erasing.
2. The chip does not have to be removed to be rewritten.
3. Does not have to be erased first for writing.
4. Program individual bytes.
5. Changing the contents does not require additional dedicated equipment.

Disadvantages of EEPROM :
1. EEPROMs are changed 1 byte at a time which makes it slow.
2. EEPROM chips are too slow to use in many products.

5.4.1.4 Electrically Alterable Read-Only Memory (EAROM)

It is a type of EEPROM that can be modified one bit at a time. Writing is a very slow process and again requires higher voltage (usually around 12 V) than is used for read access. EAROMs are intended for applications that require infrequent and only partial rewriting. EAROM may be used as non-volatile storage for critical system set-up information; in many applications.

5.4.1.5 Flash Memory

Flash memory, is a form of EEPROM that makes very efficient use of chip area and can be erased and reprogrammed thousands of times without damage.

Flash memory works much faster than traditional EEPROMs because it writes data in chunks, usually 512 bytes in size, instead of 1 byte at a time. Flash memory, uses in circuit wiring to erase by applying an electrical field to the entire chip or to predetermined sections of the chip called blocks.

Newer designs feature very high endurance (exceeding 1,000,000 cycles). This feature, along with its endurance and physical durability, has allowed NAND flash to replace magnetic in some applications (such as USB flash drives). Flash memory is sometimes called **flash ROM** or **flash EEPROM** when used as a replacement for older

ROM types, but not in applications that take advantage of its ability to be modified quickly and frequently.

In the industry, there is a convention to reserve the term EEPROM to byte-wise erasable memories compared to block-wise erasable flash memories. EEPROM takes more area than flash memory for the same capacity because each cell usually needs both a read, write and erase transistor, while in flash memory the erase circuits are shared by large blocks of cells (often 512 x 8).

Advantages of Flash memory :
1. Flash memory can be erased and rewritten faster than ordinary EEPROM,
2. In flash memory the erase circuits are shared by large blocks of cells (often 512 x 8).
3. Higher density than EEPROM.
4. High endurance and physical durability.

5.4.2 RAM Internal Memory

Accessing data or running software from a memory chip (internal memory) is much faster than from backing storage such as a hard drive. **RAM** (Random Access Memory) chips are described as volatile; the contents are lost when the computer is switched-off. RAM is a special type of chip that temporarily stores data as it is processed

When a computer is started up, the operating system is copied into the RAM. The microprocessor never accesses software directly from the computer's disk drives. Instead, the OS software loads software from the disk drives into RAM. Then the microprocessor reads the software from RAM for processing and places the results of processing back into RAM. The process of transferring data in and out of the microprocessor to RAM is repeated millions of times each second.

A moment you switch-off power to your computer, all of the data residing in RAM is erased. Because it can change so instantly, RAM is some times referred to as volatile memory. In order to safety store your work for future work sessions, you must save it to disk drive. Since RAM temporarily stores data on the computer, it is very important, to save your work before you switch-off your computer.

RAM is considered "random access" because you can access any memory cell directly if you know the row and column that intersect at that cell.

The opposite of RAM is **Serial Access Memory** (SAM). SAM stores data as a series of memory cells that can only be accessed sequentially (like a cassette tape).

Fig 5.4 : RAM

Types of RAM :

The two basic forms of semiconductor Random Access Memory (RAM) are dynamic RAM (DRAM) and static RAM (SRAM).

5.4.2.1 SRAM   [May 09, Dec. 09, May 13]

Static random access memory uses multiple transistors, typically four to six, for each memory cell but doesn't have a capacitor in each cell.

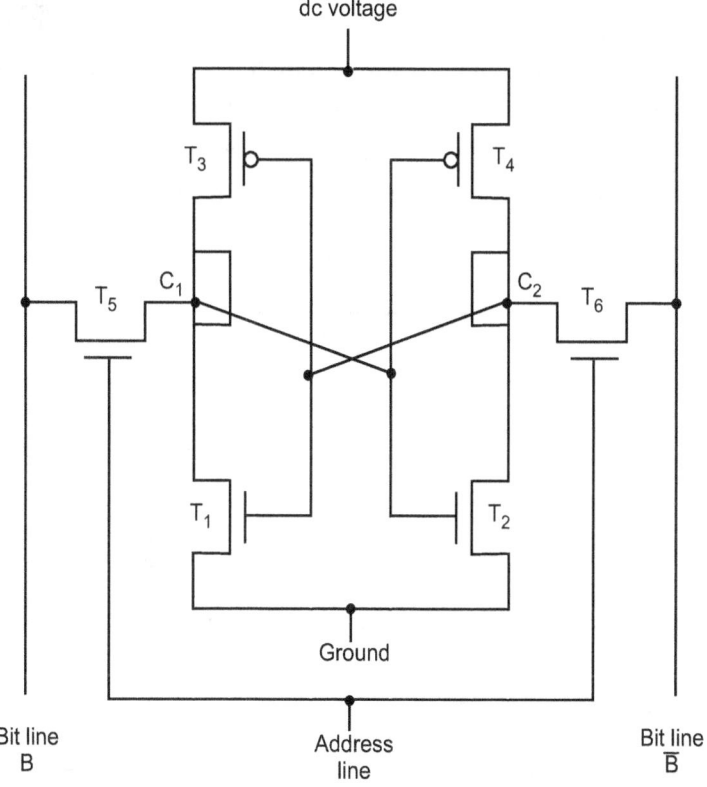

Fig. 5.5 : SRAM cell

Four transistors (T_1, T_2, T_3, T_4) are cross connected that produces a stable logical state. In logic state 0, point C_1 is low and point C_2 is high; T_1 and T_4 are on and T_2 and T_3 are off. In logic state 1, point C_1 is high and point C_2 is low; T_1 and T_4 are off. And T_2 and T_3 are on. Static Ram store each bit in a internal flip-flop which require 4 to 6 transistors.

SRAM does not need refreshing because it operates on the principle of moving current that is switched in one of two directions rather than a storage cell that holds a charge in place.

Use of SRAM : It is used primarily for cache.

Advantages :

1. SRAM does not need refreshing.
2. SRAM is faster.

Disadvantages :

1. A static memory is somewhat complex and large in size.
2. SRAM is more expensive.
3. Can not be compress so much.
4. More power consumption.
5. SRAM is less dense (less cells per unit area).

5.4.2.2 DRAM   [Dec. 09, May 13]

In the most common form of computer memory, **dynamic random access memory** (DRAM), a transistor and a capacitor are paired to create a memory cell.

DRAM is called dynamic because it must constantly be refreshed or it will lose the data which is supposed to be storing. Due to all of this refreshing it takes time and slows down the memory.

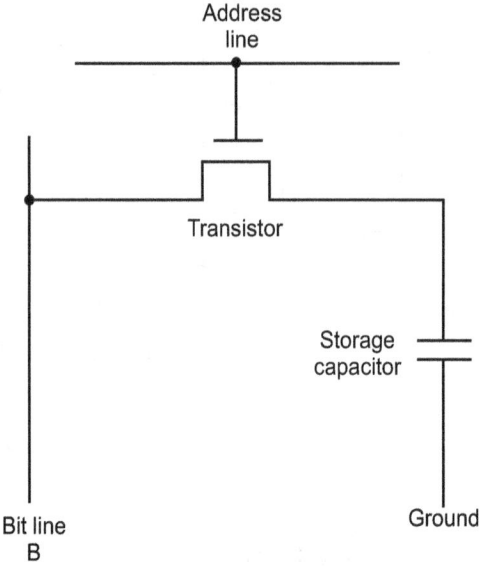

Fig. 5.6 : DRAM cell

It contains an individual cell that stores one bit. The address line is activated when the bit value from this cell is to be read or written. The transistor acts as a switch that is closed if a voltage is applied to the address line and open if no voltage is present on address line. In DRAM a data bit is stored as a charge or no charge on a tiny capacitor. All that is needed in addition to capacitor to a single transistor switch to access the capacitor. When a bit is written to it are read from it.

For write operation, a voltage signal is applied to the bit line; and then to address line, allowing a charge to be transferred to the capacitor.

For read operation, when the address line is selected, the transistor turns on and the charge stored on the capacitor is fed out onto a bit line and to a sense amplifier. The sense amplifier compares the capacitor voltage to a reference value and determines that cell contains 0 or 1. The read out from the cell discharges the capacitor, which must be restored to complete the operation.

Use of DRAM : DRAM is used for main memory.

Advantages :
1. A dynamic memory cell is simpler and smaller than static memory.
2. DRAM is more dense (more cells per unit area).
3. Can be Compress.
4. Less power consumption.
5. DRAM is less expensive.

Disadvantages:
1. It must constantly be refreshed or it will lose the data which is supposed to be storing.
2. It requires extra circuit for refreshing.
3. DRAMs are slower.

Difference Between SRAM and DRAM :

Table 5.2 : Difference Between SRAM and DRAM

Sr. No.	SRAM	DRAM
1.	It is a static RAM.	It is a dynamic RAM.
2.	SRAM consists of five or six transistors.	In DRAM a transistors and a capacitor transistors are paired to create a memory cell.
3.	SRAM does not need refreshing. It requires power continuously	It must constantly be refreshed or it will lose the data which is supposed to be storing.
4.	It doesn't require extra circuit for refreshing.	It requires extra circuit for refreshing.
5.	A static memory is somewhat complex and large in size.	A dynamic memory cell is simpler and smaller than static memory.
6.	SRAM is less dense (less cells per unit area)	DRAM is more dense (more cells per area).
7.	SRAM is more expensive.	DRAM is less expensive.
8.	SRAMs are faster.	DRAMs are slower.
9.	Can not be compress so much.	Can be Compress.
10.	More power consumption.	Less power consumption.
11.	SRAM is used for cache memory.	DRAM is used for main memory.

5.4.2.3 SDRAM (Synchronous Dynamic RAM)   [May 07]

One of the most widely used forms of DRAM is the synchronous DRAM. The traditional DRAM is asynchronous while SDRAM is synchronous. With synchronous access, the DRAM moves data in and out under control of the system clock. The processor or other master issues the instruction and address information, which is cathched by DRAM. The DRAM then responds after a number of clock cycles. Meanwhile the master can do other tasks while SDRAM is processing the request.

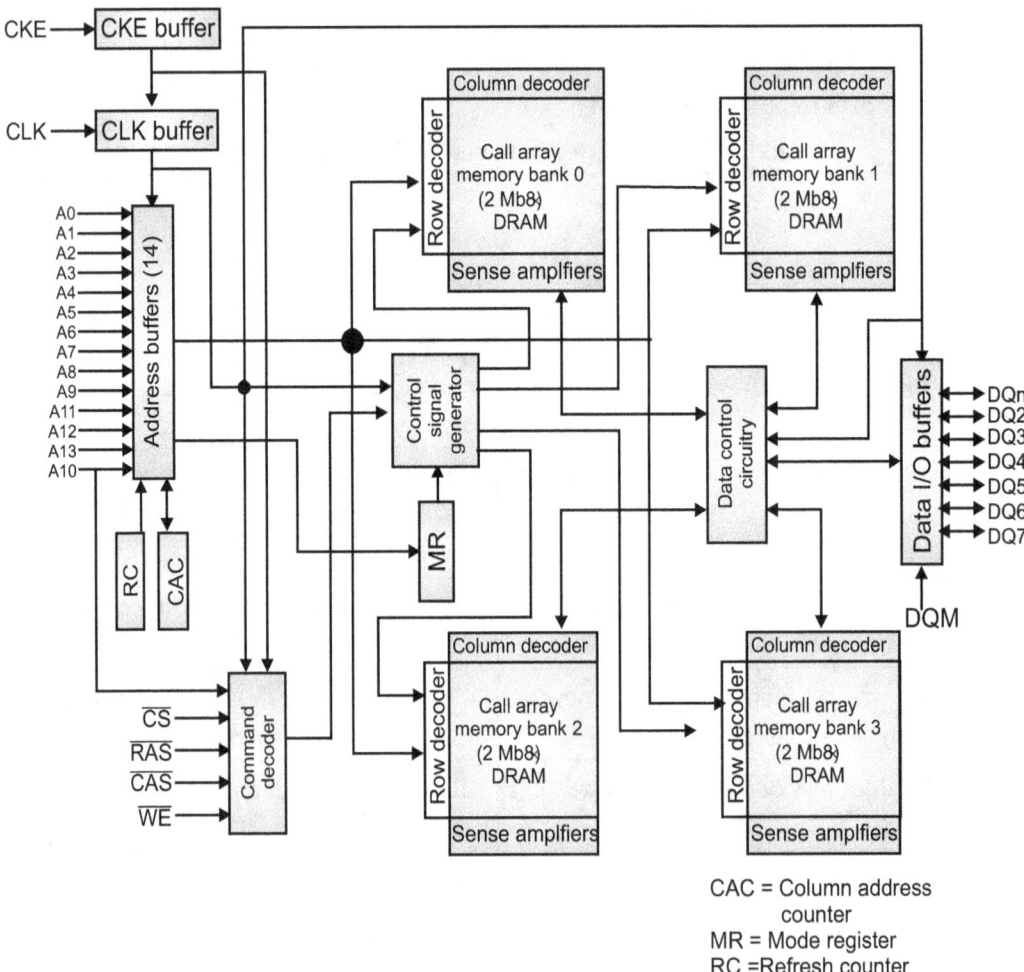

CAC = Column address counter
MR = Mode register
RC =Refresh counter

Fig. 5.7 : Synchronous Dynamic RAM (SDRAM)

Table 5.3 : SDRAM pin assignments

A0 to A13	Address inputs
CLK	Clock input
CKE	Clock enable
CS	Chip select
RAS	Row address strobe
CAS	Column address strobe
WE	Write enable
DQ 0 to DQ7	Data input/output
DWM	Data mask

SDRAM has burst mode. In this a series of data bits can be clocked out rapidly after the first bit has been accessed. This mode is useful when all the bits to be accessed are in sequence and in the same row of array.

The SDRAM has a multiple-bank internal architecture that improves on-chip parallelism.

The mode register specifies a burst length, which is the number of separate units of data synchronously fed onto the bus. It also allows the programmer to adjust the latency between receipt of a read request and the beginning of data transfer.

SDRAM performs best when it is transferring large blocks of data serially such as for applications like word processing, multimedia etc.

Normal addressing requires alternating cycles. By redesigning the basic chip interface, however, memory chips can make data available every clock cycle. Because these resulting chips can operate in sync with their computer hosts, they are termed Synchronous dynamic RAM.

To help SDRAM chips keep up with their quicker interface, a pipelined design is used. SDRAM chips are built with multiple, independently operating stages so that the chip access start to access a second address before it finishes processing first. The pipelining extends only across column addresses within a given page.

This RAM ranges from 32 MB, 64 MB, 128 MB, 256 MB, and 512 MB. This RAM is used for P II, P III, P IV processors. This RAM has 168 pins and 2 notches.

5.4.2.4 RDRAM (Rambus DRAM)

The next step up in memory speed comes from revising the interface between memory chips and the rest of the system. The leading choice is the Rambus design, developed by the company with the same name. Intel chose Rambus technology for its fastest systems designs.

The Rambus design has evolved since its beginnings. Rambus memory chips use an internal 2048 byte static RAM cache that links to the dynamic memory on the chip through a very wide bus that allows the transfer of an entire page of memory into the cache in a single cycle. The cache is fast enough that it can supply data at a 15 ns rate during hits. When the cache misses, the chip retrieves the request data from its main memory and at the same time transfers the page containing it into the cache so that it is ready for next memory operation. Because subsequent memory operations will likely come from the cache, the dynamic portion of the chip is free to be refreshed without stealing system time or adding wait states.

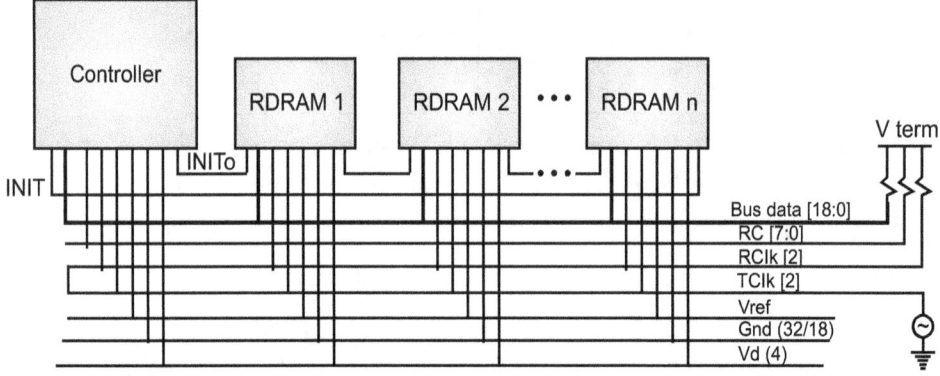

Fig. 5.8 : RDRAM Structure

Fig. 5.8 illustrates the RDRAM layout. The configuration consists of a controller and a number of RDRAM modules connected together via a common bus. The bus includes 18 data lines, 16 for actual data and 2 for parity. There is a separate set of 8 lines (RC) used for address and control signals. A RDRAM module sends data to the controller synchronously to the clock to master, and the controller sends data to RDRAM synchronously with the clock signal in the opposite direction. The remaining bus lines include voltage, ground and power source.

Because of different technology used by Rambus chips, the modules work differently with your system, too. Whereas with conventional memory it is important to match the width of the memory bus to that of the rest of your computer, such matches are unnecessary with Rambus. The memory controller recognizes the data it pulls from Rambus memory to make it fit the bus width of the host computer. Consequently, a Rambus module with a 16-bit bus works in a computer with a 64-bit bus. Usually, however, Rambus systems put two or more modules in parallel. The goal of this design is to increase memory speed or bandwidth.

This RAM ranges from 128 MB to 356 MB. Front side bus speed is 400 MHz. It is the fastest RAM. This RAM is used for only P4 processors.

Advantages :

1. Rambus systems put two or more modules in parallel. So, it increases memory speed.

2. It is not necessary to match the width of the memory bus to that of the rest of your computer.

Disadvantage :

When 256 MB RAM is used, you have to use a 0 MB RD RAM in another slot, otherwise PC would not work.

5.4.2.5 DDRRAM (Double Data rate RAM)

Memory chips that use DDR technology are rated by their effective data speed (i.e. twice their actual clock speed). Three speed ratings of chips are available. They are designed DDR 200, DDR 266, and DDR 333. The speed ratings on DDR memory modules are based on peak bandwidth rather than bus speed.

DDR memory has two buses one for addressing and one for transferring data. In DDR, only the data bus operates at double speed. The address bus still works at the standard clock speed. Consequently, DDR memory only speeds up part of the memory cycle, the part when data actually moves. Because most memory transfers now occur in bursts, this handicap is not as substantial as it might seem for some requests, DDR memory may need only one address cycle for a burst of a full page of memory, so the overhead is only one slow cycle for 4096 DDR memory transfers.

DDR RAM ranges from 128 MB to 256 MB. Front side bus speed is 133 MHz or a 232 MHz or 333 MHz. This RAM is used for P IV processors. This RAM has 184 pins and a notch slightly away from middle. This RAM has straight connections.

It is incompatible with SDRAM physically, but uses a similar parallel bus, making it easier to implement than RDRAM, which is a different technology.

5.4.2.6 Cache DRAM (CDRAM)

Cache DRAM (CDRAM) integrates a small SRAM cache (16 KB) onto a generic DRAM chip.

The SRAM on the CDRAM can be used in two ways.

First, it can be used as a true cache. The cache mode of CDRAM is effective for ordinary random access to memory.

Second, the SRAM on CDRAM can also be used as a buffer to support serial access of a block of data.

5.5   HIGH SPEED MEMORIES

Memory Hierarchy :

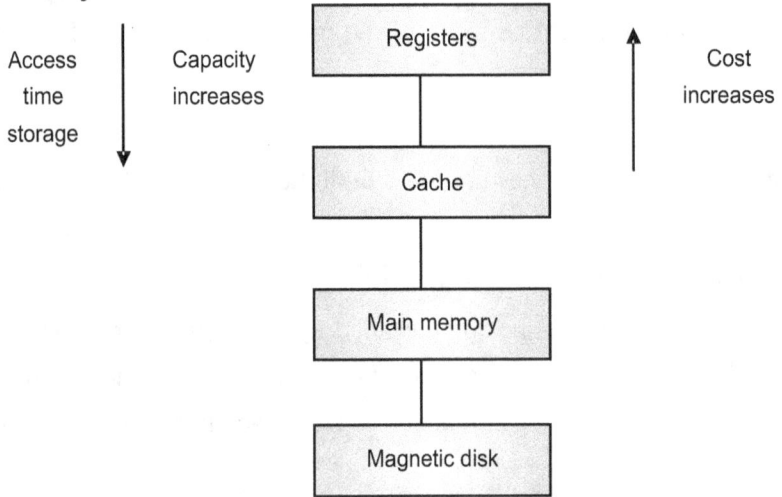

Fig. 5.9 : Memory Hierarchy

5.5.1 Cache Memory   [Dec. 06, 07, May 08, Dec. 11, May 12]

The speed of main memory is very low in comparison with the speed of modern processors. For good performance, the processor cannot spend much of its time waiting to access instructions and data in main memory.

The solution to this is to use a fast cache memory which essentially makes the main memory appear to processor to be faster than it really is.

Definition : Cache memory is random access memory (RAM) that a computer microprocessor can access more quickly than it can access regular RAM. As the microprocessor processes data, it looks first in the cache memory and if it finds the data there, it does not have to do the more time-consuming reading of data from larger memory.

- Cache is faster than main memory ==> so we must maximize its utilization.
- Cache is more expensive than main memory ==> so it is much smaller.

Consider simple arrangement as shown in Fig. 5.10. When a read request is received from the processor, the contents of a block of memory words containing the location specified are transferred into the cache one word at a time and when the program references any of the locations in this block, the desired contents are read directly from the cache.

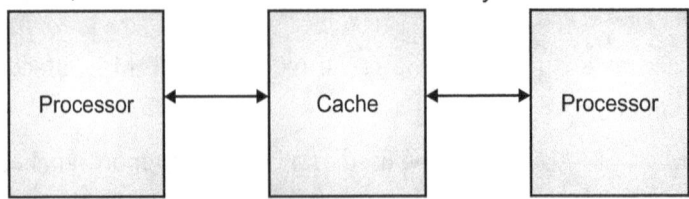

Fig. 5.10 : Use of a cache memory

Instead of fetching just one item from the main memory to the cache, it is useful to fetch several items that reside at adjacent addresses as well. We will use the term cache block/cache line to refer to a set of contiguous address locations of some size.

Locality of reference :

The principle that the instruction currently being fetched/executed is very close in memory to the instruction to be fetched/executed next. The same idea applies to the data value currently being accessed (read/written) in memory.

If we keep the most active segments of program and data in the cache, overall execution speed for the program will be optimized. Our strategy for cache utilization should maximize the number of cache read/write operations, in comparison with the number of main memory read/write operations.

So many memory requests can be handled by the primary cache has to do with two aspects of program behaviour :

Temporal Locality :

If a memory location is referenced, it is very likely that the memory location will be referenced again in the near future.

Spatial Locality :

If a memory location is referenced, it is very likely that a nearby memory location will also be referenced in the near future.

The correspondence between the main memory blocks and those in the cache is specified by a mapping function. When cache is full and required memory word is not in cache, the cache control hardware must decide which block should remove to create space for the new block. This decision is called as replacement algorithm.

Cache Hits :

When the cache contains the information requested, the transaction is said to be a cache hit.

Cache Miss :

When the cache does not contain the information requested, the transaction is said to be a cache miss.

Cache Consistency :

Since cache is a photo or copy of a small piece main memory, it is important that the cache always reflects what is in main memory.

Some common terms used to describe the process of maintaining cache consistency are :

- **Snoop :** When a cache is watching the address lines for transaction, this is called a snoop. This function allows the cache to see if any transactions are accessing memory it contains within itself.

- **Snarf :** When a cache takes the information from the data lines, the cache is said to have snarfed the data. This function allows the cache to be updated and maintain consistency. Snoop and snarf are the mechanisms the cache uses to maintain consistency.

Two other terms are commonly used to describe the inconsistencies in the cache data, these terms are :

- **Dirty Data :** When data is modified within cache but not modified in main memory, the data in the cache is called "dirty data."

- **Stale Data :** When data is modified within main memory but not modified in cache, the data in the cache is called stale data. Now that we have some names for cache functions lets see how caches are designed and how this affects their function.

5.5.2 Cache Organization   [May 13]

Caches are introduced into a system to buffer the mismatch between main memory and processor speeds. A cache is a relatively small, fast memory placed between the processor and the main memory. The cache is designed so that its access time matches the processor cycle time. Thus, if the processor is running with a 100 MHz clock the cache should be able to respond to a memory request in approximately 10 ns.

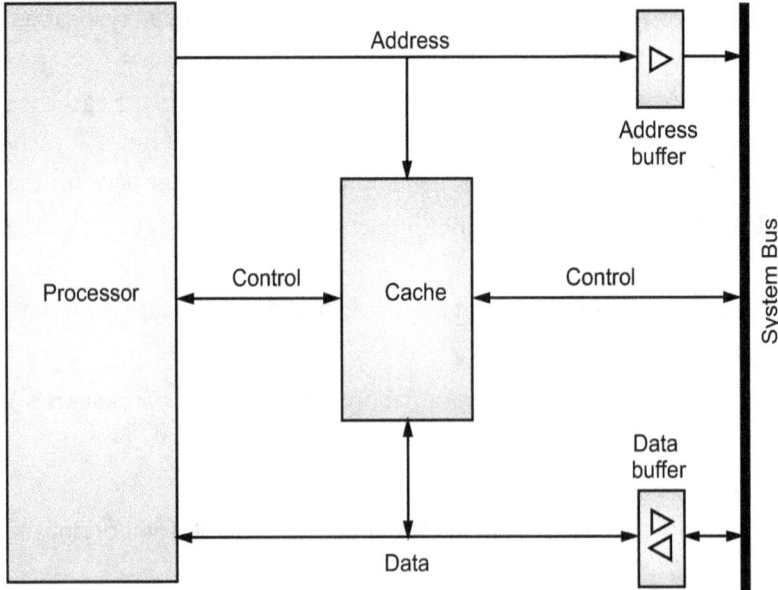

Fig. 5.11 : Typical cache organization

In the high-performance single-chip processors, the cache memory is actually built on the processor chip and separated into distinct instruction and data caches. The typical size of these caches is 8kb, for a total of 16 kB of cache on the processor chip. Many system designs also include an off-chip cache, which is called the second-level cache or the L_2 cache.

The L_2 cache can be anywhere from 128 kb to 4 Mb in size. The on-chip cache is called the first-level or primary cache. While the first-level cache must match the processor speed, the second-level cache can be somewhat slower (but not as slow as the main memory !).

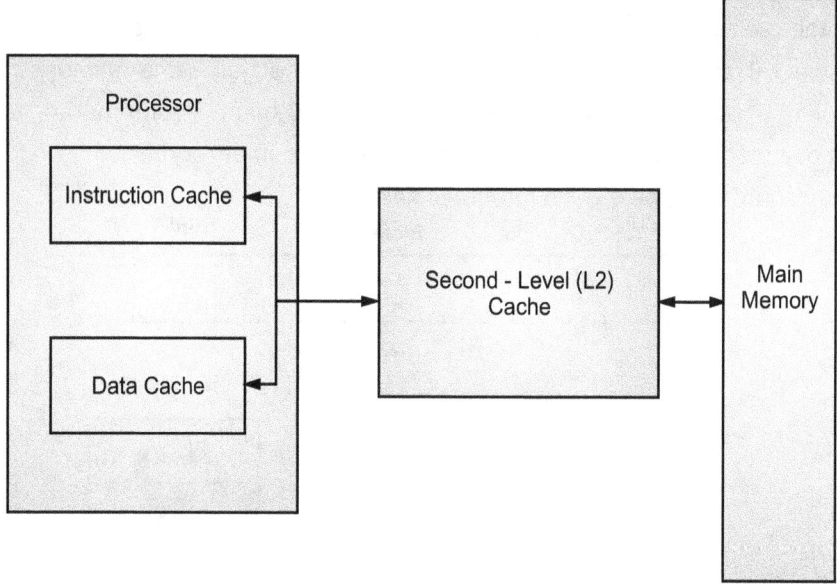

Fig. 5.12 : Caches in a typical system

When the processor makes a memory request, the request first passes to the primary cache. If the data item is found in this cache, we have a cache hit. If the data item is not found in the primary cache, we have a cache miss and the memory request is forwarded to the L_2 cache. If the data item is found in this cache, we have an L_2 cache hit and the data is passed back to the primary cache. If the data is not found in the L_2 cache, the request is finally forwarded to the main memory. When the main memory responds to the memory request, the data item is passed back to the L_2 cache and then the primary cache.

Caches work well because the memory request can usually be serviced by the primary cache. In fact, measurements show that 90% of the time the instruction cache will contain the requested instruction and 85% of the time the data cache will be able to respond to the data request. Thus, the L_2 and main memory are rarely accessed. To keep mach of which main memory locations are current action presented in 5. RAM cache the cache control uses a cache directory.

5.5.3 Mapping Techniques   [May 06, 07, 09]

Consider cache consisting of 128 blocks of 16 words each, for a total of 2048 words. Assume that main memory is addressable by 16-bit address. The main memory has 64 K words (4 K blocks of 16 words each).

1. Direct Mapping :

This is the simplest way of mapping. In this block 1 of the main memory maps onto block 1 modulo 128 of the cache, as shown in Fig. 5.13. So one of main memory blocks 0, 128, 256, is loaded in the cache, it is stored in block 0. Blocks 1, 129, 257, is loaded in the cache, it is stored in block 1 and so on. So even though cache is not full, same memory blocks are mapped onto a same cache block. In this case replacement algorithms are used. The placement of a block in the cache is determined from the memory address.

The memory address can be divided into three fields.

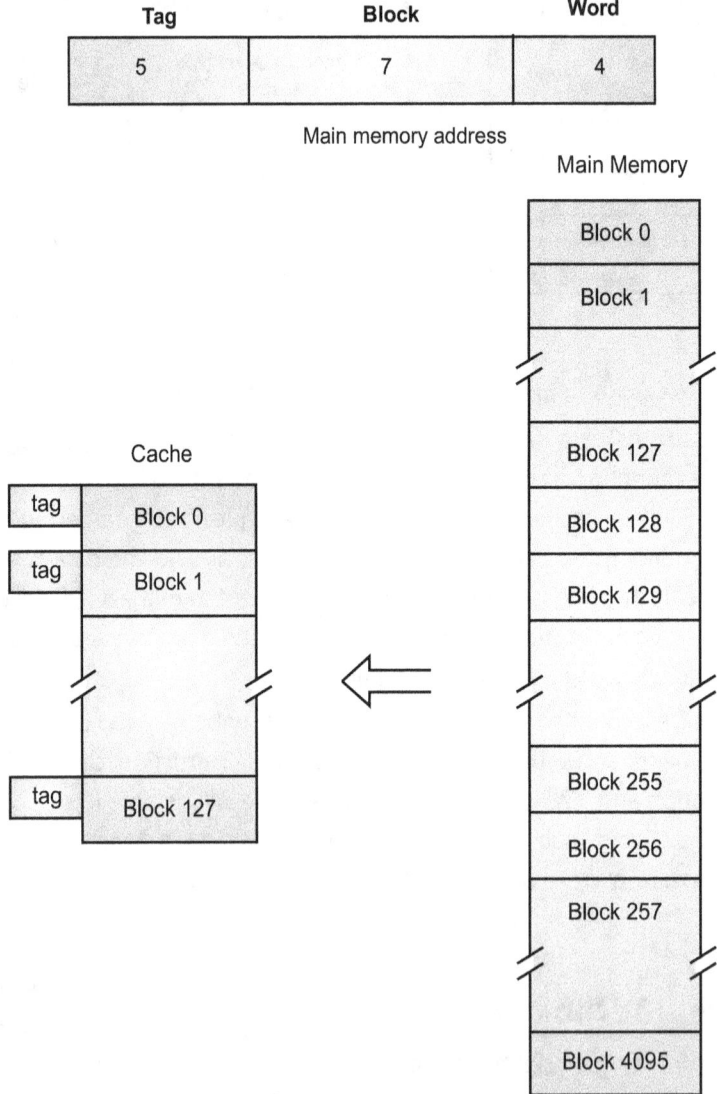

Fig. 5.13 : Direct-mapped cache

4 bits select one of the 16 words in a block. When a new block enters the cache, 7 bit cache block field determines the cache position in which this block must be stored. The high-order 5 bits of the memory address of the block are stored in 5 tag bits associated with its location in the cache. They identify which of the 32 blocks that are mapped into this cache position are currently resident in the cache. As execution proceeds, the 7 bit cache block field of each address generated by the processor points to a particular block location in the cache. The high order 5 bits of the address are compared with the tag bits associated with that cache location. If the match, then the desired word is in that block of cache. If no match, then block containing required word must be first read from the main memory and loaded into the cache.

Advantages :

1. It is very easy to implement.
2. Searching cost is less.

Disadvantages :

1. It is not very flexible.
2. Replacement is required even though cache is not full.

2. Associative Mapping :

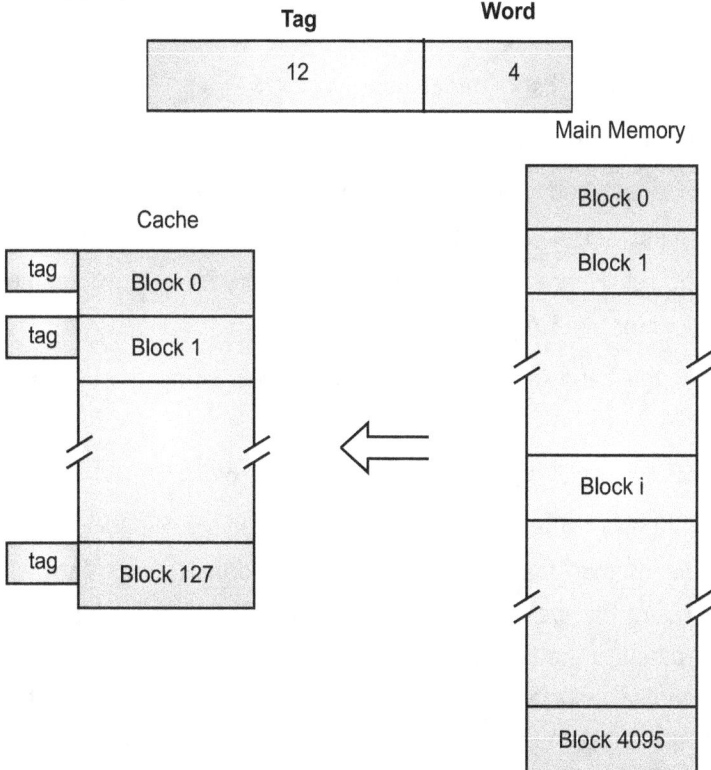

Fig 5.14 : Associative mapped cache

It is a much more flexible mapping method, in which a main memory block can be placed into any cache block position. Here, 12 tag bits are required to identify memory block when it is resident in the cache. The tag bits of an address received from the processor are compared to the tag bits of each block of the cache to see if the desired block is present. This is called associative mapping technique.

It gives complete freedom in choosing the cache location in which to place the memory block. A new block that has to be brought into the cache has to replace an existing block only if the cache is full.

The cost of associative cache is higher than the cost of direct - mapped cache because of the need to search all 128 tag patterns to determine whether a given block is in the cache. This type of search is called as associative search. For performance reasons, tags must be searched in parallel.

Advantages :

1.   It is more flexible.

2.   Replacement is required only when cache is full.

Disadvantage :

1.   Cost is higher than cost of direct mapping.

3. Set - Associative Mapping :

A combination of direct and associative mapping techniques can be used. Blocks of the cache are grouped into sets and the mapping allows a block of main memory to reside in any block of a specific set. Hence, the contention problem of the direct method is eased by having a few choices for block replacement.

At the same time, the hardware cost is reduced by decreasing the size of the associative search.

Cache consists of two blocks per set. Here, memory blocks 0, 64, 128, ...4032 map into cache set 0, and they can occupy either of the two block positions within this set.

Having 64 sets means than the 6-bit set field of the address determines which set of the cache might contain the desired block. The tag field of the address must then be associatively compared to the tags of the two blocks of the set to check if the desired block is present. This two-way associative search is simple to implement. If the controller finder that tag for a read operation correct but a line valid bit is invalid, it will read the line from main memory and write in the cache whose directory contains the tag.

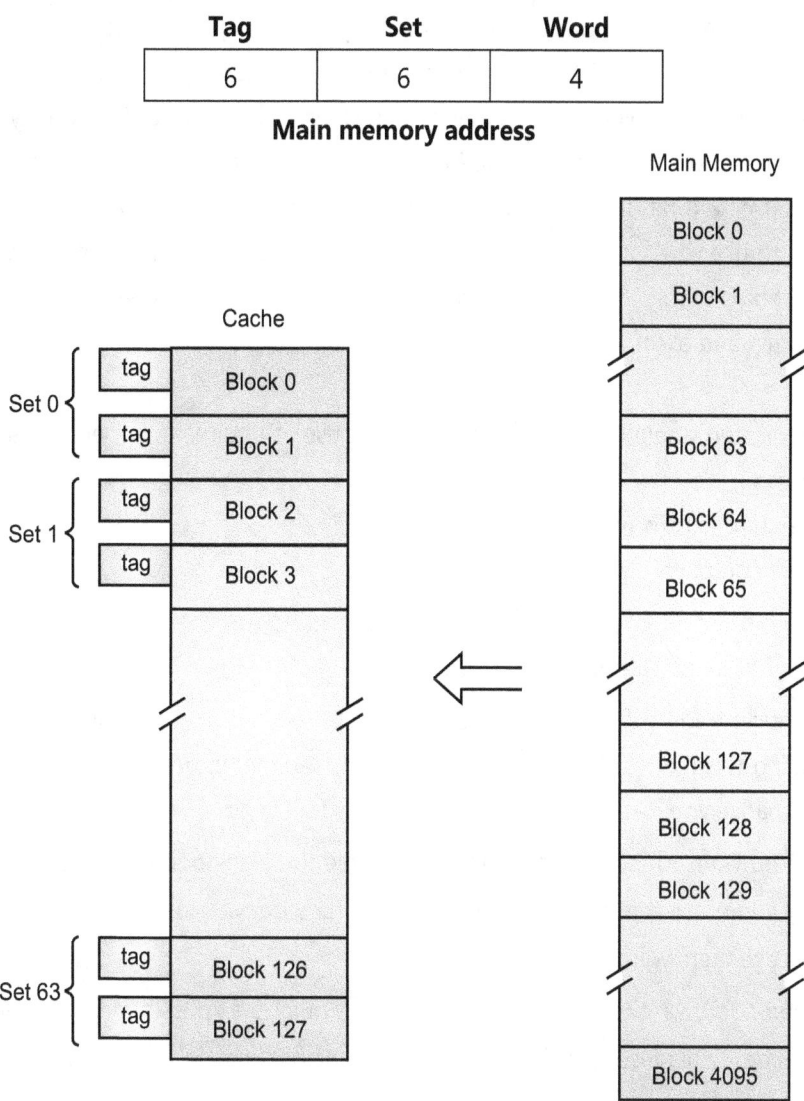

Fig. 5.15 : Set associative mapped cache with two blocks per set

Advantage :

1. This two-way associative search is simple to implement.
2. Hardware cost is reduced by decreasing size of associative search.

4. Fully-Associative Cache :

The fully associative cache has the best hit ratio because any line in the cache can hold any address that needs to be cached. This means the problem seen in the direct mapped cache disappears, because there is no dedicated single line that an address must use.

However, this cache suffers from problems involving searching the cache. If a given address can be stored in any of 16,384 lines, how do you know where it is ? Even with specialized hardware to do the searching, a performance penalty is incurred. And this penalty occurs for all accesses to memory, whether a cache hit occurs or not, because it is part of searching the cache to determine a hit. In addition, more logic must be added to determine which of the various lines to use when a new entry must be added (usually some form of a "least recently used" algorithm is employed to decide which cache line to use next). All this overhead adds cost, complexity and execution time.

Advantage :

1. No dedicated single line that an address must use as in direct mapped cache.

Disadvantages :

1.   Searching cost is more.
2.   More complex.
3.   Requires more execution time.

Comparison of Cache Mapping Techniques :

There is a critical trade-off in cache performance that has led to the creation of the various cache mapping techniques described in the previous section. In order for the cache to have good performance you want to maximize both of the following :

Hit Ratio : You want to increase as much as possible the likelihood of the cache containing the memory addresses that the processor wants. Otherwise, you lose much of the benefit of caching because there will be too many misses.

Search Speed : You want to be able to determine as quickly as possible if you have scored a hit in the cache. Otherwise, you lose a small amount of time on every access, hit or miss, while you search the cache.

Here is a summary table of the different cache mapping techniques and their relative performance :

Table 5.4 : Different mapping techniques

Cache Type	Hit Ratio	Search Speed
Direct Mapped	Good	Best
Fully Associative	Best	Moderate
N-Way Set Associative	Very Good, Better as N Increases	Good, Worse as N Increases

Difference between Direct, Associative and Set Associative Mapping :

Table 5.5 : Difference between Direct, Associative and Set Associative Mapping

Sr. No.	Direct Mapping	Associative Mapping	Set Associative Mapping
1.	Each block from the main memory has only one possible location in the cache.	A block of data from main memory can be placed into any cache block position.	A block of data from main memory can go into a particular block location of cache.
2.	Needs only one comparison.	Needs comparison with all tag bits.	Needs number of comparisons equal to number of blocks per set.
3.	Cache hit ratio decreases if processor needs to access same memory location from two different pages of the location of the main memory frequently.	Cache hit ratio has no effect if processor needs to Access same memory location from two different pages of main memory.	The effect of reduction in cache hit ratio case of frequent access to the two different pages of the main of main memory reduced.
4.	Main memory address is divided into three fields TAG, BLOCK and WORD.	Main memory address is divided into two fields TAG and WORD	Main memory address divided into three fields TAG, SET and WORD.
5.	Searching time is less.	Searching time is more.	Searching time increases with number of blocks per set.

Example 1 : A block Set-Associative cache consists of 64 blocks divided into 4 block sets. The main memory contains 4096 blocks, each consisting of 128 words of 16 bits length.

1. How many bits are there in main memory ?

2. How many bits are there in each of the TAG, SET and WORD fields ?

3. What is the size of cache memory ?

Solution :

1. Number of bits in main memory :

= No. of blocks × No. of words per block x number of bits per word

= 4096 × 128 × 16

= 8388608 bits

WORD bits : There are 128 words in each block. Therefore to identify each word (2^7 = ±28) 7 bits are required.

SET bits : There are 64 blocks and each set consists of 4 blocks. Therefore, there are 16 (64/4) sets. To identify each set (2^4 = 16) four bits are required.

TAG bits : The total words in main memory are :

$$4096 \times 128 = 524288$$

To address these words we require (2^{19} = 524288) 19 address lines. Therefore, tag bits are eight. (19 – 7 – 4).

8	4	7
TAG	SET	WORD

3. The cache memory has 64 blocks of 128 words each. Therefore, total words in cache memory = 62 × 128.

Example 2 : Consider a cache consisting of 256 blocks of 16 words each for a total number of 4096 (4 K) words and assume that the main memory is addressable by a 16 bit address and it consists of 4 K blocks. How many bits are there in each of the TAG, BLOCK/SET and WORD fields for different mapping techniques.

(a) Direct Mapping :

WORD bits : As each block consists of 16 words. Therefore, to identify each word we must have (2^4 = 16) four bits reserved for it.

SET/BLOCK bits : The cache memory consists of 256 blocks and using direct mapped technique block k of the main memory maps into block k modulo 256 of the cache. To address 128 blocks we require (2^8 = 256) eight bits.

TAG bits :   As tag bits = 16 – block bits – word bits

= 16 – 8 – 4

= 4

Main memory address :

4	8	4
TAG	SET/ BLOCK	WORD

(b) Associative Mapping :

WORD bits : The word length will remain same i.e. 4 bits.

SET/BLOCK bits : This type of techniques does not have block bits. Therefore it is 0.

TAG bits : As main memory (2^{12} = 4096). Therefore, 2 bits are required.

Therefore tag bits = 12

Main memory address :

12	4
TAG	WORD

(c) Set-Associative Mapping :

Let us assume that there is a 2-way set associative mapping. Here, the cache memory is mapped with the two blocks per set.

WORD bits : The word length will remain same as that of direct mapping i.e. 4 bits.

SET bits : As there are 128 sets (256/2). To identify each set (27 = 128) 7 bits are required.

TAG bits :   TAG bits =   16 word bits – set bits

                                  =   16 – 4 – 7

                                  =   5

Main memory address :

5	7	4
TAG	SET/ BLOCK	WORD

5.5.4 Replacement Algorithms

When a new block is brought into the cache, and cache is full one of the existing blocks must be replaced, by a new block. In case of direct mapping cache, we know that each block from main memory has only one possible location in the cache, hence there is no choice. But for associative and set associative techniques, there is a choice of replacing existing block. The replacement algorithms do the task of selecting the existing block which must be replaced.

There are four most common replacement algorithms :

1.   First in First out (FIFO)
2.   Least Recently Used (LRU)
3.   Least Frequently Used (LFU)
4.   Random

First in First out (FIFO) :

In this technique, the block which is first loaded in the cache amongst the present blocks in the cache is selected for the replacement.

Least Recently Used (LRU) :

In this technique, the block in the set which has been in the cache longest with no reference to it, is selected for the replacement.

Least Frequently Used (LFU) :

In this technique, the block in the set which has the fewest references is selected for the replacement.

Random :

Here, there are no specific criteria for replacement of any block. The existing blocks are replaced randomly.

5.5.5 Cache Coherence

In computing, **cache coherence** (also **cache coherency**) refers to the integrity of data stored in local caches of a shared resource. Cache coherence is a special case of memory coherence.

When clients in a system maintain caches of a common memory resource, problems may arise with inconsistent data. This is particularly true of CPUs in a multiprocessing system. Referring to the "Multiple Caches of Shared Resource" Fig. 5.16, if the top client has a copy of a memory block from a previous read and the bottom client changes that memory block, the top client could be left with an invalid cache of memory without any notification of the change. Cache coherence is intended to manage such conflicts and maintain consistency between cache and memory.

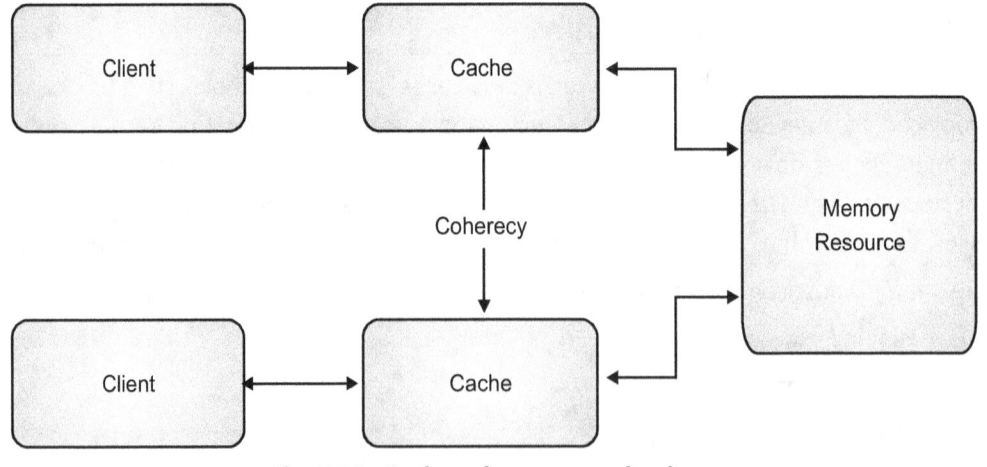

Fig. 5.16 : Cache coherence mechanisms

1. Write-through with update :

When a processor writes a new value into its cache, the new value is also written into the memory module that holds the cache block being changed and also to other caches which contains copies of this block.

Advantages :

1. READ miss never results in writes to main memory.
2. Easy to implement.
3. Main Memory always has the most current copy of the data (consistent).

Disadvantages :

1. WRITE operation is slower as we have to update both Main Memory and Cache Memory.
2. Every write needs a main memory access as a result uses more memory bandwidth.

2. Write-through based on invalidation :

When a processor writes a new value into its cache, this value is written into the memory module, and all copies in other caches are invalidated.

3. Write Back :

Multiple copies of a cache block may exist if different processors have loaded the block into their caches. If some processor wants to change this clock, it must first become an exclusive owner of this block. When the ownership is granted to this processor by the memory module, all other copies including the one in main memory module, are invalidated. Now owner of the block may change the contents of block. When another processor wishes to read this block, the data are sent to this processor by the current owner. The data are also sent to the home memory module, which reacquires ownership and updates the block to contain the latest value.

Advantages :

1. WRITEs occur at the speed of the cache memory.
2. Multiple WRITE's within a block require only one WRITE to main memory as a result uses less memory bandwidth
3. Less traffic than write-through protocol.

Disadvantages :

1. Harder to implement.
2. Main Memory is not always consistent with cache reads that result in replacement may cause writes of dirty blocks to main memory.

4. Directory-Based Coherence :

In a directory-based system, the data being shared is placed in a common directory that maintains the coherence between caches. The directory acts as a filter through which the processor must ask permission to load an entry from the primary memory to its cache. When an entry is changed the directory either updates or invalidates the other caches with that entry.

5. Snooping :

It is the process where the individual caches monitor address lines for accesses to memory locations that they have cached.

If two processors want to write the same cache block at the same time, one of the processors will be granted the use of the bus first and will become the owner. As a result the other processors copy of the cache block will be invalidated. The second processor can then repeat its write request. This sequential handling of write requests ensure that the two processors can correctly change different words in a given cache block.

6. Snarfing :

In this, a cache controller watches both address and data in an attempt to update its own copy of a memory location when a second master modifies a location in main memory.

5.5.6 Coherency Protocol

A **coherency protocol** is a protocol which maintains the consistency between all the caches in a system of distributed shared memory; the protocol maintains memory coherence according to a specified consistency model. Most of the cache protocols in multiprocessors are supporting sequential consistency model, while in software distributed shared memory more popular are models supporting release consistency or weak consistency.

Transitions between states in any specific implementation of these protocols may vary. For example, an implementation may choose different update and invalidation transitions such as update-on-read, update-on-write, invalidate-on-read, or invalidate-on-write. The choice of transition may affect the amount of inter-cache traffic, which in turn may affect the amount of cache bandwidth available for actual work. This should be taken into consideration in the design of distributed software that could cause strong contention between the caches of multiple processors.

Various models and protocols have been devised for maintaining cache coherence, such as :

- **MSI protocol**
- **MESI protocol**
- **Write-once protocol**

Choice of the consistency model is crucial to designing a cache coherent system. Coherence models differ in performance and scalability; each must be evaluated for every system design.

1. MSI Protocol :

The **MSI protocol** is a basic cache coherence protocol that is used in multiprocessor systems. As with other cache coherency protocols, the letters of the protocol name identify the possible states in which a cache line can be. So, for MSI, each block contained inside a cache can have one of three possible states :

- **Modified :** The block has been modified in the cache. The data in the cache is then inconsistent with the backing store (e.g. memory). A cache with a block in the "M" state has the responsibility to write the block to the backing store.

- **Shared :** This block is unmodified and exists in at least one cache. The cache can evict the data without writing it to the backing store.

- **Invalid :** This block is invalid, and must be fetched from memory or another cache if the block is to be stored in this cache.

These coherency states are maintained through communication between the caches and the backing store. The caches have different responsibilities when blocks are read or written, or when they learn of other caches issuing reads or writes for a block.

When a read request arrives at a cache for a block in the "M" or "S" states, the cache supplies the data. If the block is not in the cache (in the "I" state), it must verify that the line is not in the "M" state in any other cache.

Different caching architectures handle this differently. For example, bus architectures often perform snooping, where the read request is broadcast to all of the caches. Other architectures include cache directories which have agents (directories) that know which caches last had copies of a particular cache block. If another cache has the block in the "M" state, it must write back the data to the backing store and go to the "S" or "I" states. Once any "M" line is written back, the cache obtains the block from either the backing store, or another cache with the data in the "S" state. The cache can then supply the data to the requester. After supplying the data, the cache block is in the "S" state.

When a write request arrives at a cache for a block in the "M" state, the cache modifies the data locally. If the block is in the "S" state, the cache must notify any other caches that might contain the block in the "S" state that they must evict the block. This notification may be via bus snooping or a directory, as described above. Then the data may be locally modified. If the block is in the "I" state, the cache must notify any other caches that might contain the block in the "S" or "M" states that they must evict the block. If the block is in another cache in the "M" state, that cache must either write the data to the backing store or supply it to the requesting cache. If at this point the cache does not yet have the block locally, the block is read from the backing store before being modified in the cache. After the data is modified, the cache block is in the "M" state.

2. MESI protocal : The **MESI protocol** is a widely used cache coherency and memory coherence protocol. It is the most common protocol which supports write-back cache.

Every cache line is marked with one of the four following states (coded in two additional bits):

- **Modified :** The cache line is present only in the current cache, and is dirty; it has been modified from the value in main memory. The cache is required to write the data back to main memory at some time in the future, before permitting any other read of the (no longer valid) main memory state. The write-back changes the line to the Exclusive state.

- **Exclusive :** The cache line is present only in the current cache, but is clean; it matches main memory. It may be changed to the Shared state at any time, in response to a read request. Alternatively, it may be changed to the Modified state when writing to it.

- **Shared :** Indicates that this cache line may be stored in other caches of the machine and is "clean"; it matches the main memory. The line may be discarded (changed to the Invalid state) at any time.

- **Invalid :** Indicates that this cache line is invalid.

Operation :

In a typical system, several caches share a common bus to main memory. Each also has an attached CPU which issues read and write requests. The cache's collective goal is to minimize the use of the shared main memory.

A cache may satisfy a read from any state except Invalid. An Invalid line must be fetched (to the Shared or Exclusive states) to satisfy a read.

A write may only be performed if the cache line is in the Modified or Exclusive state. If it is in the Shared state, all other cached copies must be invalidated first. This is typically done by a broadcast operation known as Read for Ownership (RFO).

A cache may discard a non-modified line at any time, changing to the Invalid state. A Modified line must be written back first.

A cache that holds a line in the Modified state must snoop (intercept) all attempted reads (from all of the other caches in the system) of the corresponding main memory location and insert the data that it holds. This is typically done by forcing the read to back-off (i.e. retry later), then writing the data to main memory and changing the cache line to the Shared state.

A cache that holds a line in the Shared state must listen for invalidate or read-for-ownership broadcasts from other caches, and discard the line (by moving it into Invalid state) on a match.

A cache that holds a line in the Exclusive state must also snoop all read transactions from all other caches, and move the line to Shared state on a match.

The Modified and Exclusive states are always precise : i.e. they match the true cache line ownership situation in the system. The Shared state may be imprecise : if another cache discards a Shared line, this cache may become the sole owner of that cache line, but it will not be promoted to Exclusive state. Other caches do not broadcast notices when they discard cache lines, and this cache could not use such notifications without maintaining a count of the number of shared copies.

In that sense, the Exclusive state is an opportunistic optimization: If the CPU wants to modify a cache line that is in state S, a bus transaction is necessary to invalidate all other cached copies. State E enables modifying a cache line with no bus transaction.

5.6 VIRTUAL MEMORY [Dec. 05, 06, 07, 08, 09]

Virtual Memory is a computer system technique which gives an application program the impression that it has contiguous working memory (an address space), while in fact it may be physically fragmented and may even overflow on to disk storage. Systems that use this technique make programming of large applications easier and use real physical memory more efficiently than those without virtual memory.

Note that "virtual memory" is more than just "using disk space to extend physical memory size". Extending memory to disk is a normal consequence of using virtual memory techniques, but could be done by other means such as overlays or swapping programs and their data completely out to disk while they are inactive.

All modern general-purpose computer operating systems use virtual memory techniques for ordinary applications, such as word processors, spreadsheets, multimedia players, accounting etc.

Fig. 5.17 shows typical organization that implements virtual memory. A special hardware unit, called the MMU, translates virtual addresses into physical addresses. When the desired data (or instructions) are in the main memory, these data are fetched. If the data are not in main memory, MMU causes the Operating System to bring the data into memory from disk.

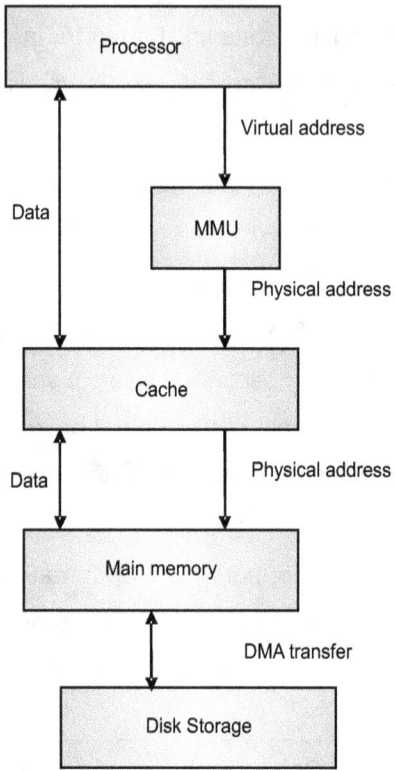

Fig. 5.17 : Virtual memory organization

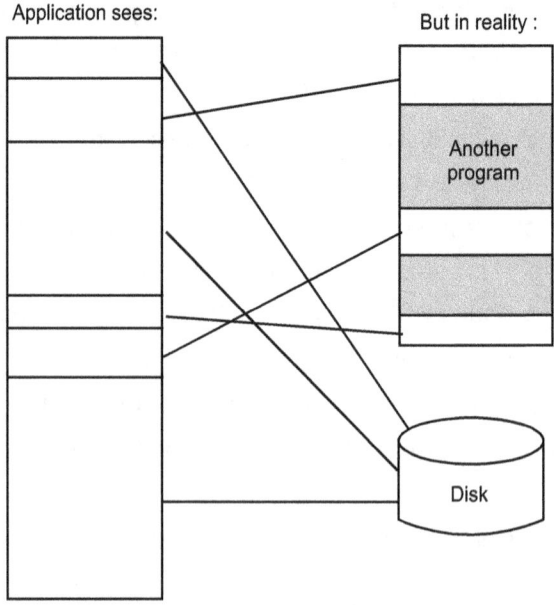

Fig. 5.18 : Virtual memory

Fig. 5.18 shows how the application sees memory and how it is in reality.

5.6.1 Segmentation

1. Memory-management scheme that supports user view of memory.
2. A program is a collection of segments. A segment is a logical unit such as Main program, Procedure, Function, Method, Object, Local variables, global variables, Common block, Stack, Symbol table, arrays.

Fig. 5.19 shows a user's view of program and Fig. 5.20 shows logical view of program.

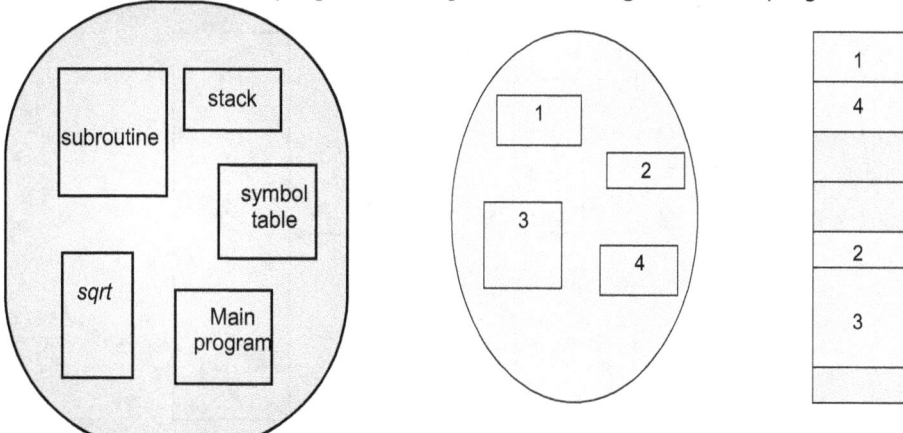

Fig. 5.19 : User's View of program   **Fig. 5.20 : Logical View of Segmentation**

Segmentation Architecture :

1. Logical address consists of a two table

2. **Segment table** - maps two-dimensional physical addresses; each table entry has

    base - contains the starting physical address where the segments reside in memory

    limit - specifies the length of the segment.

3. **Segment-table base register (STBR)** points to the segment table's location in memory.

4. **Segment - table length register (STLR)** indicates number of segments used by a program; segment number s is legal if s < STLR.

5. **Protection :**

With each entry in segment table associate

* validation bit = 0 => illegal segment
* read/write/execute privileges

6. Protection bits associated with segments; code sharing occurs at segment level.

7. Since segments vary in length, memory allocation is a dynamic storage-allocation problem.

8. A segmentation example is shown in Fig. 5.21 and Fig. 5.22.

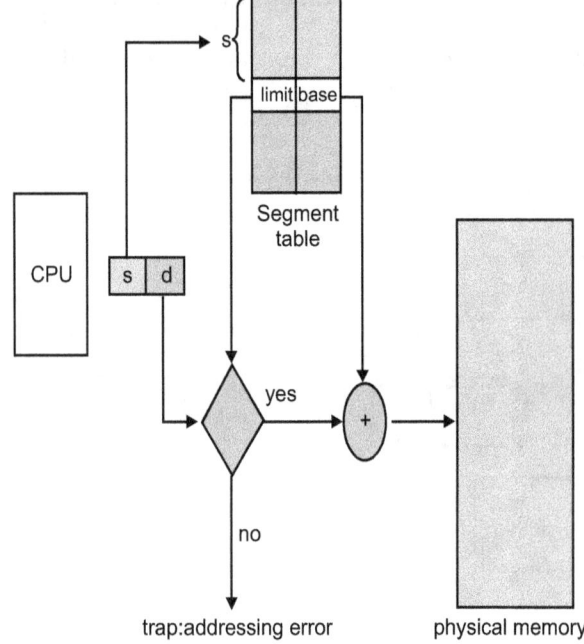

Fig. 5.21 : Segmentation Hardware

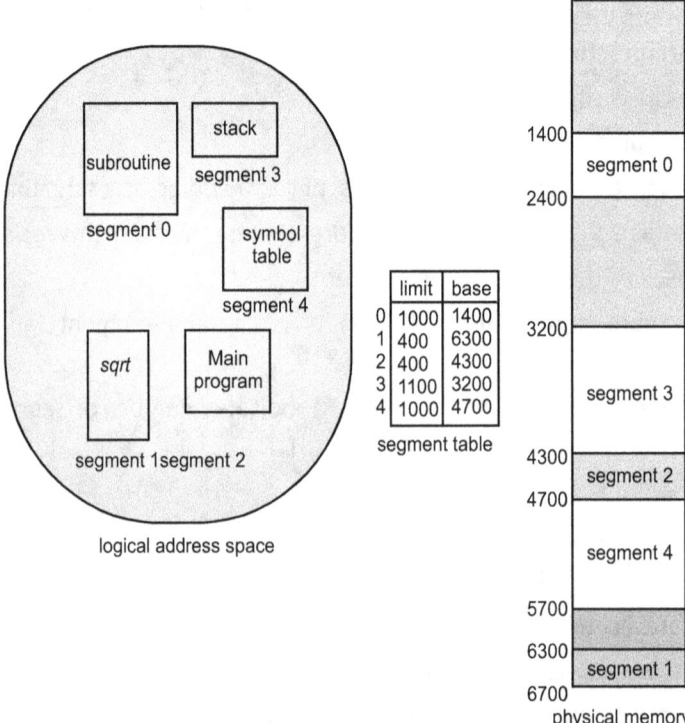

Fig. 5.22 : Example of Segmentation

5.6.2 Paging   [Dec. 05, May 06, Dec. 06, May 07, Dec. 08, May 09, 10]

In computer operating systems, there are various ways in which the operating system can store and retrieve data from secondary storage for use in main memory. One such memory management scheme is referred to as **paging**. In the paging memory-management scheme, the operating system retrieves data from secondary storage in same-size blocks called **pages**. The main advantage of paging is that it allows the physical address space of a process to be non-contiguous. Prior to paging, systems had to fit whole programs into storage contiguously which caused various storage and fragmentation problems.

Paging includes the following things :

1. Logical address space of a process can be non-contiguous; process is allocated physical memory whenever the latter is available.

2. Divide physical memory into fixed-sized blocks called frames (size is power of 2, between 512 bytes and 8,192 bytes).

3. Divide logical memory into blocks of same size called pages.

4. Keep track of all free frames.

5. To run a program of size n pages, need to find n free frames and load program.

6. Set up a page table to translate logical to physical addresses.

7. There arises problem of internal fragmentation.

Address Translation Scheme :

Address generated by CPU is divided into two parts :

1. **Page number (p) :** Used as an index into a page table which contains base address of each page in physical memory (m-n bits).

2. **Page offset (d) :** Combined with base address to define the physical memory address that is sent to the memory unit (n bits).

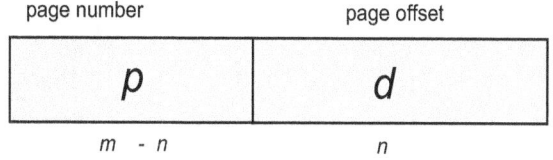

For given logical address space 2^m- and page size 2^n.

Paging Hardware :

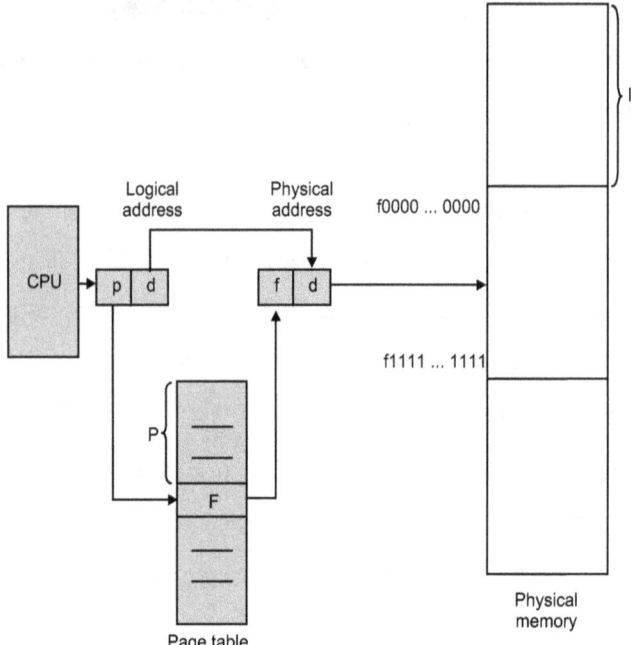

Fig. 5.23 : Paging H/W

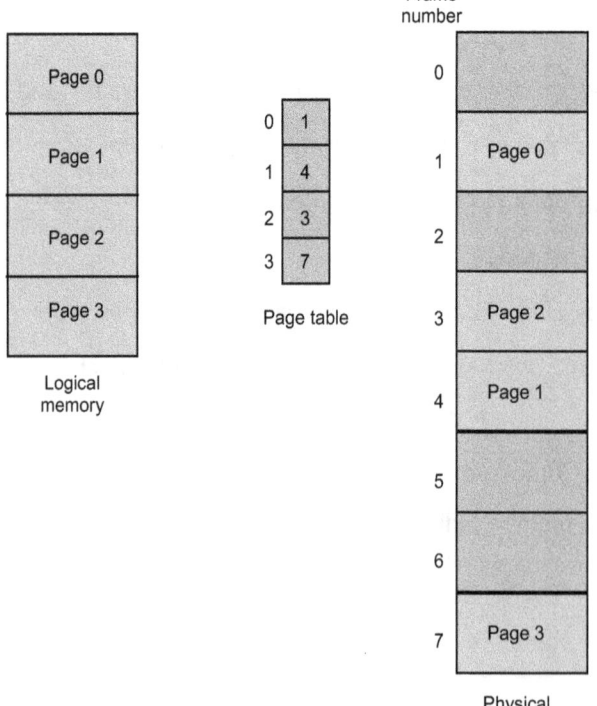

Fig. 5.24 : Paging model of logical and physical memory

Implementation of Page Table :

1. Page table is kept in main memory.

2. Page table base register (PTBR) points to the page table.

3. Page table length register (PRLR) indicates size of the page table.

4. In this scheme every data/ instruction access requires two memory accesses. One for the page table and one for the data/ instruction.

5. The two memory access problem can be solved by the use of a special fast-lookup hardware cache called associative memory or translation look-aside buffers (TLBs)

Paging Hardware with TLB :

TLB contains only a few of page-table entries. When a logical address is generated by CPU, search page number in TLB. If found, its frame number is immediately available and is used to access memory. It is very fast.

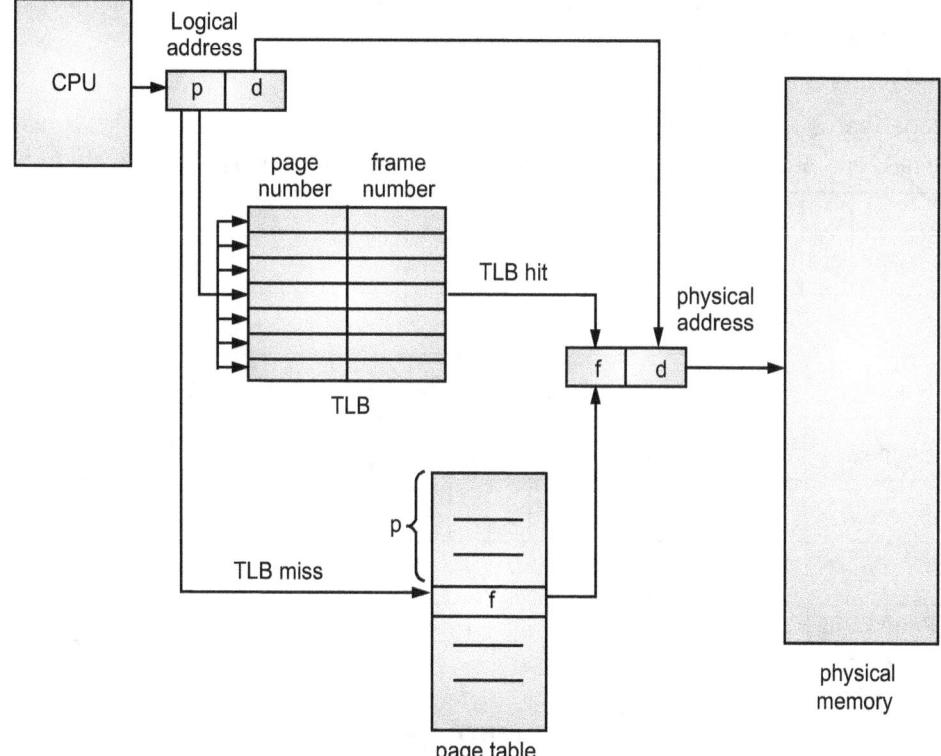

Fig 5.25 : Paging H/W with TLB

If page number is not in TLB (TLB miss), memory reference to page table must be made. When frame number is obtained, we can use it across memory. We add page number and frame number to TLB, so that they will be found quickly on next reference. If TLB is full, O.S. selects one for replacement.

5.6.2.1 Page Replacement Algorithm

Page fault : When a process is executing a with only a few pages in memory, and when an instruction is encountered which refers to any instruction or data in some other pages which is outside the main memory a page fault occurs.

Page replacement : If all the page frames in main memory are occupied and if a new page is to be brought in main memory OS has to overwrite some existing page in memory. The page to be chosen is selected by the page replacement policy. Different page replacement discussed below.

Local versus global replacement :

Replacement algorithms can be local or global.

When a process incurs a page fault, a local page replacement algorithm selects for replacement some page that belongs to that same process (or a group of processes sharing a memory partition). A global replacement algorithm is free to select any page in memory.

Page Replacement Algorithms :

1.   First in first out (FIFO) :

The page that is removed from memory is the one that entered first. This algo is easy to understand and program. This algorithm can be implemented using FIFO queue.

Page References	8	1	2	3	1	4	1	5	3	4	1	4	3	1	2	8	1	2

Frame 0	8	8	8	3	3	3	3	5	5	5	1	1	1	1	1	1	1	8	8	8
Frame 1		1	1	1	1	4	4	4	3	3	3	3	3	2	2	2	2	2	1	1
Frame 2			2	2	2	2	1	1	1	4	4	4	4	4	3	3	3	3	3	2

Page Fault	Y	Y	Y	Y		Y	Y	Y	Y	Y	Y			Y	Y			Y	Y	Y

Y = Yes (Page Fault)

Number of Page faults 15

Fig. 5.26 : FIFO algorithm

2.   Optimal (OPT) :

OPT removes a page that will be used not immediately but in the most distant future.

Let us take a random page reference string in a program. This is the sequence in which the logical page numbers are referenced during the execution of that program. To simplify the explanation, assume that there are only three page frames 0, 1, and 2 in our system. Also assume that they are empty to begin with and the list of free pages frames also maintains them in that order, e.g. 0, 1 and 2.

Therefore they will be allotted also in that order.

Page References	8	1	2	3	1	4	1	5	3	4	1	4	3	2	3	1	2	8	1	2

Frame 0	8	8	8	3	3	3	3	3	3	3	3	3	3	3	3	3	3	8	8	8
Frame 1		1	1	1	1	1	1	5	5	5	1	1	1	1	1	1	1	1	1	1
Frame 2			2	2	2	4	4	4	4	4	4	4	4	2	2	2	2	2	2	2
Page Fault	Y	Y	Y		Y		Y		Y			Y		Y		Y		Y		

Y = Yes (Page Fault)

Number of Page faults = 9

Fig. 5.27 : OPT Algorithm

3. Least recently used algo (LRU) :

When a page fault occurs LRU throws out a page that has been unused for the longest time in past.

Page References	8	1	2	3	1	4	1	5	3	4	1	4	3	2	3	1	2	8	1	2

Frame 0	8	8	8	3	3	3	3	5	5	5	1	1	1	2	2	2	2	2	2	2
Frame 1		1	1	1	1	1	1	1	4	4	4	4	4	4	1	1	1	1	1	1
Frame 2			2	2	2	4	4	4	3	3	3	3	3	3	3	3	3	8	8	8

Page Fault	Y	Y	Y	Y		Y		Y	Y	Y	Y			Y		Y		Y		

Y = Yes (Page Fault)

Number of Page faults 12

Fig. 5.28 : LRU Algorithm

5.6.3 Address Translation : Virtual to Physical

Logical versus Physical Address Space

1. Logical address : generated by the CPU; also referred to as virtual address.

   Physical address : address seen by the memory unit.

2. Logical and physical addresses are the same in compile-time and load-time address binding schemes; logical (virtual) and physical addresses differ in execution-time address-binding scheme.

Memory Management Unit (MMU) :

1. Hardware device that maps virtual to physical address.
2. In MMU scheme, the value in the relocation register is added to every address generated by a user process at the time it is sent to memory.
3. The user program deals with logical addresses; it never sees the real physical addresses.

13-bits	10-bits
Page number	offset

To convert a virtual address into a physical address, the CPU uses the page number as an index into the page table. If the page is resident, the physical frame address in the page table is concatenated in front of the offset to create the physical address.

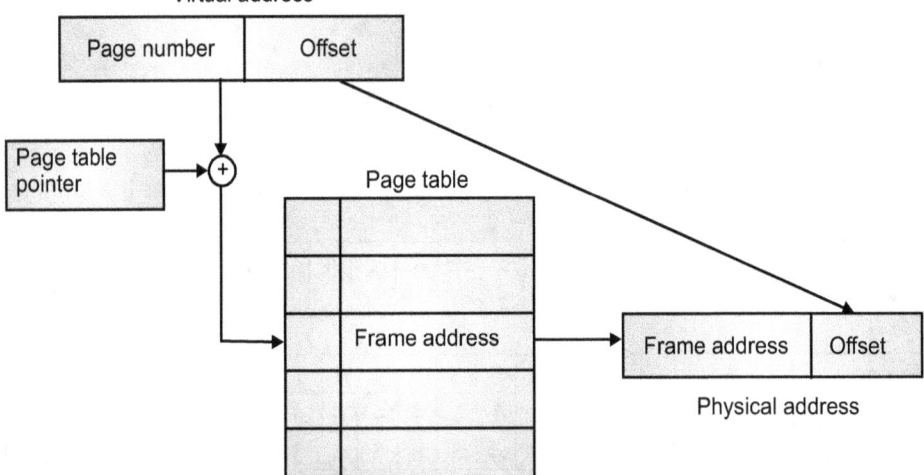

Fig. 5.29 : Virtual address translation

In a system using virtual memory, the physical memory is divided into equally-sized pages. The memory addressed by a process is also divided into logical pages of the same size. When a process references a memory address, the memory manager fetches from disk the page that includes the referenced address, and places it in a vacant physical page in the RAM. Subsequent references within that logical page are routed to the physical page. When the process references an address from another logical page, it too is fetched into a vacant physical page and becomes the target of subsequent similar references.

If the system does not have a free physical page, the memory manager swaps out a logical page into the swap area - usually a paging file on disk and copies (swaps in) the requested logical page into the now-vacant physical page. The page swapped out may belong to a different process. There are many strategies for choosing which page is to be swapped out. If a page is swapped out and then is referenced, it is swapped back in, from the swap area, at the expense of another page.

Shared Virtual Memory :

Although virtual memory allows processes to have separate (virtual) address spaces, there are times when you need processes to share memory. It is better to have only one copy in physical memory and all of the processes running share it. Dynamic libraries are another common example of executing code shared between several processes.

5.7 SECONDARY STORAGE DEVICE   [May 07, 09, Dec. 09]

A storage medium that holds information until it is deleted or overwritten. For example, a floppy disk drive or a hard disk drive is an example of a secondary storage device

5.7.1 Magnetic Disk

Magnetic disk provides the bulk of secondary storage for modern computer systems. Conceptually, disks are relatively simple. Each disk platter has a flat circular shape, like a CD. Common platter range from 1.8 to 5.25 inches. The two surfaces of a platter are covered with a magnetic material. We store information by recording it magnetically on the platters.

It is magnetically recorded and can be re-recorded over and over. Disks are rotating platters with a mechanical arm that moves a read/write head between the outer and inner edges of the platter's surface.

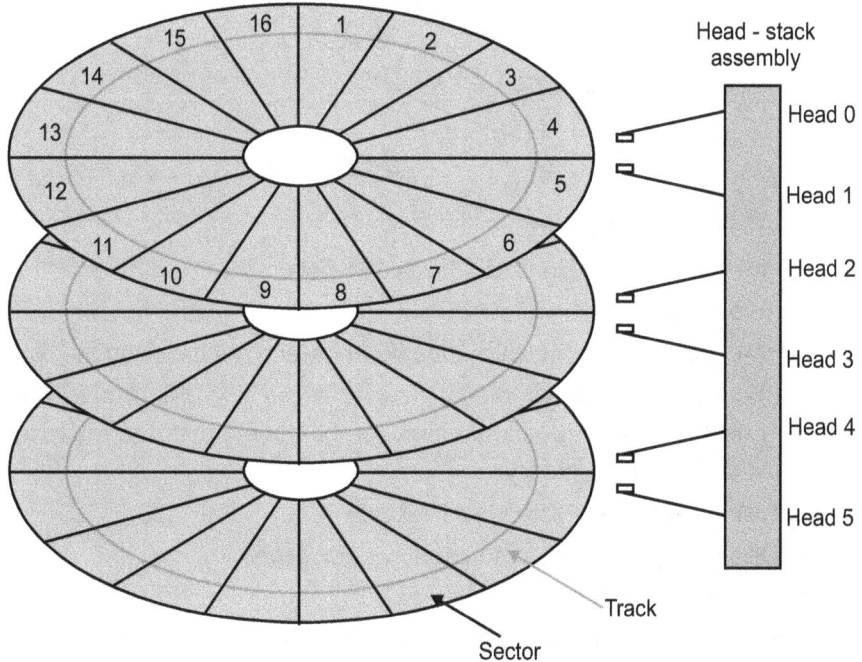

Fig. 5.30 : Components of disc drive

As shown in Fig. 5.30. The disk surface is divided into concentric tracks (circles within circles). Tracks are further divided into sectors the sector, which is typically 512 bytes, is the smallest unit that can be read or written.

The set of tracks that are at one arm position forms a cylinder.

In order to update the disk, one or more sectors are read into the computer, changed and written back to disk.

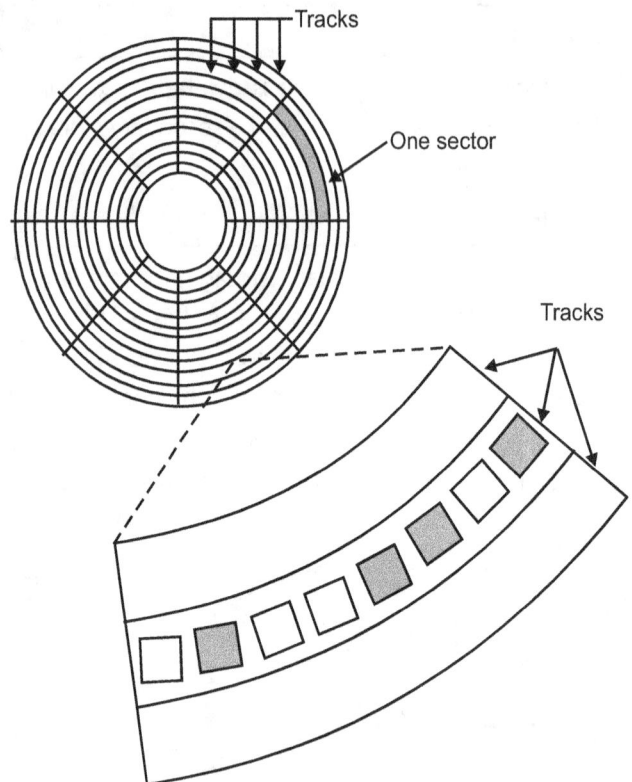

Fig. 5.31 : Surface of disc

Disc speed has two parts :

1. The transfer rate is the rate at which data flow between the drive and the computer.
2. The positioning time consists of the time to move the disk arm to the desired cylinder, called the seek time, and the time for the desired sector to rotate to the disk arm, called the rotational latency.

   Positioning time = seek time + rotational latency.

No removable Disk : It is permanently mounted in a disc drive.

E.g. Hard disk in a personal computer.

Removable disk : It can be removed and replaced with another disk. Such a disk can be moved from one computer system to another.

E.g. Floppy disks.

Single sided disks : Magnetizable coating is applied to both sides of the platter.

Double sided disks : Magnetizable coating is applied to both sides of the platter.

Single platter : Single platter is present in disk.

Multiple platters : Some disk drives accommodate multiple platters stacked vertically.

A Disk can be removable, allowing different disks to be removed as needed. Floppy discs are inexpensive removable magnetic disks.The head of floppy disk drive is designed to rotate more slowly than a hard-disk drive to reduce the wear on the disk surface. The storage capacity of a floppy disc is typically 1 MB and so.

A disk drive is attached to a computer by a set of wires called an 1/0 bus.

5.7.2 Magnetic Tape

Magnetic tape was used as an early secondary - storage medium. Although it is relatively permanent and can hold large quantities of data, its access time is slow in comparison to that of main memory.

In addition, random access to magnetic tape is about a thousand times slower than random access to magnetic disk, so tapes are not very useful for secondary storage.

Tapes are used mainly for backup and as a medium for transferring information from one system to another.

Magnetic tape is a medium for magnetic recording generally consisting of a thin magnetizable coating on a long and narrow strip of plastic. Nearly all recording tape is of this type, whether used for recording audio or video or for computer data storage. Devices that record and playback audio and video using magnetic tape are generally called tape recorders and video tape recorders respectively. A device that stores computer data on magnetic tape can be called a tape drive.

Magnetic tape allowed massive amounts of data to be stored in computers for long periods of time and rapidly accessed when needed.

Tape has been more economical than disks for archival data, but that is changing as disk capacities have increased enormously. If tapes are stored for the duration, they must be periodically recopied or the tightly coiled magnetic surfaces may contaminate each other.

Modern magnetic tape is most commonly packaged in cartridges and cassettes. The device that performs actual writing or reading of data is a tape drive.

When storing large amounts of data, tape can be substantially less expensive than disk or other data storage options. Tape storage has always been used with large computer systems.

Track Formats :

Tracks run parallel to the edge of the tape (linear recording) or diagonally (helical scan). A linear variation is serpentine recording, in which the tracks "snake" back and forth from the end of the tape to the beginning.

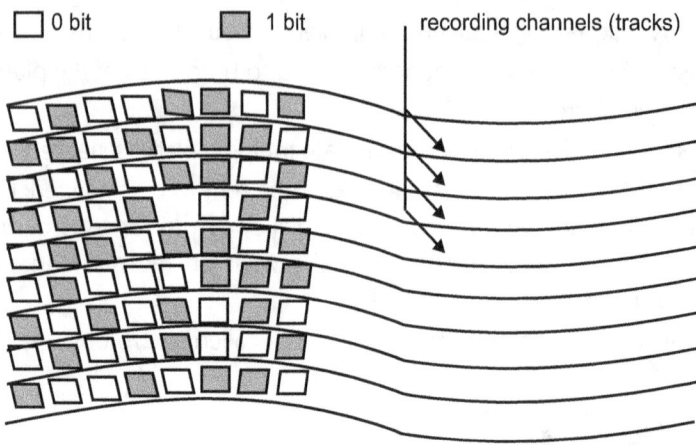

Fig. 5.32 : Tracks on Magnetic Tape

Data are recorded in blocks of contiguous bytes, separated by a space called an "interrecord gap" or "interblock gap." Tape drive speed is measured in inches per second (ips).

Advantages :

1. Less expensive when storing large amount of data.
2. Data stored is permanent.

Disadvantages :

1. The major drawback of tape is its sequential format. Locating a specific record requires reading every record in front of it or searching for markers that identify predefined partitions.
2. Updating requires copying files from the original tape to a blank tape (scratch tape) and adding the new data in between.
3. Access time is slow in magnetic tape.

5.7.3 DAT (Digital Audio Tape)

Digital Audio Tape (DAT or R-DAT) is a signal recording and playback medium developed by Sony in the mid 1980s. In appearance it is similar to a compact audio cassette, using 4 mm magnetic tape enclosed in a protective shell, but is roughly half the size at 73 mm x 54 mm x 10.5 mm. As the name suggests, the recording is digital rather than analog. DAT has the ability to record at higher, equal or lower sampling rates than a CD (48, 45.1 or 32 kHz sampling rate respectively) at 16-bits quantization. If a digital source is copied then the DAT will produce an exact clone, unlike other digital media such as Digital Compact Cassette or non-Hi-MD Mini Disc, both of which use lossy data compression.

Like most formats of videocassette, a DAT cassette may only be recorded on oneside, unlike an analog compact audio cassette.

For high-quality studio recording, effectively all of these formats were made obsolete in the early 1980's by two competing reel-to-reel formats with stationary heads.

R-DAT and S-DAT :

For a while, the DAT format was produced in two physically incompatible formats one with helical scanning heads, called R-DAT, and one with a stationary head block, called S-DAT. S-DAT failed to gain market share as it required more expensive technology in the machine, compared to the relatively simple (and much cheaper) spinning head approach of R-DAT.

Uses of DAT

1. **Professional recording industry**

   DAT was widely used in the professional audio recording industry in the 1990's, and is still used to some extent today. DAT's were also frequently used by radio broadcasters.

2. **Amateur and home use :**

   DAT was envisaged by proponents as the successor format to analogue audio cassettes in the way that the compact disc was the successor to vinyl-based recordings; however, the technology was never as commercially popular as CD. DAT recorders remained relatively expensive, and commercial recordings were generally not made available on the format. However, DAT was, for a time, popular for making and trading recordings of live music, since available DAT recorders predated affordable CD recorders.

3. **Computer data storage medium :**

   It is sequential-access media and is commonly used for backups.

5.7.4 RAID (Redundant Array of Inexpensive Disks)

[Dec. 07, 08, 09, May 10]

Disk drives have continued to get smaller and cheaper, so it is now economically feasible to attach a large number of disks to a computer system.

If the disks are operated in parallel, it improves the rate at which data can be read or written.

It offers reliability of data storage, because redundant information can be stored on multiple disks. So failure of one disk does not lead to loss of data.

To improve performance uses multiple parallel components. In the case of disk storage this leads to the development of arrays of disks that operate independently and in parallel.

1. "RAID" can divide and replicate data among multiple hard disk drives. The different schemes/ architectures are named by the word RAID followed by a number, as in RAID 0, RAID 1 etc.

2. RAID increased data reliability or increased input/output performance.

3. RAID array distributes data across multiple disks, but the array is seen by the Computer user and operating system as one single disk.

4. A failed disk may be replaced by a new one, and the lost data reconstructed from the remaining data and the parity data.

Purpose and Basics :

Redundancy is achieved by either writing the same data to multiple drives (known as mirroring), or writing extra data (known as parity data) across the array, calculated such that the failure of one (or possibly more, depending on the type of RAID) disks in the array will not result in loss of data.

Different levels of RAID :

- RAID 0 (striped disks).

- RAID 1 mirrors the contents of the disks, making a form of 1 : 1 ratio realtime backup. The contents of each disk in the array are identical to that of every other disk in the array.

- RAID 5 (striped disks with parity) combines three or more disks in a way that protects data against loss of any one disk. The storage capacity of the array is reduced by one disk.

- RAID 6 (striped disks with dual parity) can recover from the loss of two disks.

- RAID 10 (or 1 + 0) uses both striping and mirroring. "01" or "0 + 1" is sometimes distinguished from "10" or "1 + 0": a striped set of mirrored subsets and a mirrored set of striped subsets are both valid, but distinct, configurations.

RAID is not a good alternative to backing up data. Data may become damaged or destroyed without harm to the drive(s) on which they are stored. For example, some of the data may be overwritten by a system malfunction; a file may be damaged or deleted by user error and not noticed for days or weeks; and, of course, the entire array is at risk of physical damage.

RAID 0 :

Distributes data across several disks in a way that gives improved speed at any given instant. If one disk fails, however, all of the data on the array will be lost, as there is neither parity nor mirroring. The strips are mapped in round-robin way to consecutive array members.

No parity information for redundancy. A RAID 0 can be created with disks of differing sizes, but the storage space added to the array by each disk is limited to the size of the smallest disk. For example, if a 120 GB disk is striped together with a 100 GB disk, the size of the array will be 200 GB.

RAID 0

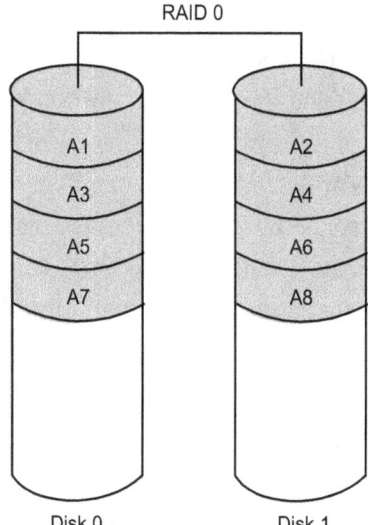

Fig. 5.33 : RAID 0 level

RAID 0 performances :

1. For reads and writes that are smaller than the stripe size, such as database access, the drives will be able to seek independently.
2. RAID 0 is useful for setups such as large read-only NFS servers where mounting many disks is time-consuming or impossible and redundancy is irrelevant.
3. RAID 0 is also used in some gaming systems where performance is desired and data integrity is not very important.

RAID 1 :

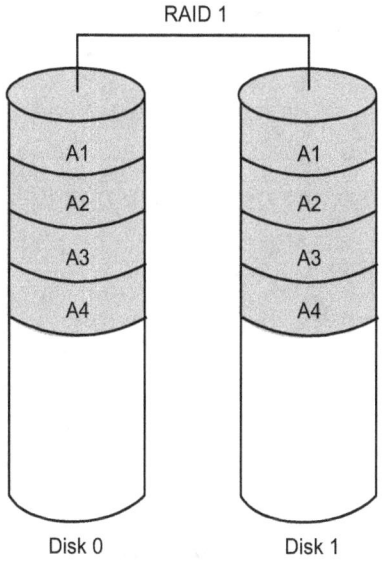

Fig. 5.34 : RAID 1 level

A **RAID 1** creates an exact copy (or **mirror**) of a set of data on two or more disks. This is useful when performance read or reliability is more important than data storage capacity. Such an array can only be as big as the smallest member disk. Since each member contains a complete copy of the data, and can be addressed independently; ordinary wear-and-tear reliability is raised by the power of the number of self-contained copies.

Advantages of RAID 1 organization :

1. Read request can be serviced by either of the two disks that contains the requested data, whichever one involves the minimum seek time plus rotational latency.
2. A write request requires that both corresponding strips be updated, in parallel.
3. Recovery from failure is simple. When a drive fails, the data may still be accessed from the second drive.

Disadvantage of RAID 1 organization :

1. Cost is more.
2. It requires twice the disk space of the logical disk that it supports.
3. If 1/0 requests are write requests, then there may be not significant performance gain over RAID 0.

RAID 2 :

A **RAID 2** stripes data at the bit (rather than block) level, here data stripping used same way as in RAID level 0 and RAID level 1. But to achieve reliability, an error correcting code is calculated across corresponding bits on each data disks and the bits of code are stored in the corresponding bit positions on multiple parity disks. It uses a Hamming code for error correction. The disks are synchronized by the controller to spin in perfect tandem. Extremely high data transfer rates are possible. This is the only original level of RAID that is not currently used.

The use of the Hamming (7, 4) code (four data bits plus three parity bits) also permits using 7 disks in RAID 2, with 4 being used for data storage and 3 being used for error correction.

Multiple-bit corruption is possible though extremely rare. RAID 2 can detect but not repair double-bit corruption.

Advantages :

1. Error correcting code is calculated.
2. Requires fewer disks than RAID.
3. Extremely high data transfer rates are possible.

Disadvantages :

1. More costly.
2. RAID 2 can detect but not repair double-bit corruption.

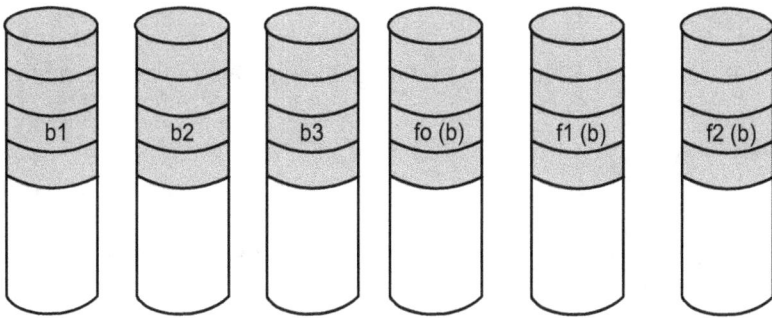

Fig. 5.35 : RAID 2 level

RAID 3 :

RAID 3 is organized in a similar fashion to RAID 2. Here data bits are organized in similar fashion to RAID level 2. The difference is that RAID 3 requires only a single redundant disk, no matter how large the disk array.

Advantages of RAID 3 organization :

1. However, the performance characteristic of RAID 3 is very consistent, unlike higher RAID levels, the size of a stripe is less than the size of a sector or OS block so that, for both reading and writing, the entire stripe is accessed every time.
2. The performance of the array is therefore identical to the performance of one disk in the array except for the transfer rate, this is multiplied by the number of data drives (i.e., less parity drives).
3. This makes it good for applications that demand the highest transfer rates, for example uncompressed video editing.

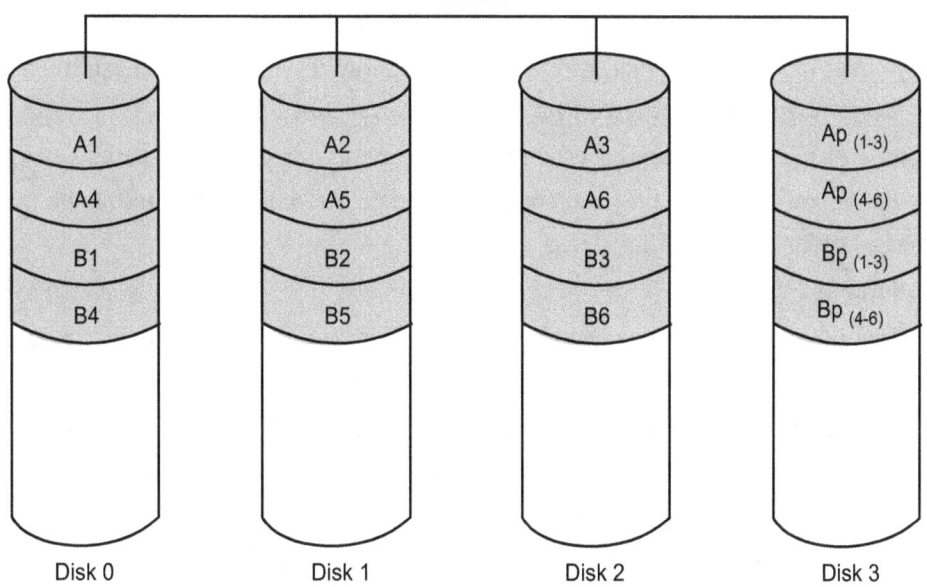

Fig. 5.36 : RAID 3 level

Disadvantage :

One of the side effects of RAID 3 is that it generally cannot service multiple requests simultaneously.

RAID 4 :

Here data stripping is used same as used in other levels, but the size of strip is large which represents one data block.

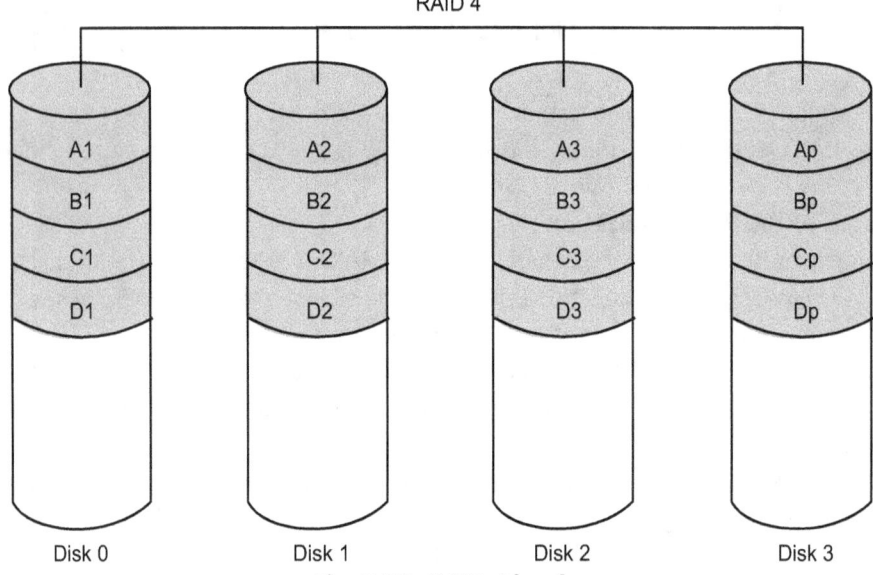

RAID 4

Disk 0   Disk 1   Disk 2   Disk 3

Fig. 5.37 : RAID 4 level

A RAID 4 uses block-level striping with a dedicated parity disk. This allows each member of the set to act independently when only a single block is requested.

Generally, RAID 4 is implemented with hardware support for parity calculations. For each read/write operation parity bits are checked for data reliability. As a result, parity disk becomes a bottleneck.

Disadvantages :

1. Every write operation must involve the parity disk, which therefore become bottleneck.

2. Each stripe write involves 2 reads and 2 writes. Because it must old 3. The performance of RAID 4 in this configuration can be very poor, but unlike RAID.

3. It does not need synchronized spindles. However, if RAID 4 is implemented on synchronized drives and the size of a stripe is reduced below the OS block size a RAID 4 array then has the same performance pattern as a RAID 3 array.

RAID 5 :

RAID 5 is organized in a similar fashion to RAID 5. The difference is that RAID 5 distributes the parity strips across all disks. A typical allocation is a round-robin scheme. For an n-disk array, the parity strip is on a different disk for the first n stripes and the pattern then repeats.

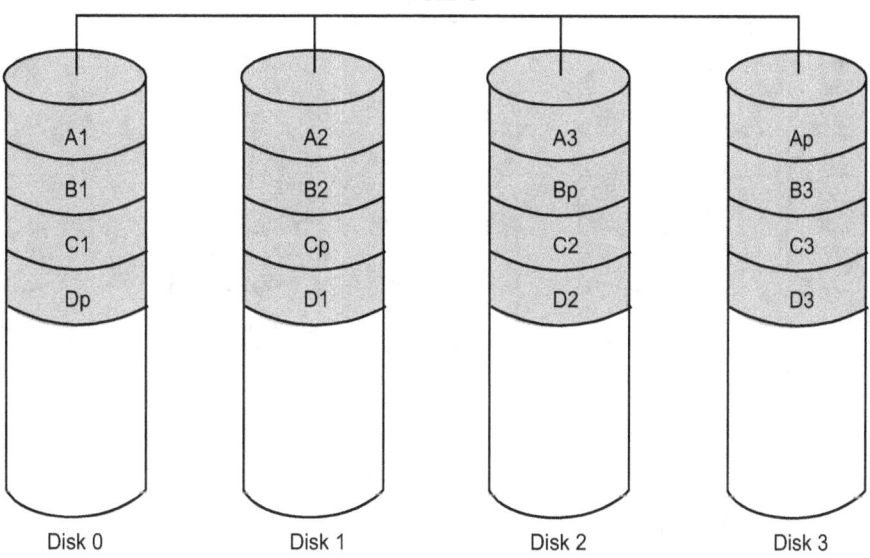

Fig. 5.38 : RAID 5 level

Advantages :

1. The distribution of parity strips across all drives avoids the potential 1/0 bottleneck.
2. Low cost of redundancy.
3. The read performance of RAID 5 is almost as good as RAID 0 for the same number of disks.

Disadvantages :

1. RAID 5 writes are expensive in terms of disk operations and traffic between the disks and the controller.
2. RAID 5 implementations suffer from poor performance when faced with a workload which includes many writes which are smaller than the capacity of a single stripe.

    This is because parity must be updated on each write, requiring read-modify-write sequences for both the data block and the parity block.
3. Random write performance is poor, especially at high concurrency levels common in large multi-user databases

RAID 6 (Redundancy and data loss recovery capability) :

RAID 6 extends RAID 5 by adding an additional parity block; thus it uses block-level striping with two parity blocks distributed across all member disks. It was not one of the original RAID levels.

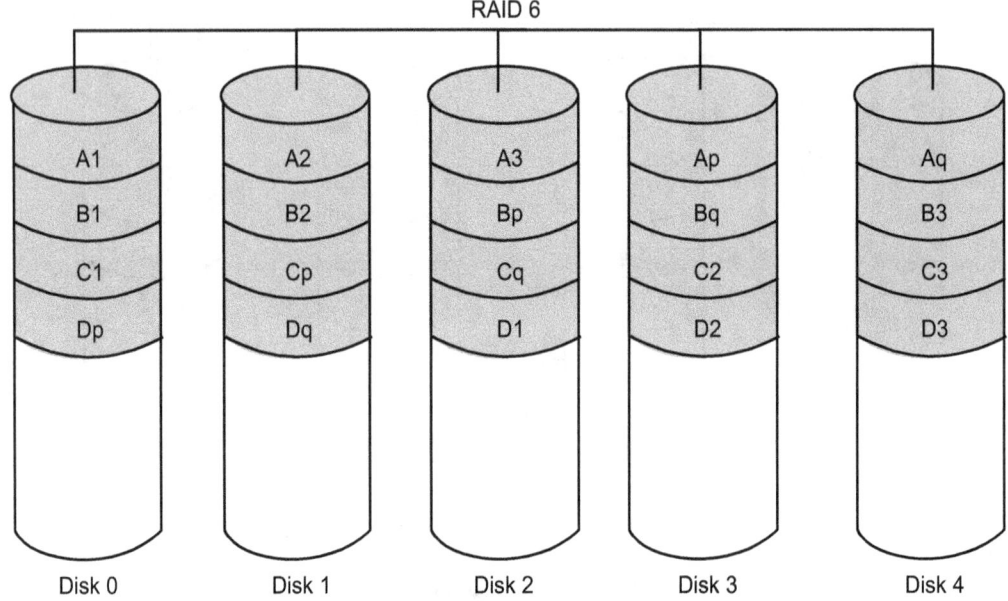

Fig. 5.39 : RAID 6 level

By adding additional syndromes it is possible to achieve any number of redundant disks, and recover from the failure of that many drives anywhere in the array.

Advantages :

1. It provides extremely high data availability.

2. RAID 6 does not have a performance penalty for read operations.

3. As arrays become bigger and have more drives the loss in storage capacity becomes less important and the probability of data loss is greater. RAID 6 provides protection against data loss during an array rebuild; by replacing a failed drive.

Disadvantages :

1. It does have a performance penalty on write operations because of the overhead associated with parity calculations.

2. RAID 6 provides protection against data loss during an array rebuild; when a second drive is lost, a bad block read is encountered, or when a human operator accidentally removes and replaces the wrong disk drive when attempting to replace a failed drive.

5.7.5 Optical Memory   [May 07]

In Optical Memory, data is stored on an optical medium (i.e., CD-ROM or DVD), and read with a laser beam. While not currently practical for use in computer processing, optical memory is an ideal solution for storing large quantities of data very inexpensively, and more importantly, transporting that data between computer devices.

5.7.5.1 CD-ROM (Compact Disc Read Only Memory)   [Dec. 07, 08, May 09]

The CD is a no erasable disk that can store more than 60 minutes of audio information on one side. It is low cost optical-disk for storage.

Discs are made from a 1.2 mm thick disc of polycarbonate plastic, with a thin layer of aluminum to make a reflective surface. The most common size of CD-ROM disc is 120 mm in diameter, though the smaller Mini CD standard with an 80 mm diameter, as well as numerous non-standard sizes and shapes are also available.

CD-ROMs are popularly used to distribute computer software, including games and multimedia applications, though any data can be stored (up to the capacity limit of a disc). Some CDs hold both computer data and audio with the latter capable of being played on a CD player, while data (such as software or digital video) is only usable on a computer (such as PC CD-ROMs). These are called enhanced CDs.

CD-ROM discs are identical in appearance to audio CDs, and data are stored and retrieved in a very similar manner.

CD-ROM is a compact disc that contains data accessible by a computer. While the compact Disc format was originally designed for music storage and playback, the format was later adapted to hold any form of binary data.

Capacity :

A standard 120 mm CD ROM holds 650 or 700 MB of data. Textual data can be compressed by more than a factor of 10, using compression algorithms.

CD ROM Drives :

CD ROM discs are read using CD ROM drives. Which are now almost universal on personal computers? A CD ROM drive may be connected to a computer via an IDE SCSI, SATA, and Fire wire or USB interface. Virtually all modern CD ROM drives can also play audio CDs as well as video CDs and other data standards.

CD-ROM Data Storage :

Two new sectors were defined, Mode 1 for storing computer data and Mode 2 for compressed audio or video/graphic data.

CD-ROM Mode 1 :

CD-ROM Mode 1 is the mode used for CD-ROMs that carry data and applications only. Data is stored in sectors, which each hold 2,352 bytes of data, with an additional number of bytes used for error detection and correction, as well as control structures.

CD-ROM Mode 2 :

CD-ROM Mode 2 is used for compressed audio/video information and uses only two layers of error detection and correction. Although the sectors of CD-ROM Mode 1 and Mode 2 are the same size, the amount of data that can be stored varies considerably because of the use of sync and header bytes, error correction and detection.

Information is retrieved from a CD or CD-ROM by a low-powered laser housed in an optical disk player or drive unit.

To achieve greater capacity, CDs and CD-ROMs do not organize information on concentric tracks. Instead, the disk contains a single spiral track, beginning near the center and spiraling out to the outer edge of the disk.

Constant Linear Velocity (CLV) is the principle by which data is read from a CD-ROM. This principal states that the read head must interact with the data track at a constant rate, whether it is accessing data from the inner or outermost portions of the disc. This is affected by varying the rotation speed of the disc, from 500 rpm at the center, to 200 rpm at the outside. In a music CD, data is read sequentially, so rotation speed is not an issue. The CD-ROM, on the other hand, must read in random patterns, which necessitates constantly shifting rotation speeds. Pauses in the read function are audible, and some of the faster drives can be quite noisy because of it.

Compared with traditional hard disks, the CD-ROM has the following advantages :

1. The optical disk together with the information stored on it can be mass replicated inexpensively - unlike a magnetic disk.
2. The optical disk is removable, allowing the disk itself to be used for archival storage.
3. It is highly reliable and efficient information storage system.
4. It provides high capacity read only memory.
5. It is light in weight and can be easily carried from one comp to another.

Disadvantages of CD-ROM :

1. It is read-only and cannot be updated.
2. It has an access time much longer than that of a magnetic disk drive.
3. Needs careful handling, because dust, finger prints, and crashes on reading surface may affect.

CD-Recordable (CD-R) :

To accommodate applications in which only one or small number of copies of set of data is needed, the write-once read-many CD, known as the CD-R, has been developed.

CD-Rewritable :

CD-RNV has the obvious advantage over CD-ROM and CD-R that it can be written and overwritten, as a magnetic disk.

5.7.5.2 DVD (Digital Versatile Disc)   [May 09, Dec. 09]

DVD, also known as "Digital Versatile Disc" or "Digital Video Disc" is an optimal disk storage media format. Its main uses are video and audio data storage. DVDs are of same dimension as CDs, as but more than six times as much data storage capacity.

DVD technology offers many improvements over earlier electronic resources. DVD disks are more durable and portable than laser discs and more resistant to scratches than CDs.

Unlike magnetic media such as floppy discs and videotapes, DVD discs are optimal media and cannot be damaged by magnet fields. They are also less sensitive to extreme temperature.

The DVDs greater capacity is due to some differences from CDs :

    1.   Bits are packed more closely on DVD.

    2.   The DVD - ROM can be two sided whereas data is recorded on only one side of a CD.

The term DVD used in describing three ways that data is stored on the disc.

    1.   DVD ROM has data which can only be a read and not written.

    2.   DVD-R can be written once and then functions as DVD ROM.

    3.   DVD RAM holds data that can be rewritten multiple times.

DVD video and audio discs respectively refer to properly formatted and structured video and audio content. Everything else including other types of DVD discs with video content is referred to as a DVD data disc. DVD is also used generically to refer to HD (high density). Video disc formats blu-ray and HD DVD.

Features of DVD :

- Backward compatibility with current CD media.
- Physical dimensions are identical to CD but with capacity at least 7 times larger than that of CD.
- Capacities of 5.7 GB, 8.54 GB etc. depending on disk structure.
- DVD is a popular optical disc storage media format used for data storage.
- Its main usage is for move software and data archiving.

DVD Recordable And Rewritable :

HP initially developed recordable DVD media from the need to store data for backup and transport. DVD recordable is now also used for consumer audio and video recording.

The different types are

    DVD – R

    DVD + R

    DVD – RW

    DV – RW

1. DVD-R :

It is a DVD recordable format. A DVD - R has a larger storage capacity than its optical predecessor, the 700 MB CD-R, typically storing 4,71 GB.

Data on DVD - R can not be changed whereas DVD-RW can be rewritten multiple (1000+) times

2. DVD + R :

A DVD+R is once writable optical discs with 5.7 GB of stored capacity. It has slightly less storage capacity than DVD–R. Unlike DVD+RW discs, DVD+R discs can only be written to once. Because of this, DVD+R discs are suited to applications such as non-volatile data storage, audio, or video. This can cause confusion because the DVD +RW alliance logo is stylized "RW". Thus, a DVD+R discs can have the RW logo but is not a rewritable.

3.DVD-RW :

A DVD-RW is a rewritable optical disc with equal storage capacity to a DVD-R typically 5.7 GB. The primary advantage of DVD-RW over DVD-R is the ability to erase and rewrite to a DVD-RW disc. DVD-RW discs are commonly used for volatile data, such as backups or collection of files. They are also increasingly used for home DVD video recorder. One benefit to using a rewritable disc is if there are writing errors when recording data, the disc is not ruined and can still store data be erasing the faulty data.

4. DVD + RW :

DVD+RW are the name of standard for optical discs; one of several types of DVD which hold up to about say 5.7 GB per disc and are used for storing films, music, or other data. DVD+RW supports random write access, which means that data can be added or removed without erasing the whole disc and starting over (up to about 1000 times). With suitable support from OS, DVD+RW media can thus be treated like a large floppy discs, in contrast to DVD-RW which must be erased before rewriting can takes place. However, they (And DVD-RW) are less popular for computer use than DVD-R or DVD+R discs because they are not suitable for permanent backup files (because non-rewritable media is significantly cheaper). For similar reasons rewritable discs are not widely used for permanent storage of home DVD video recorders as DVD-R and DVD+R. On the other hand, DVD+RW or DVD-RNV makes an inexpensive medium for multiple temporary recordings. They can be used for daily discs of backup cycle (which are overwritten after a number of days or weeks). And can become very popular for their convenience and cheapness.

DVD, also known as **"Digital Versatile Disc"** or **"Digital Video Disc"**, is an optical disc storage media format. Its main uses are video and data storage. DVDs are of the same dimensions as compact discs (CDs), but store more than six tunes as much data.

Questions

1. Compare Associative and Set-Associative mapped cache.
2. A block set-Associative cache consists of 64 blocks divided into 4 block sets. The main memory contains 4096 blocks, each consisting of 128 words of 16 bits length
   (i) How many bits are there in main memory ?
   (ii) How many bits are there in each of the TAG, SET and WORD fields ?
3. What are the page replacement algorithms ? Give the details of LRU algorithm.
4. Explain briefly :
   (i) CD-ROM   (iii) DVD
   (ii) DAT   (iv) Magnetic Disk
5. How does SDRAM differs from an ordinary DRAM ? Explain.
6. Explain briefly the seven RAID levels.
7. What is MESI protocol ? Explain the meaning of each of the four states of the MESI protocol.
8. Discuss in detail hardware cache coherent schemes.
9. What is cache memory ? Explain how a memory address is mapped into a cache memory address using set associative mapped cache. The main memory is 64 K words. The cache memory had 2048 words with block size of 128 words.

10. Explain the following :
    (i)   EPROM   (ii) EEPROM
    (iii) SRAM   (iv) DRAM
    (v)   RD RAM

11. What is mean by virtual memory ? Explain with the help of a neat diagram, the virtual memory address translation.

12. Explain
    (i)   Direct
    (ii) Set associative cache mapping techniques along with its merits and demerits.

13. Consider a cache consisting of 256 blocks of 16 words each for a total number of 4096 (4 K) words and assume that the main memory is addressable by a 16-bit address and it consists of 4 K blocks. How many bits are there in each of the TAG, BLOCK/ SET and WORD fields for different mapping techniques ?

14. Explain high speed memories:
    (i)   Associative   (ii) Interleaved

15. Explain briefly :
    (i)   Optical memory
    (ii) DVD

16. Explain DRAM and SRAM with diagram. Also give advantages and disadvantages.

17. What is virtual memory concept ? Explain the role of TLB in virtual memory organization.

18. Explain the following terms :
    (i) Cache updation policies   (ii) Cache hit and cache miss.

19. Compare SRAM versus DRAM.

20. What are the different cache mapping techniques ? Explain any one with neat diagram.

21. Write short notes on :
    (i)   Virtual memory   (ii) Cache memory

22. Compare Associative and Set Associative mapped cache.

MICROPROCESSOR

6.1 8086 MICROPROCESSOR ORGANIZATION

6.1.1 History of Intel Microprocessor

First IC is invented by Fairchild semiconductors in 1957. In 1968, Robert Noyce, Gordan Moore, Andrew Grove resigned from Fairchild Semiconductors and founded their own company Intel (Integrated Electronics).

Fig. 6.1 : INTEL 4004

In 1971 first microprocessor Introduced by Intel is 4 bit µp with clock speed 740 kHz. It had 2,300 transistors. It could execute around 60,000 instructions per second.

Fig. 6.2 : INTEL 4040

In 1974 Intel Introduced 4040 in 1974. It was also 4-bit µP.

Fig. 6.3 : INTEL 8008

In 1972 Intel Introduced 8008 in 1972. It was first 8-bit µP. Its clock speed was 500 kHz which execute 50,000 instructions per second.

Fig. 6.4 : INTEL 8080

In 1974 Intel 8080 Introduced. It was also 8-bit µP. Its clock speed was 2 MHz. It had 6,000 transistors. It was 10 times faster than 8008. It could execute 5,00,000 instructions per second.

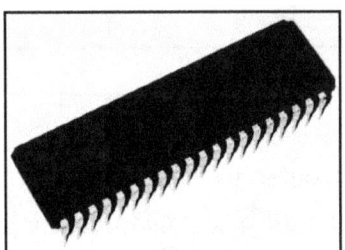

Fig. 6.5 : INTEL 8085

In 1976 Intel 8085 is Introduced. It was also 8-bit µP. Its clock speed was 3 MHz. Its data bus is 8-bit and address bus is 16-bit. It had 6,500 transistors. It could execute 7,69,230 instructions per second. It could access 64 KB of memory. It had 246 instructions.

Fig. 6.6 : Intel 8086

In 1978 Intel 8086 is Introduced. It was first 16-bit µP.

Its clock speed is 4.77 MHz, 8MHz and 10 MHz, depending on the version. Its data bus is 16-bit and address bus is 20-bit. It had 29,000 transistors. It could execute 2.5 million instructions per second. It could access 1 MB of memory. It had 22,000 instructions.

It had **Multiply** and **Divide** instructions.

8088 is Introduced in 1979. It was also 16-bit microprocessor. It was created as a cheaper version of Intel's 8086. It was a 16-bit processor with an 8-bit external bus. It could execute 2.5 million instructions per second. This chip became the most popular in the computer industry when IBM used it for its first PC.

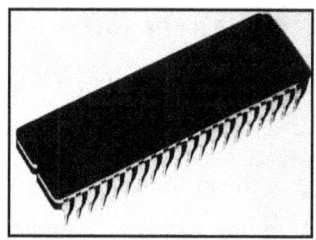

Fig. 6.7 : Intel 8088

Then intel has introduced a series of Microprocessors 80186 / 188,80286,80386DX / SX / SL / SLC/EX, 80486DX/SX/dx2/sl/dx4, Pentium, PentiumPro, Pentium MMX, Pentium II, Celeron, Pentium III, Pentium II/III Xeon, Pentium 4, Itanium, Xeon, Itanium 2 and Itanium 3 and So on.

6.1.2 Introduction to Microprocessor

A processor is a circuitry that processes the data.

Data is raw facts or raw information after processing, data becomes meaningful and we call it as information.

e.g. Dipak 32 MBA this data is not meaningful. We can not understand what the other user want to say after processing we get

My name is Dipak. I am 32 years old. I have completed MBA.

which is meaningful data and so it is called information.

The processor takes input as data process the data and provides o/p as result.

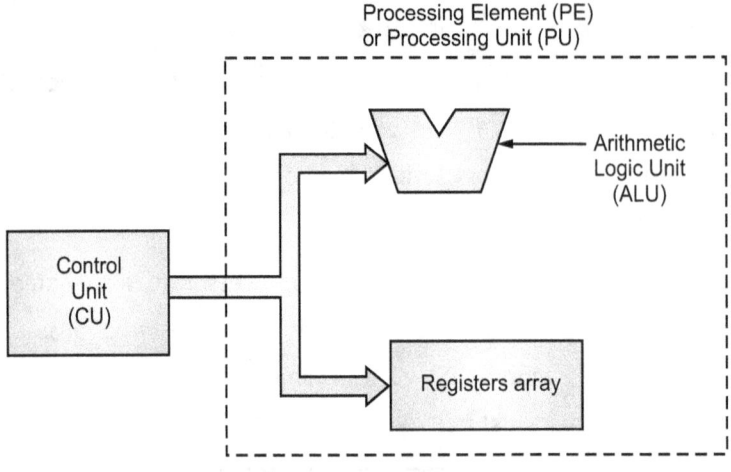

Fig. 6.8 : Processor

The components of processor are arithmetic logic unit (ALU), register array and control unit (CU).

ALU and Register array together form the Processing Element (PE) or Processing Unit (PU). As shown in Fig. 6.8. If all components of processor (ALU, register array and CU) register present on a single chip, the size of the processor reduces and the processor is called a **Microprocessor**. The microprocessor is as shown in Fig. 6.9.

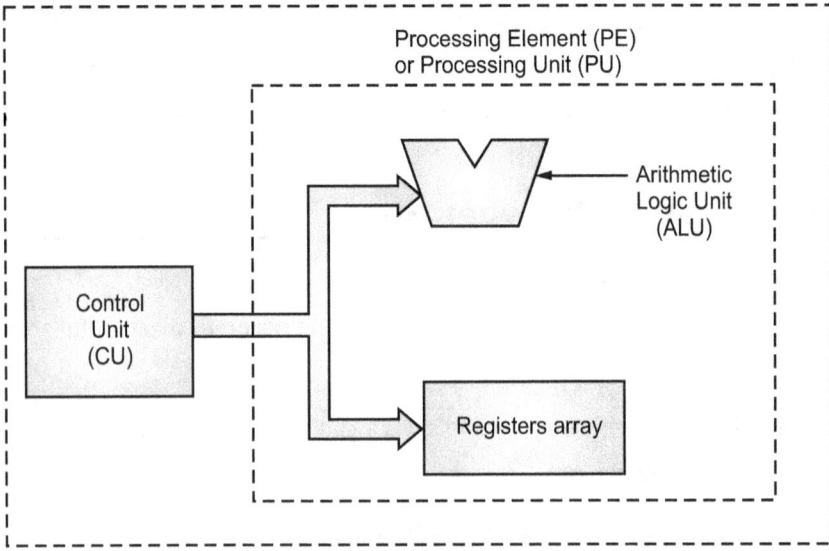

Fig. 6.9 : Microprocessor

When the processor is interfaced with memory and/or input/output (I/O) or pheripheral, the combination is called a computer. A computer is shown in Fig. 6.10.

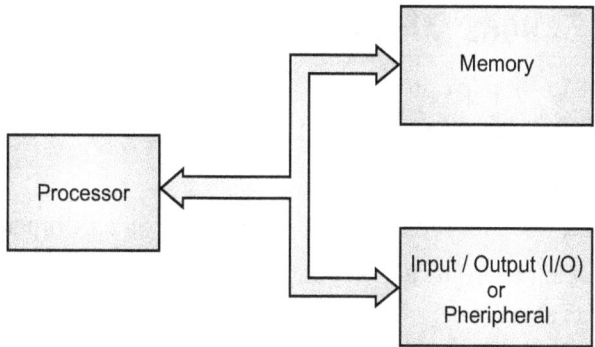

Fig. 6.10 : Computer

If the processor in the computer is a microprocessor the computer is called a Microcomputer or a Microprocessor based system.

A microcomputer or a microprocessor based system is shown in Fig. 6.11.

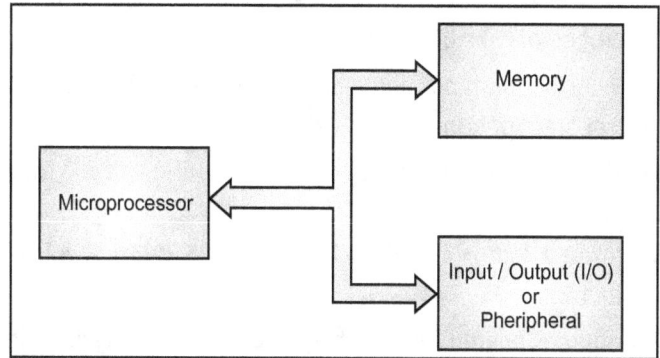

Fig. 6.11 : Microcomputers or microprocessor based system

When the microprocessor, memory and input/output (I/O) or peripherial are present on single chip it is called a single-chip microcomputer or microcontroller, when chip memory is not sufficient, the additional memory can be interfaced externally to the microcontroller Fig. 6.12 shows microcontroller.

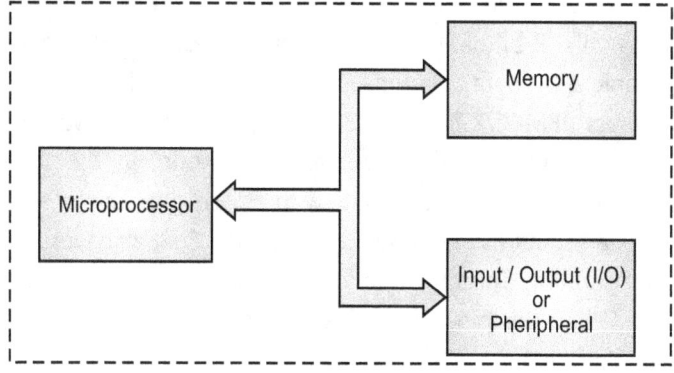

Fig. 6.12 : Microcontroller

6.1.3 Features of 8086 Microprocessor

- It was the first 16-bit microprocessor.
- It is available as 40-pin Dual-Inline-Package (DIP).
- It consists of 29,000 transistors.
- 8086 has 16-bit ALU; this means 16-bit numbers are directly processed by 8086.
- It has 16-bit data bus, so it can read data or write data to memory or I/O ports either 16 bits or 8 bits at a time.
- It has 20 address lines, so it can address up to 2^{20} i.e. 1048576 = 1 Mbytes of memory (words i.e. 16 bit numbers are stored in consecutive memory locations). Due to the 1 Mbytes memory size multiprogramming is made feasible as well as several multiprogramming features have been incorporated in 8086 design.
- 8086 includes few features, which enhance multiprocessing capability (it can be used with math coprocessors like 8087, I/O processor 8089 etc.
- Operates on +5V supply and single phase (single line) clock frequency. (Clock is generated by separate peripheral chip 8284).
- 8086 comes with different versions. 8086 runs at 5 MHz, 8086-2 runs at 8 MHz, 8086-1 runs at 10 MHz.
- It has multiplexed address and data bus like 8085 due to which the pin count is reduced considerably.
- Higher Throughput (Speed) (This is achieved by a concept called pipelining. Fetching the next instruction while current instruction is under execution is called pipelining.)

8086 is the first 16-bit microprocessor from INTEL, released in the year 1978. The term 16 bit means that it's ALU, its internal registers and most of the instructions are designed to work with 16 bit binary words. 8086 microprocessor has a 16-bit data bus and 20-bit address bus. So, it can address any one of 2^{20} = 1048576 = 1 mega byte memory locations. INTEL 8088 has the same ALU, same registers and same instruction set as the 8086. But the only difference is 8088 has only 8-bit data bus and 20-bit address bus. Hence, the 8088 can only read/write/ports of only 8-bit data at a time. The 8088 was used as the CPU in the original IBM personal computers [IBMPC/XT]. The 8086 microprocessor can work in two modes of operations. They are Minimum mode and Maximum mode. In the minimum mode of operation the microprocessors do not associate with any co-processors and cannot be used for multiprocessor systems. But in the maximum mode the 8086 can work in multi-processor or co-processor configuration. This minimum or maximum operations are decided by the pin MN/ MX(Active low). When this pin is high 8086 operates in minimum mode otherwise it operates in Maximium mode.

6.1.4 Differences Between 8086 and 8088 Microprocessors

Though the architecture and instruction set of both 8086 and 8088 processors are same, still we find certain differences between them. They are

(i)   8086 has 16-bit data bus lines whereas   8088 has 8-data lines.

(ii)   8086 is available in three clock speeds namely 5 MHz, 8 MHz(8086-2) and 10 MHz (8086-1) whereas 8088 is available is only available only in two speeds namely 5 MHz and 8 MHz.

(iii)   The memory address space of 8086 is organized as two 512kB banks whereas 8088 memory space is implemented as a single 1MX 8 memory bank.

(iv)   8086 has a 6-byte instruction queue whereas 8088 has a 4 byte instruction queue. The reason for this is that 8088 can fetch only one byte at a time.

(v)   In 8086 the memory control pin (M/IO) signal is complement of the 8088 equivalent signal (IO/M).

(vi)   The 8086 has BHE (Bank High Enable) whereas 8088 has SSO status signal.

(vii)   The byte and word data operations of 8086 are different from 8088.

(viii) 8086 can read or write either 8-bit or 16-bit word at a time, whereas 8088 can read only 8-bit data at a time.

(ix)   The I/O voltage levels for 8086 are, Vol is measured at 2.5 mA and for 8088 it is measured at 2.0 mA.

(x)   8086 draws a maximum supply current of 360 mA and the 8088 draws a maximum of 340 mA.

Nowadays 8086 are no longer used. But the concept of its principles and structures is very useful for understanding other advanced Intel microprocessors.

6.2   ARCHITECTURE OF 8086/8088

The microprocessors functions as the CPU digital computer. Its job is to generate all system timing signals and synchronize the transfer of data between memory, I/O and itself. It accomplishes this task via the three-bus system architecture previously discussed.

The microprocessor also has a S/W function. It must recognize, decode, and execute program instructions fetched from the memory unit. This requires an Arithmetic-Logic Unit (ALU) within the CPU to perform arithmetic and logical (AND, OR, NOT, compare, etc) functions.

To improve the performance by implementing the parallel processing concept, the 8086/8088 CPU is organized as two separate units-

1. Bus Interface Unit (BIU) and

2. Execution Unit (EU).

Fig. shows the Architecture of 8086 Microprocessor.

The BIU provides H/W functions, including generation of the memory and I/O addresses for the transfer of data between the outside world, outside the CPU, and the EU.

The BIU sends addresses, fetches instructions, read data from ports and memory and writes data to ports and memory. The BIU handles all transfers data and addresses on the buses required by the execution unit. Whereas the Execution Unit decodes the instructions and executes the instructions. The EU receives program instruction codes and data from the BIU, executes these instructions and store the results in the general registers. By passing the data back to the BIU, data can also be stored in a memory location or written to an output device. Note that the EU has no connection to the system buses. It receives and outputs all its data through the BIU.

6.2.1 The Execution Unit

The Execution Unit consists of a control system, a 16-bit ALU, 16-bit Flag register and four general purpose registers namely AX, BX, CX and DX, pointer registers SP, BP and Index registers SI, DI of each 16-bits.

The control unit controls all the internal operations. The instruction decoder in the execution unit decodes the instructions fetched from the memory into a series of actions. The ALU performs the operations like add, subtract, AND, OR, XOR, increment, decrement, complement, and shifting the binary numbers.

6.2.2 Bus Interface Unit

The BIU consists of a 6-byte long instruction register called Instruction Queue.

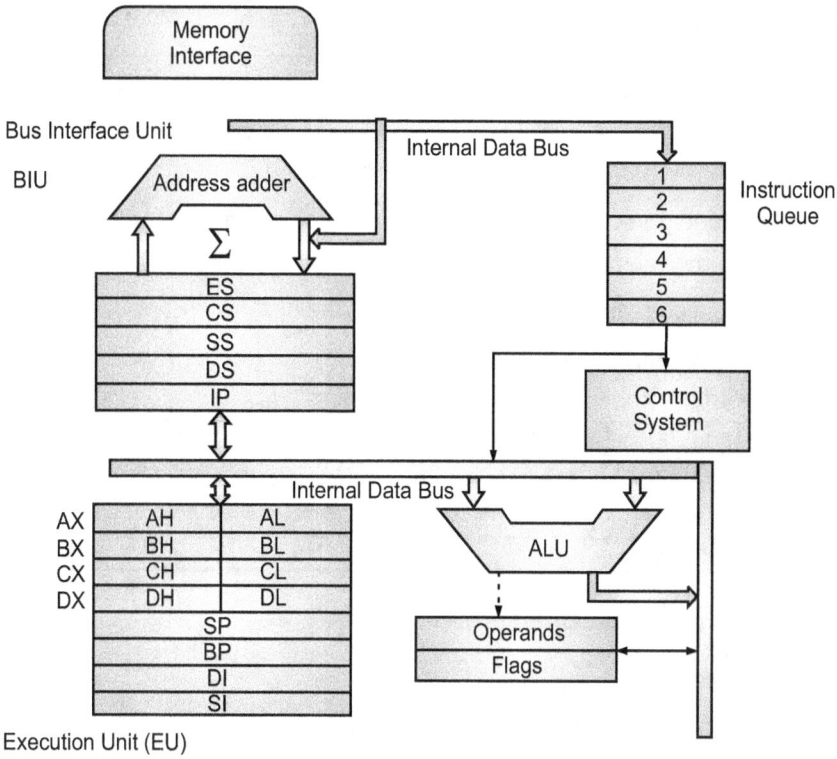

Fig. 6.13 : Architecture of 8086 Microprocessor

And four segment registers as Extra segment register ES, Code segment register CS, Stack Segment Register SS and Data Segment Register DS , one Instruction Pointer IP and an adder circuit to calculate the 20 bit physical address of a location. This bus interface unit performs all the external bus operations like fetching the instructions from the memory, read/write data from/into memory or port and also supporting the instruction Queue etc. The BIU fetches up to six instruction bytes from the memory and stores these pre-fetched bytes in a first –in first out register set called Instruction Queue. When the execution unit is ready for the execution of the instruction, it reads the byte from the Queue instead of fetching the byte/word from the memory. This will increase the overall speed of microprocessor. Fetching the next instruction while the current instruction executes is called pipelining or parallel processing.

The important point to note, however, is that because the EU is the same for each processor (8086/8088), the programming instructions are exactly the same for each. Programs written for the 8086 can be run on the 8088 without any changes.

6.2.3 Fetch and Execute

Although the 8086/88 still functions as a stored program computer, organization of the CPU into a separate BIU and EU allows the fetch and execute cycles to overlap. To see this, consider what happens when the 8086 or 8088 is first started.

1. The BIU outputs the contents of the instruction pointer register (IP) onto the address bus, causing the selected byte or word to be read into the BIU.

2. Register IP is incremented by 1 to prepare for the next instruction fetch.

3. Once inside the BIU, the instruction is passed to the queue. This is a first-in, first-out storage register sometimes likened to a "pipeline".

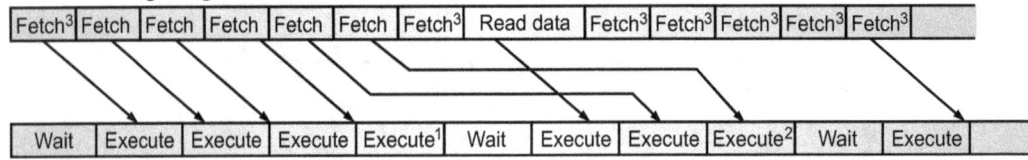

[1] This instruction requires a request for data not in the queue
[2] Jump instruction occurs
[3] These bytes are discarded

Fig. 6.14 : Fetch and Execute cycle of 8086

4. Assuming that the queue is initially empty, the EU immediately draws this instruction from the queue and begins execution.

5. While the EU is executing this instruction, the BIU proceeds to fetch a new instruction. Depending on the execution time of the first instruction, the BIU may fill the queue with several new instructions before the EU is ready to draw its next instruction.

The BIU is programmed to fetch a new instruction whenever the queue has room for one (with the 8088) or two (with the 8086) additional bytes. The advantage of this pipelined architecture is that the EU can execute instructions almost continually instead of having to wait for the BIU to fetch a new instruction.

There are three conditions that will cause the EU to enter a "wait" mode :

1. The first occurs when an instruction requires access to a memory location not in the queue. The BIU must suspend fetching instructions and output the address of this memory location. After waiting for the memory access, the EU can resume executing instruction codes from the queue (and the BIU can resume filling the queue).

2. The second condition occurs when the instruction to be executed is a "jump" instruction. In this case control is to be transferred to a new (non-sequential) address. The queue, however, assumes that instructions will always be executed in sequence

and thus will be holding the "wrong" instruction codes. The EU must wait while the instruction at the jump address is fetched. Note that any bytes presently in the queue must be discarded (they are overwritten).

3. One other condition can cause the BIU to suspend fetching instructions. This occurs during execution of instructions that are slow to execute. For example, the instruction AAM (ASCII Adjust for Multiplication) requires 83 clock cycles to complete. At four cycles per instruction fetch, the queue will be completely filled during the execution of this single instruction. The BIU will thus have to wait for the EU to pull over one or two bytes from the queue before resuming the fetch cycle.

A subtle advantage to the pipelined architecture should be mentioned. Because the next several instructions are usually in the queue, the BIU can access memory at a somewhat "leisurely" pace. This means that slow-mem parts can be used without affecting overall system performance.

6.2.4 Register Organization

Total 14 registers are available in 8086 microprocessor are these are categorized into four groups. They are General purpose data registers, Pointer & Index registers, Segment registers and Flag register as shown in the table below.

Table 6.1 : 8086 Microprocessor Register

Sr. No	Type	Register width	Name of the Registers
1	General purpose Registers(4)	16-bit	AX,BX,CX,DX
		8-bit	AL,AH,BL,BH,CL,CH,DL,DH
2	Pointer Registers	16-bit	Stack Pointer(SP) Base Pointer(BP)
3	Index Registers	16-bit	Source Index(SI) Destination Index(DI)
4	Segment Registers	16-bit	Code Segment(CS) Data Segment(DS) Stack Segment(SS) Extra Segment(ES)
5	Instruction	16-bit	Instruction Pointer (IP)
6	Flag (PSW)	16-bit	Flag Register

- **General purpose registers :** There are four 16-bit 4 general purpose registers namely (AH, AL); (BH, BL); (CH, CL); (and DH, DL) which are part of Execution unit. These registers can be used individually for storing 16-bit data temporarily. The AL register is also called the accumulator. The pairs of registers can be used together to store 16-bit data words.

It is always advantageous to store the data in these registers because the data can be accessed much more easily as these registers are already in the execution unit. Here L indicates the lower byte and H indicates the higher byte. X indicates the extended register. The general purpose data registers are used for data manipulations. The use of these registers is more dependent on the mode of addressing also.

8086 CPU has 8 general purpose registers, each register has its own name:

AX - the accumulator register (divided into **AH / AL**) :

    1.   Generates shortest machine code

    2.   Arithmetic, logic and data transfer

    3.   One number must be in AL or AX

    4.   Multiplication & Division

    5.   Input & Output

BX - the base address register (divided into **BH / BL**).

CX - the count register (divided into **CH / CL**):

    1.   Iterative code segments using the LOOP instruction

    2.   Repetitive operations on strings with the REP command

    3.   Count (in CL) of bits to shift and rotate

DX - the data register (divided into **DH / DL**) :

    1.   DX:AX concatenated into 32-bit register for some MUL and DIV operations

    2.   Specifying ports in some IN and OUT operations

The other four registers of EU are referred to as index / pointer registers. They are Stack Pointer register, Base Pointer register, Source Index register and Destination Index registers. The pointer registers contain the offset within a particular segment.

SI - source index register:

    1.   Can be used for pointer addressing of data

    2.   Used as source in some string processing instructions

    3.   Offset address relative to DS

DI - destination index register:

1. Can be used for pointer addressing of data

2. Used as destination in some string processing instructions

3. Offset address relative to ES

BP - base pointer:

1. Primarily used to access parameters passed via the stack

2. Offset address relative to SS

SP - stack pointer:

1. Always points to top item on the stack

2. Offset address relative to SS

3. Always points to word (byte at even address)

4. An empty stack will had SP = FFFEh

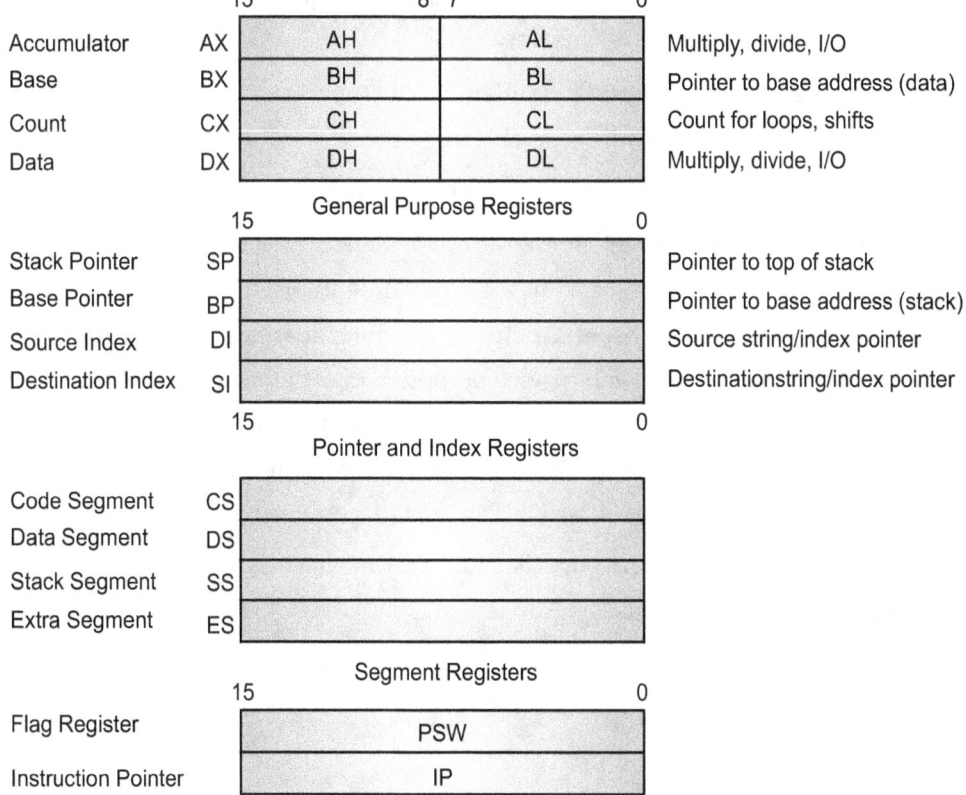

Fig. 6.15 : Register Organization

The BP and SP registers holds the offsets within the data and stack segments respectively. The Index registers are used as general purpose registers as well as for holding the offset in case of indexed based and relative indexed addressing modes. The source Index register is generally used to store the offset of source data in data segment while the Destination Index register used to store the offset of destination in data or extra segment. These index registers are specifically used in string manipulations.

- **Segment Registers :** There are four 16-bit segment registers namely code segment register (CS), Stack segment register (SS), Data segment register (DS) and Extra segment register (ES). The code segment register is used for addressing the 64kB memory location in the code segment of the memory, where the code of the executable program is stored. Similarly the DS register points to the data segment of the 64kB memory where the data is stored. The Extra segment register also refers to essentially another data segment of the memory space. The SS register is useful for addressing stack segment of memory. So, the CS, DS, SS and ES segment registers respectively contains the segment addresses for the code, data, stack and extra segments of the memory.

CS - points at the segment containing the current program.

DS - generally points at segment where variables are defined.

ES - extra segment register, it's up to a coder to define its usage.

SS - points at the segment containing the stack.

Although it is possible to store any data in the segment registers, this is never a good idea. The segment registers have a very special purpose - pointing at accessible blocks of memory. Segment registers work together with general purpose register to access any memory value. For example, if we would like to access memory at the physical address **12345h** (hexadecimal), we could set the **DS = 1230h and SI = 0045h**. This way we can access much more memory than with a single register, which is limited to 16 bit values.

The CPU makes a calculation of the physical address by multiplying the segment register by 10h and adding the general purpose register to it (1230h * 10h + 45h = 12345h):

$$
\begin{array}{r}
12300 \\
+0045 \\
\hline
12345
\end{array}
$$

The address formed with 2 registers is called an **effective address**. By default **BX, SI** and **DI** registers work with **DS** segment register; **BP** and **SP** work with SS segment register.

Other general purpose registers cannot form an effective address. Also, although **BX** can form an effective address, **BH** and **BL** cannot.

- **Instruction Pointer Register :** It is a 16-bit register which always points to the next instruction to be executed within the currently executing code segment. So, this register contains the 16-bit offset address pointing to the next instruction code within the 64 kB of the code segment area. Its content is automatically incremented as the execution of the next instruction takes place.

IP - the instruction pointer:

1. Always points to next instruction to be executed
2. Offset address relative to CS

IP register always works together with CS segment register and it points to currently executing instruction.

- **Flag Register :** This register is also called status register. It is a 16 bit register which contains six status flags and three control flags. So, only nine bits of the 16 bit register are defined and the remaining seven bits are undefined. Normally, this status flag bits indicate the status of the ALU after the arithmetic or logical operations. Each bit of the status register is a flip/flop. The Flag register contains Carry flag, Parity flag, Auxiliary flag, Zero flag, Sign flag, Trap flag, Interrupt flag, Direction flag and overflow flag as shown in the diagram. The CF, PF, AF, ZF, SF, OF are the status flags and the TF, IF and CF are the control flags.

X	X	X	X	OF	DF	IF	TF	SF	ZF	X	AF	X	PF	X	CF

Fig. 6.16 : Flag Register

CF- Carry Flag : This flag is set to 1, when there is a carry out of MSB in case of addition or a borrow in case of subtraction. Otherwise this bit sets to 0.

PF - Parity Flag : This flag is set to 1, if the lower byte of the result contains even number of 1's and for odd number of 1s in result the bit set to zero.

AF- Auxilary Carry Flag : This bit is set to 1, if there is a carry from the lowest nibble, i.e, bit three to bit four during addition, or borrow for the lowest nibble, i.e, bit three, during subtraction. (bits 0 to bit 7 take in consideration)

ZF- Zero Flag : This flag is set to 1, if the result of the computation or comparison performed by the previous instruction is zero otherwise bit is set to 0 indicating that result is non-zero.

SF- Sign Flag : This flag is set to 1, when the result of any computation (MSB is 1) is negative and set to 0 if result is positive (MSB is 0).

TF - Tarp Flag: If this flag is set 1, the processor enters the single step execution mode.

IF- Interrupt Flag: If this flag is set to 1, the maskable interrupt INTR of 8086 is enabled and if it is zero, the interrupt is disabled. It can be set by using the STI instruction and can be cleared by executing CLI instruction.

DF- Direction Flag: This is used by string manipulation instructions. If this flag bit is '0', the string is processed beginning from the lowest address to the highest address, i.e., auto incrementing mode. Otherwise, the string is processed from the highest address towards the lowest address, i.e., auto decrementing mode.

OF- Over flow Flag: This flag is set, if an overflow occurs, i.e, if the result of a signed operation is large enough to accommodate in a destination register. The result is of more than 7-bits in size in case of 8-bit signed operation and more than 15-bits in size in case of 16-bit sign operations, then the overflow will be set.

6.3 PIN DIAGRAM OF 8086

Fig. 6.17 shows signal description of 8086 microprocessor.

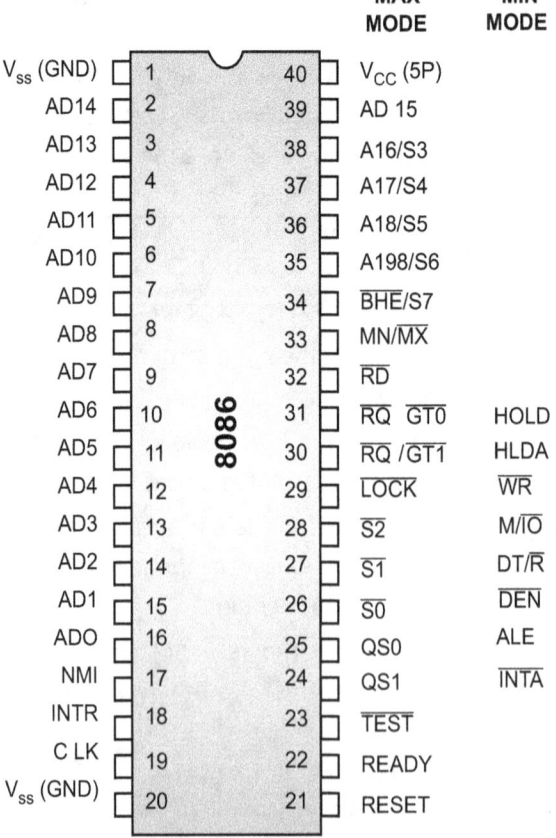

Fig. 6.17 : Pin Diagram of 8086

Intel 8086 is a 16-bit microprocessor. It is available in 40 pin DIP chip. It uses a 5 V d.c. supply for its operation. The 8086 uses 20-line address bus. It uses a 16-line data bus. The 20 lines of the address bus operate in multiplexed mode. The 16-low order address bus lines are multiplexed with data and 4 high-order address bus lines are multiplexed with status signals.

AD_0-AD_{15} (Bidirectional) : Address/Data bus. These are low order address bus. They are multiplexed with data. When AD lines are used to transmit memory address the symbol A is used instead of AD, for example, A_0-A_{15}. When data are transmitted over AD lines the symbol D is used in place of AD, for example, D_0-D_7, D_8-D_{15} or D_0-D_{15}.

A_{16}-A_{19} (Output) : High order address bus. These are multiplexed with status signals.

Table 6.2 : Common Pins of 8086

AD_7-AD_0	The 8086/8088 **address/data bus** lines compose the multiplexed address data bus of the 8086/8088.
A_{15}-A_8	The 8086/8088 **address bus** provides the upper-half memory address.
AD_{15}-AD_8	The 8086 **address/data bus** lines compose the upper multiplexed address/data bus on the 8086.
A_{19}-S_6 **A_{16}/S_3**	The **address/status bus** bits are multiplexed to provide address signals A19-A16 and also status bits S6-S3.
$\overline{RD}$	Whenever the read signal is a logic 0, the data bus is receptive to data from the memory or I/O devices connected to the system.
INTR	Interrupt request is used to request a hardware interrupt.
NMI	The non-maskable interrupt.
RESET	The reset input causes the microprocessor to reset.
CLK	The clock pin provides the basic timing signal to the microprocessor.
MN/$\overline{MX}$	The minimum/maximum mode pin selects either minimum mode or maximum mode operation for the microprocessor.
$\overline{BHE}$ /S7	The bus high enable pin is used in the 8086 to enable the most significant data bus bits (D15-D8) during a read or a write operation. The state of S7 of always a logic 1.

Table 6.3 : Minimum Mode Pins

IO/$\overline{\text{M}}$ or M/$\overline{\text{IO}}$	The IO/$\overline{\text{M}}$ (8088) or the M/$\overline{\text{IO}}$ (8086) pin selects memory or I/O.
$\overline{\text{WR}}$	The write line is a strobe that indicates the 8086/8088 is outputting data to a memory or I/O device.
$\overline{\text{INTA}}$	The interrupt acknowledge signal is a response to the INTR input pin.
ALE	Address latch enable shows that the 8086/8088 address / data bus contains address information.
DT/$\overline{\text{R}}$	The data transmit/receive signal shows that the microprocessor data bus is transmitting (DT/R = 1) or receiving (DT/R = 0) data.
DEN	Data bus enable activates external data bus buffers.
HOLD	The hold input requests a direct memory access (DMA).
HLDA	Hold acknowledge indicates that the 8086/8088 has entered the hold state.
$\overline{\text{SS0}}$	The $\overline{\text{SS0}}$ status line is equivalent to the S0 pin in maximum mode operation of the microprocessor. This signal is combined with IO/$\overline{\text{M}}$ and DT/$\overline{\text{R}}$ to decode the function of the current bus cycle.

Table 6.4 : Maximum Mode Pins

Maximum mode signals (MN / $\overline{\text{MX}}$ = GND)		
Name	**Function**	**Type**
RQ/ $\overline{\text{GT1, 0}}$	Request / Grant Bus Access Control	Bidirectional
$\overline{\text{LOCK}}$	Bus Priority Lock Control	Output, 3-State
$\overline{\text{S}}_2$ – $\overline{\text{S}}_0$	Bus Cycle Status	Output, 3-State
QS1, QS0	Instruction Queue Status	Output

A_{16}/S_3, A_{17}/S_4, A_{18}/S_5, A_{19}/S_6 : The specified address lines are multiplexed with corresponding status signals.

BHE (Active Low)/S7 (Output) : Bus High Enable/Status. During T1 it is low. It is used to enable data onto the most significant half of data bus, D8-D15. 8-bit device connected to upper half of the data bus use BHE (Active Low) signal. It is multiplexed with status signal S7. S7 signal is available during T2, T3 and T4.

RD (Read) (Active Low) : The signal is used for read operation. It is an output signal. It is active when low.

READY : This is the acknowledgement from the slow device or memory that they have completed the data transfer. The signal made available by the devices is synchronized by the 8284A clock generator to provide ready input to the 8086. The signal is active high.

INTR-Interrupt Request : This is a triggered input. This is sampled during the last clock cycles of each instruction to determine the availability of the request. If any interrupt request is pending, the processor enters the interrupt acknowledge cycle. This can be internally masked by resulting the interrupt enable flag. This signal is active high and internally synchronized.

NMI (Input) : Non-maskable interrupt : It is an edge triggered input which causes a type 2 interrupt. A subroutine is vectored to via an interrupt vector lookup table located in system memory. NMI is not maskable internally by software. A transition from LOW to HIGH initiates the interrupt at the end of the current instruction. This input is internally synchronized.

INTA : Interrupt acknowledge. It is active LOW during T_2 ,T_3 and T_w of each interrupt acknowledge cycle.

MN/ MX MINIMUM / MAXIMUM : This pin signal indicates what mode the processor is to operate in.

RQ/GT RQ/GT0 : REQUEST/GRANT : These pins are used by other local bus masters to force the processor to release the local bus at the end of the processor's current bus cycle. Each pin is bidirectional with RQ/GT having higher priority than RQ /GT1.

LOCK : Its an active low pin. It indicates that other system bus masters are not to allowed to gain control of the system bus while LOCK is active LOW. The LOCK signal remains active until the completion of the next instruction.

TEST : This input is examined by a 'WAIT' instruction. If the TEST pin goes low, execution will continue, else the processor remains in an idle state. The input is synchronized internally during each clock cycle on leading edge of clock.

CLK - Clock Input : The clock input provides the basic timing for processor operation and bus control activity. Its an asymmetric square wave with 33% duty cycle.

RESET (Input) : RESET : causes the processor to immediately terminate its present activity. The signal must be active HIGH for at least four clock cycles.

Vcc – Power Supply (+5V D.C.)

GND – Ground

QS$_1$, QS$_0$ (Queue Status) : These signals indicate the status of the internal 8086 instruction queue according to the table shown below

Table 6.5

QSI	QSO	Status
0 (LOW)	0	No Operation
0	1	First Byte of Op Code from Queue
1 (HIGH)	0	Empty the Queue
1	1	Subsequent Byte from Queue

DT/R : DATA TRANSMIT/RECEIVE : This pin is needed in minimum system that desires to use an 8086/8087 data bus transceiver. It is used to control the direction of data flow through the transceiver.

DEN : DATA ENABLE : This pin is provided as an output enable for the 8086/8087 in a minimum system which uses the transceiver. DEN is active LOW during each memory and I/O access and for INTA cycles.

HOLD/HLDA : HOLD indicates that another master is requesting a local bus .This is an active HIGH. The processor receiving the "hold" request will issue HLDA (HIGH) as an acknowledgement in the middle of a T$_4$ or T$_1$ clock cycle.

6.4 PROGRAMMERS MODEL OF 8086

As a programmer of the 8086 or 8088 you must become familiar with the various registers in the EU and BIU of 8086.

The detail Register organization we seen in the section 6.2.4.

The data group consists of the accumulator and the BX, CX, and DX registers. Note that each can be accessed as a byte or a word. Thus, BX refers to the 16-bit base register but BH refers only to the higher 8 bits of this register. The data registers are normally used for storing temporary results that will be acted on by subsequent instructions.

The pointer and index group are all 16-bit registers (you cannot access the low or high bytes alone). These registers are used as memory pointers. Sometimes a pointer register will be interpreted as pointing to a memory byte and at other times a memory word. As you will see, the 8086/88 always stores words with the high-order byte in the high-order word address.

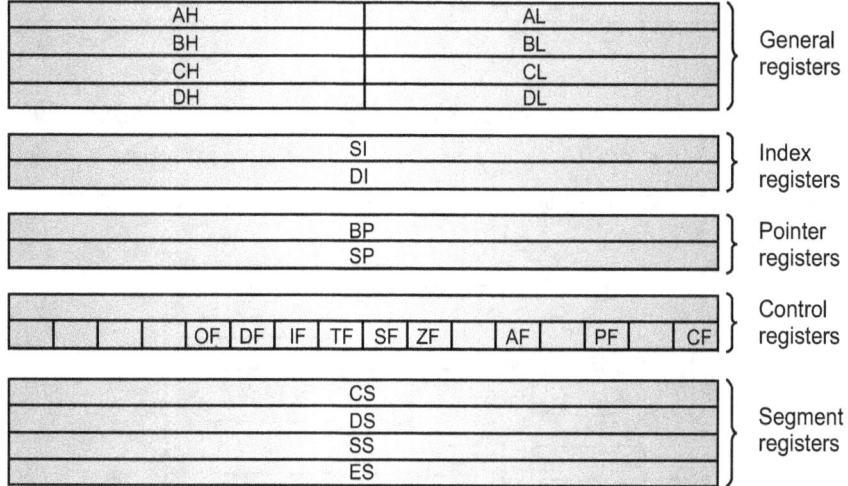

Fig. 6.18 : Programmers model of 8086

Register IP could be considered in the previous group, but this register has only one function to point to the next instruction to be fetched in to the BIU. Register IP is physically part of the BIU and not under direct control of the programmer as are the other pointer registers.

Six of the flags are status indicators, reflecting properties of the result of the last arithmetic or logical instructions. The 8086/88 has several instructions that can be used to transfer program control to a new memory location based on the state of the flags.

Three of the flags can be set or reset directly by the programmer and are used to control the operation of the processor. These are TF, IF, and DF.

The final group of registers is called the segment group. These registers are used by the BIU to determine the memory address output by the CPU when it is reading or writing from the memory unit. To fully understand these registers, we must first study the way the 8086/88 divides its memory into segments.

6.5 MEMORY SEGMENTATION

- The total memory size is divided into segments of various sizes. A segment is just an area in memory. The process of dividing memory this way is called Segmentation.

- In memory, data is stored as bytes. Each byte has a specific address. Intel 8086 has 20 lines address bus. With 20 address lines, the memory that can be addressed is 2^{20} bytes 2^{20} = 1,048,576 bytes (1 MB).

- The 8086 processor provides a 20-bit address to access any location of the 1 MB memory space. The memory is organized as a linear array of 1 million bytes, addressed as 00000(H) to FFFFF(H).

- The memory is logically divided into code, data, extra data, and stack segments of up to 64 K bytes each .

- Each of these segments are addressed by an address stored in corresponding segment register. These registers are 16-bit in size. Each register stores the base address (starting address) of the corresponding segment. Because the segment registers cannot store 20 bits, they only store the upper 16 bits.

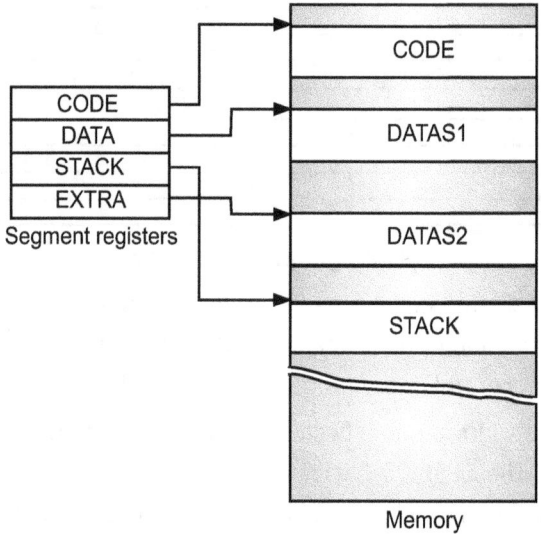

Fig. 6.19 : Segment Registers

Physical memory address pointed by segment:offset pair is calculated as:

address = (* 16) + <offset>

The memory is divided as

- **Program memory** - Following program can be located anywhere in memory. Jump and call instructions can be used for short jumps within currently selected 64 kB code segment, as well as for far jumps anywhere within 1 MB of memory. All conditional jump instructions can be used to jump within approximately +127 to –127 bytes from current instruction.

- **Data memory** - The processor can access data in any one out of four available segments, which limits the size of accessible memory to 256 kB (if all four segments point to different 64 KB blocks). Accessing data from the Data, Code, Stack or Extra segments can be usually done by prefixing instructions with the DS:, CS:, SS: or ES: (some registers and instructions by default may use the ES or SS segments instead of DS segment).

Word data can be located at odd or even byte boundaries. The processor uses two memory accesses to read 16-bit word located at odd byte boundaries. Reading word data from even byte boundaries requires only one memory access.

- **Stack memory :** can be placed anywhere in memory. The stack can be located at odd memory addresses, but it is not recommended for performance reasons

- **Reserved locations :**
  - 0000h - 03FFh are reserved for interrupt vectors. Each interrupt vector is a 32-bit pointer in format segment:offset.

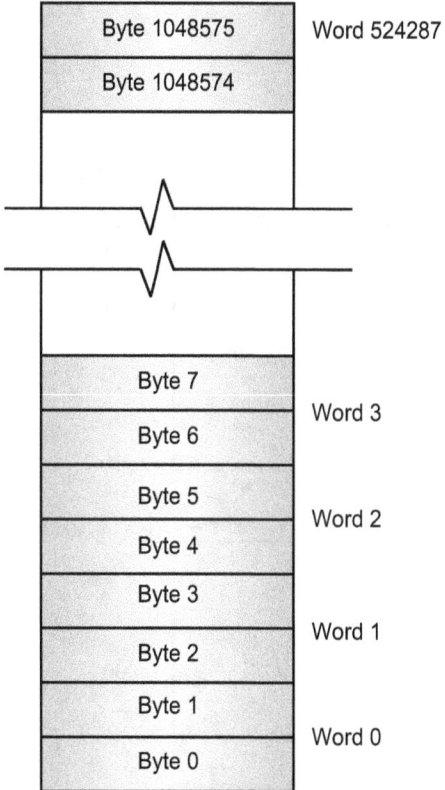

Fig. 6.20 : Memory layout

FFFF0h - FFFFFh - after RESET the processor always starts program execution at the FFFF0h address.

- With 20 bits, 1,048,576 different combinations are available. Each memory location is assigned a different combination. Each memory location is 1 byte wide. Therefore, the memory space of the 8086 consists of 1,048,576 bytes or 524,288 16-bit words.

- The 8086 has a 20-bit address bus. Therefore, it can access 1,048,576 bytes of memory. How many bits and how many HEX digits are required to access 1 M memory?

$2^N = 1M$ (where N is in bits)

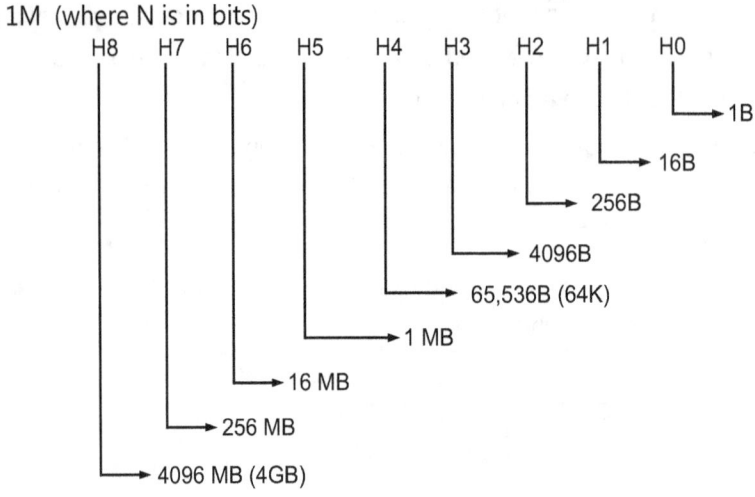

N = 20 bits   20/4 = 5 HEX digits

Fig. 6.21 : Positional Notation (Hex Digits)

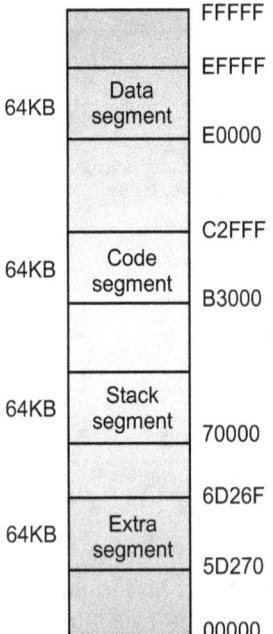

Fig. 6.22 : Segmented Memory

N = 20 bits = 20/4 = 5 HEX digits

- Within the 1 MB of memory, the 8086 defines 4 64 kB memory blocks. The segment registers point to location 0 of each segment. (The base address)
- Segments are variable-sized areas of memory used by a program containing either code or data.

- Segmentation provides a way to isolate memory segments from each other. This permits multiple programs to run simultaneously without interfering with each other. A segment selector is a 16-bit value stored in a segment register. A logical address is a combination of a segment selector and an offset(16-bit for 8086).

How is a 20-bit address obtained if there are only 16- bit registers?

- The 20-bit address of a byte is called its **Physical Address**. But, it is specified as a **Logical Address**. Logical address is in the form of: **Base Address : Offset**.

Offset is the displacement of the memory location from the starting location of the segment.

Example :

The value of Data Segment Register (DS) is 2222 H. To convert this 16-bit address into 20-bit, the BIU appends 0H to the LSBs of the address. After appending, the starting address of the Data Segment becomes 22220H. If the data at any location has a logical address specified as: 2222 H : 0016 H   Then, the number 0016 H is the offset. 2222 H is the value of DS. To calculate the effective address of the memory, BIU uses the following formula:

Effective Address = Starting Address of Segment + Offset

To find the starting address of the segment, BIU appends the contents of Segment Register with 0H. Then, it adds offset to it. Therefore :

EA = 22220 H
+ 0016 H

22236 H

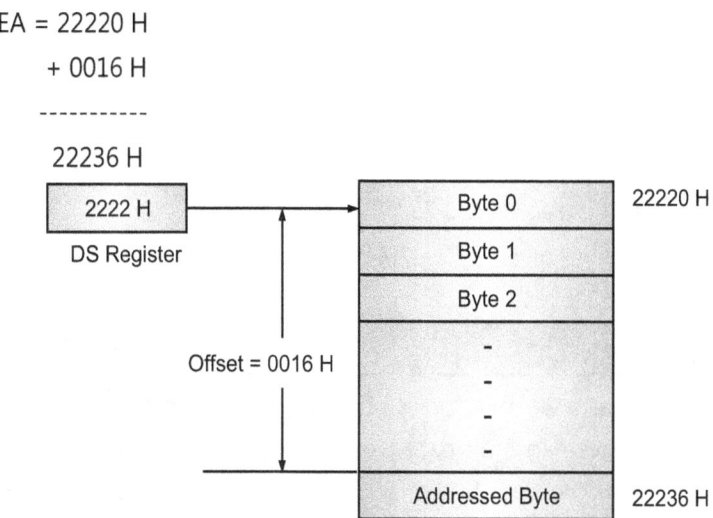

Fig. 6.23 : Memory layout for example

All offsets are limited to 16-bits. It means that the maximum size possible for segment is 2^{16} = 65,535 bytes (64 kB). The offset of the first location within the segment is 0000 H. The offset of the last location in the segment is FFFF H.

Table 6.6

Segment	Offset Registers	Function
CS	IP	Address of the next instruction
DS	BX, DI, SI	Address of data
SS	SP, BP	Address in the stack
ES	BX, DI, SI	Address of destination data (for string operations)

For example, the contents of the following registers are :

$$CS = 1111 \text{ H}$$
$$DS = 3333 \text{ H}$$
$$SS = 2526 \text{ H}$$
$$IP = 1232 \text{ H}$$
$$SP = 1100 \text{ H}$$
$$DI = 0020 \text{ H}$$

Calculate the corresponding physical addresses for the address bytes in CS, DS and SS.

1. CS = 1111 H

The base address of the code segment is 11110 H.

Effective address of memory is given by 11110H + 1232H = 12342H.

2. DS = 3333 H

The base address of the data segment is 33330 H.

Effective address of memory is given by 33330H + 0020H = 33350H.

3. SS = 2526 H

The base address of the stack segment is 25260 H.

Effective address of memory is given by 25260H + 1100H = 26350H.

6.6 MEMORY ORGANIZATION

We know that the 8086 has a 20 bit Address bus. So it can address 2^{20} or 1,048576 address. At each address we can store an 8 bit data i.e. 1 byte. Hence the total memory capacity of 8086 is 1M byte. However the data bus of 8086 is 16 bit and the processor is capable of processing 16 bit data i.e. words.

The question is how to write a word i.e. 16 bit data into segmented memory.

The answer is that a word is written into two consecutive memory addresses. That means the lower byte is writeen into the specified memory address.

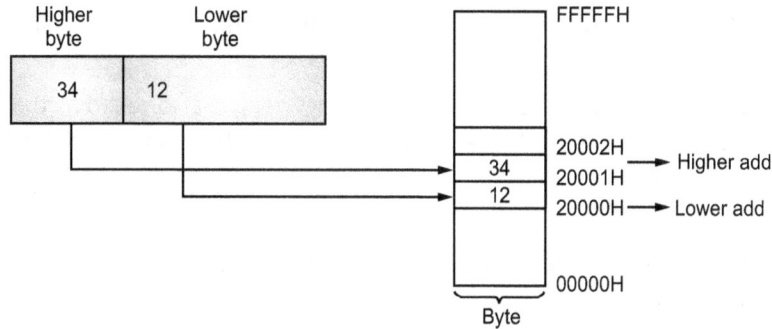

Fig. 6.24 : Data storage in 8086 memory

To read or write a word with one machine cycle; the memory of 8086 is divided into two bank of upto 524, 288 bytes. i.e. 50014 bytes each as shown in Fig. 6.24.

The two memory banks are known as

(1) The even addressed memory bank

(2) The odd addressed memory bank

The even addressed memory bank contains all the bytes which have even addresses such as 00000, 00002, 00004 etc. The odd addressed memory bank, contains all the bytes which have odd addresses such as 00001, 00003, 00005 etc.

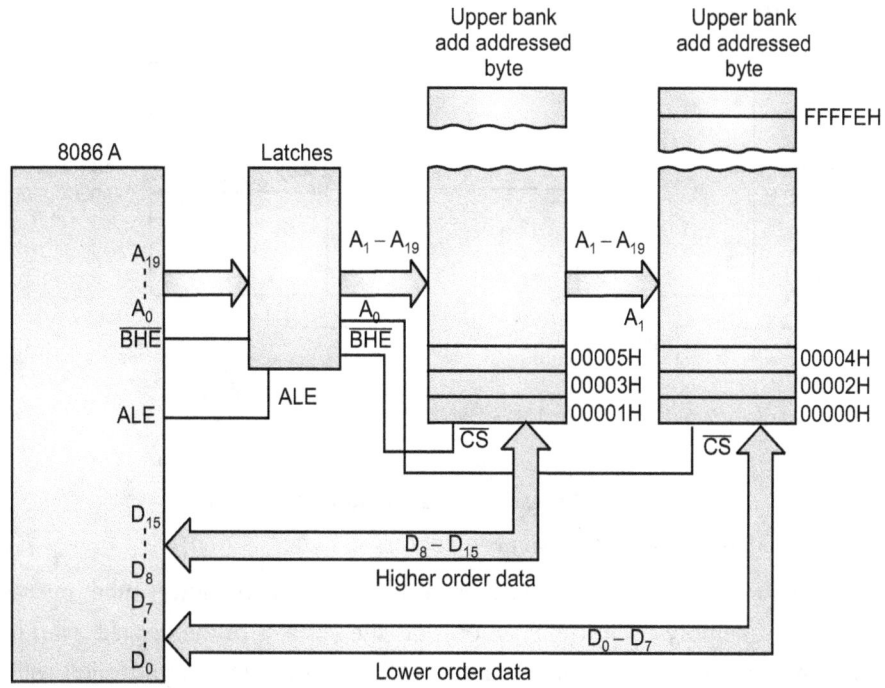

Fig. 6.25 : 8086 memory banks block diagram

- The even addressed bank is also called as lower bank and the data present on the lines $D_0 - D_7$ of 8086.
- The odd addressed bank is also called as the upper bank is also called as the upper bank and the data lines of this bank are D_8-D_{15} of 8086. Address line A_0 is used to used to enable the lower memory bank and $\overline{BHE}$ BHE is used to eneable the higher memory bank.
- Add lines A_1-A_{19} are used for selecting the desired memory address in the lower and upper memory bank.
- ALE signal is used to strobe in the address into the external latch. The same latch stores the $\overline{BHE}$ signal.

Table 6.7 : Signals for the byte and word operations

Add	Data type	$\overline{BHE}$	A_0	Bus Cycle	Data lines
0000	Byte	1	0	one	D_0-D_7
0000	Word	0	0	one	D_0-D_{15}
0001	Byte	0	1	one	D_8-D_{15}
0001	Word	0	1	first	D_0-D_7
		1	0	Second	D_8-$1D_{15}$

(I) Accessing even addressed byte :

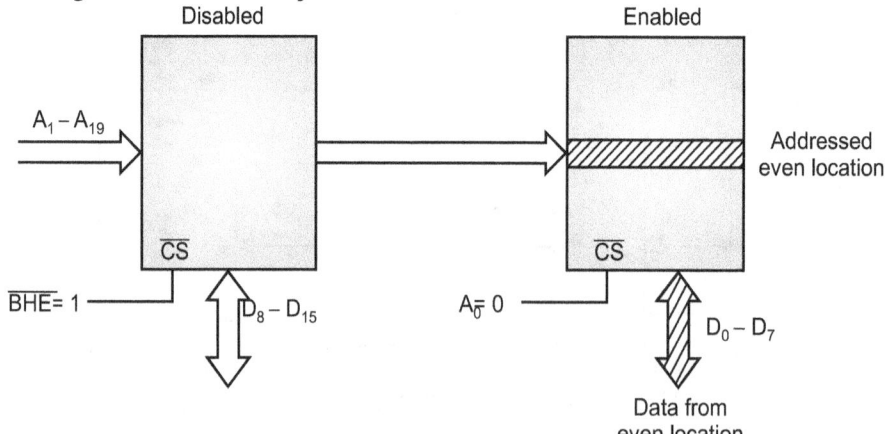

Fig. 6.26 : Accessing an even addressed byte

Fig. 6.26 shows the process to access an even addressed byte.

The 8086 forces A_0 line to low and $\overline{BHE}$ high. This will enable the lower memory bank and disable the higher memory bank. The 8086 outputs the address of the desired even memory location on the address lines A_1 to A_{19}. The data stored at even memory location will appear on D_0-D_7 lines.

(II) Accessing the odd addressed byte : Fig. 6.27 shows the process involved in accessing the odd addressed byte.

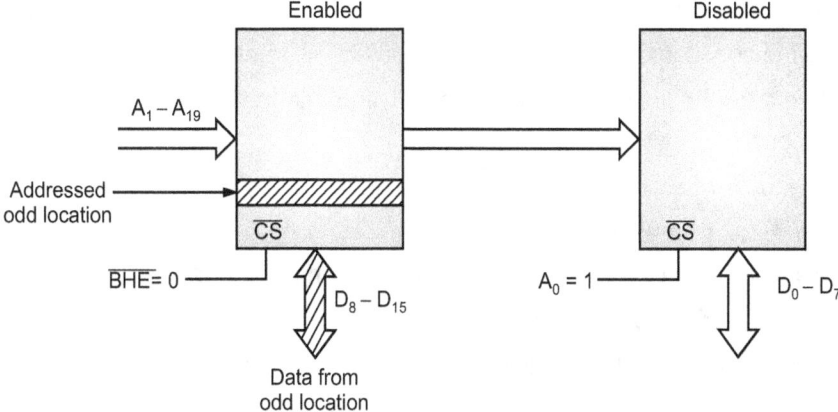

Fig. 6.27 : Accessing an odd addressed byte

The 8086 forces $A_0 = 1$ (High) and $\overline{BHE} = 0$ (low). This will disable the lower memory bank and enable the upper memory bank.

The 8086 will output the address of desired memory, location on A_1-A_{19} Address lines.

The data byte from odd location will appear on D_8-D_{15} data lines.

(III) Accessing even addressed word :

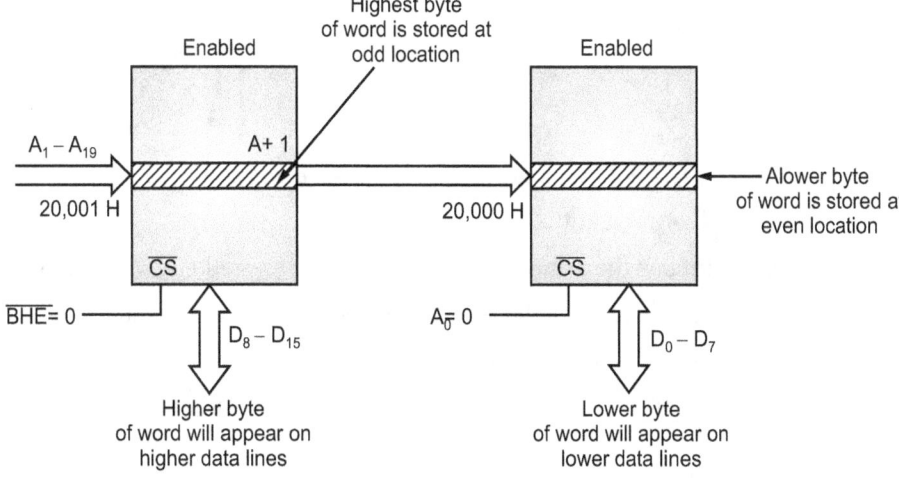

Fig. 6.28 : Accessing an even addressed word

• The lower byte of this word is stored first and the higher byte is stored first and the higher byte is stored at the next higher.

- The lower byte of the word has been stored at the even memory location 20,000 H and the higher byte of the same word has been stored at the next location 20,001 H which is odd location.

- Both the memory banks are enabled because 8086 will force A_0 and $\overline{BHE}$ to low.

- The address on the lines A_1-A_{19} will point towards the locations 20,000 H and 20,001 H simultaneously.

- The lower byte of word will appear on the data lines D_0-D_7 and the higher byte will appear on D_8-D_{15} simultaneously.

- To read a word from even address the 8086 needs only one bus cycle.

(IV) Accessing an odd addressed word :

- To access odd addressed word 8086 required two bus cycles. Because the lower byte is stored at odd address and the upper byte of the word is at even address. Fig. 6.29 show the situation.

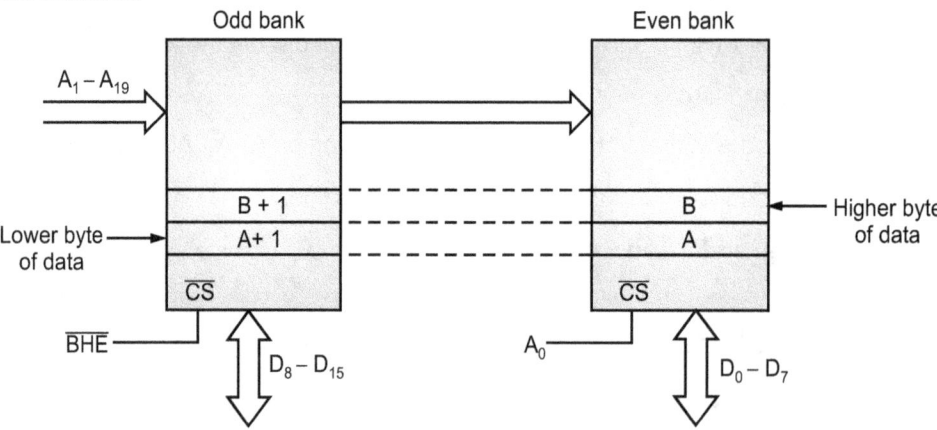

Fig. 6.29 : Accessing odd addressed word

The locations A + 1 and B are not at the same level.

Therefore the 8086 cannot use the same address for both these locations, A+ 1 and B.

Therefore, for it is not possible for 8086 to read all 16 bits of word at same time.

Hence the 8086 needs two bus cycles to read the 16 bit word. One bus cycle is required to read the contents of locations (A + 1) and other to read the contents of location B.

(a) First bus cycle

In first cycle the 8086 forces $A_0 = 1$ and $\overline{BHE} = 0$ to enable the odd bank.

It then outputs the A_1-A_{19} lines to point to location A + 1.

The contents of A + 1 location will appear on the data lines $D_8 - D_{15}$.

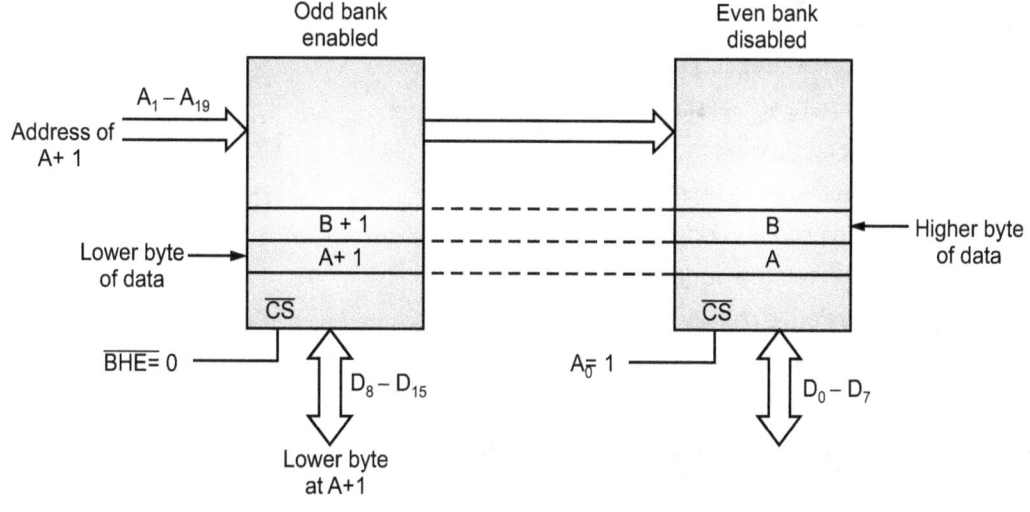

Fig. 6.30 : First bus cycle

Fig. 6.31 : Second bus cycle

In the second bus cycle the 8086 forces. $A_0 = 0$ and $\overline{BHE} = 1$ to enable the lower i.e. even bank.

Then it outputs the new address on the A_1–A_{19} lines to put at location B.

Then the contents of location B will appear on D_0–D_7 data line.

6.7 8086 ADDRESSING MODES

The way in which an operand is specified is called the *Addressing Mode*. Different addressing modes may take different amount of time to compute the effective address.

The x86 instructions use five different operand types : registers, constants, and three memory addressing schemes. Each form is called an addressing mode.

The x86 processors support :

- The register addressing mode.
- The immediate addressing mode.
- The direct addressing mode.
- The indirect addressing mode.
- The base plus index addressing mode.
- The register relative addressing mode.
- The base relative plus index addressing mode.
- The memory addressing mode.

6.7.1 The Register Addressing Mode

Instructions using the registers are shorter and faster than those that access memory.

Most 8086 instructions can operate on the 8086's general purpose register set. By specifying the name of the register as an operand to the instruction, you may access the contents of that register. Consider the 8086 MOV (move) instruction:

MOV   destination, source

This instruction copies the data from the source operand to the destination operand. The 8 and 16 bit registers are certainly valid operands for this instruction. The only restriction is that both operands must be the same size. Now let's look at some actual 8086 MOV instructions:

MOV   AX, BX ; Copies the value from BX into AX
MOV   DL, AL ; Copies the value from AL into DL
MOV   SI, DX ; Copies the value from DX into SI
MOV   SP, BP ; Copies the value from BP into SP
MOV   DH, CL ; Copies the value from CL into DH
MOV   AX, AX ; Yes, this is legal!

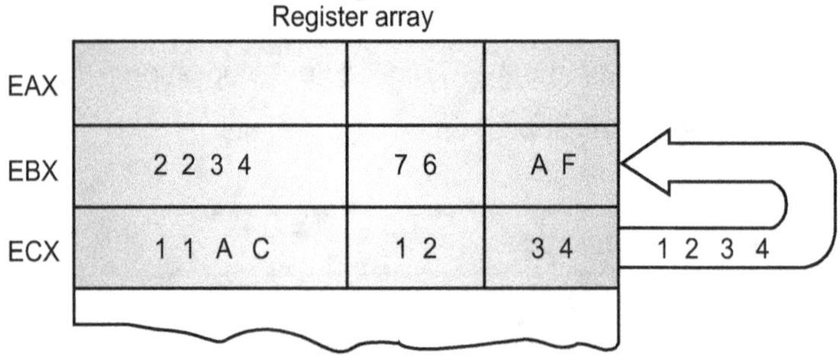

Fig. 6.32 : Register Addressing Mode e.g. MOV BX,CX

You should never use the segment registers as data registers to hold arbitrary values. They should only contain segment addresses.

6.7.2 The Immediate Addressing Mode

The term immediate implies that the data immediately follow the hexadecimal opcode in the memory. Immediate are constant data. The MOV immediate instruction transfers a copy of the immediate data into a register or a memory location

Fig. 6.33 shows the source data (sometimes preceded by #) overwrite the destination data. The instruction copies the 1345H into register AX.

e.g. MOV AX, 1345 H

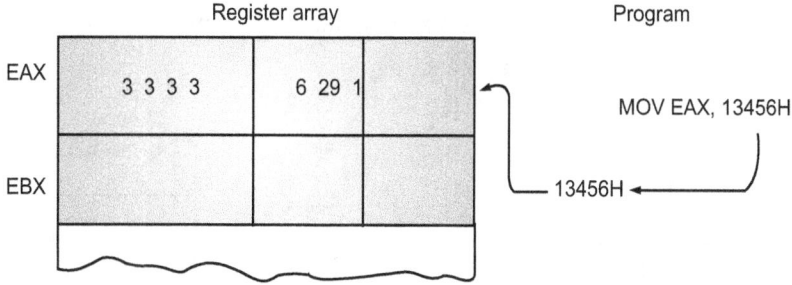

Fig. 6.33: Immediate addressing mode e.g. MOV EAX, 13456H

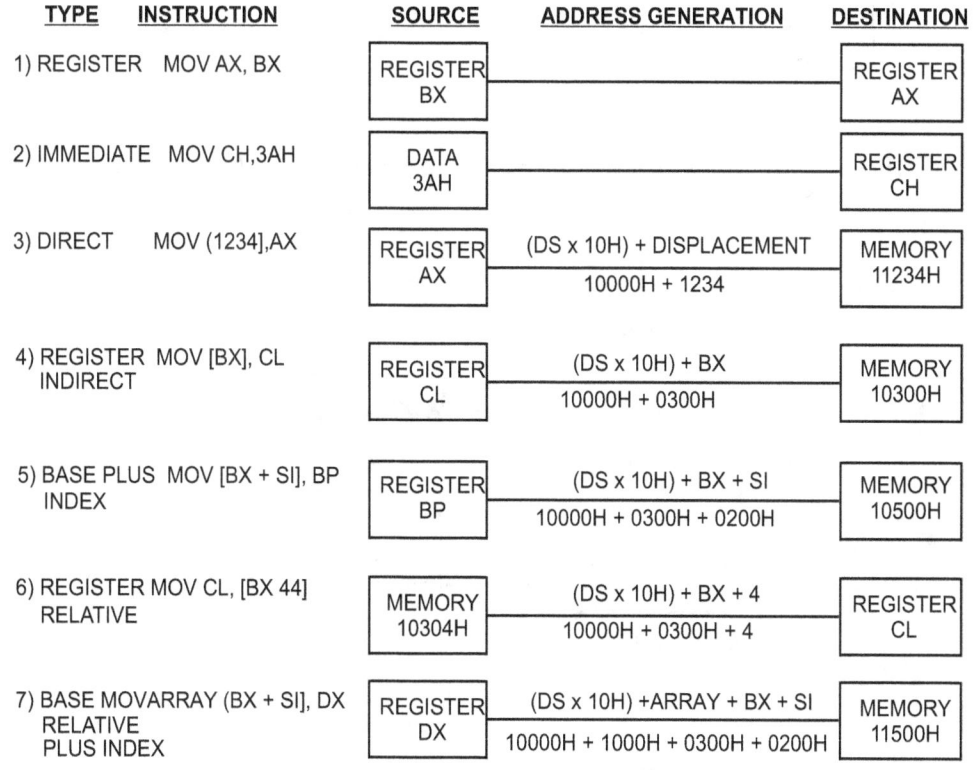

TYPE	INSTRUCTION	SOURCE	ADDRESS GENERATION	DESTINATION
1) REGISTER	MOV AX, BX	REGISTER BX		REGISTER AX
2) IMMEDIATE	MOV CH,3AH	DATA 3AH		REGISTER CH
3) DIRECT	MOV (1234),AX	REGISTER AX	(DS x 10H) + DISPLACEMENT 10000H + 1234	MEMORY 11234H
4) REGISTER INDIRECT	MOV [BX], CL	REGISTER CL	(DS x 10H) + BX 10000H + 0300H	MEMORY 10300H
5) BASE PLUS INDEX	MOV [BX + SI], BP	REGISTER BP	(DS x 10H) + BX + SI 10000H + 0300H + 0200H	MEMORY 10500H
6) REGISTER RELATIVE	MOV CL, [BX 44]	MEMORY 10304H	(DS x 10H) + BX + 4 10000H + 0300H + 4	REGISTER CL
7) BASE RELATIVE PLUS INDEX	MOV ARRAY [BX + SI], DX	REGISTER DX	(DS x 10H) +ARRAY + BX + SI 10000H + 1000H + 0300H + 0200H	MEMORY 11500H

Fig. 6.34 : Addressing modes

6.7.3 The Direct Addressing Mode

The most common addressing mode, and the one that's easiest to understand, is the displacement-only (or direct) addressing mode. The displacement-only addressing mode consists of a 16 bit constant that specifies the address of the target location. The displacement-only addressing mode is perfect for accessing simple variables.

Intel named this the displacement-only addressing mode because a 16 bit constant (displacement) follows the MOV opcode in memory. On the x86, a direct address can be thought of as a displacement from address zero. On the 80x86 processors, this displacement is an offset from the beginning of a segment.

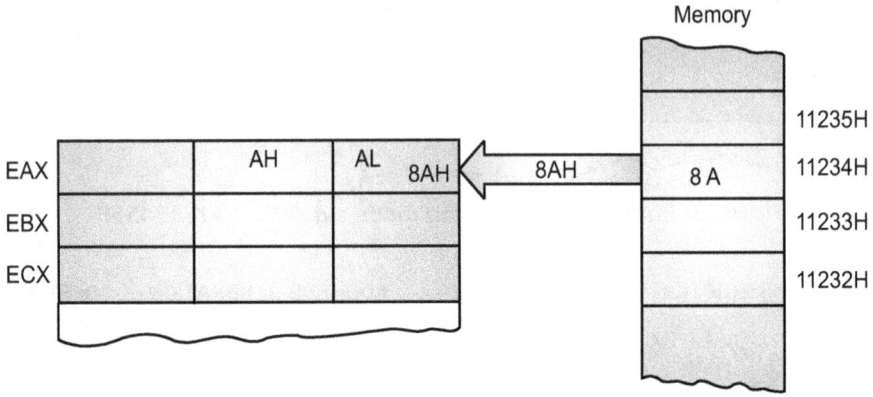

Fig. 6.35 : Direct /Displacement Addressing Mode e.g. MOV AL, [11234H]

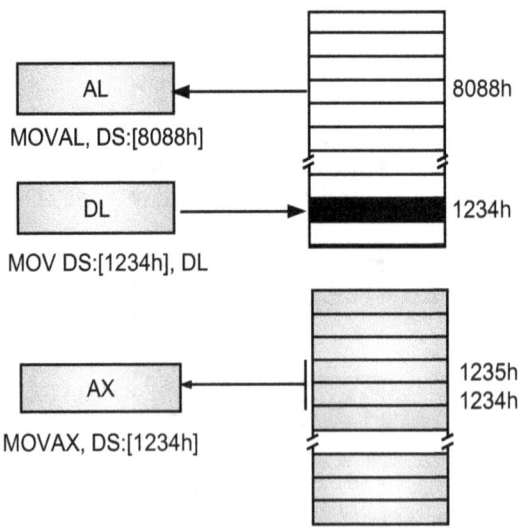

Fig. 6.36 : The direct addressing mode

There are two basic forms of direct data addressing :

- Direct addressing, which applies to a MOV between a memory location and AL, AX or EAX.
- Displacement addressing, which applies to almost any instruction in the instruction set.

e.g. Dierct Addressing: MOV AL, DATA ; MOV instruction is 3-byte long instruction.

Displacement Addressing: MOV CL, DATA almost identical with direct addressing except that the instruction is four bytes wide.

6.7.4 The Register Indirect Addressing Modes

The 80x86 CPUs let you access memory indirectly through a register using the register indirect addressing modes. There are four forms of this addressing mode on the 8086, best demonstrated by the following instructions:

        MOV   AL, [BX]
        MOV   AL, [BP]
        MOV   AL, [SI]
        MOV   AL, [DI]

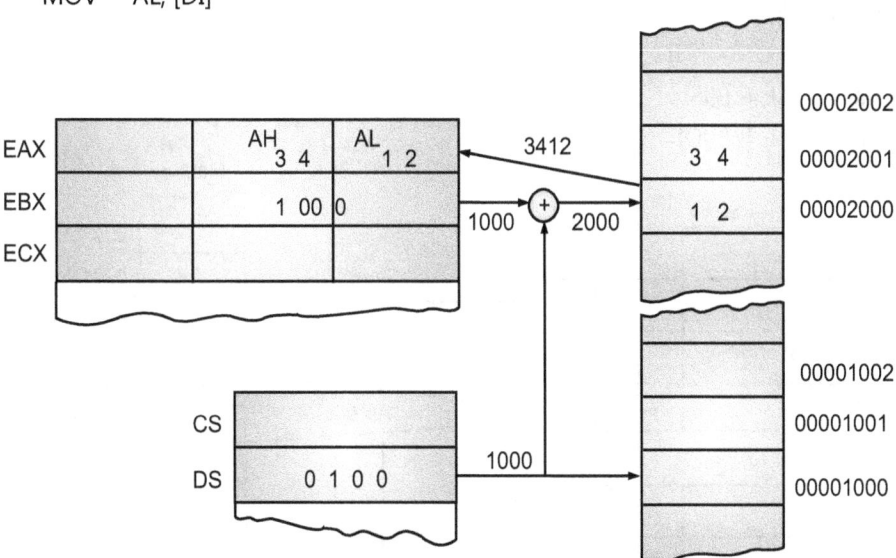

Fig. 6.37 : Register indirect addressing modes

This addressing modes reference the byte at the offset found in the BX, BP, SI, or DI register, respectively. The [BX], [SI], and [DI] modes use the DS segment by default. The [BP] addressing mode uses the stack segment (SS) by default.

You can use the segment override prefix symbols if you wish to access data in different segments. The following instructions demonstrate the use of these

MOV   AL, CS:[BX]

MOV   AL, DS:[BP]

MOV   AL, SS:[SI]

MOV   AL, ES:[DI]

Fig. 6.37 shows the operation of instruction MOV AX, [BX] when BX = 1000H and DS = 0100H.

6.7.5 Indexed Addressing Modes

Indexed Addressing mode: address is available in any index register SI,DI

MOV AX,[SI]

6.7.6 Based Indexed Addressing Modes

The based indexed addressing modes are simply combinations of the register indirect addressing modes. These addressing modes form the offset by adding together a base register (BX OR BP) and an index register (SI OR DI). The allowable forms for these addressing modes are

MOV   AL, [BX][SI]

MOV   AL, [BX][DI]

MOV   AL, [BP][SI]

MOV   AL, [BP][DI]

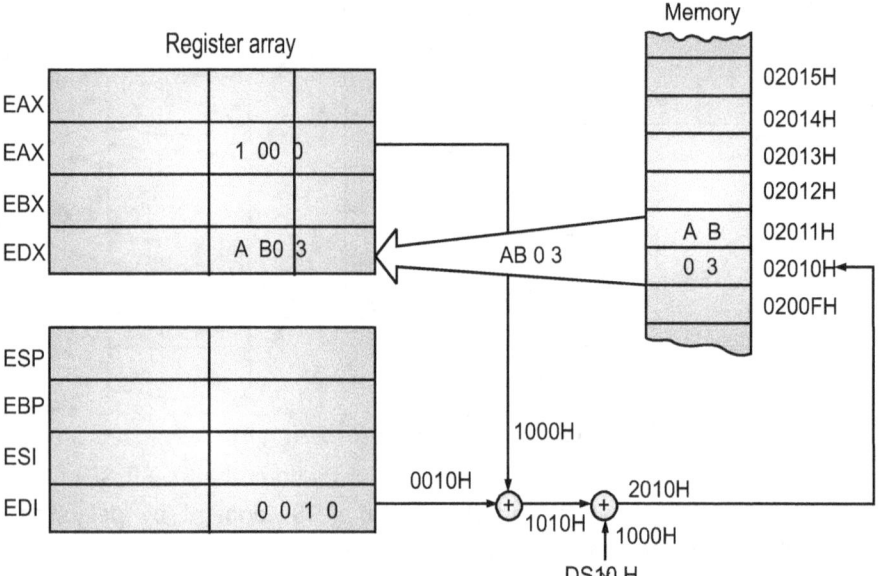

Fig. 6.38 : Based Indexed Addressing Modes

Suppose that BX contains 1000h and SI contains 880h. Then the instruction

    MOV   AL, [BX][SI]

would load AL from location DS:1880h. Likewise, if BP contains 1598h and DI contains 1004, MOV AX,[BP+DI] will load the 16 bits in AX from locations SS:259C and SS:259D.

The addressing modes that do not involve BP use the data segment by default. Those that have BP as an operand use the stack segment by default.

Fig. 6.38 shows the operation of Instruction MOV DX, [BX + DI] where DS = 0100H, BX = 1000H and DI = 0010H.

6.7.7 Register Relative Addressing Mode

In its, the data in a segment of memory are addressed by adding the displacement to the contents of a base ro and index register (BP, BX, DI, or SI)

E.g. MOV AX,[BX+ 1000H]. The displacement can be a number added to the register within the [ ], as in MOV AL, [DI+2], or it can be a displacement substracted from the register, as in MOV AL,[SI-1]. It is possible to address array data with register relative addressing such as one does with base-plus-index addressing. Fig. 6.39 shows the operation of instruction

    MOV AX, [BX+1000H] when BX = 0100H and DS = 0200H

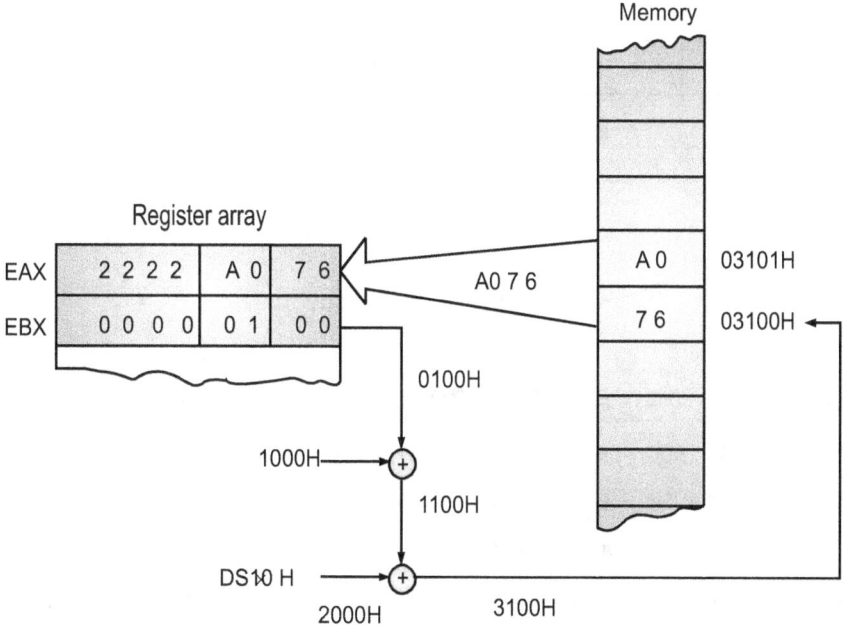

Fig. 6.39 : Register Relative Addressing Mode

6.7.8 Based Indexed Plus Displacement (Relative) Addressing Mode

These addressing modes are a slight modification of the base/indexed addressing modes with the addition of an eight bit or sixteen bit constant. The following are some examples of these addressing modes:

       MOV   AL, DISP[BX][SI]

       MOV   AL, DISP[BX+DI]

       MOV   AL, [BP+SI+DISP]

       MOV   AL, [BP][DI][DISP]

Fig. 6.40 shows the operation of instruction MOV AX, [BX+SI+100H] when DS = 1000H.

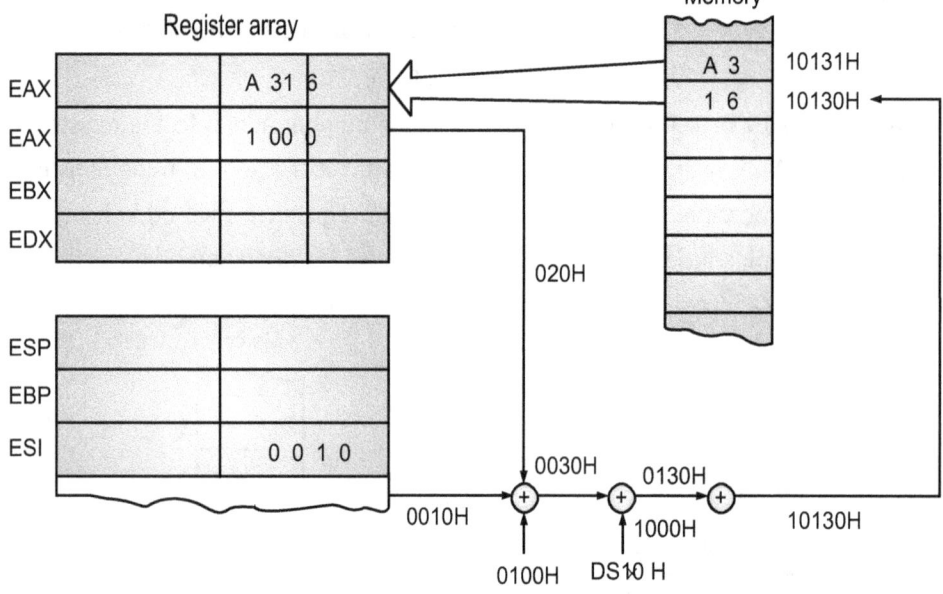

Fig. 6.40 : Based Indexed Plus Displacement Addressing Mode

6.7.9 Memory Addressing Modes

The 8086 provides 17 different ways to access memory. The key to good assembly language programming is the proper use of memory addressing modes.

The addressing modes provided by the 8086 family include displacement-only, base, displacement plus base, base plus indexed, and displacement plus base plus indexed. Variations on these five forms provide the 17 different addressing modes on the 8086.

6.8   8086 INTERRUPT STRUCTURE

Computer Interrupt is a signal indicating that an event, needing immediate attention. An interrupt is an external event which informs the CPU that a device needs its service.

Interrupts are useful when interfacing I/O devices at relatively low data transfer rates, such as keyboard inputs. Interrupt processing allows the processor to execute other software while the keyboard operator is thinking about what to type next. When a key is pressed, the keyboard encoder debounces the switch and puts out one pulse that interrupts the microprocessor.

- **Types of Interrupts :**

There are two main types of interrupts in the 8086 microprocessor, **internal and external interrupts**. External interrupts occur when a peripheral device asserts an interrupt input pin of the microprocessor. Whereas internal interrupts are initiated by the state of the CPU (e.g. divide by zero error) or by an instruction.

    (1) External - generated outside the CPU by other hardware

    (2) Internal - generated within the CPU as a result of an instruction or operation

X86 has internal interrupts: INT, INTO, Divide Error and Single Step. The internal and external interrupts of X86 comes in the following types:

    (1) Hardware Interrupt

    (2) Software Interrupt

    (3) Processor Interrupt

- Intel processors include two hardware pins (INTR and NMI) that request interrupts...
- And one hardware pin (INTA) to acknowledge the interrupt requested through INTR.
- The processor also has software interrupts INT, INTO, INT 3, and BOUND.
- Flag bits IF (interrupt flag) and TF (trap flag), are also used with the interrupt structure and special return instruction IRET, IRETD in the 80386, 80486, or Pentium

The 8086/88 microprocessors allow normal program execution to be interrupted by external signals or by special instructions embedded in the program code. When the microprocessor is interrupted, it stops executing the current program and **calls** a procedure which **services** the interrupt. At the end of the **interrupt service routine**, the code execution sequence is returned to the original, interrupted program.

An interrupt can be generated by one of three sources. First, an interrupt can be generated as a result of a processor state violation, called an exception. An example would be a divide-by-zero interrupt produced when the DIV instruction is interpreted to have a zero divisor. Program execution is automatically interrupted and control transferred to an interrupt handler. Conditional interrupts such as this are referred to as internal interrupts.

An interrupt can also be generated by an external device requesting service. This happens when a device signals its request on either the non-maskable interrupt (NMI) or on the INTR interrupts input lines of the processor. The NMI interrupt is generally used to signal the occurrence of a catastrophic event, such as the immanent loss of power. The INTR interrupt is used by all other devices. An interrupt caused by a signal applied to either the NMI or INTR input is referred to as **hardware interrupt**.

Since there is only one INTR input, and multiple devices may have an interrupt capability, an Intel 8259A Programmable Interrupt Controller (PIC) can be used to manage multiple interrupt requests. The PIC receives requests from peripheral equipment, decides which request has the highest priority and issues an interrupt request to the CPU.

Finally, interrupts may be generated as a result of executing the INT instruction. This is referred to as **software interrupt**.

- In 8086/8088 there are a total of 256 interrupts: INT 00, INT 01,..., INT FF.
- When an interrupt is executed, the microprocessor automatically saves
    - Flag register
    - Instruction pointer
    - Code segment register
- On the stack and goes to a fixed memory location.

6.8.1 Interrupt Vector Table

- Interrupt vectors and the vector table are crucial to an understanding of hardware and software interrupts.
- The **interrupt vector table** is located in the first 1024 bytes of memory at addresses 000000H–0003FFH.
    - Contains 256 different four-byte interrupt vectors.
    - An interrupt vector contains the address (segment and offset) of the interrupt service procedure.
    - The first five interrupt vectors are identical in all Intel processors.
    - Intel reserves the first 32 interrupt vectors.
    - The last 224 vectors are user-available.
    - Each is four bytes long in real mode and contains the starting address of the interrupt service procedure.
    - The first two bytes contain the offset address.
    - The last two contain the segment address.

IVT format

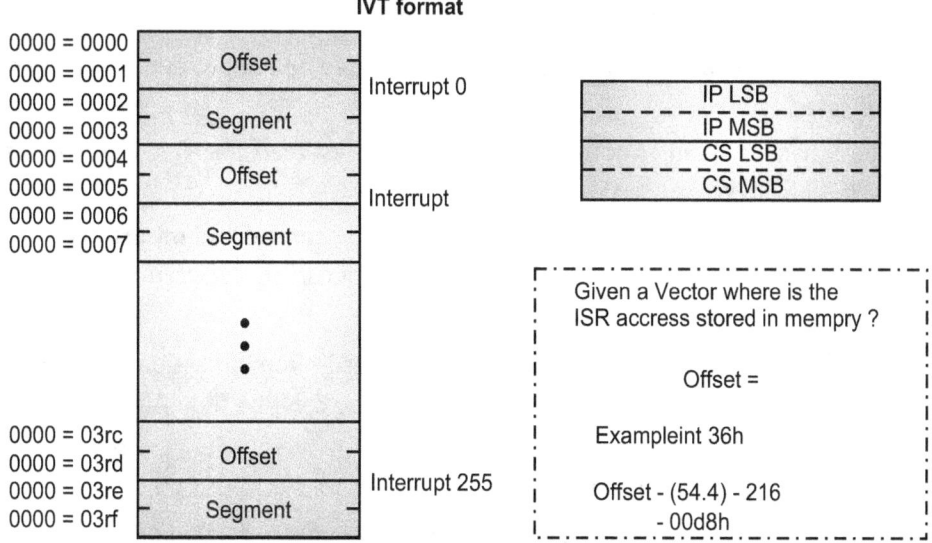

Fig. 6.41 : IVT format

Memory address (in Hex)

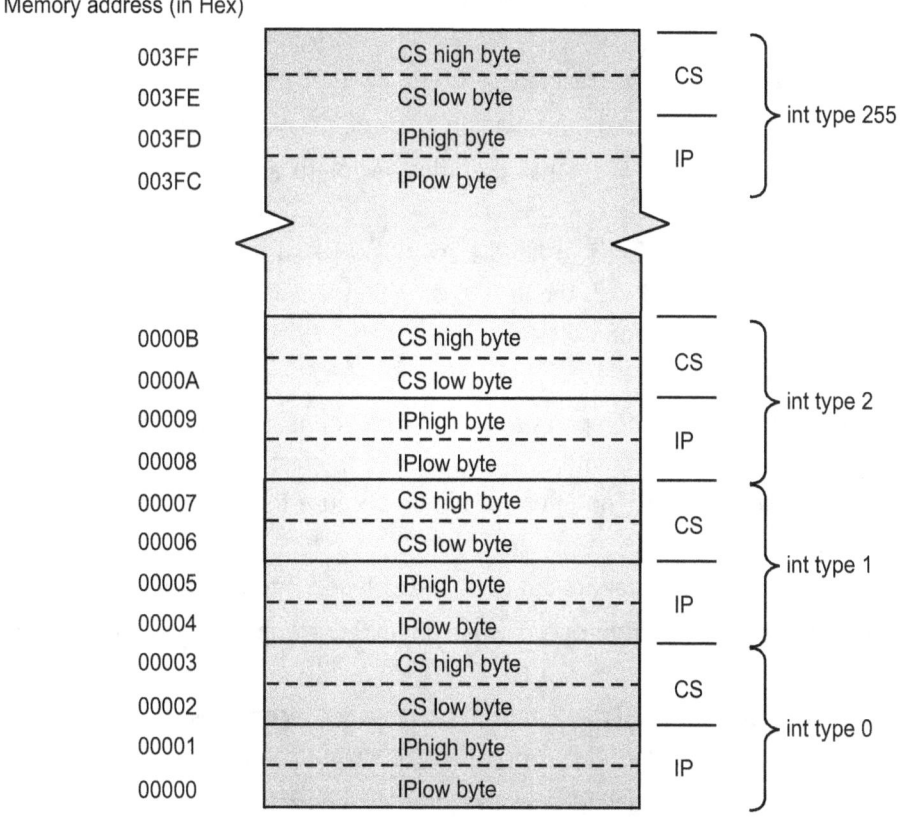

Fig. 6.42 : Interrupt vector table

256 INTERRUPTS OF 8086 ARE DIVIDED INTO THREE GROUPS

- Type 0 to type 4 interrupts : These are used for fixed operations and hence are called **dedicated interrupts.**
- Type 5 to type 31 interrupts not used by 8086, **reserved** for higher processors like 80286, 80386 etc.
- Type 32 to 255 interrupts available for user, called **user defined interrupts** these can be h/w interrupts and activated through intr line or can be s/w interrupts.

(a) Dedicated interrupts :

Type 0 : divide error interrupt occurs whenever the result from a division overflows or an attempt is made to divide by zero that is quotient is large can't be fit in AL/AX or divide by zero

Type 1 : single step interrupt used for executing the program in single step mode by

setting trap flag to set trap flag. Single-step or trap occurs after execution of each instruction if the trap (TF) flag bit is set. Upon accepting this interrupt, TF bit is cleared

Type 2 : non-maskable interrupt occurs when a logic 1 is placed on the NMI input pin to the microprocessor.

- non-maskable - it cannot be disabled

Type 3 : break point interrupt used for providing break points in the program.

A special one-byte instruction (INT 3) that uses this vector to access its interrupt-service procedure.

Type 4 : over flow interrupt used to handle any overflow error after signed arithmetic. Overflow is a special vector used with the INTO instruction. The INTO instruction interrupts the program if an overflow condition exists.

(b) Intel Reserved Interrupts

Type 5 : The **BOUND** instruction compares a register with boundaries stored in the memory. If the contents of the register are greater than or equal to the first word in memory and less than or equal to the second word, no interrupt occurs because the contents of the register are within bounds.

- if the contents of the register are out of bounds,a type 5 interrupt ensues

Type 6 : An **invalid opcode** interrupt occurs when an undefined opcode is encountered in a program.

Type 7 : The **coprocessor not available** interrupt occurs when a coprocessor is not found, as dictated by the machine status word (MSW or CR0) coprocessor control bits.

- if an ESC or WAIT instruction executes and no coprocessor is found, a type 7 exception or interrupt occurs

Type 8 : A **double fault** interrupt is activated when two separate interrupts occur during the same instruction.

Type 9 : The **coprocessor segment overrun** occurs if the ESC instruction (coprocessor opcode) memory operand extends beyond offset address FFFFH in real mode.

Type 10 : An **invalid task state** segment interrupt occurs in the protected mode if the TSS is invalid because the segment limit field is not 002BH or higher.

- usually because the TSS is not initialized

Type 11 : The **segment not present** interrupt occurs when the protected mode P bit (P = 0) in a descriptor indicates that the segment is not present or not valid.

Type 12 : A **stack segment overrun** occurs if the stack segment is not present (P = 0) in the protected mode or if the limit of the stack segment is exceeded

Type 13 : The **general protection fault** occurs for most protection violations in 80286–Core2 in protected mode system.

Type 14 : Page fault interrupts occur for any page fault memory or code access in 80386, 80486, and Pentium–Core2 processors.

Type 16 : Coprocessor error takes effect when a coprocessor error (ERROR = 0) occurs for ESCape or WAIT instructions for 80386, 80486, and Pentium–Core2 only.

Type 17 : Alignment checks indicate word and doubleword data are addressed at an odd memory location (or incorrect location, in the case of a doubleword).

- interrupt is active in 80486 and Pentium–Core2

Type 18 : A machine check activates a system memory management mode interrupt in Pentium–Core2

These interrupts may be -

1. Edge or Level sensitive Interrupts

- Edge level interrupts are recognized on the falling or rising edge of the input signal. They are generally used for high priority interrupts and are latched internally inside the processor. If this latching was not done, the processor could easily miss the falling edge (due to its short duration) and thus not respond to the interrupt request.
- Level sensitive interrupts overcome the problem of latching, in that the requesting device holds the interrupt line at a specified logic state (normally logic zero) till the processor acknowledges the interrupt. This type of interrupt can be shared by other devices in a wired 'OR' configuration, which is commonly used to support daisy chaining and other techniques.

- The interrupt request input (INTR) is level-sensitive, which means that it must be held at a logic 1 level until it is recognized.
  - INTR is set by an external event and cleared inside the interrupt service procedure
  - INTR is automatically disabled once accepted.
  - re-enabled by IRET at the end of the interrupt service procedure.

2. Maskable Interrupts

The processor can inhibit certain types of interrupts by use of a special interrupt mask bit. This mask bit is part of the flags/condition code register, or a special interrupt register. In the 8086 microprocessor if this bit is clear, and an interrupt request occurs on the Interrupt Request input, it is ignored.

3. Non-Maskable Interrupts

There are some interrupts which cannot be masked out or ignored by the processor. These are associated with high priority tasks which cannot be ignored (like memory parity or bus faults). In general, most processors support the Non-Maskable Interrupt (NMI). This interrupt has absolute priority, and when it occurs, the processor will finish the current memory cycle, and then branch to a special routine written to handle the interrupt request.

The **non-maskable interrupt** (NMI) is an edge-triggered input that requests an interrupt on the positive edge (0-to-1 transition).

- After a positive edge, the NMI pin must remain logic 1 until recognized by the microprocessor.
- Before the positive edge is recognized, NMI pin must be logic 0 for at least two clocking periods.
- The NMI input is often used for parity errors and other major faults, such as power failures.

Power failures are easily detected by monitoring the AC power line and causing an NMI interrupt whenever AC power drops out

6.8.2 Advantages of Interrupts

Interrupts are used to ensure adequate service response times by the processing. Sometimes, with software polling routines, service times by the processor cannot be guaranteed, and data may be lost. The use of interrupts guarantees that the processor will service the request within a specified time period, reducing the likelihood of lost data.

6.8.3 The Operation of an Interrupt Sequence on the 8086 Microprocessor

1. External interface sends an interrupt signal, to the Interrupt Request (INTR) pin, or an internal interrupt occurs.

2. The CPU finishes the present instruction (for a hardware interrupt) and sends Interrupt Acknowledge (INTA) to hardware interface.

3. The interrupt type N is sent to the Central Processor Unit (CPU) via the Data bus from the hardware interface.

4. The contents of the flag registers are pushed onto the stack.

5. Both the interrupt (IF) and (TF) flags are cleared. This disables the INTR pin and the trap or single-step feature.

6. The contents of the code segment register (CS) are pushed onto the Stack.

7. The contents of the instruction pointer (IP) are pushed onto the Stack.

8. The interrupt vector contents are fetched, from (4 x N) and then placed into the IP and from (4 x N +2) into the CS so that the next instruction executes at the interrupt service procedure addressed by the interrupt vector.

9. While returning from the interrupt-service routine by the Interrupt Return (IRET) instruction, the IP, CS and Flag registers are popped from the Stack and return to their state prior to the interrupt.

QUESTIONS

1. Draw and explain Architecture of 8086 microprocessor.

2. Draw and explain block diagram of 8086 microprocessor.

3. Explain programmers model of 8086 microprocessor.

4. Draw and explain pin diagram of 8086 microprocessor.

5. Explain Minimum and Maximum mode pins of 8086 microprocessor.

6. Explain following pins

    BHE#, INTR, RESET, RQ#/GT#, DEN,ALE,HOLD,HLDA,READY,LOCK#

7. Explain Register organization of 8086 microprocessor.

8. Explain Memory segmentation of 8086 microprocessor.

9.   Explain in detail different addressing modes of 8086 microprocessor.

10. Write a short note on Interrupt Vector Table.

11. What are different types of interrupts in 8086 microprocessor.

12. Explain Even and Odd Memory Banks of 8086 microprocessor.

13. Explain flag register of 8086 microprocessor in detail.

14. How to convert Logical address into physical address in 8086 microprocessor Explain with the help of example.

15. Explain following bits of flag register in detail with the help of example.

     AF, CF, OF, PF, SF

www.ingramcontent.com/pod-product-compliance
Lightning Source LLC
Chambersburg PA
CBHW081143020726
47504CB00009B/1977